More praise for

A Hot and Sultry Night for Crime . . .

"Deaver's own 'Ninety-eight Point Six,' which opens the collection, is indicative of the whole anthology: compelling, quick-moving, and packing a trick ending . . . Readers will find what they're looking for in this anthology."

—*Romantic Times*

"A steamy theme . . . starting with Edgar-nominee Deaver's own nicely twisted 'Ninety-eight Point Six.' Another bright spot is Ronnie Klaskin's 'Child Support,' in which a woman has to cope with unreliable men. Toni L. P. Kelner's 'Old Dog Days' features a retired police chief who manages to turn a hunt for a missing dog into a neat trick. In newcomer Ana Rainwater's arresting 'Night Rose,' a young woman with a difficult mother celebrates adulthood. Angela Zeman's 'Green Heat' brings a Chicago hit man out of the cold and into the sweltering heat of West Virginia, where he gets a surprising education . . . Loren D. Estleman, John Lutz, Jeremiah Healy . . . should attract fans."

—*Publishers Weekly*

"The stories run the gamut of crime fiction with a few seemingly more thriller than mystery. The contributors make up some of the top talent in the genre . . . All of the tales are solid and entertaining . . . a few are superb."

—*Under the Covers*

A Hot and Sultry Night for Crime

Edited by Jeffery Deaver

BERKLEY PRIME CRIME, NEW YORK

A HOT AND SULTRY NIGHT FOR CRIME

A Berkley Prime Crime Book / published by arrangement with the authors

PRINTING HISTORY
Berkley Prime Crime hardcover edition / February 2003
Berkley Prime Crime mass-market edition / December 2003

ISBN: 0-425-19369-1

Berkley Prime Crime Books are published
by The Berkley Publishing Group,
a division of Penguin Group (USA) Inc.,
375 Hudson Street, New York, New York 10014.
The name BERKLEY PRIME CRIME and the BERKLEY PRIME CRIME
design are trademarks belonging to Penguin Group (USA) Inc.

PRINTED IN THE UNITED STATES OF AMERICA

10 9 8 7 6 5 4 3 2 1

Contents

Introduction   ix
  Jeffery Deaver

Ninety-eight Point Six   1
  Jeffery Deaver

The Last of the Bad Girls   26
  David Handler

Child Support   48
  Ronnie Klaskin

Old Dog Days   59
  Toni L. P. Kelner

Body in the Pond   75
  Suzanne C. Johnson

Lady on Ice   102
  Loren D. Estleman

El Palacio   118
  John Lutz

Heat Lightning   140
  Gary Brandner

Too Hot to Die   162
Mat Coward

Green Heat   180
Angela Zeman

No Lie   208
Robert Lee Hall

The Stay-at-Home Thief   217
Tim Myers

War Crimes   229
G. Miki Hayden

The Slow Blink   251
Jeremiah Healy

Hot Days, Cold Nights   273
Alan Cook

Prom Night   286
David Bart

Night Rose   299
Ana Rainwater

Neighborhood Watch   317
Sinclair Browning

Splitting   335
Marilyn Wallace

What the Dormouse Said   351
Carolyn Wheat

INTRODUCTION

WHAT is there about heat and crime?

They go together like, well, gunpowder and a match.

Tempers *boil*.

Jealousies *flare*.

People kill in the *heat of passion*.

There might be some crime stories in which perpetrators are driven to murder by snowflakes, but I sure can't think of any. Winter is hot cocoa, Christmas, cozy fireplaces, and—at the most macabre—a tasteful if stiff body on a frosty moor. No, summer is the perfect season for mayhem, and so we asked a number of Mystery Writers of America authors to come up with some original stories whose theme is hot and sultry crime. Voilà: out of the oven came this harrowing collection.

The genres represented here are as varied as stifling rain forests differ from sizzling deserts.

Maybe it's my imagination, but do the private eyes get their best assignments on hot days? In "Heat Lightning," Gary Brandner's PI escapes from the heat into an icy movie theater, only to find the action among the audience is far more intriguing than that on the screen (and bravo to the author for managing to mention Blatz beer—my first brew ever—in the opening line). In "Neighborhood Watch," Sinclair Browning's Trade Ellis, irrepressible private investigator and rancher, finds that the July heat doesn't slow up criminal misdoings, even in sweltering Tucson, Arizona.

Several of our stories transport the reader to steaming foreign shores. One gives us a wrenching look at a Japanese prisoner-of-war camp, where the conditions—and the heat—drive men to extremes: G. Miki Hayden's "War Crimes." In John Lutz's "El Palacio," we join a cast right out of *The Treasure of the Sierra Madre*: local thugs and American expatriates, who drink and sweat . . . and learn an answer to a mystery that will echo in all readers' minds. And after reading Mat Coward's "Too Hot to Die," I, for one, won't be popping by any British pubs for a pint of bitters in the near future, no matter how muggy the weather.

While it's not exactly set in a foreign location, Jeremiah Healy's "The Slow Blink" definitely explores exotic territory: Florida, a state that *must* be represented in any anthology that dares to call itself hot and sultry. The Left Coast also makes an appearance here in David Handler's "The Last of the Bad Girls," a Hollywood tale that might be called *Get Shorty* with a twist.

Passion and murder—and heat—are timeless, of course, and in her story, "Body in the Pond," Suzanne C. Johnson takes us back to an era when there was no air-conditioning to cool down feverish lusts and tempers.

A cold case—an old, unsolved crime—is the ironic theme of Angela Zeman's "Green Heat," which finds us in a sweltering West Virginia burgh, where all is not what it seems to be. The story features a delightful buddy team: a stranger in town on a dangerous mission and some locals with a unique approach to fighting crime.

Speaking of cold: the theme of our collection may be heat, but several authors use low temperatures to great advantage in their stories. Ronnie Klaskin's "Child Support" is one of these but, ever cautious about giving away twists, I'm not going to spoil the ending by mentioning exactly how freezing figures in her story. In Loren D. Estleman's "Lady on Ice," temperatures—and tempers—prove as hot on the skating rink as they do outside on the gritty streets of Detroit. And Alan Cook gives us "Hot Days, Cold Nights," with another surprise ending that leaves us—okay, sorry—chilled to the bone.

The familiar activities and recreations of summertime are explored by some of our authors. The innocent pastime of growing flowers and the drone of a lawn mower are motifs in two tales of relationships that move from dysfunctional to deadly: respectively, Ana Rainwater's "Night Rose" and "No Lie," by Robert Lee Hall. What do parents do during the summer? Balance chauffeuring the kids to their activities while trying to keep up with the demands of one's job, which is particularly difficult if the profession in question happens to be burglary, as Tim Myers illustrates in "The Stay-at-Home Thief." And in "Prom Night," by David Bart, a single mom goes a-courting and learns that dating later in life is a lot different from those idyllic June evenings back in high school.

Of course, no collection of short stories on our theme would be complete without some reference to a particularly well-known phrase about the lethargy of summer afternoons, and Toni L. P. Kelner obliges with "Old Dog Days," which has, as you might've guessed, a double meaning.

An overheated car on a deserted highway in Michigan leads to some very twisted goings-on in my own story, "Ninety-eight Point Six."

So, open a cold beer (Blatz or otherwise) or pour an iced

tea. Lounge back in the pool recliner or on your beach blanket, apply your sunscreen, and read on. Relax, enjoy the sun, bask in the balmy air. Though while you do, you might want to keep in mind English writer Sydney Smith's comment about surviving a particularly vicious heat wave: "Heat, ma'am! It was so dreadful . . . that I found there was nothing left for it but to take off my flesh and sit in my bones."

—JEFFERY DEAVER

NINETY-EIGHT POINT SIX

Jeffery Deaver

Former journalist, folksinger, and attorney Jeffery Deaver's novels have appeared on a number of best-seller lists around the world, including the *New York Times*, the *London Times*, and the *Los Angeles Times*. The author of seventeen novels, he's been nominated for five Edgar Awards from the Mystery Writers of America and an Anthony Award, is a two-time recipient of the Ellery Queen Reader's award for Best Short Story of the Year, and won last year's British Thumping Good Read Award. His book *A Maiden's Grave* was made into an HBO movie starring James Garner and Marlee Matlin, and his novel *The Bone Collector* was a feature release from Universal Pictures, starring Denzel Washington and Angelina Jolie. Turner Broadcasting is currently making a TV movie of his novel *Praying for Sleep*. His most recent novels are *The Stone Monkey*, *The Blue Nowhere*, and *The Empty Chair*. He lives in Virginia and California. Readers can visit his web site at **www.jefferydeaver.com** or the web site for *The Blue Nowhere* at **www.thebluenowhere.com**.

———

SUIT jacket slung over his shoulder, the man trudged up the long walk to the bungalow, his lungs aching, breathless in the astonishing heat, which had persisted well after sundown.

Pausing on the sidewalk in front of the house, trying to catch his breath, he believed he heard troubled voices from inside. Still, he'd had no choice but to come here. This was the only house he'd seen along the highway.

He climbed the stairs to the unwelcomingly dark porch and rang the bell.

The voices ceased immediately.

There was a shuffle. Two or three words spoken.

He rang the bell again, and finally the door opened.

Sloan observed that the three people inside gazed at him with different expressions on their faces.

The woman on the couch, in her fifties, wearing an over-washed sleeveless housedress, appeared relieved. The man sitting beside her—about the same age, rounding and bald—was wary.

And the man who'd opened the door and stood closest to Sloan had a grin on his face—a thick-lipped grin that really meant, *What the hell do you want?* He was about Sloan's own age—late thirties—and his tattooed arms were long. He gripped the side of the door defensively with a massive hand. His clothes were gray, stained dungarees and a torn work shirt. His shaved scalp glistened.

"Help you?" the tattooed man asked.

"I'm sorry to bother you," Sloan said. "My car broke down—it overheated. I need to call Triple A. You mind if I use your phone?"

"Phone company's having problems, I heard," the tattooed man replied, nodding toward the dense, still, night sky. "With the heat—those rolling brownouts or black-outs, whatever."

He didn't move out of the doorway.

But the woman said quickly, "No, please come in," with curious eagerness. "Our phone just rang a bit ago. I'm sure it's working fine."

"Please," echoed the older man, who was holding her hand.

The tattooed man looked Sloan over cautiously, as people often did. Unsmiling by nature, Sloan was a big man, and muscular—he'd worked out every day for the past three years—and at the moment he was a mess; tonight he'd trekked through the brush to take a shortcut to the lights of this house. And like anyone walking around on this overwhelmingly humid and hot night, every inch of his skin was slick with sweat.

Finally, the tattooed man gestured him inside. Sloan noticed a bad scar across the back of his hand. It looked like a knife wound, and it was recent.

The house was overly bright and painfully hot. A tiny air conditioner moaned but did nothing to cool the still air. He glanced at the walls, taking in fast vignettes of lives spent in a small bubble of the world. He deduced careers with Allstate Insurance and a high school library and nebulous involvement in the Rotary Club, church groups, and parent-teacher organizations. Busmen's holidays of fishing trips to Saginaw or Minnesota. A vacation to Chicago memorialized in framed, yellowing snapshots.

Introductions were made. "I'm Dave Sloan."

Agnes and Bill Willis were the couple. Sloan observed immediately that they shared an ambiguous similarity of manner that characterized people long married. The tattooed man said nothing about himself. He tinkered with the air conditioner, turning the compressor knob up and down.

"I'm not interrupting supper, I hope."

There was a moment of silence. It was eight P.M., and Sloan could see no dirty dishes from the night's meal.

"No" was Agnes's soft reply.

"Nope, no food here," the tattooed man said with a cryptic edge to the comment. He looked angrily at the air conditioner as if he were going to kick it out the window, but he controlled himself and walked back to the place he'd staked out for himself: an overstuffed Naugahyde armchair that still glistened with the sweat that'd leached from his skin before he stood to answer the door.

"Phone's in there." Bill pointed.

Sloan thanked him and went into the kitchen. He made his call. As soon as he stepped back into the living room, Bill and the younger man, who'd been talking, fell silent fast.

Sloan looked at Bill and said, "They'll tow it to Hatfield. The truck should be here in twenty minutes. I can wait outside."

"No," Agnes said, then seemed to decide she'd been too forceful and glanced at the tattooed man with a squint, almost as if she was afraid of being hit.

"Too hot outside," Bill said.

"No hotter'n in here," the tattooed man replied caustically, with that grin back. His lips were bulbous, and the top one was beaded with sweat—an image that made Sloan itch.

"Set yourself down," Bill said cautiously. Sloan looked around and found the only unoccupied piece of furniture, an uncomfortable couch covered in pink and green chintz, flowers everywhere. The gaudy pattern, combined with the still heat in the room and the nervous fidgeting of the large, tattooed man set him on edge.

"Can I get you anything?" the woman asked.

"Maybe some water if it's not too much trouble." Sloan wiped his face with his hand.

The woman rose.

"Notice," the tattooed man said coolly, "they didn't introduce me."

"Well, I didn't mean—" Bill began.

The man waved him silent.

"My name's Greg." Another hesitation. "I'm their nephew. Just stopped by for a visit. Right, Bill? Aren't we having a high old time?"

Bill nodded, looking down at the frayed carpet. "High old time."

Sloan was suddenly aware of something—a curious noise. A scraping. A faint bang. No one else seemed to hear it. He looked up as Agnes returned. She handed Sloan the glass, and he drank half of it down immediately.

She said, "I was thinking, maybe you could look at Mr. Sloan's car, Bill. Why don't you and Greg go take a look at it?"

"Dave," Sloan said. "Please. Call me Dave."

"Maybe save Dave some money."

"Sure—" Bill began.

Greg said, "Naw, we don't wanna do that. Too much work in this heat. 'Sides, Dave looks like he can afford a proper mechanic. He looks like he's rollin' in dough. How 'bout it, Dave? Whatta you do?"

"Sales."

"Whatcha sell?"

"Computers. Hardware and software."

"I don't trust computers. Bet I'm the only person in the country without E-mail."

"No, a good eighty million people don't have it, I heard," Dave told him.

Bill piped up. "Children, for instance."

"Like me, huh? Me and the kiddies? Is that what you're saying?"

"Oh, no," Bill said quickly. "I just was talking. Didn't mean any offense."

"How about you, Greg?" Sloan asked. "What line're you in?"

He considered for a minute. "I work with my hands. . . . Want to know what Bill does?"

A dark look crossed Bill's face; then it vanished. "I was in insurance. I'm between jobs right now."

"He'll be working someday soon, though, won't you, Bill?"

"I hope to be."

"I'm sure you will," Agnes said.

"We're *all* sure he will. Hey, Sloan, you think Bill could sell computers?"

"I don't know. All I know is I enjoy what I do."

"You good at it?"

"Oh, I'm very good at it."

"Why computers?"

"Because there's a market for what my company makes right now. But it doesn't matter to me. I can sell anything. Maybe next year it'll be radiators or a new kind of medical laser. If I can make money at it, I'll sell it."

"Why don't you tell us about your computers?" Greg asked.

Sloan shrugged dismissively. "It's real technical. You'd be bored."

"Well, we don't want to bore anybody now, especially us kiddies. Not if we're having such an enjoyable party, the family all together . . . family." Greg thumped the arm of the chair with his massive hands. "Don't you think family's important? I do. You have family, Dave?"

"They're dead. My immediate family, that is."

"All of 'em?" Greg asked curiously.

"My parents and sister."

"How'd they die?"

Agnes stirred at this blunt question, but Sloan didn't mind. "An accident."

"Accident?" Greg nodded. "My folks're gone, too," he added emotionlessly.

Which meant that, because he was their nephew, Bill and Agnes had lost a sibling, too. But Greg didn't acknowledge their portion of the loss.

The sound of the air conditioner seemed to vanish as the silence of four mute human beings filled the tiny, stifling room. Then Sloan heard a faint thumping. It seemed to come from behind a closed door off the hallway. No one else noticed. He heard it again; then the sound ceased.

Greg rose and walked to a thermometer tacked up on the wall. A silver wire ran through a hole sloppily drilled through the window jamb. He tapped the circular dial with his finger. "Busted," he announced. Then he turned back to the threesome. "I heard the news? Before? And they said that it was ninety-eight degrees at sunset. That's a record round here, the newscaster said. I got to thinking. Ninety-eight point *six*—that's the temperature of a human body. And you know what occurred to me?"

Sloan examined the man's eerie, amused eyes. He said nothing. Neither did Bill or Agnes.

Greg continued. "I realized that there's no difference between life and death. Not a bit. Whatta you think about that?"

"No difference? I don't get it." Sloan shook his head.

"See, take a bad person. What sort of person should we use, Bill? Maybe a person who doesn't pay his debts. How's that? OK, now what I'm saying is that it's not his *body*, it's his *soul* that's a welcher. When he dies, what hangs around? A welcher's soul. Same thing with a good man. There's a good soul hanging around after a good body goes. Or a murderer, for instance. When they execute a murderer, there's a killer's soul still walking around."

"That's an interesting thought, Greg."

"The way I see it," the intense man continued, "a body is just a soul warmed to ninety-eight point six degrees."

"I'd have to think about it."

"OK, our folks are dead, yours and mine," Greg continued.

"True," Sloan replied.

"But even when they're gone," Greg said philosophically, "you can still have trouble because of them, right?" He sat back in the slick, stained chair and crossed his legs. He wore no socks, and Sloan got a look at another tattoo— one that started on his ankle and went north. Sloan knew that tattoos on the ankle were among the most painful on the body, since the needle had to hit bone. A tattoo there was more than body painting; it was a defiant reminder that pain was nothing to the wearer.

"Trouble?"

"Your parents can cause you grief after they're dead."

Any psychiatrist'd tell you that, Sloan thought, but he decided that this was a bit too clever for Greg.

The young man rubbed his massive hand over his glistening crew cut. That was quite a scar he had. Another one was on his opposite arm. "There was this thing happened a few years ago."

"What was that?" Bill asked.

Sloan noticed that Agnes had shredded the napkin she was holding.

"Well, I'm not inclined to go into specifics with strangers," he said, irritated.

"I'm sorry," Bill said quickly.

"I'm just making a point. Which is that somebody who was dead was still causing me problems. I could see it real clear. A bitch when she was alive, a bitch when she was dead. God gave her a troublemaker's soul. You believe in God, Sloan?"

"No."

Agnes stirred. Sloan glanced at three crucifixes on the wall.

"I believe in selling. That's about it."

"That's *your* soul then. Warmed to ninety-eight point six." A rubbery grin. "Since you're still alive."

"And what's your soul like, Greg? Good, bad?"

"Well, I'm not a welcher," he said coyly. "Beyond that, you'll have to guess. I don't give as much away as you do."

The lights dimmed. Another dip in the power.

"Look at that," Greg said. "Maybe it's the souls of some family hanging around here, playing with the lights. Whatta you think, Bill?"

"I don't know. Maybe."

"A family that died here," Greg mused. "Anybody die here that you know of, Bill?"

Agnes swallowed hard. Bill took a sip from a glass of what looked like flat soda. His hands shook.

The lights came back on full. Greg looked around the place. "Whatta you think this house's worth, Sloan?"

"I don't know," he answered calmly, growing tired of the baiting. "I sell computers, remember? Not houses."

"I'm thinking a cool two hundred thousand."

The noise again from behind the door. It was louder this time, audible over the moaning of the air conditioner. A scraping, a thud.

The three people in the room looked toward the door. Agnes and Bill were uneasy. Nobody said a word about the sound.

"Where've you been selling your computers?" Greg asked.

"I was in Durrant today. Now I'm heading east."

"Times're slow round here. People out of work, right, Bill?"

"Hard times."

"Hard times here, hard times everywhere." Greg seemed drunk, but Sloan smelled no liquor and noticed that the only alcohol in sight was a corked bottle of New York State port and a cheap brandy, sitting safely behind a greasy-windowed breakfront. "Hard times for salesmen, too, I'll bet. Even salesmen who can sell *anything,* like you."

Sloan calmly asked, "Something about me you don't like, Greg?"

"Why, no." But the man's steely eyes muttered the opposite. "Where'd you get that idea?"

"It's the heat," Agnes said quickly, playing mediator. "I was watching this show on the news. CNN. About what the heat's doing. Rioting in Detroit, forest fires up near Saginaw. It's making people act crazy."

"Crazy?" Greg asked. "Crazy?"

"I didn't mean you," she said fast.

Greg turned to Sloan. "Let's ask Mr. Salesman here if I'm acting crazy."

Sloan figured he could have the boy on his back in a stranglehold in four or five minutes, but there'd be some serious damage to the tacky knickknacks. And the police'd come, and there'd be all sorts of complications.

"Well, how 'bout it?"

"Nope, you don't seem crazy to me."

"You're saying that 'cause you don't want a hassle. Maybe you *don't* have a salesman's soul. Maybe you've got a liar's soul. . . ." He rubbed his face with both hands. "Damn, I've sweated a gallon."

Sloan sensed control leaving the man. He noticed a gun rack on the wall. There were two rifles in it. He judged how fast he could get there. Was Bill stupid enough to leave an unlocked, loaded gun on the rack? Probably.

"Let me tell you something—" Greg began ominously, tapping the sweaty arms of the chair with blunt fingers.

The doorbell rang.

No one moved for a moment. Then Greg rose and walked to it and opened the door.

A husky man with long hair stood in the doorway. "Somebody called for a tow?"

"That'd be me." Sloan stood and said to Agnes and Bill, "Thanks for the use of the phone."

"No problem."

"You're sure you don't want to stay? I can put some supper on. Please?" The poor woman was now clearly desperate.

"No. I have to be going."

"Yeah," Greg said, "Dave's got to be going."

"Damn," the tow operator said. "Hotter in there than it is outside."

You don't know the half of it, Sloan thought and started down the steps to the idling flatbed.

THE driver winched Sloan's disabled Chevy onto the bed, chained it down, and then the two men climbed inside the cab of the truck. They pulled out onto the highway, heading east. The air conditioner roared, and the cool air was a blessing.

The radio clattered. Sloan couldn't hear it clearly over the sound of the AC, but the driver leaned forward and listened to what was apparently some important message. When the transmission was over, the driver said, "They still haven't caught that guy."

"What guy?" Sloan asked.

"The killer. The guy who escaped from that prison earlier."

"I didn't hear about that."

"I hope it makes it on *America's Most Wanted.* You ever watch that show?"

"No. I don't watch much TV," Sloan said.

"I do," the tow driver offered. "Can be educational."

"Who is this guy?"

"Sort of a psycho killer, one of those sorts. Like in *Silence of the Lambs.* How 'bout movies, you like movies?"

"Yeah," Sloan responded. "That was a good flick."

"Guy was in the state prison about twenty miles west of here."

"How'd he escape? That's a pretty high-security place, isn't it?"

"Sure is. My brother . . . uhm, my brother had a *friend* did time there for grand theft auto. Hard place. What they said on the news was that this killer was in the yard of that prison and, what with the heat, there was a power failure. I guess the backup didn't go on either or something, and the lights and the electrified fence were down for, I dunno, almost an hour. By the time they got it going again, he was gone."

Sloan shivered as the freezing air chilled his sweat-soaked clothes. He asked, "Say, you know that family where you picked me up? The Willises?"

"No, sir. I don't get out this way much."

They continued driving for twenty minutes. Ahead, Sloan saw a band of flashing lights.

The driver said, "Roadblock. Probably searching for that escapee."

Sloan could see two police cars. Two uniformed officers were pulling people over.

The salesman said to the tow driver, "When you get up there, pull off to the side. I want to talk to one of the cops."

"Sure thing, mister."

When they pulled over, Sloan got out and told the driver, "I'll just be a minute." Sloan inhaled deeply, but no air seemed to get into his lungs. His chest began to hurt again.

One of the officers glanced at Sloan. The big man, his tan shirt dark with sweat, approached. "Hold up there, sir. Can I help you?" He held his flashlight defensively as he walked toward Sloan, who introduced himself and handed over a business card. Sloan observed the man's name badge:

Sheriff Mills. The law enforcer looked the card over and then Sloan's suit and, satisfied that he wasn't the man they were looking for, asked, "What can I do for you?"

"Is this about that fellow who escaped from the prison?" He nodded at the squad car.

"Yes, sir, it is. You seen anything that might help us find him?"

"Well, it might be nothing. But I thought I should mention it."

"Go ahead."

"What's the prisoner look like?"

"Just escaped about two hours ago. We don't have a picture yet. But he's in his midthirties, beard. Six feet, muscular build. Like yours, more or less."

"Shaved head?"

"No. But if I was him, I mighta shaved it the minute I got out. Lost the beard, too."

"Tattoo?"

"Don't know. Probably."

Sloan explained about his car's breaking down and about his stop at the Willises' house. "You think that prisoner would come this way?"

"If he had his wits about him, he would. To go west'd take him fifty miles through forest. This way, he's got a crack at stealing a car in town or hitching a ride on the interstate."

"And that'd take him right past the Willises'?"

"Yep. If he took Route 202. What're you getting at, Mr. Sloan?"

"I think that fellow might be at the Willises' house."

"What?"

"Do you know if they have a nephew?"

"I don't think they ever mentioned one."

"Well, there's a man there now—sort of fits the description of the killer. He claimed he was Bill's nephew, visiting them. But something didn't seem right. I mean, first of all, it was suppertime, but they hadn't eaten and they weren't cooking anything and there were no dirty dishes in the kitchen. And anything Greg told them to do, they did. Like they were afraid to upset him."

The sheriff found a wad of paper towel in his pocket and wiped his face and head. "Anything else?"

"He was saying weird stuff—talking about death and about this experience he had that made him look at dying differently. Like it wasn't that bad a thing . . . Spooked me. Oh, and another thing: he said he didn't want to mention something in front of strangers. He might've meant me, but then why'd he say 'strangers,' not 'a stranger'? It was like he meant Bill and Agnes, too."

"Good point."

"He also had some bad scars. Like he'd been in a knife fight. And he mentioned somebody who died—a woman, who gave him as much grief after she was dead as before. I was thinking he meant trouble with the law for killing her."

"What'd their daughter say?"

"Daughter?"

"The Willises have a daughter. Sandy. Didn't you see her? She's home from college now. And she works the day shift at Taco Bell. She should've been home by now."

"Jesus," Sloan muttered. "I didn't see her. . . . But I remember something else. The door to one of the bedrooms was closed, and there was a sound coming from inside it. Everybody there was uneasy about it. You don't think she was, I don't know, tied up inside there?"

"Lord," the sheriff said, wiping his face, "that escapee—he was arrested for raping and murdering girls. College girls." He pulled out his radio. "All Hatfield police units. This's Mills. I have a lead on that prisoner. The perpetrator might be out at Bill Willis's place off 202. Leave one car each on the roadblocks, but everybody else respond immediately. Silent roll up, with lights out. Stop on the road near the driveway, but don't go in. Wait for me."

Replies came back.

The sheriff turned to Sloan. "We might need you as a witness, Mr. Sloan."

"Sure, whatever I can do."

The sheriff said, "Have the driver take you to the police station—it's on Elm Street. My girl's there; Clara's her name. Just tell her the same thing you told me. I'll call her and tell her to take your statement."

"Be happy to, Sheriff."

The sheriff ran back to his car and jumped in. His deputy climbed into the passenger seat, and they skidded 180 degrees and sped off toward the Willises' house.

Sloan watched them vanish and climbed back in the truck, said to the driver, "Never thought I'd end up in the middle of this."

"Most exciting call *I've* ever had," the man replied, "I'll tell you that."

The driver pulled back onto the highway, and the flat-bed clattered down the asphalt toward a faint band of light radiated by the heat-socked town of Hatfield, Michigan.

"I DON'T see anybody but the Willises," the deputy whispered.

He'd made some fast reconnaissance of the bungalow through a side window. "They're just sitting there talking, Bill and Agnes."

Three male officers and two women—five-eighths of the Hatfield constabulary—surrounded the house.

"He might be in the john. Let's go in fast."

"We knock?"

"No," the sheriff muttered, "we don't knock."

They burst through the front door so fast that Agnes dropped her soda on the couch, and Bill made it two steps to the gun rack before he recognized the sheriff and his deputies.

"Lord of mercy, you scared us, Hal."

"What a fright," Agnes muttered. Then: "Don't blaspheme, Bill."

"Are you OK?"

"Sure, we're OK. Why?"

"And your daughter?"

"She's out with her friends. Is this about her? Is she all right?"

"No, it's not about her." Sheriff Mills slipped his gun away. "Where is he, Bill?"

"Who?"

"That fellow who was here?"

"The guy whose car broke down?" Agnes asked. "He left in the tow truck."

"No, not him. The guy calling himself Greg."

"Greg?" Agnes asked. "Well, he's gone, too. What's this all about?"

"Who is he?" the sheriff asked.

"He's my late brother's son," Bill said.

"He really is your nephew?"

"Much as I hate to say it, yeah."

The sheriff put the gun away. "That Sloan, the man who called the tow truck from here—he had this idea that maybe Greg was that escapee. We thought he'd held you hostage."

"What escapee?"

"A killer from that prison west of here. A psychopath. He escaped a couple of hours ago."

"No!" Agnes said breathlessly. "We didn't have the news on tonight."

The sheriff told them what Sloan had mentioned about

how odd Greg had behaved and how the Willises clearly
didn't want him there, were even afraid of him.

Agnes nodded. "See, we . . ."

Her voice faded and she glanced at her husband, who
said, "It's OK, honey, you can tell him."

"When Bill lost his job last year, we didn't know what
we were going to do. We only had a little savings and my
job at the library, well, that wasn't bringing in much
money. So we had to borrow some. The bank wouldn't
even talk to us, so we called Greg."

Clearly ashamed, Bill shook his head. "He's the richest
one in the family."

"Him?" Sheriff Mills asked.

Agnes said, "Yep. He's a plumber. . . . No, sorry, a
'plumbing contractor.' Makes money hand over fist. Has
eight trucks. He inherited the business when Bill's brother
died."

Her husband: "Well, he made me a loan. Insisted on a
second mortgage on the house, of course. And plenty of
interest, too. More'n the banks woulda charged. Was real
obnoxious about it, since we never really had him and his
dad over when he was growing up—my brother and me
didn't get along too good. But he wrote us a check, and
nobody else would. I thought I'd have another job by now,
but nothing came up. And unemployment ran out. When
I couldn't make the payments to him, I stopped returning
his phone calls. I was so embarrassed. He finally drove over
here tonight and stopped by unannounced. He gave us
hell. Threatening to foreclose, drive us out in the street."

"That's when Mr. Sloan showed up. We were hoping
he'd stay. It was a nightmare sitting here listening to Greg
go on and on."

"Sloan said he was scarred. Like knife wounds."

"Accidents on the job, I guess," Bill said.

"What'd he mean about a woman who died a few years ago?"

Nodding, Bill said, "He wouldn't tell us exactly what he meant." He looked at Agnes. "I'd guess that must've been his girlfriend. She died in a car wreck, and Greg sort of inherited her son for a few months. It was a mess— Greg's not the best father, as you can imagine. Finally, her sister took the boy."

The sheriff remembered something else that Sloan had said. "He said he heard something in the other room. It seemed suspicious to him."

Agnes blushed fiercely. "That was Sandy."

"Your daughter?"

A nod. The woman couldn't continue. Bill said, "She came home with her boyfriend. They went into her room so she could change out of her uniform before they went out. The next thing you know—well, you can figure it out. . . . I told her to respect us. I told her not to be with him when we were home. She doesn't care."

So it was all a misunderstanding, Sheriff Mills reflected.

Bill laughed faintly. "And you thought Greg was the killer? That's wild."

"Wasn't that far-fetched," the sheriff said. "Think about it. The guy escaped at five tonight. That'd be just enough time to steal a car and get to your place from Durrant in early evening."

"Guess that's right," Bill said.

The sheriff returned to the door and started to open it.

Bill said, "Wait a minute, Hal. You said Durrant?"

"Right. That's where the prison is that guy escaped from."

Bill looked at Agnes. "Didn't that fellow Sloan say he'd just come here from Durrant?"

"Yeah, he did. I'm sure."

"Really?" the sheriff asked. He returned to the Willises, then asked, "What else do you know about him?"

"Nothing much really. Just that he said he sold computers."

"Computers?" The sheriff frowned. "Around here?"

"That's what he said."

This was odd; Hatfield was hardly a high-tech area of the state. The closest retail computer store was fifteen miles south of here. "Anything else?"

"He was pretty evasive, now that I think about it. Didn't say much of anything. Except he did say his parents were dead."

"And he didn't seem very upset about it," Agnes offered.

The sheriff reflected: "And Sloan was about the same age and build as the killer. Dark hair, too."

Damn, he thought to himself: I didn't even look at his driver's license, only his business card. He might've killed the real Sloan and stolen his car.

"And that was another thing. He said his car overheated," Bill pointed out. "You'd think a salesman'd be in a new car. And you ever hear about cars overheating nowadays? Hardly ever happens. And at night?"

"Mary, Mother of God," Agnes said, crossing herself, apparently finding an exception to the rule about blasphemy. "He was right here, in our house."

But the sheriff's mind continued further along this troubling path. Sloan, he now understood, had known there'd be a roadblock. So he'd disabled his car himself, called Triple A, and waltzed right through the roadblock. *Hell, he even walked right up to me, ballsy as could be, and spun that story about Greg to lead the law off.*

And we let him get away. He could be—

No!

And then he felt the punch in his gut. He'd sent Sloan to police headquarters. Where there was only one other person at the moment: Clara. Twenty-one years old. Beautiful.

And whom the sheriff referred to as "his girl" not out of any vestigial chauvinism but because she was, in fact, his daughter, working for him on summer vacation from college.

He grabbed the Willises' phone and called the station. There was no answer.

Sheriff Mills ran from the house, climbed into his car. "Oh, Lord, please no. . . ."

The deputy with him offered a prayer, too. But the sheriff didn't hear it. He dropped into the seat and slammed the door. Ten seconds later, the Crown Vic hit eighty as it cut through the night air, hot as soup and dotted with the lights from a thousand edgy fireflies.

No reconnaissance this time.

On Elm Street downtown, the sheriff skidded to a stop against a trash can, knocking it over and scattering the street with empty soda bottles and Good Humor sticks and wrappers.

His deputy was beside him, carting the stubby scatter-gun, a shell chambered and the safety off.

"What's the plan?" the deputy asked.

"This." Sheriff Mills snapped and slammed into the door with his shoulder, leveling the gun as he rushed inside, the deputy on his heels.

Both men stopped fast, staring at the two people in the room, caught in the act of sipping Arizona iced teas. Dave Sloan and the sheriff's daughter, both blinking in shock at the hostile entrance.

The officers lowered their weapons.

"Dad!"

"What's the matter, Sheriff?" Sloan asked.

"I—" he stammered. "Mr. Sloan, could I see some ID?"

Sloan showed his driver's license to the sheriff, who examined the picture; it was clearly Sloan. Then Mills shamefacedly told them what he'd suspected after his conversation with the Willises.

Sloan took the news good-naturedly. "Probably should've asked for that license up front, Sheriff."

"I probably should have. Right you are. It was just that things seemed a little suspicious. Like you told them that you'd just come from Durrant—"

"My company installs and services the prison computers. It's one of my big accounts." He fished in his jacket pocket and showed the sheriff a work order. "These blackouts from the heat are hell on computers. If you don't shut them down properly, it causes all kinds of problems."

"Oh. I'm sorry, sir. You have to understand—"

"That you got a killer on the loose." Sloan laughed again. "So they thought I was the killer. . . . Only fair, I suppose, since *I* thought Greg was."

"I called before," the sheriff said to his daughter. "There was no answer. Where were you?"

"Oh, the AC went out. Mr. Sloan here and I went out back to see if we could get it going."

A moment later, the fax machine began churning out a piece of paper. It contained a picture of a young man, bearded, with trim, dark hair: the two-angle mug shot of the escapee.

The sheriff showed it to Sloan and Clara. He read from the prison's bulletin. "Name's Tony Windham. Rich kid from Ann Arbor. Worth millions, trust funds, prep school. Honors grad. But he's got something loose somewhere. Killed six women and never showed a gnat of regret at the trial. Well, he's not getting through Hatfield. Route 202 and 17're the only ways to the interstate, and we're checking every car." He then said to the deputy, "Let's spell the boys on the roadblocks."

Outside, Sheriff Mills pointed Dave Sloan to the garage where his Chevy was being fixed and climbed into his squad car with his deputy. He wiped the sweat with a soggy paper towel and said good night to the salesman. "Stay cool."

Sloan laughed. "Like a snowball in hell. Night, Sheriff."

IN Earl's Automotive, Sloan wandered up to the mechanic, who was as stained from sweat as he was from grease.

"Okay, she's fixed," the man told Sloan.

"What was wrong with it?"

"The cap'd come loose, and your coolant shot out is all. Feel bad charging you."

"But you're going to anyway."

The man pulled his soggy baseball cap off and wiped his forehead with the crown. Replaced it. "I'd be home in a cold bath right now, it wasn't for your wheels."

"Fair enough."

"Only charged you twenty."

Any other time, Sloan would have negotiated, but he wanted to get back on the road. He paid and climbed into the car, fired it up, and turned the AC on full. He pulled onto the main street and headed out of town.

Ten miles east of Hatfield, near the interstate, he turned into the parking lot of a Greyhound bus station. He stopped the car in a deserted part of the lot. He climbed out and popped the trunk.

Looking inside, he nodded to the young, bearded man in prison overalls. The man blinked painfully at the brilliant lights above them and gasped for air. He was curled up fetally.

"How you doing?" Sloan asked.

"Jesus," Tony Windham muttered, gasping, his head lolling around alarmingly. "Heat . . . dizzy. Cramps."

"Climb out slow."

Sloan helped the prisoner out of the car. Even with the beard and sweat-drenched hair, he looked much more like a preppy banker than a serial killer, though those two activities weren't mutually exclusive, Sloan supposed.

"Sorry," the salesman said. "It took longer than I'd thought for the tow to come. Then I got stuck in the sheriff's office waiting for them to come back.

"I went through two quarts of that water," Windham said. "And I still don't need to pee."

Sloan looked around the deserted lot. "There's a bus on the hour going to Cleveland. There's a ticket in there and a fake driver's license," he added, handing Windham a gym bag, which also contained some toiletries and a change of clothes. The killer stepped into the shadow of a Dumpster and dressed in the jeans and T-shirt, which said, "Rock and Roll Hall of Fame." Windham pitched his prison outfit into the Dumpster. Then he hunched over and shaved the beard off with Evian water and Edge gel, using his fingers to make certain he'd gotten all the whiskers. When he was finished, he stuffed his hair under a baseball cap.

"How do I look?"

"Like a whole new man.

"Damn," the boy said. "You did it, Sloan. You're good."

The salesman had met Tony Windham in the prison library a month ago when he was supervising upgrades of the penitentiary computer systems. He found Windham charming and smart and empathic—the same skills that had catapulted Sloan to stardom as a salesman. The two hit it off. Finally, Windham made his offer for the one thing that Sloan could sell him: freedom. There was no negotiation. Sloan set the price at three million, which the rich kid had arranged to have transferred into an anonymous overseas account.

Sloan's plan was to wait for one of the hottest days of the year, then, pretending there'd been a momentary electric blackout, he would shut down the power and security systems at the prison using the computers. This would give Windham a chance to climb over the fence. Sloan would then pick up the killer, who'd hide in the trunk, specially perforated with air holes and stocked with plenty of water.

Since he'd be coming from the prison, Sloan had assumed that every car would be searched at roadblocks, so he'd stopped the car outside one of the few houses along Route 202 and left his coolant cap off so the car would overheat. He'd then asked to use the phone. He'd intended to learn a little about the homeowners so he could come up with a credible story about suspicious goings-on at the house and distract the cops, keep them from searching his car. But he'd never thought he'd find as good a false lead as the crazy plumber, Greg.

"I realized that there's no difference between life and death. Not a bit. Whatta you think about that?"

Sloan gave Tony Windham five hundred in cash.

The killer shook Sloan's hand. Then he frowned. "You're probably wondering, now that I'm out, am I going to clean up my act? If I'm going to, well, keep behaving like I was before. With the girls."

Sloan held up a hand to silence him. "I'll give you a lesson about my business, Tony. Once the deal closes, a good salesman never thinks about what the buyer does with the product."

The boy nodded and started for the station, the bag over his shoulder.

Sloan got back in his company car and started the engine. He opened his attaché case and looked over the sales sheets for tomorrow. Some good prospects, he reflected happily. He turned the AC up full, pulled out of the parking lot, and headed east, looking for a hotel where he could spend the night.

"You believe in God, Sloan?"

"No. I believe in selling. That's about it."

"That's your *soul then."*

Dave Sloan reflected, *It sure is.*

Warmed to ninety-eight point six.

THE LAST OF THE BAD GIRLS

David Handler

David Handler was born and raised in Los Angeles, where "The Last of the Bad Girls" takes place, and he published two highly acclaimed novels about growing up there, *Kiddo* and *Boss*, before resorting to a life of crime fiction. He has written eight novels featuring the witty and dapper celebrity ghostwriter Stewart Hoag, including the Edgar and American Mystery Award–winning *The Man Who Would Be F. Scott Fitzgerald*. He has also written extensively for television and films on both coasts and coauthored the international best-selling thriller *Gideon* under the pseudonym Russell Andrews. With the publication of *The Cold Blue Blood* in October 2001, he launched a new mystery series featuring the mismatched crime-fighting duo of New York film critic Mitch Berger and Connecticut state trooper Desiree Mitry. Mr. Handler presently lives in a 200-year-old carriage house in Old Lyme, Connecticut.

"I CAN'T believe it—that's *Mildred Todd*," Lieutenant Marco Gianfriddo of the NYPD whispered to me excitedly. He and I were eating breakfast in the coffee shop of the Sportsman's Lodge on Ventura and Coldwater, and he was still a little starstruck. Make that a lot starstruck.

"Not a chance. Mildred Todd has been dead for years."

"Oh, yeah? Tell that to the little old lady who's sitting over there by herself in the corner, sipping hot tea."

"Marco, there are *three* little old ladies sitting over there by themselves, sipping hot tea."

I should point out that the coffee shop of the Sportsman's Lodge was, in pitch parlance, Schwab's Drugstore meets *The Day of the Locust* meets *Jurassic Park*. If you sat there long enough, you'd see virtually everyone who'd been anyone in Hollywood—and wasn't anymore—hanging out at a table, working on her needlepoint, passing around pictures of his grandkids, or just plain dozing. It was a combination coffee klatch, clan gathering, and seniors' center. If they ever drove a getaway car on *Mannix*, they were in there. If they ever took a ride on *The Loveboat*, they were in there.

We were in there because we'd flown out from New York to pitch a new series to the network, and I always stayed at the Lodge, that wonderfully indomitable survivor of the Rat Pack era with its exotic gardens and its man-made streams stocked with rainbow trout. Kids used to fish for them while their parents were seated inside the sumptuous dining room, knocking back martoonis. More recently, it had gotten a bit seedy and faded, and you didn't see anyone fishing for anything. But I still vastly preferred it to the Four Seasons and those other high-priced spreads. The Lodge was a place where everyone had a story to tell. Being an ex-newspaperman, which is to say a newspaperman for life, I always gravitated toward such places. Besides, from the Lodge you could stroll right down Ventura to the big sound stages on Radford. Plus there was a Hughes supermarket directly across the street open twenty-four hours a day and an all-night deli, Jerry's, two doors down. If you were a New Yorker, you could almost feel at home there.

Not quite, but almost.

Our pitch, which was essentially *Donnie Brasco* meets *The Brothers McMullen*, had gone over unbelievably well. The suits grew goggle-eyed with excitement when we wanted them to, laughed when we wanted them to, and—

most significantly—said yes when we wanted them to. They *wanted* to make a deal with us. After all, I was already running their top-rated drama, *The Street Life*, a gritty cop show that came out of my own youthful experiences as a police beat reporter for one of the New York City tabloids. And Gianfriddo was the real thing: a squarely built homicide detective in his forties who possessed the calm self-assurance of a man who has seen it all. I had discovered him, if you want to call it that, when he started sending me unsolicited scripts. They showed tremendous promise; his dialogue positively crackled. Intrigued, I invited him to sit in on our story meetings. Soon he was writing episodes for us. And I was helping him develop a drama about a closely knit family of cops based on his own home life. Now we had ourselves a network pilot deal and the rest of the day to start writing it outside by the pool with our shirts off. It had been thirty-five degrees when we left New York. In Studio City, it was a bright and balmy ninety. Our plane home didn't leave until four.

If only I could get him to stop staring at that little old lady sipping her tea.

I had never seen such unabashed adoration on this man's face—all for an ancient, albeit fine-boned, woman wearing an oversized man's dress shirt, lime green stretch pants, and perforated orthopedic shoes. She had the palest blue eyes I'd ever seen, delicate features, and milky white hair that was pulled back in a ponytail. She appeared to be reading her horoscope in that morning's *Times* as she drank her tea and nibbled on a piece of dry toast.

"That little lady over there was *the* queen of film noir," he said in a low, appreciative voice. "You do remember her, don't you, Alex?"

Of course I did. There had been a choice handful of actresses who specialized in playing the bad girls in those wonderfully dark, brooding, black-and-white thrillers of the late forties and early fifties. Jane Greer and Marie Windsor come to mind. So do Gloria Graham and Jan Sterling. But none of them could touch Mildred Todd—especially in *Ten Cents a Dance*, the tough-talking 1950 noir classic in which she drove the boys wild as a smoldering, scheming little dance hall girl named Lorelei Evans. The plot had to do with an armored car heist. There was a falling-out among the thieves. There was a double cross. And there was Mildred, right in the middle of it, playing Robert Mitchum off against Edmond O'Brien. She had a laconic, mocking air, bedroom eyes, pouty lips, and flaring nostrils. She was steamy and she was tough and nobody got the best of her. Not even Mitchum. But her heyday was a short one. When it became a Doris Day, Technicolor world, she was banished to grade Z sci fi films about slimy, one-eyed swamp creatures. And then she was over and out. I couldn't remember seeing her in anything in years. She had to be pushing eighty.

"Man, I loved her when I was a kid," Gianfriddo gushed. "She was my dream girl."

"So why don't you go tell her. You'll make her day."

"Nah, I couldn't."

"Marco, you're producing your own network series. You're hot stuff now."

"Hey, maybe we could create a part for her."

I must confess I was thinking the same thing. *Roseanne* had gotten great press mileage a few years back by bringing Shelley Winters out of retirement. Maybe we could lure the great Mildred Todd back as our hero's tough-as-nails Brooklyn grandmother. "Go feel her out," I suggested.

"Will you come with me?"

I went with him, Marco drawn to her like a yellow jacket to a glass of Kool-Aid, me hanging back a little.

"May we join you, Miss Todd?" he asked her.

She looked up at us, startled. "Excuse me?"

"You *are* Mildred Todd, aren't you?"

She breathed slowly in and out several times, as if to assuage a panic attack. The come-hither look of her glorious youth had been replaced by wide-eyed fear. "Who is Mildred Todd?" Her voice was faint, the inflection more Philadelphia Main Line than it was Canarsie.

"You are, and you darned well know it," Gianfriddo said. "My partner and I are doing a new show, and we think there may be a part in it for you. May we sit?" On her slight, unsure nod, we sat. "We're writers, you see. Well, Alex is the real writer. He's Alex Koffman, the man behind *The Street Life*. I'm just a cop who's moonlighting."

The old lady blanched. "You're a *policeman*?"

"I am but I'm not. I'm on the wrong coast right now."

"Honey, I've been on the wrong coast since nineteen hundred and forty-four."

He let out a laugh, delighted that she'd shown us a dash of her old vinegar. "It's such an honor to meet you, Miss Todd. I am a huge fan."

Mildred shot a quick, anxious glance at the door, as if she were dying to run through it. Then she turned her gaze back to Gianfriddo, looking him up and down. "You weren't even born when I was making pictures."

"I used to sit up half the night watching you on the late-late show."

"Then you must be a very, very baaad boy."

"Wait, wait . . . you said that to Edmond O'Brien in *Ten Cents a Dance*. Am I right? That scene in the cab right after he picked you up in the dance hall."

"He just *thought* he picked me up." She sniffed.

"*You* picked *him* up," Gianfriddo said quickly, nodding.

She arched an eyebrow at him. "So you *are* a fan."

"What I've been telling you. So what are you doing with yourself?" he asked. "Are you retired?"

This drew a scornful laugh. "Actors don't retire. First your agent stops returning your calls. Then people stop making eye contact with you in restaurants. And then, poof, you cease to exist. Except you don't." She glanced around at her fellow has-beens. "We're still here. All of us are still very much . . ." Now she trailed off. Again, I noticed that she seemed uncommonly preoccupied and edgy. Every time someone came in the door, she would tense up. Meanwhile, she hadn't pressed us for any information about the part. From an actress, this was unheard of.

Gianfriddo noticed it, too. "Is something wrong, Miss Todd? Is there anything we can do?" The man was blessed with a wonderfully calming bedside manner. As well as eyes that were as warm and moist as a stray spaniel's.

She reached across the table and put her translucent, thin-boned hand over his, where it commenced to throb and twitch like a dying parakeet. "You ask me if there's anything you can do as if it's the most natural thing in the world. . . ."

"Anything, Miss Todd."

"It so happens . . ." She lowered her eyes, hesitating. "You see, I *am* in terrible trouble."

"What kind of trouble?"

"He wants to kill me!" Now she was trembling, her voice spiked by an urgency that bordered on terror.

"Who wants to kill you?" I asked.

"It's because I know the truth. It's because I *know*."

I peered across the table at her doubtfully. The word *Alzheimer's* came to mind. But her eyes were clear and sharp, her gaze steady. "*Who* wants to kill you?"

Her response came in a whisper: "Max Diamond."

"*Max Diamond?*" Max Diamond had been running Pan-

orama Studios for over a half century. There was no bigger
mogul or power broker on the West Coast. You didn't
become governor or president or a star without his en-
dorsement. Max Diamond *was* the Hollywood establish-
ment. And even though he was presently pushing ninety,
he was still chairman of the board, still The Czar. "What
about Max Diamond?" I asked.

Mildred reached for her tea. "He's trying to kill me, like
I told you," she said, sipping it.

"Now why would he want to do that?" Gianfriddo asked
gently.

"Because I want my money. It's a good deal of money.
One hundred thousand dollars, if you must know. And it's
mine. I've earned it. And I want it."

"Have you got anything on paper?" I asked. "If he's
trying to cheat you out of the back end of your contract,
a good lawyer should be able to——"

"No, no," she broke in. "This is not studio business. It's
personal, between Max and myself. He promised to take
care of me if I kept quiet. I know the truth about him,
you see. I know how he got his job. No one else knows.
Just Max and me. And it's the only asset I've got left. I
have no car. No savings. I'm practically subsisting on dog
food. And I told him so. I need my money. I must have
it—or else. And now I-I'm being followed. Someone is
following me."

"If that's the case, I do know some fellows on the force
out here," Gianfriddo offered. "I can make some calls."

"No cops," she responded sharply.

"Why not, Miss Todd?"

"Because then I'll never see one penny of the money. I
may be an old woman, but I am no fool." She reached into
her worn leather purse and took out a mirror and lipstick
and went to work on her mouth with a garish shade of
magenta. "Max knows people who can do it, too. Bump

me off, I mean. They'll fly in from Vegas or Detroit. They'll conk me over the head. And everyone will think I fell down in the bathtub or whatever it is that happens to decrepit old women who live alone. . . ." She faltered, her chest rising and falling as if she had just run up five flights of stairs. I knew actresses. Actresses were friends of mine. And this one wasn't hamming. She was genuinely frightened.

"Well, how *did* he get his job?" I asked her.

"No, no . . ." Mildred leaned across the table at me. "Not here. Too many people are listening. And they'd sell me out in a heartbeat for one day's work. A part, any part." She moistened her freshly painted lips with the tip of her tongue. "Do you gentlemen know where Kowloon Gardens is?"

"We can find it," Gianfriddo said.

"Meet me there at noon. Come alone. Bring no one. Do you hear me? Bring no one."

KOWLOON Gardens was a small, rather tired-looking neighborhood Chinese restaurant located three blocks down Ventura from the Lodge. Mildred was on her third mai tai in the dimly lit cocktail bar when we got there at noon with no one. She sat alone, a floppy straw hat pulled down low over her face.

"Help me out here, Marco," I said as we paused there in the doorway. "The premise of this scene is what?"

"We're helping someone who's in trouble," he said quietly. "This is my day job, Alex. This is what I do. If you want out, I'll understand."

"No way. You might be a grizzled veteran of the mean streets, but when it comes to Hollywood, you are strictly Felicity. Someone needs to watch your back."

I wasn't just watching it, I was talking to it. He was

already plowing across the restaurant to join his celluloid dream girl.

"I've been thinking it over. . . ." she said to us after he and I had ordered beers. "If you can collect what's owed to me, I'll give you half."

"We don't want your money, Miss Todd," Gianfriddo said.

"But I can't ask you to do this for nothing," she insisted, slurring her words slightly.

"Why don't you just tell it to us from the beginning," he said soothingly.

"Well, OK," she allowed. "But first let me ask you something. Is there a statute of limitations on murder?"

Gianfriddo raised an eyebrow at her. "No, there is not."

"Good, because Max Diamond killed a man once. Shot him dead. It was a long, long time ago. And it wasn't just anyone. . . ." She broke off, lunging for her drink. Her hand shook as she raised it to her lips.

"Who was it, Miss Todd?" I asked.

When she said the victim's name, Gianfriddo and I immediately stopped breathing.

She was right. It wasn't just anyone.

After a long moment, I said, "How do you know this?"

"Because I was right there when it happened," she replied, her voice turning low and flat. "I was Maxie's girl at the time—the standard off-camera role for every new contract cutie. . . . It was June 1947. The twentieth. It was a warm evening, just before eleven. We were supposed to be on our way to Ciro's in Maxie's black Caddy. He told me he had to make a stop first. It was at a big house on Linden Drive, just south of Sunset. The number was 810. He got out and fetched an Army rifle out of his trunk. And he waited there in the shadow of a rose-covered pergola, resting the barrel of it on a crossbar of the latticework, waiting for someone to open the living room drapes. He fired through the window exactly nine times. I can still remember that. Then he jumped in the car, and we drove on to Ciro's as if nothing had happened. I wore a gold lamé gown cut down to here and a diamond necklace that belonged to studio wardrobe. When I came down that staircase, every man in the place wanted me, every single one of them. God, I was something. . . ." Briefly, she got a fond, faraway look in her eyes. Then she snapped back to here and now and added, "That's how he got the job. It was payback. That's how he took over the studio."

When she'd finished with the details, I said, "Miss Todd, if what you say is true—"

"Oh, it's true. Every single word of it."

"Then you're sitting on one of the biggest stories in the entire history of show business."

"What do you think I've been trying to tell you?" she said tartly.

"My point is this: if it's money you're after, why don't you sell it to the tabloids? It's bound to fetch huge bucks."

"No tabloids," she sniffed. "I know how they operate. All of the sleaze will end up rubbing off onto me."

"Okay, do a memoir then. Publishers will line up to buy it after they hear this story."

"I'm no writer."

"They'll hire you one."

Mildred shook her head slowly from side to side. "I will only deal with Max. He made a promise to me. And I intend to hold him to it. I've tried to call him. Only he won't take my calls. And now . . . now I'm scared. Because *he's* scared. See, he wants them to name that new children's wing at Cedars Sinai after him. He's put up millions for it. But they won't name a hospital wing after a murderer, will they?"

"Well, it probably wouldn't be the first time," Gianfriddo said, rubbing his chin thoughtfully.

Mildred's pale blue eyes gave him a thorough undressing. "You're an awfully nice-looking fellow, you know that? Shy, sweet smile. Big shoulders. Good strong wrists. I always measure a man by his wrists." She reached across the table and gripped him by his, clinging to him like a small skiff lashed to a sturdy dock in a storm. "There was a time when I could have gone for you in a big way," she purred.

"Likewise," he said, enjoying this hugely.

"Are you married, handsome?"

"Very happily, yes." And poor Rosalie thought it was the Heather Locklears of the world she had to worry about.

"Well, don't you dare double-cross me," she said to him with sudden vehemence.

"Now why would I do that?" he protested.

She let out a harsh laugh. "You're a man, aren't you?"

I paid the check, and we escorted her outside into the bright, hot sunlight. Mildred was tiny. Barely five feet tall. And she was clearly feeling the effects of those drinks. She leaned heavily against Gianfriddo for support.

"You're awfully . . . awfully tall," she murmured, gazing up at him. Her eyes seemed to be having trouble staying in focus. "Care to dance . . . ?"

"I thought we already were," he replied, smiling at her.

Our rented Grand Am was parked at the curb, our bags loaded into the trunk. I unlocked it and helped her into the backseat. By the time Gianfriddo and I got in front, she'd begun to snore, small bubbles of saliva forming on her thin lips.

"Okay," I sighed helplessly. "This is the moment where one of us turns to the other and says, 'Remember, pardner, we have a four o'clock plane to catch.' "

"Not a problem, Alex. We'll run the lady home, and then we'll head straight for the airport."

"And two hours from now we'll be high over the Grand Canyon, eating shrimp cocktails and laughing about this."

"We may be eating shrimp cocktails," he said somberly, "but I don't think we'll be laughing about this."

"You got that right. You don't suppose there's any truth to her story, do you?"

"Not a chance. Why, do you?"

"No way." I reached over the seat for the old lady's purse and opened it, releasing a strong smell of mothballs. The first thing I found in there was a gun—a small derringer that looked like a prop gun she might have once worn stuffed in her garter. "Is this thing loaded?" I asked, handing it to him.

He examined it expertly. "It sure is."

"Could she actually kill someone with it?"

"If she got close enough, sure."

I kept searching. I found cheap drugstore cosmetics, a packet of tissues, a pair of reading glasses, a coin purse. I found a worn-looking bankbook from Glendale Federal, the kind you never see anymore unless you rummage through an old person's belongings. She had $12.39 in her account. I found a wallet. According to her driver's license, which had expired four years ago, she lived on Woodman Avenue in Van Nuys. And was eighty-one years old.

Her place was out in the sun-baked flats near Victory Boulevard. It was a limp, dreary neighborhood full of limp, defeated people. Mildred lived in a faded two-story apartment house that had probably been pumpkin color at one time. But never very nice. There were eight units. The apartments facing the street had tinfoil taped over their windows to deflect the sun's searing rays.

When I shut off the engine, Mildred stirred and started to get out. Gianfriddo helped her. She leaned against him for support, but she was able to walk. Her unit was around in back, up a flight of stairs. We took them slowly, one step at a time.

It wasn't until we'd reached the upstairs landing that we discovered that her door was half open, the lock smashed.

Someone had broken in.

"I told you," Mildred cried forlornly. "He's trying to scare me. Didn't I tell you?"

"You told us," I admitted.

Gianfriddo pulled his service piece and shoved the door open wide. "You'd better wait here," he warned, starting inside with his gun drawn.

He hadn't taken more than two steps through the door when suddenly a bulked-up young pit bull with a shaved head and a nose ring came lunging out from behind it and grabbed Mildred by the scruff of the neck, lifting the poor old thing half off of her feet. She let out a feeble moan as he clutched her against his chest with a big left arm, using her as a human shield. He had a semiautomatic handgun in his meaty right hand. This he held against her trembling head.

"I am out of here," he growled at us. "You won't try to stop me, will you?"

Gianfriddo's jaw muscles tightened. Otherwise, he was motionless. "We won't try."

"Good." He shoved her at Gianfriddo and took off, ramming me out of his way as he flew down the stairs. I bounced hard off of the wall and went down, feeling as if I'd just been hit by a medium-size sport utility vehicle. By the time I'd scrambled back up and gone after him, he had jumped in his car and sped away. I did not see what he was driving.

Back upstairs, Gianfriddo had helped Mildred over to the sofa, where she was stretched out, looking very tired and pale. It occurred to me, from the way he stood there gazing down at her, that there had once been a time when this would have been his most tumid of fantasies. He and Mildred Todd, together in her apartment. But that was yesterday. Today she was just a lost little old lady.

"Is she okay?"

He nodded and found a blanket in the bedroom and put it over her. It was warm and stuffy in her apartment, but she was shaking so badly her teeth were chattering.

The apartment was small and plainly furnished. Over the sofa hung a truly smashing oil portrait that a studio artist had painted of Mildred when she was at her sexiest best. It belonged over a mantel in Beverly Hills, not here. It was the only indication of who she had once been. There were no photos of her on display, no memorabilia.

We looked the place over. It had been thoroughly tossed. The boxes of rice and dry cereal in her kitchen cupboards had been dumped into the sink. Her bedroom closet had been ransacked, her dresser drawers emptied. She had hundreds of pairs of old shoes stashed in there. Designer stuff from the fifties. The rest of her wardrobe was strictly from today's JCPenney. The contents of her jewelry box had been dumped on the floor. Strictly costume stuff available at any drugstore.

"I should phone this in, Alex," Gianfriddo said to me in a low, grim voice. "I should report this."

"And say what—that someone is trying to scare her?"

"Not someone. Max Diamond."

"So now you believe her story?"

"Don't you?"

"Marco, I don't know what to believe. All I know is that in less than one hour, our plane is leaving."

"I'm staying over," he said, sticking his jaw out at me. "I can't leave her alone like this. You want to head home, go right ahead. I won't hold it against you."

But I wasn't going anywhere either, and we both knew

it. Because he was right; Mildred was alone and defenseless. And because he and I were partners now. Partners stuck together.

Mildred couldn't stay there, not without a lock on the door, so we packed her a bag and drove her back to the Lodge and checked her in there, along with ourselves.

"How do we get to see Max Diamond?" Gianfriddo wanted to know after we'd unpacked for the second time and bumped our flight back by twenty-four hours.

"There are ways."

And our agent knew all of them. That was why he was our agent.

After dark, Gianfriddo and I drove over the hill on Coldwater to Sunset and headed down the Strip to Massimo's, with its windows overlooking the glittering lights of the city and its tables crowded with a revolving A-list of Hollywood stars and power brokers. Max Diamond ate dinner there every Wednesday night. He always got there at six. And he always cleared out before the eight o'clock crowd arrived.

There was valet parking, and that spot in the driveway where the patrons waited for their cars to be delivered was considered prime buttonhole territory. This was where an ambitious agent—or a pair of writers masquerading as white knights—could grab twenty precious seconds of face time with the one and only Max Diamond.

At precisely seven-thirty, he came strolling out with his third wife on his arm and a toothpick in his mouth. He was eighty-eight years old now, but still tall and broad-shouldered and commanding with his long beak of a nose and magnificent pompadour of silver hair. The Hawk, they'd always called him. He was immaculately tailored in a black suit, black tie, and sparkling white dress shirt with French cuffs and sapphire cuff links. His wife, the former torch singer Bonnie Morgan, was equally well decked out.

"Good evening, Mr. Diamond," I spoke up, extending my hand. "Alex Koffman."

"Love your show," he said pleasantly, gripping it. "Heard you just sold them another one, you little pisher. This must be your cop friend, am I right?" He grinned at Gianfriddo. "Sure I am. After all of these years I can still smell a cop." And he still knew everything there was to know. That was what made him Max Diamond. That and the fact that he genuinely terrified people.

"We ran into an old friend of yours today, Mr. Diamond," I said quickly. "She told us an incredibly wild story about you."

"Is that so?" he responded as his vintage Bentley came pulling up smartly before us. "Who was it?"

"Mildred Todd," Gianfriddo said.

When he heard that name, Max Diamond's expression changed instantly. His eyes got hard, his jaw tight. His fists clenched. He shot a quick, worried glance over at his wife, who was being helped into the car by the valet parking kid, then turned back to us. "Not here," he said between gritted teeth. "My office. Come to my office tomorrow morning at ten. We'll talk then, okay?"

HIS personal elevator brought us to the top floor of Panorama's Burbank office tower at two minutes before the appointed hour. The carpeting in Max Diamond's suite was thick, the flowers fresh, the lighting muted. A crisply efficient secretary led us through the tall double doors into his private corner office, which had floor-to-ceiling windows looking out over the studio's vast back lot, most of it now a theme park for tram loads of Japanese tourists. The sound stages were still in use, though. I'd churned out shows in them a couple of times.

Max Diamond's walls were adorned with photos of him

taken with seven different U.S. presidents, with Nelson Mandela and Bishop Tutu, with Elvis, with Frank Sinatra, with the Beatles. There were dozens of honorary awards from charitable foundations. Also a collection of ten Oscar statuettes on display inside a locked glass case.

The Hawk was seated in a high-backed black leather chair behind a desk that was one long slab of ebony. Not a hair was out of place. Not a thing was on his desk other than a phone and a large jar of red jelly beans. He was dressed exactly as he had been the night before: black suit, black tie, white shirt, and sapphire cuff links. It was the only outfit he ever wore. Supposedly he kept at least three dozen black suits in his closet at all times, because after he'd worn a suit once, he gave it away. There were waiters, bartenders, and car attendants all over town wearing Max Diamond's old suits. This was a famous little quirk of his.

"How did you fellows get mixed up with Mildred?" he asked coolly after we sat down across from him.

"We thought she might be right for a part in our new show," I answered.

"Just between us, I don't think so," he confided, pursing his lips thoughtfully. "But I'm glad you mentioned her; she's been on my mind lately."

"Why is that?"

"Because she's been driving me nuts, that's why. Phoning me over and over and over again. *'I'm gonna destroy you, Maxie,'* she keeps telling me. *'You won't get away with this, Maxie.'* She phones me here. She phones me at my house, at my club. I've even caught her hanging around outside my house, like some kind of crazy stalker. I call her a cab and send her home. Next day, she's right back again. I really, really don't want to go to court on this. If I get an injunction filed against her, it'll end up in the newspapers. And that would be just tragic. Mildred and me, there was a time she meant a lot to me. I don't want to see her name dragged through the mud. But she's scaring my poor wife half to death, and I honestly don't know what the devil she wants from me."

"Mr. Diamond, we may be able to shed some light on that."

He laid his large, manicured hands on the desk, palms up. "Please do."

"She thinks you've put out a hit on her," Gianfriddo said.

"A *hit?*" Max Diamond stared down his long beak at us, flabbergasted. "Assuming I even knew how to do that, which I don't, why on earth would I want to bump off *Mildred Todd?*"

"Because she knows a deep, dark secret about you," I responded. "Or so she claims. She also claims that you promised to pay her for her silence."

"*What* deep, dark secret?"

Gianfriddo took a deep breath and said, "Mr. Diamond, Mildred told us that you're the man who shot Bugsy Siegel."

Max Diamond bristled, his cold, hard eyes flickering at us. For a brief instant, I was certain that Mildred's story was true. But then he threw back his head and laughed and laughed, and my certainty evaporated. "You've got to be kidding me!" he roared, wiping his eyes with a linen hankerchief.

"No joke," said Gianfriddo. "She told us that she was there with you when you shot him. She gave us a very detailed description of how it went down. And why. According to Mildred, you were brought out here after the war from Detroit by Meyer Lansky to strong-arm the unions. She said that you reported directly to Ben Siegel, who soon got himself embroiled in a turf war with Mickey Cohen and Jack Dragna. When it was time for him to go, Lanksy chose you to carry out the order because you were a neutral party; if you did it, there'd be no bloodbath. As payment for the job, Lanksy saw to it that you took over Panorama Studios."

Max Diamond shook his regal, pompadoured head at us. "My god, she's even crazier than I thought."

"You're saying she has made all of this up?" I asked.

"Of course she has," he responded, his pale tongue flicking at his lips. "One of Jack Dragna's trigger men shot Ben. Everybody knows that. Everybody knows the details, too. She must have read them in a book. Hell, that shooting's been almost as well-documented as the JFK killing."

"Did you know Ben Siegel?" Gianfriddo asked.

"Everyone in the business knew him," he said easily. "Ben was a real character. Handsome, charismatic, charming . . ."

"Did you work for him?"

"Never. He was a thug."

"Was Mildred ever your girl?"

"They were all my girls," he said, gazing out the window at his empire. For a moment he was back there, remembering it, relishing it. Then, abruptly, he shook himself and returned to us. "Look, fellows, there's something you have to understand about Mildred. She was never all there to begin with. And now that she's getting on in years, well, I wouldn't be surprised if she's had a couple of those small strokes that are so common in people our age. Happened just last month to an old hoofer I know. Sweetest, most generous guy in the world. Now he thinks all his old friends are trying to steal from him. If we stop by to visit, he calls the police. . . . Just exactly how much did she say I was going to pay her?"

I told him.

"And she offered to split this hundred grand with you, am I right?" He made a pained face. "This is straight out of an old script, fellows. She's turning into a character in one of those B pictures of hers. This is a sad, sad thing."

"But someone *did* ransack her apartment yesterday," Gianfriddo pointed out.

"Did you happen to get a look at him?"

"We did."

"Was he a bodybuilder type with a shaved head and a nose ring?"

"That's him," I affirmed.

"That's no hit man. That's her grandson, Tommy."

"He had a gun."

"I don't know a single performer who doesn't carry a gun in their glove compartment these days."

"You mean he's an actor?"

"Actor slash bum," Max Diamond replied sourly. "I got him some bit roles playing heavies on *Baywatch, Hunter,* that sort of crap. He couldn't hack it. Showed up late, unprepared, high. Now he's just a druggie. When he gets hard up for cash, he cleans poor Mildred out. Not that she's got much left. Just her Social Security check and her memories. She never made more than a couple of thou a week, and the gonif who she married lost every penny of it in the real estate business." He paused, running a hand across his tanned, lined face. "Will you be seeing her again?"

"We will."

He produced a slim silver money clip from his pocket and peeled off five crisp $100 bills and slid them across the desk to me. "Tell her to buy herself a new pair of shoes. She was always mad for shoes. Pairs and pairs of them. She took a size five double-A. Funny the things you remember, isn't it?" The Hawk sat back in his chair, his hands folded in his lap. "Mildred Todd could do more with the simple gesture of lighting a cigarette than Streep can do with a hundred pages of dialogue. But that was all make believe.

She was never really that smart or that tough. She was just a beautiful, not-too-bright little thing from Akron, Ohio, who loved nice clothes and dance bands. We used to go down to the Aragon Ballroom together, out on the pier. Light as a feather in my arms, she was. That's why I gave her the part in *Ten Cents a Dance*. Because she was the best dancer on the lot. But the Mildred Todd who you fellows know from her old movies—that Mildred Todd was strictly an illusion. As soon as the director yelled, 'Cut,' she vanished into thin air. That's why they call them actors." Something in his eyes slammed shut now. He climbed to his feet, his manner turning brusque. "Now, if you will excuse me, I've got a contingent from Sacramento waiting."

"Could you find a part in a movie for her?" Gianfriddo asked. "For old times' sake?"

"There are no old times. In this business, there's today and there's tomorrow."

"But she's Mildred Todd," Gianfriddo protested.

The Hawk let out a short laugh and said, "Who is Mildred Todd?"

She was an old lady in a floppy hat who was waiting for us back in the coffee shop of the Sportsman's Lodge. I gave her Max's $500, plus another $500 that Marco and I threw in, and I told her what Max had said to us about her story.

In response, she said, "And you believed him, you fools?"

She didn't say anything else. Didn't thank us. Didn't even pay her breakfast check, come to think of it. She just grabbed her money and left.

Like I said before, everyone at the Sportsman's Lodge had a story to tell. I still don't know which one of them to believe. Gianfriddo thinks that Max Diamond really did kill Bugsy Siegel. Some sort of cop's intuition. And maybe Max did. I have no idea. I also have no idea what happened to Mildred after that. We gave the role in our new show to another actress.

And, after that, we started staying someplace else when we came to town.

CHILD SUPPORT

Ronnie Klaskin

Ronnie Klaskin has had short stories in *EQMM*, Whittle Communications' *Special Report*, and *The West Side Spirit*, among others. She has won prizes for her short stories and poetry. She has been active in Mystery Writers of America, Sisters in Crime, and The International Association of Crime Writers. She has an MFA in fiction writing from Vermont College.

—————

IT is not easy being a hot and sultry woman on a hot and sultry night. Too much sweat and stickiness. No seductive lingerie from Victoria's Secret. Just an old fan blowing on naked, overheated skin.

The air conditioner is not working again.

But all Carl wants of me is passion. Passion always, whether I feel it or not. He hardly even sweats. Not even at the gym where I met him. And he works out hard. I know. I was his personal trainer when we met. He was surprised at how strong a woman like me can be.

I'm five six but slender. A hundred and thirty pounds. But solid. I look thinner.

Carl is not much taller, five eight and weighs maybe a hundred and fifty. But he's very muscular with broad shoulders and narrow hips. He's very handsome with black curly hair and dark brown eyes, so dark they are almost opaque.

Carl is not my husband.

Philip is long gone. He lost interest soon after Samantha was born. Even though he was awarded visitation rights, he never visited except once. And he stopped paying the allotted child support. He left for places unknown, and no one's been able to find him.

Samantha is eleven now. She's very pretty and petite with blonde curls and blue eyes. Soon she'll have boys hovering around her.

I hear her moan in her hot bedroom. She has a fan, but there's still not much of a breeze. Her door is closed. She will not open it when Carl is sleeping here. Even if it is stifling.

She doesn't like Carl. She says he looks at her in a funny way. It makes her uncomfortable.

Carl moves his warm body next to mine. I don't need more heat. I don't need someone blocking the air from the window. I wish he would go home. And not come back till winter. He's getting on my nerves.

Carl kisses me again. His beard feels like sandpaper on my face. He blows in my ear. "I have some good news for you," he whispers.

"What?" I murmur.

"I found your husband. I found Philip."

I sit up, banging Carl hard in the chin with my head.

"Ouch," Carl says. He rubs his chin. "That hurt."

"Sorry," I say.

"I hired an Internet detective," Carl said. "He located Philip. Now you can sue for back child support. You won't have to live in this hellhole."

My house isn't that bad. It's a small, two-bedroom ranch and not in good repair. It could use a paint job, inside and out. The plaster is peeling, and the air conditioners don't work. The bathroom and the basement are mildewed, and the kitchen cabinets are old. But it is mine. I grew up in it. I inherited it from my father. So it was not community property.

I resent Carl for disparaging it.

The cicadas' hum fills the air. Raccoons trill. A cat howls. A cricket adds to the cacophony.

"He won't pay it," I say. "And then what? They'll throw him in jail. What good will that do anyone?"

"You have to try," Carl says.

Have to? What right has he to tell me what I have to do? What right has he to hire a detective to search for Philip? I never asked him to. If I wanted to find Philip, I would. It is my business, not Carl's.

Oh, yes, Carl would like to make me his business. He would like to control me just like Philip did. Carl makes me wear my blonde hair long, below my shoulders. It is hot on my neck. I should cut it short and punk. But Carl doesn't like that. He doesn't even want me to put it up when he's here. And the underwear, the fancy underwear. Not my style at all, but it's what Carl wants, and the short skirts and high heels. They make my feet hurt. I'm more comfortable in sneakers.

Philip was just the opposite. He did not want me to look sexy. When I was with him, my hair was short and its natural mousy brown. Mostly I wore jeans and oversized shirts. He hated it if I even smiled at another man. Then he had the nerve to be jealous of Samantha. His own baby. And to say that maybe she wasn't really his. As if another man would even look at me, the way Philip made me dress.

Well, OK, he did marry me because I was pregnant. But I had never slept with anyone besides him. Not in my entire life. I was too busy taking care of Daddy after my mother died.

Philip was the first and only man. I was twenty-four and

still a virgin, hard to believe. Daddy had just passed away. I needed a job. I didn't have a lot of skills. I finally got work in a department store, in the boys' clothing department.

That's where I met Philip. He was a customer. He was shorter than I was, only five four and slim. He had to buy his clothes in the boys' department. But he had a nice face. Big blue eyes, like Samantha has, and a bushy mustache.

He was the first man I ever slept with. Philip said we didn't need to use anything because it was not the right time of the month. Like a fool, I believed him. And right away, I got pregnant.

We got married by a justice of the peace. I was an only child, and both my parents were dead. Neither Philip nor I wanted a big, fancy wedding.

Philip moved into my house. He had it good.

He chose the furniture. All of it was his taste, not mine. A surprise, he said. One day I came home from work, and there it was. He had thrown out all of my parents' stuff without consulting me. Even the comfortable reclining chair that Daddy used to relax in. I loved that chair.

I came home from work and walked into the house. Philip was home, sitting on a black leather sofa. "Surprise!" he said.

I looked around the room. Hard-backed chairs. Barrel-shaped tables. Even the pictures my mother had so carefully chosen were gone, replaced by hunting scenes.

I began to cry.

"What's wrong?" Philip asked. "I thought you'd love it."

"My parents' stuff, the pictures? Where are they?"

I hoped he had at least stored them in the basement.

"Salvation Army," Philip said. "We'll get a good tax rebate." Philip was an accountant.

Philip wanted me to cook everything well done and

keep the house spotlessly clean. After Samantha was born, he wanted me to keep her quiet. She was colicky. He said the sound of her crying interfered with his listening to his opera CDs. He said they were the only thing that relaxed him after a hard day at work. He hated his job. He said I should give her the bottle and not nurse her. He said it made my breasts sag.

I guess he had to be bossy to compensate for his lack of size.

One day, when Samantha had the croup, he walked into her bedroom.

"I've had enough," he announced. "I'm leaving. I want a divorce."

Luckily, I was smart about one thing. I had a bit of money saved that I had planned to use for college. I had never told Philip about that.

I was able to use it to get myself a good attorney. Philip had to pay a lump sum of maintenance and a decent amount of child support.

AT least Carl makes me feel sexy. Desirable. He tells me I'm beautiful. He says I'm great in bed. But that, too, has its cost. Sometimes I don't feel like it. I just want to be left alone.

Now Carl says I should sell the house.

"You could get a lot of money for the land," he says. "They will tear the house down and build something larger."

Sure, one of those mansions on a 40 by 100 plot with no land, just big houses hugging one another. They destroy the feeling of the neighborhood. The house is in the suburbs, backing on a nature preserve. So there are no back door neighbors. Just trees and birds and bugs, raccoons and possum, groundhogs, lots of squirrels, an occasional turtle in the stream that edges my property. Or a duck. Flocks of Canada geese.

"The preserve would allow you to get even more money for it. At least it gives the illusion of a backyard," he says.

"And where would I go?" I ask. "It's not expensive living here. The mortgage is paid off. And because the house is old, the taxes are not that high. They're low by Long Island standards."

"You could move in with me," Carl says.

Sure, and then he would try to spend all the money from my sale. He liked showy things, showy women, showy cars, showy clothes.

He wouldn't have to help support Samantha if Philip paid back child support.

When he was ready to leave me, he would just kick me out.

It all made sense now. He'd have spent the money, and I'd have nothing left. I couldn't afford a new house at today's prices.

I've learned how to take care of myself. And of Samantha.

The moon is shining in through the bedroom window. I'm glad no one lives behind us. It's a bright, full moon tonight.

I hear Samantha's door open. She walks into the hall to the bathroom. She's naked. Her blonde hair falls around her shoulders. The moon shines on her budding breasts. She is maturing early, just like I did.

Carl sits up and watches her. "Nice little body she's got there," he says.

"Stop looking at her," I say. He'd better not touch her.

MY daddy tried touching me once, on the breast. I was nearly eighteen. It was soon after we lost my mother to cancer.

"Don't you dare do that," I told him. "Touch me again, and I'll move away."

Then he had a stroke, and he needed me to take care of him. So he behaved himself. As if he could do anything from the wheelchair.

I gave up any plans I had to go to college.

Daddy was only fifty, so he was not eligible for Medicare. An aide would have been expensive. But if I stayed home with him, I couldn't get a job.

Daddy owned a chain of dry cleaners. He had a partner named George, a fat, balding man who was married and had five children.

When Daddy left the hospital for rehab, George came to visit me. "I don't know what I'm going to do," I said.

"I can't afford to buy Oscar out," George said. "But I have an idea. It's a gamble for both of us. I can leave you and Oscar on the firm's medical care. I can pay you thirty thousand dollars a year as long as Oscar's alive. Then, when he dies, the business will be mine. How does that sound?"

"Fifty thousand," I said. I figured I was driving a hard bargain.

"Forty," George counteroffered.

I agreed.

I stayed home with Daddy for over five years. Had to lift him in and out of the bed and change his diapers. It's lucky I was strong.

When he died of a second stroke nearly six years later, I discovered the business had been worth several million dollars. Men can screw you in many ways.

I HEAR the toilet flush. Samantha trudges back to her room. I cover Carl's eyes with my hand.

Carl pulls down my hand, and he kisses it. He kisses

my lips and my neck and my breasts. His lips are hot. I feel like he's branding me with them.

Even the air smells heavy. The aroma of honeysuckle wafts into the room.

Then I smell burning. An electrical odor.

There is a sputtering noise. The fan stops.

Dead.

I pull out the plug.

"Oh, no," I mutter. I want to cry.

"Do you have another fan?" Carl asks.

"In the basement," I say. An old window fan. "I think it still works."

IT was Philip's. One day, six months after the divorce, he came home. I had just come back from work, and I saw his car parked in front of the house. I walked into the living room, and there he was sitting on one of the uncomfortable, hard-backed chairs.

"I've come to list the furniture," he said. "And my other things. I'm thinking of buying a house. I'll need them."

"You can't have them," I said.

"I paid for them," he said. "You got to keep the house."

"It was my daddy's house. You threw out all of Daddy's things. I never wanted to throw them out. You never even asked me what I wanted.

"You never liked this furniture anyhow," he said. "You preferred that old junk."

"I can't afford new stuff now," I said.

"You get child support. Use that," he said.

"I need it for Samantha. There are doctor's bills and clothing. There's diapers and baby food. I don't get paid a lot."

I was a receptionist at the gym then. It was good because

they had free child care. At least I didn't have to pay for that.

"I want the lawn mower, too," Philip said. "And the garden spade, the hand cart, the microwave, the fan, the VCR, the coffeemaker, and the stereo. I paid for all of those."

"You can't have them," I said.

Philip opened the door to the basement. He walked down the stairs. He looked around.

I followed him down. "You touch one thing, and I'm calling 911," I said.

"I'll be back when I find a house," Philip said. "I want the barbecue grill. And the lawn furniture, too. I'll be back with a couple of guys and a truck when I'm ready. It's too much to move myself."

"You can't have any of it," I said.

"Maybe I'll take you to court," Philip said. "Maybe I'll sue for custody of Samantha."

"You don't even like Samantha," I said. "You don't want custody."

"Right," he said. "But if I sue, it will cost you. We can bargain down my child support. And I can get all the furniture and stuff."

I looked at him as if he was crazy.

A mouse scurried across the basement floor. Philip picked up a broom and whacked at it.

"I could move," Philip said. "I could change my identity. Then you could never find me. I hate my job, anyway."

"You'd do this to your own child," I said. "I can't believe you'd be so selfish."

"She's not mine," Philip said. "I'll have them take a blood test. That should prove I'm not the father. You're just a whore. Sleeping with any man who came along. And you're not even any good in bed. I've had a lot better."

The next day, I changed the locks. I should have done it as soon as he divorced me.

Philip never came back. He never took the furniture. He didn't pay me any more child support. I never heard from him again.

CARL walks ahead of me to the basement. We are both not wearing any clothes.

The basement smells musty. But it is a bit cooler than the rest of the house. A dying water bug lies on its back. Its legs wave in the air.

I push the garden spade aside. I roll the handcart out of the way. A centipede scuttles out from behind it. "Here's the fan," I say.

It's a bit rusted. I hope it works. I pull it into the middle of the room.

Carl makes no attempt to help me. He just stands there and watches. I wish I had put on clothes.

"That kid of yours is quite the sexpot," Carl says. "The boys are going to be all over her soon."

He has an erection.

I pick up the spade. It's heavy and sharp-edged.

"I wouldn't mind fucking her myself," he says. He inspects the fan.

I lift the spade above my head.

"Nice little tits," he says.

The spade comes down on his head.

Again and again and again.

I drag the body to the freezer. I lean him in a sitting position against it.

The freezer is half full. I remove a couple of chickens and some boxes of peas and broccoli. I take out pints of chocolate and cookie dough ice cream and a large loaf of bread. I remove some hamburger patties and a couple of pound cakes.

I find two plastic drop cloths. They're splattered with yellow paint from the last time I tried to paint the kitchen. I use the larger one to line the bottom of the freezer.

I kneel and place my hands under Carl's arms. I hoist him up and drop his torso into the freezer. I then lift his legs and place the rest of his body there.

I put the second drop cloth on top of Carl's carcass. Then I cover it with the frozen food.

When we get some rain and the ground is soft, I will bury him in the preserve.

I pick up the fan and carry it upstairs. I put it in the window. I plug it in and turn it on. I don't need a man to do these things for me.

It works.

A cool breeze wafts through my bedroom.

I tiptoe to Samantha's room and open her door. She will be cooler now.

She doesn't have to worry about Carl anymore.

I shower. I need to get rid of Carl's scent.

I lie down in my bed, alone and comfortable now. The breeze from the fan feels good on my damp body.

I close my eyes.

I wonder who the man the Internet detective found is.

Of course, I know it's not Philip.

OLD DOG DAYS

Toni L. P. Kelner

Though Toni L. P. Kelner's books have all featured Southern sleuth Laura Fleming, she frequently turns to secondary characters from the imaginary town of Byerly, North Carolina, to populate her short stories. This story's protagonist, Andy Norton, has appeared in one other short story, and his daughter, Junior Norton, and former deputy Mark Pope figure prominently in Kelner's book *Mad as the Dickens*. When not taking fictional trips down South, Kelner lives just north of Boston, Massachusetts, with her husband Steve and daughters Maggie and Valerie. As a full-time mother and a full-time writer, she laughs at the idea of hobbies but is a beginning student in the martial art Chung Moo Doe.

"**WHEN** did you last see him?" Andy asked Payson Smith, but instead of answering, Payson glared at his wife Doreen.

"Around five-thirty, when I got back from Hardee's with dinner," Doreen said. "I cook most nights, but it was so hot that day that I hated to get the kitchen heated up."

Andy nodded understandingly, which he'd done for so many years that it looked pretty convincing. "Five-thirty yesterday evening."

Then Brian piped up with, "It couldn't have been yesterday. We had Kentucky Fried Chicken yesterday, and pizza the night before that. It must have been Wednesday." The boy smirked, pleased with himself for proving his stepmother wrong, not to mention the dig he'd gotten in about her cooking.

"Jesus Christ, Doreen!" Payson exploded. "Are you saying my dog's been missing for three solid days, and you didn't even notice?"

"You know I never go out back," she whined, "especially not as hot as it's been. Maybe if we got one of those above-ground pools . . ." Then, probably realizing that it wasn't a good time to bring that up, she said, "Besides, it's Brian's job to take Wolf his food and water. He's the one who should have figured out he was gone."

Payson turned his glare onto his son, and it was Doreen's turn to smirk.

"Well?" Payson prompted.

"You know I was over at Earl's every day," he said, whining just like his stepmother. *"She* knew that."

"Since when do you tell me where you're going to be?" Doreen shot back.

Andy could tell this was an old argument, so he spoke over them. "Then the last time either of you saw Wolf was Wednesday night, and since Payson was gone until late Friday night, nobody noticed he was gone until this morning. Is that right?"

Doreen and Brian nodded while Payson tried to decide which one deserved to be glared at more.

Andy wouldn't have minded glaring a little himself, but his target wasn't handy. Deputy Mark Pope was probably still at the police station, sitting at a desk he didn't deserve.

If Andy's wife had been there, she'd have told him it was his own fault. It's just that after having been Byerly's chief of police for so long, it was hard to keep from sticking his nose in. He did resist most of the time. After all, he'd trained his daughter Junior as his replacement, and he knew she could handle pretty much anything that came along. Plus she had enough sense to ask for help when she needed it. But Junior was out of town, which left Mark Pope in charge, and that was a horse of a different color.

Mark had been Andy's deputy before he was Junior's, so Andy knew the man wasn't stupid, exactly, but he also knew he didn't have the first bit of imagination. Since Andy figured it was nigh unto impossible to solve a tricky case without a little imagination, when he heard about Missy Terhune's murder, it only seemed polite to go down to the station and offer advice.

That's when Andy discovered that Mark had some imagination after all; he imagined that he'd been done wrong when Junior was made police chief over him. Andy didn't know if it was because Mark was a man and Junior was a woman or because Mark was older or what, but Mark sure thought he deserved Junior's job. With her out of town, he was bound and determined to prove it by solving this case on his own.

Not that Mark said that, of course. All he actually said was that he had the situation under control, but the color his face turned when Andy pushed for details meant that the murder was a long way from being solved. When Andy made a couple of suggestions, Mark got mad.

That's when he said there was something Andy could do to help, and Andy said he would, not knowing what Mark had in mind. He'd even let Mark deputize him for the day, the way they did folks who helped with parking at the Walters Mill picnic. Only then had he given Andy the missing dog report and told him to take care of it. To add insult to injury, the dog lived on Butler Street, just two doors down from the murder site.

Still, if Andy had learned one thing in his years as police chief, it was that people can get just as upset over a missing dog as over a murder, so he had to take it seriously.

"Was Wolf all right when you saw him Wednesday night?" he asked Doreen.

"I guess," she said. "Maybe suffering a little from the heat, but then again, so was I." She wiped her forehead and sighed, probably still thinking about that swimming pool.

"Did you hear anything out of him that night? Or any time after that?"

"Not a peep," she said. "Now that you mention it, that must mean he was gone Wednesday night."

"How do you figure that?"

"Because I *didn't* hear anything. That fool dog barks his head off any time anybody comes near the house, any hour of the day or night."

"He's supposed to bark," Payson said, outraged. "He's a watchdog."

Doreen just sniffed.

"Are y'all sure he didn't get out on his own?" Andy asked. Lord knows, if he only had Doreen and Brian to depend on, he'd get away any way he could.

"Yes, sir," Payson said firmly. "Come take a look at his pen." He led the way out the back door, and Andy noticed that neither Doreen nor Brian made a move to leave the air-conditioned house.

What little grass there was in the backyard was brown, making Andy wonder if lawn care was Brian's responsibility, too. Next to the house was a large chicken-wire pen enclosing a patch of dusty red earth and a bone-dry metal water bowl. There was a nice-sized dog house for shade, but Andy kept looking at that water bowl, wondering how long Doreen and Brian had let Wolf go without water during the hottest part of Byerly's long summer.

Payson must have been thinking the same thing because he said, "I don't understand how Brian can treat that dog so bad. Wolf's been part of the family nearly as long as he has. Hell, me and my ex fought more over who was going to get Wolf than we did over who was going to get Brian."

Andy didn't say anything, but he thought that might be the problem right there.

"And Doreen loves dogs," Payson went on. "When my ex wanted to keep Wolf, Doreen fought it tooth and nail. She said she needed him for company while I'm on the road, but we hadn't been married but a month when she found out she's allergic, so I had to put him outside. I made him this pen and got the best dog house I could find, but I know the old fellow thought he'd done something wrong."

Though everybody in Byerly knew Doreen had broken up Payson's first marriage, and Andy figured that she'd insisted on keeping the dog to spite the ex-wife, Andy kept what he was thinking to himself as he walked around the pen. There were no holes dug under the fence and no gaps anywhere big enough for anything larger than his daughter Denise's toy poodle to have slipped out. "Wolf is a big dog, isn't he?"

"One of the biggest German shepherds Dr. Josie's ever seen," Payson said proudly. "We took him to her when we first got him, and she could tell that he was going to be a big, strong dog. Smart as a whip, too."

Andy fiddled with the latch on the gate, but not even a canine genius could have opened it by himself. "I don't want to cause any trouble, Payson, but are you sure nobody left the gate open?"

"You heard Doreen—she never comes out here. And Brian would have owned up to it if he had. Somebody must have taken him." He could tell Andy wasn't convinced, because he added, "I called the pound as soon as I found him gone, but they haven't picked up any German shepherds all week. Then I called Dr. Josie, but she didn't know anything about him either. If he'd gotten loose, he'd have ended up at one place or the other."

"Those would be the two places I'd call," Andy said. In

fact, he'd have called Dr. Josie first. A lot of people wouldn't take a dog to the pound for fear they'd put it to sleep, but everybody knew Josie Gilpin didn't do that unless it was absolutely necessary. The veterinarian thought dogs and cats had as much right to live as human beings, maybe more so.

Right about then, Andy saw movement a couple of back yards away, behind the late Missy Terhune's house. Mark Pope was walking around, examining the ground as though there was something there to find. He looked over, saw Andy, and gave a mock salute. Andy had such a hard time resisting the kind of salute he wanted to return that all he could manage was a nod.

Payson saw Mark, too. "Wolf must have been gone by Thursday night, or he'd have let folks know there was a stranger nosing around, and Missy might still be alive."

"It doesn't look like it was a stranger," Andy said. "More like Miz Terhune let somebody inside the house and turned her back for a minute. Then whoever it was bludgeoned her with a cast-iron doorstop." Andy didn't mind telling Payson this because it was common knowledge already. Besides, Payson was a long-haul trucker who never hit town until late Friday night, so he wasn't a suspect.

"Didn't anybody see him going into the house?"

"Afraid not. I guess she had company coming by at all hours of the day and night, and folks didn't pay much attention." Since her own husband left her, Missy had been cutting quite a swath through the men of Byerly, married and single. It wasn't too hard to imagine that one of them hadn't appreciated sharing and made sure that it wouldn't happen again.

"She was a handsome woman," Payson said, sounding almost regretful. "Of course, it's a shame for that to happen to anybody. And I sure don't like a killing this close to

Doreen. If you can't find Wolf, I'm going to have to ask Dr. Josie to help me find a new watchdog."

In most cases, Andy would have told him not to give up so quickly, but he wasn't feeling real hopeful. Still, he owed it to Payson to do the best he could. He turned his back on Mark Pope and said, "Tell you what. I'll see what I can find out and get back to you." He left Payson staring at the empty pen.

Andy had gotten used to having a radio in his squad car to get in touch with people, so a few months after retirement, he'd broken down and gotten a cell phone. He climbed into his car, turned on the air conditioner full blast, and reached for the phone. There were a couple of calls he needed to make that he didn't want Payson to hear.

The thing was, Andy just couldn't see why anybody would have stolen that dog. According to Payson, Wolf was ten years old, and ten-year-old dogs aren't big resale items. While Andy had heard of dognapping rings that sold stolen dogs to laboratories, he'd never known such a ring to operate in Byerly and didn't think a professional would have risked grabbing a barking dog from a pen right next to a house.

What he thought was that somebody had opened the pen, if not Doreen or Brian, then a neighborhood kid. Either way, chances were that the dog had ended up on the road, which meant that he'd most likely been hit by a car.

So Andy called the public works people to find out if they'd picked up any dead dogs. They had disposed of three that week, but no German shepherds. Next he called the dump, but none of the garbagemen had brought in a dead dog, either.

Andy still thought Wolf was dead—there were plenty of places a dog's body could be without anybody noticing for a while—but he hated to tell Payson that. Besides,

Mark Pope picked that minute to come out of Missy Terhune's house and amble over to Andy's car. Andy reluctantly rolled down his window, and Mark leaned over, looking for all the world as if he was giving Andy a ticket.

"How's the investigation going?" Mark said with a shit-eating grin.

"Pretty routine," Andy said as evenly as he could. "You making any headway in your case?"

Mark shrugged nonchalantly. "Got a few ideas, waiting for some tests to come in. A murder's a lot more complicated than a lost dog, you know."

Andy thought about reminding him how many murders he'd solved, but decided it wasn't worth the effort. "I guess you're right."

Mark seemed disappointed but kept grinning as he said, "Let me know if you have any problems."

"You bet," was what Andy said, but he was thinking something different as Mark headed for the squad car and screeched away as if he had someplace important to go.

Andy wasn't about to give up after that, so he decided to take the so-called investigation to the next step: questioning possible witnesses. In other words, he talked to Payson's neighbors.

Old Miz Farley, whose house was to the left of Payson's, spent five minutes telling Andy what he should be doing about Missy Terhune's murder before he could explain that he wasn't working on that case. Then he had to listen to ten minutes of complaints about Wolf's barking. According to Miz Farley, she couldn't go outside to water her rosebushes without Wolf barking loud enough to wake the dead. Unfortunately, Miz Farley couldn't remember the last time she'd heard that barking, and she hadn't seen anybody messing with the dog.

Miz Farley hadn't seen anybody near Missy Terhune's house the night she was killed, either, but that didn't stop her from declaring that it wouldn't have happened if more of Terhune's friends had stayed at home with their wives. Andy couldn't resist asking for details, but Miz Farley insisted that she wasn't one to gossip. He probably could have wheedled more out of her, but instead he reminded himself that it wasn't his case, and he went to the next house on the street.

Miz Cranford wanted to talk on the porch because her husband Roy was on the night shift at the mill and was asleep inside. She hadn't noticed that Wolf was gone, but now that Andy mentioned it, it had been quiet the last half of the week. Since she worked days at the mill and was home alone at night, sometimes Wolf's barking made her nervous, and it kept Roy up during the day.

Miz Cranford also said she didn't blame the dog for running off because the way Doreen neglected him was a disgrace. She'd started filling his water bowl herself when she watered her lawn. In her opinion, people like that shouldn't have dogs in the first place.

Her indignation made Andy wonder if she'd taken Wolf, but he couldn't figure out how she could be hiding him in her house. Noisy watchdogs didn't turn quiet overnight, not even when given enough water.

The Cranford house was the last on the block, so Andy backtracked to the Titus house on the other side of Payson's, but Mr. Titus couldn't tell him anything; he was so deaf he'd never even noticed Wolf barking. The next house was Missy Terhune's, and the one after that was vacant and for sale.

The vacant place was the last on that side of the street, and though he wasn't sure if he was being thorough or foolish, Andy crossed the street to talk to the people over there. He didn't hear anything other than more complaints about Wolf barking too much and gossip about Missy Terhune's sunbathing in a bikini in her front yard, and he got the distinct impression that nobody was going to miss either of them.

Fortunately, there weren't any houses behind Payson's house, just a patch of woods that blocked the houses from Johnson Road, or Andy would probably have felt obligated to question the folks back there, too. Instead, he retreated to his car to try to think of anything he might have missed.

What about the ex-wife? Payson had said they fought over custody of Wolf. Andy couldn't remember her name, so he used the cell phone to call his wife, who always knew such things. It turned out that the ex-wife was on her honeymoon with her new husband, which was why Brian was staying with Payson and Doreen, and Andy couldn't imagine even a devoted dog lover cutting short a trip to Branson to steal a dog.

Andy was sure he'd taken all the reasonable steps, but Mark Pope's grin was still fresh in his mind. The only thing more humiliating than getting stuck with a trivial case would be messing it up. So he was going to have to do something unreasonable.

He thought about walking through the woods behind Payson's house to see if Wolf had found his way in there and died, and if it hadn't been so hot, he might have done it. Instead, he looked at the sky above the woods. There weren't any birds circling, meaning that there probably wasn't any carrion as big as a dog out there, and if Wolf were still alive, somebody would have heard him barking. So Andy just couldn't make himself go traipsing through the woods when all it was likely to get him was a bunch of ticks.

That dog *had* to be dead on the side of the road some-where, or at best, injured and nearly dead. Either way, it would be right foolish to drive around looking, so there was no reason for Andy to start driving other than the fact that he didn't want Mark Pope to come back by and find him sitting in his car as if he didn't know what he was doing.

An hour later, he'd driven down every road in Byerly, even those so far away that no ten-year-old dog could have gotten there, especially not with the heat and the condition Wolf must have been in. Andy knew he ought to give up and admit to Mark that he couldn't even find a lost dog anymore. Maybe what they said about old dogs not learning new tricks was true; he and Wolf probably had a lot in common.

As tempted as he was to confess over the phone, he knew Mark would crow that much more if Andy avoided talking to him in person. He pulled into the first driveway he came to, meaning to turn around and head back to the police station, but the driveway turned out to be the one that led to Dr. Josie's place. He decided it couldn't hurt to stop and ask if anybody had brought Wolf by since Payson called. His wife would have said he was only delaying the inevitable, which he was, but he was thirsty, and maybe Dr. Josie would give him something to drink.

Dr. Josie only saw patients in the morning on Saturdays, so Andy knew the office would already be closed, but since she lived as well as worked at the old farmhouse, he figured she'd be around. Since she came outside when he stopped the car, she must have seen him drive up. Or maybe her dogs had let her know he was there—even with the door closed, he could hear all manner of barks and yelps.

"Hey," she said as he got out of the car.

"Hey there. How're you doing?"

Normally, he'd have expected a lengthy answer. Dr. Josie wasn't the most talkative person in Byerly, but she was a Southerner. This time her only answer was, "Fine." While Andy tried to think of what he'd done to offend her, she said, "What can I do for you?"

"I've got some questions about Payson Smith's dog Wolf, if you've got a minute."

Her mouth got tight, and she crossed her hands over her chest. "If you think I'm giving that dog back, you've got another think coming, and you're not getting into my house without a court order."

Andy worked hard not to show how got away with he was. Of course, it did make sense, now that she'd confessed. There wasn't a dog in Byerly that wouldn't come running if Dr. Josie snapped her fingers. "Why'd you do it?" he asked, trying to make it sound like he'd known all along that she was involved.

"If you could have seen that dog, you wouldn't even ask. Skinny as a rail, dehydrated—he'd have been dead by now if I hadn't taken him."

"I don't suppose you had any problem getting him."

"Not a bit. Parked my pickup on Johnson Road and went through the woods to get to Payson's yard." Obviously she didn't share Andy's dislike of ticks, but then again, she couldn't afford to, in her line of work. "Poor fellow couldn't hardly walk. He did his best to follow me when I called him, but I had to carry him most of the way to the truck. No creature on earth deserves to be treated like that."

Andy thought for a while. As police chief, maybe he'd have felt differently, but as Mark Pope had taken such pains to demonstrate, he wasn't police chief anymore. Maybe Payson was fond of the dog, but it wasn't fair to Wolf to make him go back to that pen with its empty water bowl.

Dr. Josie was getting nervous. "What are you going to do?"

"Nothing, but this is what *you're* going to do. You're going to call Payson and tell him somebody from out of town hit Wolf with a car and brought him here. You did your best but couldn't save him. Then tell him you buried Wolf already, and you might better put up a marker in case he wants to come see."

"That could work," she said slowly.

"Of course, you're going to have to make sure Payson never sees Wolf again, but unless he gets another dog, he won't have any reason to come out here."

"He better not get another dog," she said ominously.

"Tell him that, too, how bad off the dog was, how maybe he'd have lived if he'd been in better condition. Then suggest that he get a burglar alarm."

She smiled. "Andy, you're my kind of cop. Hey, wait a minute! You're not a cop anymore."

"Nope, I'm retired. Just like Wolf."

She finally invited him in for a Coca-Cola and let him see Wolf. The old dog did look pretty rough, but Dr. Josie thought he'd live another year or two.

It wasn't until Andy was fixing to leave that he thought of something else. "How did you find out about Wolf being without water, anyway?"

"A little bird told me."

He just looked at her.

"I mean it. I got an anonymous phone call. Whoever it was must have been talking through a handkerchief, because it sounded funny, but he said Wolf was in bad shape. I didn't know if it was a trick or not, but as soon as I saw the old fellow, I knew I had to bring him home with me."

"You don't know who it was?"

She shook her head.

"Would you tell me if you did?"

She smiled again, so Andy just patted Wolf and headed for his car.

The former police chief was feeling mighty pleased with himself. Mark might make a few noises about tracking down whoever it was who'd supposedly hit Wolf, but nothing would come of that. Then he'd make fun because it was only a dog that got hit by a car, but the fact was that Andy had solved his case, when Andy would bet money that Mark wasn't a bit closer to finding Missy Terhune's murderer than he had been that morning.

Imagining about how he'd have handled the murder reminded Andy of what Payson had said about it being a shame Wolf hadn't been around the night it happened. Dr. Josie took the dog on Wednesday night, and Terhune was killed on Thursday night. Like Andy told Payson, she must have known her killer because there was no sign of a break-in, and everybody had been assuming that the killer had come to the front door like so many men had. But what if the killer had come to the back door?

Somebody could have parked on Johnson Road just like Dr. Josie had, snuck through the woods, and shown up at Terhune's door without anybody in the neighborhood being the wiser. Of course, Wolf would have barked if he'd still been there, but only a neighbor would have known that.

Then Andy thought about how he could see Terhune's backyard while standing in Payson's. In fact, he could see all the yards down the block; nobody had fences or hedges, and it was hard to tell where one yard ended and the next began. As hot as it had been all week, even at night, nobody had been spending much time outside their air-conditioned houses, so somebody could have walked from one end of the block to the other without ever coming out onto the street and without anybody noticing. Unless, that is, Wolf barked. But Wolf was already gone the night Terhune was killed because somebody had called Dr. Josie. And that somebody was almost certainly a neighbor, because they were the ones who'd have seen how Wolf was suffering.

That's when Andy headed for Butler Street. He was still

deputized, so he had a legal right to do what he had in mind. Of course, he didn't have a gun or handcuffs, but he'd rarely used them before retirement, and he thought he could handle one more arrest without them.

Fortunately, she was alone when he rang the bell, and it didn't take much to convince her that she'd be better off if she came willingly. He'd been planning to take her to the police station, but when they came out the door, Mark Pope was standing in front of the Terhune house, talking to Hank Parker, the *Byerly Gazette*'s only full-time reporter, and damned if Mark didn't flash that shit-eating grin again when he saw Andy. That's when Andy changed his mind. He escorted Miz Cranford over there and announced that he'd just arrested her for Missy Terhune's murder. Mark was too flabbergasted to speak, but Hank had plenty of questions.

Andy explained how Miz Cranford had found out her husband hadn't spent all day resting for the night shift. Instead, he'd been calling on Missy Terhune. Like many women in her situation, Miz Cranford had blamed the other woman instead of the husband and decided to get rid of her. Getting to Terhune's house without being seen was easy. All she had to do was walk through the backyards. The only problem was Wolf's barking.

Miz Cranford considered poisoning the dog's water but decided Wolf didn't deserve that, so she called Dr. Josie, knowing she'd rescue him. Like the vet, Miz Cranford was more soft-hearted with dogs than she was with people, because she didn't hesitate for a second when it came to killing Missy Terhune.

Once Andy had realized that Wolf's disappearing the night before the murder was no coincidence, it was easy to figure out that Miz Cranford was the murderer. It had to be a neighbor, because only a neighbor would have known about Wolf's barking, and only the people on the same side of the block as Payson would have been worried about rousing Wolf. That limited the suspects.

There was Mr. Titus, who was deaf and didn't even know Wolf barked, and Miz Farley, but Andy couldn't imagine what motive she could have had. Then there were the Cranfords. Roy Cranford worked at night, so he couldn't have done it, but with him gone and Wolf out of the way, the coast was clear for Miz Cranford.

Mark finally started talking then, trying to make it sound like he'd known all along that the missing dog and the murder were connected, and that Andy had only been following his orders. When he insisted on carrying Miz Cranford to the station in the squad car, lights flashing, Andy knew Mark was going to write up the arrest as his own.

Andy didn't care. He knew the real story, and so did Mark. Besides, Mark hadn't fooled Hank for a minute, and once everybody in Byerly read Hank's article in the *Gazette*, they'd know who had really solved the case.

As he drove back home, Andy decided that even if you can't teach an old dog new tricks, sometimes the old tricks work just as well as they ever did.

BODY IN THE POND

Suzanne C. Johnson

Edgar Allan Poe and Nancy Drew. An unlikely pair? Not according to Suzanne C. Johnson, who confesses that the duo lured her as a school-age, reluctant reader into the addictive world of books. Not until much later, though, would the Author's Muse snare her. "Body in the Pond" is a product of Suzanne's background in psychology and her love of mystery, language, and a city and period from the life of Poe. It is her first short story. She also admits to a case of writer's split personality. Evidence: released in 2001 by Knopf/Random House, her first book is for young children, a "hilarious ... high-octane romp," according to reviewers. So, living on a lake in Washington State with her husband and son, Suzanne slips back and forth between books for children and the heady realm of adult mystery.

---

13 JUNE 1835. QUARTER PAST NINE O'CLOCK P.M.

I am forever weighing. Right or Wrong. Truth or Lies. Good or Evil.

Evil that my study is on the second floor. Spring has withered into a steamy Virginia summer, and upper floors swelter as night descends.

The second floor is Good, too. It affords its Master views into chambers belonging to a certain neighbor.

And now a fortuitous breeze bears sweet scents of her garden and of memories, oh, of her skin! Widow

Ashcroft, a woman of regularity of habit (thank the Heavens!) and of impatience to rid herself of gown and corset each sweltering eve.

Verdict: Praise the second floor! . . .

From the Diary of Judge Jacob Danby

On the heels of each summer dawn, Stella roamed the sun-kissed cloister of her garden.

Dressed in loose muslin, no binding corset, no hampering petticoats, hair tucked beneath wide-brimmed straw hat, she followed any whim of honeysuckle scent or bee buzz. Here she was free of the need to coax and contrive for the financial rescue of her modest bookshop. Free of lectures, be they on Homer or Cicero, to pen with Father by eye-wearying lamplight. Free of Mother's salon gatherings where ladies indulge their tastes for tea and honey cakes, occasional juleps, and ubiquitous Richmond gossip.

Yet such freedom was not to be had by Stella Taylor Ashcroft this sultry Virginia morn.

At the edge of the small pond deep among the laurels and magnolias of the lower garden, she stood with First Officer of Police W. D. Page. But for the ripplings made by fish, the pond surface was as glass.

Beneath lay the body, faceup, of Judge Jacob Danby.

"You found him just like this, Mrs. Ashcroft?" Mr. Page spoke with a voice hushed in respect for both dead and living, since the Danby property was neighbor. Its vast lawn sloped up to the home some distance away; its garden house stood yards from Stella's pond.

Despite the heat, she shivered, drawing tightly the shawl she had plucked from a kitchen peg to disguise her lack of corset. "I found him as you see him, Mr. Page."

Jacob Danby: short, trim, tailored in every gentlemanly detail, except that his cravat was loose, its end floating like a flattened fish. The man's features, fine and younger than his fifty or so years, were clean-shaven but for sidewhiskers. He lay inches from air. Inches from life.

Mr. Page tossed a pebble in the water to keep fish from nibbling.

Stomach churning, Stella stepped back. "I cannot stay here anymore!"

"Beg pardon, ma'am, but I need to notify the mayor, see how he wants to handle this." The officer, dressed in a common black suit, hair and mustache the color of sand, gave a nod in the direction of the pond. "Would you please keep nearby? I want no animals coming round, nothing more than fish, leastways."

Stella bit her lip. "My duty, of course. But do hurry."

Three strides, then he came back. "One thing. How is it Judge Danby is in your pond?"

The question made her mouth go dry, yet she forced herself to answer, even meeting his inquiring eyes: "I have no utter idea, Mr. Page."

LAST night Stella had met Jacob Danby's eyes, too. For several evenings from her bedchamber upstairs she had noticed a figure standing at a second-floor window of the Danby home. Yesterday near dusk, armed with her father's birding glass, she awaited the figure. When it appeared, she stepped back into shadows and held up the glass.

Judge Danby stood between narrowly opened draperies, his own spyglass aimed her way.

Taking a steadying breath, glass to her eye, she stepped to her window. At that instant, the judge jerked backwards, stumbling out of view.

Later came the confrontation. This man so revered for his legal acumen, philanthropy, flawless comportment— how dare he! How long, she wanted to know, had he been violating her privacy? She would expose his scandalous nature to his fragile wife, Myra, to his son, Creed, to all of Richmond if he did not desist!

Stella stepped to the pond again and made herself look. Jacob Danby would bother her no more. Alive, that is. In death he might prove to be bothersome a hundred times over.

Early that morning, once she had sent for the police, she'd paced the garden, glad of one thing—that her parents were gone to Baltimore, thus escaping the inevitable inquisition by every friend and acquaintance and perhaps by authority. She'd wandered the wide, pebbly path to the berry patch, then to the laurel hedge at the Danby line. Over the years, blight had taken a few of the laurels. It was in one of these sparse places that the grass showed trampling, and Stella found, with a quickening of her pulse, the small torn piece of cotton cloth snagged on a low stem. A graceful pattern of peach and robin's-egg blue. She'd freed it and plucked the stem clean of every thread.

Yards away, crammed in a hollow of dogwood trunks, was the woolen blanket. Bloodstained. She'd heaped on extra plant debris as further disguise. How she needed time to think!

Now, standing watch near the pond as Mr. Page had bidden, Stella had time but as yet no capacity for thinking.

Sounds of horses, a wagon, voices of the returning officer and assistance.

Reaching into her pocket, fingers icy, Stella worried the torn fabric into a tight wad. She knew it well. It was hers.

THE sodden body lay pondside. Flies worked.

Stella sheltered herself beneath pines and kept out of the men's way.

"Dear God!" Creed Danby, alarmingly pale, was steadied by two officers. "We thought, Mother and I, he was in his study upstairs. He does that, works all night, sleeps until noon some days." Tall and lanky, in shirtsleeves and vest, Creed raked his fingers through his hair. "My dear mother!"

Out of the young lawyer's earshot, the doctor lectured Mr. Page, his hand chopping the air at each turn of his theory. "Misstep in the dark. Backward fall against pond stones—quite a nasty gash back of the head. Unconscious. Drowned." He clicked his tongue. "I declare, such a loss to Richmond! Have the body taken to my surgery."

Mr. Page and two officers roamed the garden, particularly the path to the laurels, then to the Danby side. Stella followed, not too closely, and strained to hear any call signifying a find. None came.

"Jacob! Jacob!" Myra Danby, sobbing, tore at the laurels as she sought a way into Stella's yard.

Creed ran past Stella. "Mother! It's no good! Rose, thank God you're here, take her home. I'll ask the doctor to come by with something to calm her."

Through a narrow break in the hedge, Stella watched. No. She spied. Rose Walters, the only free servant in the Danby household, murmured tenderly as she supported the inconsolable figure of her mistress across the lawn. Even in this crushing moment, Rose presented a strikingly lithe, lovely, and capable figure. Creed's narrow shoulders sagged as he awaited the women's entrance into the house, then he trudged back to seek the doctor. Stella viewed them as if for the first time, as if she were neither acquaintance nor friend. Had Jacob Danby felt so detached, so coldly alone, as he'd spied upon her just a half day ago? Somehow, she doubted that.

Another hour passed, and everyone left. Or so Stella thought.

"Is this yours, Mrs. Ashcroft?"

She spun around.

W. D. Page held up several inches of gold chain, substantial links of a geometric pattern, end links twisted open. The officer's hand and the chain dripped water.

Stella shook her head. "It's unfamiliar to me but from the pond, I assume, so perhaps it's a portion of Judge Danby's watch chain."

"I reckon so. Broken somehow in his fall." He slipped it into his pocket and tipped his hat. "Been a trying mornin', hasn't it, ma'am?"

This time she avoided his gaze, fixing hers upon the tiny orange wings of a flitting ladybird beetle. "A definite understatement, Mr. Page."

WITHIN a half hour of the officer's departure, Stella had inspected every inch of her pond, turning stones, swirling vegetation, as she sought assurance that not a vestige of Jacob Danby was left. Something glinted in a twinkling of sunlight through the dense canopy.

Soaking her sleeve, she plucked the find: several more inches of chain identical to what Mr. Page had found. She searched further but was soon convinced that the bit of chain was the last remnant of the judge.

She slipped the links into her pocket next to the damning piece of cloth.

THAT afternoon, Mr. Burwell Bassett planted his portly frame on the couch in Stella's parlor. His melodic voice soothed while his gaze—a piercing blue from under shadowed brow—unsettled. A perfect combination for a city magistrate. Banker by trade, he had been appointed by the mayor to inquire into the death.

A smile spread across his broad face. "Your parents, Mrs.

Ashcroft, I understand they are in Baltimore for the summer."

Stella sat in her father's mahogany rocker and smoothed her fresh frock of violet-dusted ivory. "Father is lecturing, 'Orations of Cicero.' Mother is visiting her sisters."

" 'Tis best they are gone." Mr. Bassett nodded in the direction of the Danby home. "This is a delicate business, and thus I come to your parlor unaccompanied." He pointed to the front window, to where Mr. Page leaned against the trunk of the great oak that sheltered the front half of the Taylor home. "Even Page will not be party to our conversation."

It was just like Burwell Bassett to toy with her: a gentleman's game when the gentleman did not much like the lady. His daughters had more than once participated in her bookshop's Ladies' Study Circle, where the topics often strayed beyond the customary domesticity to the unaccustomed women's rights, public education, literacy for black citizens, and, though whispered, abolition. Recently, when she had applied at his bank for a small loan for her bookshop, he had made it clear that funds would be available only if she curtailed her ladies' group. Stella had declined. Mr. Bassett had made sure the other banks in town likewise refused her.

Here in her parlor she would take Mr. Bassett's bait. "Death is delicate," she said, "but I fail to imagine what it is that you wish not to discuss in front of Mr. Page."

"I will be more direct. Did you arrange to meet Judge Danby last night in his garden house?"

Stella straightened. "Preposterous!"

"There was a note carried to him last night asking for an eleven o'clock meeting."

"Why on earth would you think it was from me?"

He pulled a folded paper from his coat pocket and held it out. "It is signed *W. A.*"

The pen had been wielded hurriedly: *Must see you. Tonight. Eleven o'clock. Garden house again.*

Stella looked up, still puzzled. "My question still stands. Why would you think I—?"

"Come, now! *W* for *Widow. A* for *Ashcroft.*"

At this, Stella could laugh. "Two letters of the alphabet? Is that what ties this note to me?" She sat back in her father's rocker. "I have been a widow for nearly ten years of my seven and twenty. No woman would entitle herself 'Widow' after ten years' passing. Come, now, Mr. Bassett! Besides," she leaned forward, pointing to the note, "I'm not convinced the *A* is an *A.* It's a bit malformed and could be, perhaps, an *O* or a *D.*"

But the magistrate was not swayed. "I contend that *Widow Ashcroft* and so *W. A.* were code names between you and His Honor." He put up his hand to halt her protest. "Believe me, madam, I do not want this lurid information in the public domain any more than you do."

Stella stood abruptly and marched, petticoats rustling, to the writing table. She snatched up her household journal and thrust it at the magistrate. "Compare my handwriting to that of the infamous note!"

He gave a cursory glance. "Handwriting can be disguised." With a grunt he stood, his piercing gaze upon her as he reached once more into his pocket. This time he pulled out a small gold-trimmed book. "The Judge's personal diary, not something I care to show you, but I see that I must." He opened it to a ribbon marker and pointed to the entry dated the prior eve. "His last. Read, please."

The leather felt clammy in Stella's hands. *I am forever weighing. . . . Good or Evil . . . second floor . . . a certain neighbor . . . memories, oh, of her skin . . . Widow Ashcroft . . . gown and corset . . .*

Heat surged up Stella's neck. "An abomination!" She shoved the book at Mr. Bassett.

"Have you read it all? No?" He firmly guided it back into her view, his words quite gentle. "Disclosure is vital to your welfare."

Stella swallowed—*Damn him!*—and reaffixed her eyes upon the judge's perfect penmanship: *Verdict: Praise the second floor! She offers magnificent views to hold me until our next garden rendezvous. Until later this night, my Widow Ashcroft!*

Stella furiously flipped pages. Beyond the entry, the leaves were blank, but prior it was *Ashcroft . . . Ashcroft . . . Ashcroft!* One fancied assignation after another! She slammed the book shut, pulse throbbing in her fingertips. She fortified herself with a deep, slow breath and with the hope that Mr. Bassett would respond to reason. "You are correct about something."

He smiled indulgently. "Yes?"

"This is a delicate business. The cost to Judge Danby's legacy and to his legal firm which, no doubt, will pass to his son . . . well, this sordid book of . . . of *imaginings* could destroy a lifetime of work."

"Agreed. In part."

"And it would damage me and those I hold dear." Gossip and censure marked a woman, and so her family, as deeply and permanently as some terrible disfigurement. Disfigurement, at least, brought with it pity.

Mr. Bassett nodded. "Which is why I wish to strike a deal with you." He repocketed the book and note. "In return for keeping both of these from public eyes—forever, mind you—you will confess to causing—accidentally, of course—the death of His Honor."

Stella's hands clenched, nails biting palms. She dared not speak, not even breathe, else she would either dissolve or explode.

"By the way, Mrs. Ashcroft, the doctor found no water in the lungs. He was dead before he lay in the pond. A blow to the back of the head. Is that how it happened?"

Defiance rode the bitter bile in her throat. "Get out!"

Mr. Bassett, though pinking at his meaty ears and cheeks, remained undaunted. "Our fine city need only think that he was sleepwalking and you mistook him, quite innocently, dark as it was, for a trespasser."

She struck him down—a fleeting victory—with a simple statement of fact. "The moon, sir, was full last night."

His broad forehead glistened with perspiration as he leaned toward her. "A man of Judge Danby's intelligence, which tolerated only facts, would not enter 'imaginings' into his diary. And I will not allow the guilty party to go free, even if I must use that diary as evidence. Furthermore, once the proverbial dust settles, I believe the public would forgive and forget his little indulgence in light of his great deeds and gifts to the Commonwealth. But, of course, I would rather not go that route."

You must, for I will never—! She began it in her head but seemed powerless to force the declaration to her lips. Powerless because she knew she was just that. She could instruct him on lunar phases, but, armed with Judge Danby's diary, reputation, and station, armed with Mr. Bassett's own position and connections, the magistrate could indeed do exactly what he threatened.

He headed for the entryway. "I will be in touch tomorrow. The inquest is set for the day following." At the door, he turned. "Young Creed and his mother put up a handsome reward. It is below my station to collect, but Page, who knows of the note but not of the diary, is—shall we say?—eager to augment his slender salary."

* * *

THE magistrate departed. W. D. Page remained, though discreetly, across the road.

Stella could postpone no longer a task she'd dreaded.

Her frock was too festive for calling on such a somber occasion, but time was precious, so she hoped a simple gray bonnet would assuage any offense. She pretended no awareness of the officer as she walked to the corner and turned up the bricked path to the richly polished Danby front door. Chandeliers of swirled iron hung from the columned porch roof. With a steady hand, she struck the brass knocker.

Jackson, his skin the patina of aged black leather, offered a silver tray for her card, guided her into the expansive hall, but was startled out of his decades-old routine by her request: "Please fetch Rose."

"You meanin' Miz Myra, ma'am?"

"I'm not wishing to disturb your mistress or Mr. Creed. Rose, please. But wait." Stella lowered her voice. "Judge Danby's death was quite unfortunate."

"Yes'm."

"I understand a message came for him last eve. Did you receive it?"

"I took it from the young'un, Jem."

"Jem Rafferty?" An entrepreneurial street boy.

Jackson nodded.

Stella chanced another question. "Mr. Bassett, Mr. Page, did they ask you who brought the message?"

She knew the answer would be *no* before he shook his head. The deliverer, of course, had been hired by "Widow Ashcroft." One would hope modern-day authorities might not operate on assumptions, that they would at least seek to verify their theories. But large rewards often blinded police, an issue the subject of colorful editorials. As to the magistrate: even if someone other than the "Widow Ashcroft" had sent the note, it would not erase the damning diary.

But for Jackson's fading footsteps and the ponderous ticking of a clock, the Danby home was quiet. Somewhere down in the basement, preparations were surely under way for the receipt of the Judge's body, then the washing, dressing, and eventual laying out in the parlor for visitation by Richmond society.

Rose might be in the basement, her seamstressing skills needed. Seamstressing was how Stella had met her three years prior, inquiring at the tiny lodging rooms behind Krause's Cook Shop and securing Rose's adroit skills for the making of a spring frock. There had been more than frocks since then.

"You ever teach school?" Rose had asked one winter day, rain driving against the narrow panes, the seamstress on her knees, pins pressed between lips as she tucked the hem of a cloak. Her two girls, ages eight and seven, sat crosslegged, mannered, dark eyes fixed upon their mother's efficient motions.

The cloak was draped upon Stella. "I have never taught." With mincing steps, she turned a circle for Rose. "Why do you ask?"

Rose worked her way around the hem until her lips were free of pins. She stood, half a head taller than Stella, and spoke in a husky whisper. "I'll give you all your sewin' needs. No charge." She motioned her girls to gather at her skirt.

How much time passed? Seconds? Minutes? Stella recalled only that those six brown eyes did not leave her face until she nodded. "I will do it! Gladly!"

The very next day, Stella had begun to teach three eager students in those rooms behind Krause's Cook Shop. A bold commitment by both Rose and herself, since teaching a Negro to read and write was illegal in Richmond. The eagerness with which Rose and her children had received Stella's lessons these past two years compensated her beyond the making of frocks and overshadowed the worry of discovery.

And when Myra Danby had mentioned months ago she was in need of a personal maid, Stella had recommended Rose.

The clock in the Danby hall was as yet the only source of sound as Stella awaited Rose, who was probably needed upstairs, too, where Myra Danby would be gathering her strength, setting out a black gown, petticoats, gloves. Certainly, the new widow would grace her bodice with her always-present ruby cluster pin which secured a petite watch. Stella and her parents had attended the anniversary gala when the judge, with quite the fanfare, had bestowed the gift upon his wife.

And what of Creed now? Was he in his father's study? That room from which Judge Danby had let his lurid mind and eye roam? Creed might be pacing there, his mind, his eye upon his own issues: had experience equipped him for the role of head of the house, head of the law firm, leader in Richmond? Daunting for a young man.

A noise as faint as a mouse scratch.

Stella turned.

Creed stood before her, understandably haggard of face, neatly appointed in black suit and tie. He held her card and bowed slightly.

"Mrs. Ashcroft, Rose is assisting my mother right now. Whatever it is you came for, I can probably help you, though time . . ." He ran his hand down the embroidered silk vest and tucked her card partway into the watch pocket. "Time is short. I'm sure you understand."

"Oh, I do! And I had not meant to disturb you or your mother." The torn fabric plucked from the laurels lay tucked in her skirt pocket. "This seems so selfish now, but I came to ask Rose if . . . if she had finished a frock for me, one she'd been working on for weeks." The armor of de-

ception, so necessary at times, was comforting yet so fragile.

He frowned, surely impatient with triviality, but Stella
went on. "A dark gray frock, which would be most appropriate for paying my respects." She waved her hand at the
parlor doors.

"Ah." The frown vanished. "Not selfish at all. In fact,
quite generous that you should—" He turned at a sound
from the far end of the hall. "Mother?"

Myra Danby, a forlorn figure seeming to float on a black
cloud of mourning attire, looked exactly as Stella had
imagined, though missing was the ruby watch pin. Indeed,
it might now be too painful to wear such a dear gift.

"Rose?" Myra's voice was barely audible. "Where is
Rose?"

Creed clasped both her hands. "I'll find her for you."

He had slipped naturally into the role of protector. Stella
had often seen son and mother strolling their slope of lawn,
arm in arm. And in public Myra gazed upon Creed with
unmistakable adoration.

"Who is that?" Myra peered round him, her drawn face
framed by wisps of graying hair. Always frail and flighty,
she now was even more these things. Grief, shock, and
possibly the doctor's laudanum enhanced the mix. "Our
neighbor? Stella?"

At that moment, Rose stepped into the hall, turned red-
rimmed eyes onto Stella, then shrank back out of view.

"Rose?" Stella said.

No answer. No appearance. Grief? Confusion? These
emotions did not explain these actions by the resilient Rose
Walters.

Stella asked Creed, "May I please speak to her?"

Myra had begun to weep.

"Rose," said Creed, "Mother needs you."

A few moments, and Rose reappeared, scurried across

the hall, her look fixed upon Creed, then, without even a glance at Stella, ushered away her distressed mistress.

Fear? Distrust? Stella blinked at the sting of them.

"Perhaps you can return later, Mrs. Ashcroft," said Creed, "although Rose has her hands full, as you can see." He walked toward Stella, smoothing his vest again, pushing her card all the way into his watch pocket. "I must leave for another meeting with Burwell Bassett."

Stella's face flushed with the sudden realization—though it should have come as no surprise—that Creed must surely know now of his father's diary. And what of the accusation of murder? Was he in concurrence with the magistrate, or was that theory's author only Mr. Bassett? The young Danby's gaze was unreadable, not because he was naive or ignorant, Stella believed, but because he had been bred a Virginia gentleman.

And what of Myra? Did she know of the diary, of her husband's wandering attentions? Maybe that was why the poor woman, shortly upon seeing Stella, had wept.

As she had that morning, Stella felt as if she lived on one side of the James River and the rest of the world lived on the other.

Murmuring a hasty "Good day," she escaped out the Danby front door.

And to the surveillance of Officer Page.

EXCHANGING her gray bonnet for summer-weight ivory and a parasol, Stella buggied Richmond's bumpy streets to the city's center. Mr. Page followed on horseback at a proper distance.

It was less than fashionable for a woman to command a buggy, but living far from her bookshop, having no husband to drive her and a father who, when home, offered but clearly would rather be managing pens than reins,

Stella drove herself. Mother had at last accepted it and deftly lied to her friends that a lady at the reins was considered in Paris by some to be, well, fashionable.

This afternoon, however, Stella did not head for her shop. The Closed sign must remain in her window today.

She left the buggy at the livery and found young Jem Rafferty hefting feed sacks at Miller & Able. Coins brought a sweep of his cap, a shock of red hair, and an answer to Stella's question.

"Got the note last night at the Danby and Son office, an' I ran it straight to Judge Danby."

"Who hired you? A clerk working late?"

"Ain't sure he was a clerk, but name was Mr. Wick Arbogast."

Stella drew a sharp breath. *W. A.*

Jem added, "An' I carried back the Judge's answer."

"Which was—?"

" 'Yes.' "

Yes. I will meet you, Wick Arbogast, in my garden house at eleven o'clock tonight.

Jem squinted into the sun. "I carried back the answer to where he lives." He opened his small callused palm. "Want me to take you?"

IN the parlor of Mrs. Yarrington's rooming house, Stella smoothed her fan pleats, and Jem flipped coins and caught them.

"Mr. Arbogast!" announced the efficient Mrs. Yarrington with a sweep of the parlor door.

Unshaven, curly hair disheveled, tie administered with haste, vest buttoned unevenly but watch attached and pocketed, he tugged at his suit coat. "Forgive me! I've been working on several cases, up all night, or has it been two?" He smiled disarmingly, one corner jauntily tipped. He palmed her card and read, " 'Mrs. Stella Taylor Ashcroft.' You are in need of legal services?"

She kept her eyes on the man, but her words were meant for Jem. "Is this he?"

"Yes'm."

Mr. Arbogast chuckled. "Jem! Didn't see you." His tone sobered. "What may I do for you, Mrs. Ashcroft?"

Was she now standing before the last or *one* of the last persons to see the judge alive? And what, if anything, could that mean?

Her fingers tightened around the parasol handle. "This morning Judge Danby was found dead in my pond."

Jem let out a low whistle. Mr. Arbogast backed up to a chair and sat. "But-but—!" He threw his hands up. "But I met with him last night! In that garden house of his. He was healthy as a bull. Fact is, he was angry as a bull when he read my report, every line of three pages, questioned me, lightning quick as always. Yes."

"He was angry with you?" asked Stella.

"No, no. At what I'd uncovered in some research I did for him."

He stood, paced, his hazel eyes intent on inward thoughts. "Oh, he was furious, but when I left him, he was alive with that fury! The anger must have dealt his heart a blow."

"He wandered to my yard? Fell over dead in my pond? According to the doctor, Judge Danby was struck on the back of the head."

Arbogast frowned.

"Jem," said Stella. He scrambled to her side, and she planted another coin in his hand. "Fetch Police Officer Page. He's probably not far from the front door."

"Hurry, Jem!" Mr. Arbogast tossed the boy an extra coin. He turned to Stella. "I am grieved for the loss of a great legal mind, for the loss to his family, for the shock you, dear lady, must have endured."

Stella did not know what to think of this Wick Arbogast. Either he was the most genuine person she had met all day, or he was a consummate actor.

Guardedly, she thanked him for his generous sympathies, then asked, her voice tense with hope, "Could there be something inherent in the information you brought Judge Danby that might have contributed to his death?"

He shook his head. "My report was not concerning some case gone wrong. No vendetta by an irate client or felon. It was a personal matter for the judge. I'm sure you understand I can divulge no particulars. But I assure you no one involved would have harmed him." Assurances or not, Mr. Arbogast's brow furrowed.

"And the report?" she asked. "What did he do with it?"

"Put it in his coat pocket. Yes. Then shook my hand, albeit somewhat grimly, and I departed."

"Here he is!" Jem sauntered into the parlor. "Like you said, ma'am, he was close by."

W. D. Page, hat in hand, strode in. He looked sheepishly from Stella to the lawyer and back.

She had failed to reason with Mr. Bassett, had failed in her mission to talk with Rose, had failed to extract anything of value from Mr. Arbogast. Nevertheless, she shrugged off the weighty cloak of disappointment to relish a most singular satisfaction.

"Mr. Page!" She flourished a hand in the direction of Wick Arbogast. "Please, kind sir, meet the Widow Ashcroft!"

STANDING out of the path of passersby and sheltered by her parasol, Stella waited.

"Mr. Page!" she called as the officer closed Mrs. Yarrington's gate.

He turned, startled.

"It is unsettling," she said, "to find you are being followed, is it not?"

His cheeks took on a red hue. "It is, ma'am." He thumbed toward the boardinghouse. "Beg pardon for the mistake, us thinking you were the writer of the note. It would not have taken much brains to find him." The red hue deepened. "I-I mean, I didn't mean—"

"You are correct, Mr. Page. It did not take intelligence to find Mr. Arbogast." She savored one last morsel. "However, it did take operating outside one's assumptions."

"Yes, ma'am, but, unfortunately, Mr. Bassett says there is more than just the note."

The word *unfortunately* did not pass by her. Perhaps Mr. Page was in a frame of mind to share information. "Did you manage to find out from Mr. Arbogast the subject of the unsettling report he delivered to the judge?"

He shook his head. "He says it's all legal confidences."

A most convenient reply if the lawyer had something to hide. "I presume he told you it was his opinion the report had nothing to do with the judge's death."

"Yes, ma'am."

"I would be more comforted to know that *you* had made that determination, Mr. Page." But her comfort, she assumed, was the last thing on his mind. "Did you find Mr. Arbogast's report in the judge's pocket?"

"Wouldn't be much left of paper, ma'am, soaking all night in your pond."

"Not even remnants of some pulpy mass?"

"No. And I went through his pockets myself. Speaking of that—" From his own pocket he pulled out the inches of chain. "From the pond, you remember? Must be your father's or somebody else's, 'cause I found Judge Danby's chain and watch intact on the body."

The officer spoke on, but Stella pondered the now familiar links. "Forgive me," she finally said. "What were you saying?"

"Judge's watch and chain had to be plain as day for you and me to see as we looked down on him in the water. Memory plays its tricks."

"Especially when one is staring death in the face."

"You have a way of puttin' things, ma'am." He tipped his hat and stepped aside for her to pass.

On her way to the livery, Stella stopped briefly to see Jem and arrange that he arrive at her home just before nightfall. For an assignment. *If*, she told herself, she had the mettle to execute it.

IN twilight shadows, Mr. Page stationed himself across the road from the Taylor home. A determined bounty hunter, though he would probably take offense at the term.

Stella prepared a small package for Jem's delivery: one-half the fabric snagged at the laurels and a note. *It is mine. It is yours. Near where found is hidden another telling detail.* No signature.

The boy came, and, before she could falter in her resolution, she sent him on his way. Then she went up to her darkened room and sat at the open window. Her father's birding glass lay in the lap of her dark blue skirt. The heat, as crushingly heavy as her heart and her hopes, remained unstirred by a faint breeze. Night rhythms—crickets, frogs, plaintive whippoorwill—and moon's rise marked time's passing.

At last, a yellowish light, as if a giant firefly, traveled in haste down the Danby lawn. Her chest tightening with each breath, Stella leaned forward, spyglass poised.

Dependable Jem had done his job.

Silently, swiftly, Stella headed downstairs and through her garden. Even in the dark of a new moon, she could have found her way past every bush, tree, and bed, along every stretch and crook of path.

At the cage of dogwood trunks, a lantern lighted the figure of Rose Walters wresting the bloodstained blanket.

"Rose!" whispered Stella.

The woman bolted upright, stifled a scream.

Hand trembling, Stella held out her half of the torn cloth.

Two months ago she'd carried the frock of peach and robin's-egg blue to the rooms behind Krause's Cook Shop.

"It needs some of your magic," Stella had told Rose. "It's never looked right on me."

Rose had embraced the gown to her own waist with one hand, to her neck with the other. She cooed with unself-conscious delight. And Stella had laughed. "The colors are ravishing on you! It's *yours*, Rose!"

But now, on this night of the day of discovery of Jacob Danby's murdered corpse, Rose stared at another fabric: bloodstained wool.

"I wanted—" Her voice broke. "I wanted him *away!*" Eyes huge, she looked more like one of her children caught in a swirl of guilt and regret. "The pond was yours! I knew it, but I wasn't thinkin' straight! Oh, Stella!"

Stella gripped Rose's lean, strong arms. "With the blanket you dragged the body to the pond. But it was not you who killed him?" Doubt and dread compromised certainty.

Rose uttered nothing. Tears spilled.

"For your children's sake," Stella pleaded, "this is not a time to shield someone! Was it . . . was it Myra Danby?"

A man's voice shot from the dark: "What are you doing here?"

Stella and Rose swung around as one.

Creed Danby stepped into the lantern's light. His mother clung to him, only part of her in the yellow glow— curve of face, blinking eye, a slender segment of her gaunt frame. The rest of her in her son's shadow.

A deep breath, and Stella said, "I am seeking the truth, Mr. Danby."

"The truth?" his mother asked.

He caressed her arm. "Hush, now."

But Myra stepped fully into the light, pressing her fingers to her temples as if to assuage incessant pain. "A note came, and Jacob refused to tell me from whom. Secret messages had come many, many times in the past, but not since he'd promised with the lovely ruby watch pin." She touched her bodice, barren of the gift.

"Mother . . ." There was heartbreak in Creed's voice. "You mustn't."

She went on, as if recounting some dream. "From my room I watched him slip from the house. I stole into his study. The note was there. And a *diary!*"

"Every word untrue!" Stella spoke, though she knew the woman would not hear.

"A tryst in our garden house!" Myra cried. "But the woman of the diary, the woman of the note, she was gone when I arrived, yet before I could speak one word, Jacob was angry. *I was angrier!* 'Jacob! I will live with treachery no more!' Then, something in my hand! He went down! I killed my husband!" She sobbed.

Rose fixed her eyes upon Creed as he put his arms around his mother and rocked her.

And into the lighted circle stepped W. D. Page.

"How long have you been here?" Creed's voice deepened with wariness.

Mr. Page's Adam's apple slid. "Beg pardon, Mr. Danby, I think I'll fetch Mr. Bassett to talk with your mother."

To know, at last, that Rose had not ended the life of the judge was cause to rejoice, but no celebration could be had amid the ruin of Myra Danby. The gentlewoman had waited so long to stand her ground that when she finally did, the venom had burst forth, catapulting herself and her husband to disaster.

Yet . . . something still did not fit.

Stella pulled from her pocket the short length of chain she'd scavenged from the pond. She held it to the light and asked Myra, "Where is your ruby watch pin?"

"In her room," answered Rose, "in pieces."

"I-I smashed it." Myra's face was soaked with tears.

Stella fingered the golden segment's bold pattern. "You smashed the pin and the watch, but their chain is intact, is it not?"

Myra nodded.

Why hadn't Stella realized it before? These links were unsuitable for a woman's delicate piece.

To Creed she said, "My calling card—you tucked it in your empty watch pocket. Odd. And when you spoke of *time,* your hand passed where your chain should have hung and went to where your watch should have been."

Even now, his fingers fidgeted along the bottom of his vest, but he hastily dropped his hands to his side.

Stella went on. "Your mother returned home, frenzied. Your singular purpose to protect her, you fled to the garden house. You found your father not quite dead? You found a damning report in his pocket? You had words, perhaps, when he roused? And in the tussle, your chain snared—in his fingers? on his clothing?—during your father's last desperate motions." She held up the links. "This piece of chain I found in my pond and, I would guess, it is yours, Creed."

Rose let out a feeble cry. Myra looked about in confusion.

Creed jerked around to the officer. "She flings accusations as one might throw darts! Is this some cruel parlor game?"

"Mrs. Ashcroft—" began Mr. Page.

"Danby and *Son* . . ." Myra reached out and ran her finger down the dangling links. "The watch and chain were Jacob's gift. Oh, he was so full of hope." She pointed to the house. "I found your watch, Creed, in your suit coat this morning." Again, she pointed to the links held by Stella. "The rest of your broken chain is there. A shame, but I'm sure the goldsmith—"

Creed pulled her close.

Rose had not taken her eyes off Creed. It was now no wonder that Rose of late had spent increasing time at the Danby home, missing lessons, leaving notes for Stella with the girls: *Sorry. Work at Danbys'.* And no wonder Creed had been so shocked at the sight of his father's body *in the pond.*

To Rose, Stella said, "You dragged the body off to shield Creed."

The woman said not a word. Tears trailed down her cheeks.

Creed's mouth hardened. "Where is my motive, Mr. Page?"

The officer brushed a finger across his mustache. "A Mr. Wick Arbogast came calling on me and the magistrate late today. He'd been thinking over some papers he'd left with the judge last night in the garden house. Said he figured they had no bearing on the death—surely no upstanding son, he said, would harm his father over money troubles—but he thought it best we knew just the same. Gambling, he said, and *borrowing,* you might call it, from law office accounts. Trust accounts, was what he named 'em."

Creed swallowed. "I admit to differences with my father, but, surely, nothing to warrant—" His voice choked.

He had not planned to kill, Stella believed. A moment ripe with fear for his future, with frustration at a life, perhaps, under the judge's thumb, with a wish for the effortless path through life. The moment came. And once passed, it was too late to undo.

Rose spoke softly. "Miz Myra was at the house cryin', beside herself, sayin' Judge Danby was dead. Creed—Mr. Creed—ran, and I followed, thinkin' I could help. Through the garden house window I saw the judge was down. Mr. Creed took papers from his father's pocket, and soon the judge was stirrin', and—"

"Page!" Creed clenched his fists. "You believe the wench?"

Rose flinched. "And the judge was stirrin', and Creed tore off his own jacket, bunched it up, and held it on his father's face till there was no more stirrin'!"

Creed flung a hand toward her. "It matters not what she says! You know the law, Page!"

Everyone in Richmond knew that Negroes—black or mulatto, free or slave—could not testify against whites.

Law be damned! Stella shoved the piece of chain toward Creed. "This must surely be proof!"

"Mr. Page!" Creed held himself as if he were about to deliver the penultimate judicial victory speech. "Based on my father's diary, I'm sure you will agree, Mrs. Ashcroft's word would be as worthless in court as Rose Walter's!"

Mr. Page extracted from his pocket inches of chain. He held it next to Stella's. "I, sir, found this piece, identical, in the pond under the lifeless body of your father. Thanks to Mrs. Ashcroft here, I now know, among other things, it's yours. I think it's 'bout time we talk with Mr. Bassett."

EQUIPPED with a bouquet of lavender roses and heliotrope, Stella knocked at the door behind Krause's Cook Shop. A morning breeze off the James stirred a stew of the flowers' sweet scents and the pungent ones of the cook shop—

cracklings, corn cakes—and of the docks—sweat, fish, to-bacco.

It took a second knock, but finally the door opened. Inches. "No!" came a breathless voice.

"Please!" Stella thrust the bouquet to the opening.

The door flung wide and Rose, hair loose, muslin limp, stood straight-backed, chin puckered. Her girls peered from the shadows.

Stella pressed the shank of the bouquet into the woman's hands. "A gift not of condolence but of congratulations."

"Congratulations?"

"For your having fallen for your devil. Did you not know it happens once for every woman? Now you are done with your turn. An angel next!"

Rose caught her lip, her face contorting as if in angst over whether to cry or laugh.

Stella whispered loudly enough for the girls to hear, "Lessons resume tomorrow," then turned, skirts swishing.

"And what 'bout you, Stella?" called Rose, the sharpness of her tone more show than true. "Have you had your turn at a devil?"

Stella was saved the reply, for at the corner of the building, she stopped. "Mr. Page!"

The officer doffed his hat. "Mornin'. Mr. Bassett asked me to tell you he 'burned it.' " He shrugged. "I think he was talking about that diary Creed Danby mentioned."

The irony of the judge's fanciful entries had never been lost on Stella. Her fierce "confrontation" with her neighbor concerning his voyeurism had been her own fantasy written in her own journal. A mere vicarious triumph—as vicarious a triumph as Jacob Danby's diary might have been for him. She had learned long ago to choose her battles with care, and crossing swords with Judge Danby would have been a loss for her from the start. Her journal was often her weapon of choice. Perhaps too often.

"Any reply to the magistrate, ma'am?" asked Mr. Page.

The incendiary deed had not been done for *her*.

She shook her head. "It was kind of you to seek me out, Mr. Page. You are quite adept at that talent."

He mumbled awkwardly, and, as he walked her to her buggy, she added, "My condolences."

"Condolences?"

"That the Danby reward was withdrawn. Understandably, of course."

A smile flickered beneath the mustache. "You do have a way of puttin' things, Mrs. Ashcroft."

LADY ON ICE

Loren D. Estleman

Loren D. Estleman has published nearly fifty novels in the fields of mystery, historical Western, and mainstream. His Amos Walker detective series has earned four Notable Book of the Year mentions from the *New York Times Book Review*, and *The Master Executioner* was featured by *Publishers Weekly* in "The Year in Books" (2001). The recipient of sixteen national writing awards, he has been nominated for the Edgar Allan Poe Award, England's Silver Dagger Award, the National Book Award, and the Pulitzer Prize. His latest Amos Walker novel, *Sinister Heights*, was published in February 2002. Estleman is the current president of the Western Writers of America. He lives in Whitmore Lake, Michigan, with his wife, author Deborah Morgan.

———

OUTSIDE, it was eighty-nine degrees at ten P.M., with percentage of humidity to match, and I was experiencing the early stages of frostbite.

I was sitting on a bench otherwise occupied by semi-professional hockey players, each of whose pads, jerseys, and weapons-grade adrenaline were more effective insulation against the proximity of the ice than my street clothes. The arena had been conjured up out of an old Michigan Company stove warehouse on the Detroit River, with the Renaissance Center undergoing a public-friendly renovation on the one side and twenty toxic acres being parceled out to gullible buyers wanting riverfront condos on the other. Veteran Detroiters were aware that asbestos and car batteries had been leaking poisons into the earth there since Henry Ford, and so the athletes on the ice outnumbered the fans in the bleachers.

I wasn't playing, and I was only half paying attention to the game. When I want to see apes brawl, I can always tune in to the Discovery Channel. I was providing security for a Detroit Lifters guard named Grigori Ivanov who, at the moment I realized I could no longer feel my face, was busy pummeling a French-Canadian center skating for the Philadelphia North Churches. Ivanov didn't seem to need my help with that.

The team owner, a Fordson High School dropout who'd made a couple of hundred million selling pet grooming products over the Internet, had gambled most of his capital on the notion that a summer hockey league would go over as big as Sergeant Spaniel's Tickbuster Spray. Now he was finishing out the team's second season under a court order forcing him to play his team or pay off the remaining time on the players' contracts.

In the midst of all this, Ivanov had started receiving letters from an anonymous party threatening to throw acid in his face if he didn't remand his salary over to a fund to save the Michigan massassauga rattlesnake from extinction. Since most people, particularly those with small children, aged relatives, and beloved pets, would just as soon see the region's only venomous viper go the way of the passenger pigeon, and since hockey stars in general looked as if someone had already thrown acid in their faces, no one was taking the threats seriously.

No one, that is, except the owner's attorneys, who warned him of the legal consequences on the off chance Mr. Anonymous wasn't just blowing smoke. But Ivanov was a reclusive type, with relatives in the Ukraine awaiting money from him to make the journey to America and no wish for any undesirable publicity that might move the State Department to deny them entry visas. That ruled out the police. I'd come recommended on the basis of an old personal-security assignment that had wound up with no one dead or injured (three cracked ribs didn't count, since they were mine), and since I was on my sixth week without a client and considering trading a kidney for the office rent, here I was on the night of the hottest day of summer, rubbing circulation into my face while visions of hot toddies danced in my head.

The score was lopsided in Philadelphia's favor. By the final buzzer, the only audience left was either too drunk on watered-down beer to move or sweeping up Bazooka Joe wrappers in the aisles. I pried my stiff muscles off the bench and moved in close to Ivanov as the Lifters started down the tunnel toward the showers.

The kid had on a bright green T-shirt, or I might not have spotted him bobbing upriver through the red-and-yellow jerseys. The concrete walls were less than ten feet apart, and the players averaged six feet wide. It was a tight crowd, and I had to wedge myself in sideways to keep from being squeezed to the back, which is no place for a bodyguard. As it was, I couldn't get to my gun and had to body-check Ivanov out of the way when the kid's arm swept up and yellow liquid sprayed out of the open vial in his hand.

I hadn't time to see where the liquid went. I hurled myself between two padded shoulders, grabbed a fistful of green cotton, and pulled hard. A seam tore, but the kid's forward momentum started him toward the floor, and I came down on top of him and grasped the wrist of his throwing arm and twisted it up behind his back. The empty vial rolled out of his hand and broke into bits on the concrete floor.

I placed a knee in the small of his back and ran a hand over him for weapons. He hadn't any. By this time, the players had backed off to give us room. I got to my feet, pulling the kid up with me by his twisted arm, and slammed him into the wall, pinning him there while I looked at Ivanov.

"He get you?" I asked.

He'd put a hand against the wall to catch himself when I'd shoved him aside. He pushed himself away from it and touched his face, a reflexive gesture; the lawyers weren't the only ones who'd suspected something was behind the letters besides a crank. "No. I am OK."

The kid was shouting something. I took hold of his hair and pulled his face away from the wall to hear it.

"I didn't want to hurt anybody!" he was saying. "I just wanted to scare him. It was just colored water."

I looked at the wall farther up the tunnel. It had been painted green until a moment before. Now there was a large runny patch with smoke tearing away from its bubbling surface. A patch about the size of a man's face.

"YOUR name's Amos Walker?"

I'd seen the speaker once or twice at police headquarters, but we'd never exchanged a word except maybe to ask for a button to be pushed on the elevator. He was a big Mexican in his forties who bought his sport coats a size too large to leave room for his underarm rig and wore matching shirt-and-tie sets to save himself time dressing. His graying hair was thick enough to be a rug but wasn't, and he had a red, raw face that looked as if he exfoliated with emory paper. The name on the ID clipped to his lapel was Testaverde. He was a detective sergeant with Special Investigations.

I said my name was Amos Walker. He was holding my

ID folder, so there didn't seem any point in denying it. We were standing in a hall at headquarters by the two-way glass looking into the interview room where the kid with the stretched-out T-shirt was answering a detective's questions in front of a camcorder. The air conditioner wasn't working any better than it did in any other government building, which was all right with me. My nose was still running from the chill in the arena.

Testaverde returned the folder. "That was quick thinking. Baby-sitting your specialty?"

"I almost never do it. Hours of sitting around on your hip pockets, seasoned by ten seconds of pure terror. But a job's a job."

"One might say *our* job. Why do people pay taxes if they're going to hire the competition?"

"If they refused, you'd arrest them. Anyway, this one had a muffler on it. It's the only edge I've got. You've got all the people and whirlygigs."

"Well, the rabbit's out of the hutch now. Let's have a listen." He flipped the switch on an intercom panel next to the window. The kid's shallow voice wobbled out of the speaker.

". . . vegetable dye, I don't remember what kind. All I know is there wasn't any kind of acid."

The detective, a well-dressed black man named Clary, read from his notebook. " 'High concentration of sulphuric and hydrochloric acid.' That's what Forensics scraped off the wall. It scarred the concrete, Michael. Think what it would have done to Ivanov's face."

"I filled the tube from the tap and put in the coloring. I wouldn't even know where to lay hands on that other stuff."

"Hydrochloric you can get in any hardware store. People soak their faucet filters in it to remove rust. Sulphuric you can drain out of an ordinary car battery. I want to believe your story, Michael, but you're not helping much. Who could have switched the tubes?"

"I don't know." His mouth clamped shut on the end.

Clary scratched his chin with a corner of the notebook. "Let's go back to those letters you wrote. You said you were jealous of Ivanov's success."

Testaverde switched off the speaker. "Robin Williams is funnier. But he has to make sense. This punk's got serious problems if he's jealous of a third-rate stickman on a crummy semipro hockey team."

"Red Wings players are harder to get close to."

I was barely listening to myself. Michael Nash was seventeen but could pass for two years younger: an undernourished towhead in an old T-shirt without lettering, faded carpenter's jeans, appropriately baggy, and pretend combat boots. He was only an exotic dye job and a couple of piercings away from the common run of self-esteem—challenged youths you saw taking up space at the mall. Nothing about his story made sense unless you fitted in the one piece he was leaving out. After that, it came together like a Greek farce. I didn't bother suggesting this to Sergeant Testaverde; he'd already have thought of it. Cops aren't stupid, just overworked.

GRIGORI Ivanov got away from the Criminal Intelligence Division after recording his statement and autographing a hockey puck for an officer whose kid followed the Lifters. I waited and rode down with Ivanov in the elevator. I asked him who wrote the letters.

He gave me that eyebrowless look you saw a lot of on Eastern European faces before the Iron Curtain rusted through; the one they showed KGB agents and officials of the U.S. State Department. "The boy," he said. "Michael Nash?"

"You wouldn't show me the letters before. Can I see them now?"

"What is point? It is over. Send bill."

"You said they weren't typewritten. I'd like to see the handwriting."

He smiled. It would take a good dentist to decide which teeth hadn't grown in his mouth. "You wish to determine personality?"

"No, and I don't read head bumps either. But I can usually tell a man's writing from a woman's."

"What woman?"

"The kid's protecting someone. When you're a seventeen-year-old boy, the someone is usually female. But then, you'd understand that. You're protecting the same person."

The elevator touched down on the ground floor. He gathered himself to leave. I mashed my thumb against the Door Close button. He grew eyebrows then. I'd seen that same look when he was trying to pry off the Philadelphia center's head with his stick.

"It's a theory, anyway," I said. "The cops will buy it; they don't care as long as the case closes. If there's another reason and I have to go out and find it, I might take the long way back, past Immigration."

The fight went out of him then. In a sport coat and silk shirt, he looked smaller than he did in pads, and now he was almost human scale. "We go somewhere?"

The cop shop is just off Greektown, which is always open, thanks to the casino. The street was speckled with zombified strollers whose air-conditioning had broken down at home. There was a scorched-metal smell in the air, peculiar to that city of wall-to-wall automobiles on a heated summer night. We ordered coffee in a corner booth in a place that reeked of hot grease and burnt cheese. Ivanov hunkered over his cup, looking like a nervous goalie. "She is—was—underage."

"What's her name, and how far did it go?"

His story started in the old country. Trinka Svetlana, a Ukrainian figure skater with Olympic hopes, had met Ivanov when he was skating for a team in Kiev. He was twenty-three; she was sixteen. When Detroit bought his contract and started unwinding red tape to import him, the pair had been living together secretly for six months. He promised to send for her the moment he had the cash. That was three years ago. In the meantime, she'd made her way over with an aunt's help and was living with her in Rochester Hills. Trinka surprised Ivanov one night, waiting for him outside the arena. She'd expected a joyful reunion, but the look on his face when he recognized her ended that. He'd been married to the daughter of the owner of the Lifters for a year.

She fled when he broke the news. Two weeks later, the first of the letters came, threatening to throw acid in Ivanov's face if he didn't agree to leave his wife and return to her.

"What about the Massassauga Relief Fund?" I asked.

"I read about some such thing in the newspaper. Everyone in America supports a cause, no? I thought it would, how you say, throw off the suspicion." His eyebrows disappeared again. "This thing, it is like that movie. *Fatal Extraction?*"

I didn't correct him. His dumb hunkie act had worn through. "She hasn't assimilated," I said. "The thing to do in America is to bring charges against you for statutory rape and contributing to the delinquency of a minor, not to mention encouraging the hopes of innocent rattlesnakes under false pretenses. That means deportation. No wonder you wanted private protection instead of going to the cops."

"Well, she is scared off now. What is your interest?"

"There's a kid in Holding because he thought he was throwing a pie in your face, and it turned out to have a rock in it. I'm curious to meet the person who put it there."

"What pie? What rock?"

I got up and put down money for the coffee. He seized my wrist in an athlete's grip.

"You won't tell Immigration?"

I broke the grip with a maneuver I hadn't used since Cambodia. "Too busy. I need to get an estimate on putting the Berlin Wall back up." I went out into the scorched-metal air.

THERE was a V. Svetlana listed in Rochester Hills. I tried the number from a booth, and a husky female voice confirmed the number and told me to leave a message. I disobeyed.

I opened the window in the car, mostly to let out the stale air. My congestion was clearing, and I had just begun to feel the heat. Coming up on one A.M., and the stoops of apartment buildings and single-family houses were occupied by men in damp undershirts and women in shorts and tank tops, smoking and drinking from cans beaded with moisture. Some of them looked as if they'd been hit over the head with something, but most were smiling and laughing. Winter had been long and cold and not so far back.

It was one of the homes in the older section of Rochester Hills, which means it didn't look as if it came with a heliport. The roof was in good shape, it had been painted recently, and the lawn would pass inspection, free of miniature windmills and lighthouses.

"Mrs. Svetlana?" I asked the creature who answered the doorbell.

She looked at me with slightly sloping Tartar eyes in a face that had given up its first wrinkle—a vertical crease above the bridge of the nose—and probably got something well worth having in the trade. Her hair was an unassisted auburn, cut short at the neck but teased into bangs to lighten the severity. The nose was slightly aquiline, the cheekbones high. Stradivari had made a pass at her lips and taken the rest of the week off. She had on a blue satin dressing gown and flat-heeled sandals and looked me square in the eye at six feet and change.

"Miss," she corrected. "It's late for visitors."

"Not many women would open the door this late." I showed her my ID. "Are you Trinka Svetlana's aunt?"

"You woke me up to ask me that?"

I liked her accent: Garbo out of *Ninotchka* by way of Nadia Komanich. "Trinka's boyfriend is in jail. I want to ask her a couple of questions about how he got there."

A light glimmered in the Oriental eyes. "Grigori?"

"Michael."

Her face shut down. It had never been fully open. "She's a beautiful girl. I can't keep track of her young men." She started to push the door shut. I leaned against it.

"I'm betting she can. Girls are organized about that kind of thing."

"She isn't here." She pushed harder. She had plenty of push, but I had thirty pounds on her, and it was too hot to move. She gave up then. "She's at the rink downtown, practicing her routine." She rolled the *r*.

"Routine?"

"Her figure skating act. Everything today is a show. To skate expertly is no longer enough. She wants to go to the Olympics."

"She wanted that in the Ukraine. She wanted Grigori, too. Does she still want Grigori?"

"Grigori is a pig." Spittle flecked my cheek.

"No argument from the U.S. Which rink?"

"There is only one."

I straightened, and she pushed the door shut. By that time it was redundant. With women like V. Svetlana around, it was a wonder there weren't still missiles in Cuba.

THE Iceland Skating Rink's quarter-page ad in the Yellow Pages said it closed at midnight. There was a light on in the city block of yellow brick building when I parked in a lot containing only a two-year-old Geo and a Dodge Ram pickup with a toolbox built onto the bed. When no one came to the front door, I walked around to the side and kicked at a steel fire door until it opened wide enough to show me a large, black, angry-looking face and a police .38.

"What part of Closed you need me to explain to you?" It was a deep, well-shaped voice. Motown had a lot to answer for when it moved to L.A.

"You left a light on. I'm with Detroit Edison."

He looked at my ID. "That ain't what it says."

"One of us is lying. I need a minute with Trinka."

"Don't know no Trinka."

"Yeah. I'm just the scrub team. The first string won't like that answer any more than I do. It's a long drive from Thirteen Hundred and a hot night. They'll be sore."

Thirteen Hundred is the address of Detroit Police Headquarters. He opened the door the rest of the way and put away the .38. His uniform was soaked through. The air-conditioning budget at Iceland went into keeping the rink from turning into a swimming pool.

I followed him down an unfinished corridor to a glass door. "See if you can get her to go home," he said. "I like her, but I need this job." He left me.

Inside, a trim figure in a royal blue leotard glided around on the ice. It was just her and me and Sarah Vaughan singing "Dancing in the Dark" on a portable CD player propped up on the railing that surrounded the rink. I leaned next to it and violated another rule by lighting up a Winston.

Trinka Svetlana was as tall as her aunt and could have been her daughter. Her hair was longer and a lighter shade of red, but disregard fifteen years and the laws of physics, and I might have been looking at the same woman. She had an athletic build and muscular legs, more shapely than the broken Popsicle sticks they use to sell hose on television. Her white skates cut wide, nearly silent loops on the ice.

I found the volume on the CD player and turned it down. I didn't want to startle her by switching it off. She noticed the change and slowed down, looking at me. She didn't stop.

"Nice form," I said. "I give it a ten, but my favorite's the luge."

"Who are you?" Her accent was heavier than her aunt's, but she didn't sound any more rattled.

"Not important. Michael's in jail."

Even that didn't stop her. She drew a wide circle around the edge of the rink. "Michael?"

"Nash. *N* as in *nice-to-a-fault*. *A* as in *adolescent*. *S* as in *stupid*. *H* as in *hell*. Or *Holding*. Same definition. He threw a bottle of acid at Grigori. Grigori Ivanov? *I* as in *infidelity*—"

"I know who he is." It was the first emotion she'd shown. "Michael's a nice boy. Why would he want to do that?"

"He believed your letters. Don't say, 'Letters?' No more spelling bees." My face was stiffening all over again. That night in summer was the coldest winter I'd ever spent.

"He thought it was colored water in the vial. Any thoughts on where he got that idea?"

She skated in silence. Sarah had stopped singing. I switched off the player.

"He said he filled it himself from the tap," I said, "but I figure he lied about that, too. Whoever filled it used hydrochloric and sulphuric acid in concentrate. Very hard on the complexion."

She stumbled and almost fell. She caught her balance and skated up to the rail. Her eyes were larger than her aunt's, but they hadn't been so large a moment before. "Who sent you?"

I told her.

"Aunt Vadya?" She was breathing heavily, and her face glowed with moisture. It had collected in beads along the top of her collarbone. On TV you never saw how much they were sweating.

"She didn't rat you out. In the Ukraine she grew up in, she learned how much truth to tell when. What I want to know is, why didn't you do the job yourself? Your aim probably would've been more accurate."

"It *was* water. I filled it and put in the coloring. Are you the police? Why did you arrest Michael? He's just a boy."

This sounded like truth. It didn't have the ring of conviction that went with a lie. But then she was a performer.

I put cop in my voice. "We arrest them whether it's nitro or Kool-Aid. If it's Kool-Aid, we don't hold them. When it's something else, we try them as adults."

She believed me then. I wouldn't have bet money on it a minute earlier. "Grigori. Did—?"

"Did his face melt? Six inches this way or that, and it would've. It sure made a mess out of a painted concrete wall. Not that he'd have had to look at himself in a mirror. He'd have had to skate for a team for the blind."

"That's impossible! I never—it—"

She stopped, not because I'd interrupted her. Something had clicked for both of us.

"Was that vial ever out of your sight after you filled it?" I asked.

She started shivering.

I TOLD her she could pick up her car later. I drove her to 1300, got Sergeant Testaverde out of his office, and introduced him to her. He locked himself up with her for twenty minutes. At the end of it, he sent a car to Rochester Hills.

The four of us waited in the office. Michael Nash and Trinka sat on the vinyl-upholstered sofa—close, but not touching, and without speaking. She'd put on a sweatsuit over her leotard and changed from her skates into a pair of pink running shoes. Dressed like that and with her hair twisted into a ponytail, she looked younger than nineteen, closer to Michael's age. She stared at the linoleum, he looked at a CPR chart on the wall and chewed his lower lip. The sergeant, seated behind his desk, mopped at his face and neck with a hand towel and glowered at me sipping hot coffee from a Styrofoam cup in the scoop chair.

"Do you have to guzzle that in front of me?" he snarled. "It just makes me hotter."

"That's your problem. I think I'm coming down with a cold."

"You can stay home and nurse it after Lansing jerks your license. Impersonating an officer."

"I did an impression of one. There's a difference."

"I'd sure as hell like to know what it is."

"It wouldn't do you any good. You have to shut off half your brain, and half's all you got."

"That a Mexican joke?"

"I don't know any Mexican jokes. They haven't been up here long enough. It's a cop joke. Force of habit. You'd have got around to Trinka after you finished sweating Beaver Cleaver."

"Thanks for the vote of confidence." He reached back and twisted the knob on the window fan, looking for a speed faster than High. Maintenance turned off the air conditioner at midnight.

A uniform poked his head in and said the suspect was in Interview Room 3. Testaverde stood and pulled his shirt away from his back. "Keep these two company." He stabbed a finger at me. "Let's find out what half your brain turned up."

Detective Clary was still at his post, but he wasn't asking many questions. Vadya Svetlana, having changed into a simple but by no means unfashionable green dress, but otherwise looking much as she had standing on her own doorstep, sat at the table Michael Nash had occupied, speaking directly to the video camera.

"You Americans talk of family until it means nothing," she said. "You couple it with other words—family *values*, family *workplace, extended* family—as if it needed the help. I will tell you about family. When the Nazis shelled Leningrad, my grandmother was visiting friends outside the city. She tried to sneak back in, carrying her baby—my uncle—and holding her firstborn's hand—my mother's hand—and almost stumbled into an SS patrol. She took cover in a doorway. When the baby began to cry, she smothered it with her hand so the soldiers wouldn't hear and slaughter them all. She killed her son to save her family."

After a moment, Clary cleared his throat. "Let's move closer to the present. Why did you replace the colored water in the vial with acid?"

"Because my niece is a fool."

The camera whirred, wanting more.

"Most kids are," prompted the detective. "Most guardians don't turn it into a reason for mayhem."

"Most guardians don't have Cossack blood. When someone dishonors you, the name of your family, you don't just scare him. You say, 'Boo!' What is that? No, you say it with a knife in the belly."

"If you feel that way, why didn't you do it yourself?"

"The boy wanted to do it. He said it was too dangerous for a girl. When a boy wishes to play at soldiers, it is not a woman's place to interfere."

"Except in the business of the vial."

"You frighten a pig, he runs away squealing. The fright goes away, the pig comes back. What you expect, he will stop being a pig? If you want a pig to stop being a pig, for the honor of your family, you must kill him."

"But you didn't try to kill him."

She shrugged. It was an entirely Slavic gesture, not to be imitated. "It is America. You make the adjustment."

Officer Clary was silent. We were silent. She lifted her eyebrows and looked directly at us. The glass was a blank mirror on her side.

"What did I say?" she asked. "It is my English?"

Testaverde switched off the intercom. I thought he shuddered a little. It could have been the cold.

EL PALACIO

John Lutz

John Lutz is the author of more than 35 novels and approximately 250 short stories and articles. His work has been translated into virtually every language and adapted for almost every medium. He is a past president of both Mystery Writers of America and Private Eye Writers of America. Among his awards are the MWA Edgar, the PWA Shamus, The Trophee 813 Award for best mystery short story collection translated into the French language, the PWA Life Achievement Award, and the Golden Derringer Lifetime Achievement Award for short mystery fiction. He is the author of two private eye series, the Nudger series, set in his hometown of Saint Louis, and the Carver series, set in Florida, as well as many nonseries suspense novels. His novel *SWF Seeks Same* was made into the hit movie *Single White Female*, starring Bridget Fonda and Jennifer Jason Leigh, and his novel *The Ex* was made into the HBO original movie of the same title, for which he coauthored the screenplay. His latest books are *The Nudger Dilemmas*, a collection of short stories, and *The Night Caller*, a suspense novel.

MARTIN watched Graham Firling stumble out through El Palacio's swinging doors into the buzzing evening heat. Some of the buzzing was from insects. Some was from the transformer mounted on the crooked wooden pole just outside the doors. In Port Lios, located in an almost inaccessible cove on the coast of Mexico, electricity, like a lot of other things, came and went pretty much on its own whim.

Port Lios might have been an actual commercial port at one time, Martin figured, but now it would take a lot of dredging for anything larger than a shrimp boat to berth here. Hurricanes had stirred the ocean bottom, and the ships that carried the countryside's weak crops of sugarcane, bananas, and mango, stopped docking there years ago, after one of the rusty tramp steamers had run aground. The port itself had fallen into disrepair and then ruin. The town had followed suit. The name of the crude and disreputable waterfront bar where Martin sat was a joke. El Palacio was no palace; it was a dive. The kind of drinkers you'd expect to find in it were like Graham Firling and Martin. And the big man in the sweat-stained, cream-colored suit who had stood up and was now tacking toward Martin's table.

He stood staring at Martin, sweat streaming down his broad face. He was in his late forties, gone to fat but with plenty of muscle underneath. Why he didn't at least remove his suit coat was something Martin didn't understand. *The guy must think he's a character in one of those old Hollywood movies set in the tropics, where everybody wore white suits.* That notion suggested ego, something Martin had lost long ago, and he didn't feel like talking or listening to anyone with ego. He took a sip of warm Scotch and tried to ignore the looming presence, which wasn't easy, considering the man's cloyingly sweet-smelling cologne that obviously substituted for bathing.

"My name's Rondo," the man said. He had a gentle, soothing voice for such a big man.

"First name or last?"

"Both."

Mr. Mysterious, Martin thought. He said nothing, hoping the man would leave.

Instead, chair legs scraped the rough plank floor, and he sat down across the table from Martin, casually brushing away a dead fly.

"I couldn't help but overhear your conversation with the man who just left," Rondo said. "Not that I understood anything you said, just caught a word now and then, and I gathered both of you are American. As I'm an American, and there aren't many of us in a godforsaken place like this, I thought I'd introduce myself."

"I'm Martin," Martin finally said, knowing the man wasn't going to leave.

"You seem to be a good listener," Rondo said. He caught the bartender's attention with a hard stare and raised two fingers for a fresh round of drinks. "The other man was doing most of the talking."

"Graham likes to talk."

"Do you?"

"Not particularly."

"Me either. Very close-mouthed am I. My friends tell me anything, knowing it will go no further. I'm like that little waste basket icon on your computer screen; you drop information there, and there it stops, and eventually it will be deleted entirely."

"I don't know much about computers. Anyway, I stay in a place without electricity. Most of the buildings in town don't have any kind of power."

Both men were silent while the bartender, a sullen, graceful man named Enrico, brought their drinks and accepted Rondo's pesos. Rondo absently waved away any thought of change. When Enrico was back behind the bar, and out of earshot like the three other customers in El Palacio, Rondo said, "Shall I be honest?"

"Christ, no!"

Rondo smiled his broad and almost toothless smile. "I

will be anyway, to clear the air. You and your friend have had an ounce or so too much to drink. When people get that way, sometimes it's because there's something they need to talk about but seldom do." A bead of perspiration broke from Rondo's receding hairline near the temple and raced like an insect down a fleshy cheek. "Do you collect?"

"Fleas. Odd people in bars."

"I'm what you might call a collector of true tales, other people's experiences. Your friend who left—Graham?—he obviously told you his story. I thought now you might want to take a turn, if I supplied myself as listener." He tugged a wrinkled white handkerchief from an inside pocket and dabbed at his sweaty forehead. Hollywood again.

"I think you've seen too many movies," Martin said.

"Oh, I don't think that's possible. I love movies. The worlds they create."

"So do I," Martin said, which was true, though it had been a long time since he'd seen one.

"Adventure and romance. Enhanced reality."

"I guess so," Martin said. He wiped his damp wrist across his equally damp forehead. It wasn't as effective as Rondo's handkerchief. Martin thought he might start carrying a handkerchief, be in his own movie like Rondo. He knocked back what was left in his glass, then sipped at the new Scotch. It was the same biting rotgut that was in his other glass, the only Scotch available in El Palacio. Hundred malt or some such.

But it did the job. Which included loosening the tongue.

"No one winds up in Port Lios except reluctantly," Rondo said. "You must have a story."

"You're here. Do you have a story?"

"We'll trade," Rondo said with his beefy smile. Martin really noticed his eyes for the first time, heavy-lidded and pale blue, tiny and sleepy, dreamy in a way that disturbed.

Martin had had enough of the man, of the talk, of the nauseating stench of perfumed cologne and stale sweat. He said, "I don't think so," and he stood up, almost falling. He realized he'd had way too much to drink and had been talking too freely to this stranger.

But it was hard not to drink too much in this hole of a town, with the jungle all around it supposedly occupied by guerillas who were against about everything, including *Norte Americanos* with little visible means of support. Martin knew what he looked like, what his reputation was among the townspeople. They saw him as every inch a bum. He was past the point where the guerillas would mistake him for a *turista* who might be worth robbing. He would simply be sport to them. Probably they would torture him before murdering him without fear of consequence. Just last month, the decomposed body of an unknown man was discovered at the edge of the jungle. It was assumed he was an American or Englishman, though a search of the body revealed no identification.

"Are you all right, my friend?" Rondo was asking.

"Fine," Martin assured him, trying to fight down the persistent nausea. It was the Scotch and the damned heat. Not to mention the floor tilting this way and that.

Without looking back at Rondo, he managed to make it to the swinging doors, then outside into the steaming night and around the corner of the clapboard building. There he vomited, then sat, leaning his back against a tree trunk in the darkness until he felt well enough to stand up.

He wrestled a battered pocket watch from his badly wrinkled pants, angling its face to the faint moonlight so he could see its hands. Not yet eight o'clock. Early yet. Too early to go to his stifling, odorous room and stare at the walls and cockroaches.

Licking his lips, then spitting out as much of the vomit

taste as he could, he drew several deep breaths, then tucked in his shirt and set off for the town square. If he had his days right, or nights, there was supposed to be some kind of celebration there tonight. The town was a hundred years old, if he recalled. He had to smile at that one. It sure as hell looked its age.

He was walking OK, feeling almost OK, trodding a straight path and occasionally swatting away a gnat or mosquito that kept trying to fly up his nose. No one seemed to be staring at him as if he were drunk. Most people looked away as he approached.

He could hear strains of music, a mariachi band, and see tinted light from colored paper lanterns ahead as he strode the rutted dirt road that led to the square. When he was nearer, shouting and laughter became audible, muffled by the night so oppressively humid it lay like warm velvet on Martin's flesh. Then he could see children, dancers, vendors hawking colorful if crude merchandise.

The town square was the usual one, built along plans laid out by conquering Spaniards centuries ago. There was the town hall, the *mercado*, a modest cathedral. In the center of the square was a long-dry fountain, built around the statue of a horseman whose identity no one seemed to know but who was rumored to be the founder of *Puerto Lios*. Tonight the small square was crowded with merchants and peasants and a kind of desperate cheer, all for a time when decaying Port Lios thrived and there was a healthy market for crops and the shrimp were still there for the taking in a bountiful sea. All before the hurricanes, the crash of the local economy, the crushing poverty. There was no end in sight to the plight of these people. What was left to them but to celebrate?

A boy about ten years old broke from a knot of children and dashed toward Martin. He was grinning. In his raised right hand was a colorful object that Martin knew was a brightly dyed egg. For weeks the townspeople had been carefully draining eggs, not breaking them except for two small openings through which, when the eggshells were dry, confetti would be stuffed.

Martin, in a better mood now, knew what the boy was up to and ducked down and grinned back at him. The boy broke the egg against Martin's forehead, scattering confetti through Martin's hair and down his sweat-soaked shirt. Then he laughed and darted back to his rollicking friends. Martin wished that someday he could again have that kind of mindless, innocent fun. That he could feel some emotion not tainted by fear.

"Martin, my friend!" a voice called.

Martin turned and saw Rondo seated at one of the outdoor tables near the fountain. He looked too large for his tiny, elaborate iron chair.

"Come have a drink with me," Rondo implored. He patted his forehead with his wadded handkerchief. "It's such a hot night! A man could almost swim in the humidity. *Cerveza* this time, hey? No more of that vile Scotch!"

Martin swallowed. His throat was dry. His lips were stuck together, and all the moisture of his body seemed to be oozing out as perspiration.

He veered to his right and dropped into a chair across the round, iron table from Rondo, trying not to breathe in too deeply the scent of sweat and cologne. Not that he smelled so great himself.

Rondo caught the eye of a man from the café, who was waiting tables, and raised his Corona bottle, signaling for two more of the same.

When the beers arrived, Rondo paid for both of them with crinkled, sweat-damp pesos, poured his and half of Martin's beer, then tapped his glass mug against Martin's.

"To better days like we used to have," he said. "Like the ones this unknown blight on the coast is celebrating."

Both men tilted back their mugs and took long, deep swallows of the lukewarm beer.

"I think they're celebrating their survival," Martin said.

Rondo smiled at him. "Yes, even if they don't know it." He gazed across the square for a few seconds, where a gang of shirtless boys was lustily beating a *piñata* with long sticks. "You were telling me about your job," he said.

"Was I?" Like Rondo's, Martin's gaze was fixed on the violence across the square. The *piñata* suddenly ruptured, spilling candy and prizes out as a reward. The boys swarmed over the bounty.

"Well, your former occupation."

"For your story collection?"

"Only for that."

Martin knew Rondo wasn't going to give up. The big man had about him a desperate persistence that clung to him like his cologne. He wanted reassurance that life was like movies, with logical beginnings, middles, and ends. Okay. Rondo wanted a story, he'd get a story.

"I used to work cleaning up messes," Martin said, "for people who could afford to pay well. Personal messes, if you catch my meaning."

Rondo turned to face Martin and leaned forward, obviously interested. "Are you saying you were a hit man?" His smile was wide and dark as the night, as if he didn't believe Martin. As if he couldn't believe he'd found such a priceless nugget for his collection.

Martin shrugged. "You're saying it. I'm not disagreeing. But let's just say I'm talking about someone else, make it easier."

"Agreed," Rondo said, making a pink tent of sausage-sized fingers. "Please go on."

"I—this guy I'll call *I,* used to work sometimes with a partner we'll call Evan."

Rondo nodded, tiny eyes almost closed, making mental notes.

"Evan and I got instructions—no need to say who from—to take care of this woman who'd backed down on paying a big tab for cocaine supplied to her by . . . well, let's just say my employers. There was no way to get the coke back or the money, you understand, so an example had to be made of her."

"Like in the movies," Rondo said. "Gangsters living by the code, not to mention sound business practices." Out came the damp handkerchief again so he could pat his glistening forehead. "And where did this occur?"

"Let's say L.A."

"Where else?" Rondo said. The smile again.

"This wasn't a movie star or anything, just an attractive woman who lived off rich men who supported her and her habit in exchange for you know what."

"I know," Rondo said, maybe a bit too avidly.

"So her death wouldn't be looked into all that closely. Especially considering the crowd she ran with. Big-money drug crowd. She knew lots of dangerous men, most of them rich enough to hire even more dangerous men. So Evan and I were given our usual packet, stuff in an envelope so we could learn about our intended target, name, photographs, address. No employer in this case. She was between men who'd pay her way, so she was staying with a friend. She'd been there several days, at the address we were given."

Rondo dabbed at his forehead with his handkerchief again, then wiped his fleshy, stubbled jowls. "How did you intend to dispatch . . . to complete your assignment?"

"The how was left up to us. In this case, since the hit was going to be in a quiet kind of neighborhood where a shot might draw attention, we figured we'd go with knives. They're quick and efficient if you know how to use them. And if you understand something about human anatomy and you're nice and nimble, you can avoid getting even a little blood on you."

"Not so nice but nimble, you mean."

"Huh? Oh, yeah, I guess so."

"That would take a real pro," Rondo said thoughtfully. "The part about avoiding all the blood."

"Evan and I, you better believe we were real pros. In fact, this assignment promised to be pretty routine. The woman kept late hours and was careless even though she owed money to the wrong people. Party type using her looks while they lasted, had to have her fun even if it killed her."

"I know the type well," Rondo said.

Martin doubted it. "And there wouldn't be any problem identifying our target. She was a tanned and lovely California beach beauty, great legs, long blonde hair, boob job, the whole package."

"A shame to harm such a creature," Rondo said.

"Do you really think so?" Martin asked.

Rondo grinned. "No, not really. You're telling your story, but you're learning about me."

Martin sipped his beer and nodded. "It can work that way, as you must know. So Evan and me, we drove to the address about nine in the evening just to look the place over and consider our options. That was when serendipity took over."

Rondo raised both arched eyebrows. "Pardon me?"

"Serendipity. Fate. Whatever you want to call it."

"Fate," Rondo said.

"Okay. What fate did was deliver us our target like a gift that first night. We're sitting in our rental car trying to figure the best way in and out of the building, which was a ritzy condo, when out she walks. She came out of the right address, a town house with its own entrance, and we could see she fit the description perfectly, even in the dim light. She was kind of dressed up, wearing what they call a cocktail dress, like she was going to meet someone, but there was nobody else around.".

"In times like that," Rondo said, "men of opportunity act without hesitation."

"That was us, men of opportunity. We didn't even have to discuss it beforehand, just nodded to each other. We climbed out of the car and crossed the street, smiling when the woman noticed us, like we were on our way to visit someone in the building and wasn't it a nice night? She didn't suspect anything was wrong till Evan shoved her back in the shadows of the walkway she'd come down, back among some shrubbery. The surprise took the breath out of her, and she didn't make a sound. Evan was fast and he was good. We both were. He got behind her and yanked her head back by the hair. I got behind her too, alongside Evan, and used the knife on her throat. It was all so quick she didn't hardly suffer."

"Merciful," Rondo said.

Martin swirled beer in his glass. "Why not?" He swatted away a mosquito that had taken a liking to him. The damned thing was substantial enough that it went about ten feet and maybe wouldn't find its way back. *Go bother somebody else!*

"Then you made your escape," Rondo said.

Martin shook his head. "No. Just then something hit me in the shoulder, and I saw Evan go flying. And all of a sudden we were in a tussle with this guy who happened along."

"Fate, again," Rondo said.

"Fate with a hell of a lot of fight in him. We finally took care of him, but it wasn't easy, and it was a mess. We left footprints, got some blood on us, got some dogs to barking somewhere in the neighborhood. Then we got out of there fast. Evan had some bad cuts on his hand, and some tooth marks. I noticed for the first time both my gloves had been pulled off in the struggle. They were leather, and it was a hot, humid night like this one."

"Slippery with sweat," Rondo said. "Unexpected things can happen when you're slippery with sweat. But all ended well and as planned. Except for the unfortunate Sir Galahad who happened along and was too brave."

"Not exactly," Martin said. "Fate wasn't finished with us. Evan and I got the papers and checked the TV news early the next morning. Turns out Sir Galahad was a parking valet at a restaurant the victim had been to earlier that night. He realized he'd brought around the wrong car for her, one that was the same make and model as hers, even the same color. She'd been drinking and hadn't even noticed, just drove the thing home and parked it in the street. So he phoned from the restaurant, which wasn't far away, and offered to drive her car over, park it in her rear driveway, then walk around and exchange keys with her so he could drive the other car back and complete the switch. She knew when he was coming and walked out to meet him."

"Then he wasn't anyone of great importance, either. I mean, not a movie star or famous director or anything of that sort. You seem to have avoided celebrity involvement."

"Well," Martin said, "here's the thing. It seems we accidentally took out a woman who wasn't our target. The woman who lived in the condo our intended hit was staying at was pretty much the same type, especially considering we saw her at night."

"She mistook another car for hers, and you mistook her for another woman. Isn't that just how fate operates, with a wicked sense of humor and symmetry? I tell you, Martin, there are no coincidences in this life. It unfolds like a movie script. And it seems to me this tale is taking on a disturbing familiarity."

"Uh-huh. There's more, and it's all trouble for the hero. The woman we killed just happened to be the former wife of a celebrity. A famous retired ballplayer."

Rondo swallowed and leaned forward over the table. A bead of perspiration that had been clinging to the tip of his nose lost its grip and plummeted into his beer. "My God! You don't really mean . . ."

Martin nodded somberly. "Mountain Davis. The best third baseman that ever played in the National League. A power hitter with a gold glove and an arm like a rocket launcher. Ten years out of the game, but still all over TV and movies. A national sports hero."

"And you and this Evan accidentally killed his ex-wife and the parking valet."

"That's right," Martin said. "Cynthia Davis and Brad Leonard."

Rondo sat back. He was breathing heavily. "You stun me, Mr. Martin. You absolutely stun me!"

"Martin is my first name."

"Yes, it would be . . ." Rondo seemed shaken. He tossed down the rest of his beer and motioned for the waiter.

No one said anything as the drinks were delivered and the waiter withdrew.

"The trial lasted almost a year," Rondo said. "The country, the world, was spellbound by it. But what would you have done if Davis had been found guilty?"

Martin said nothing.

Rondo finally nodded, making his sweaty jowls spill over his stained white collar. "I see. It didn't matter to you what the verdict was."

"But it did," Martin said. "It mattered very much. Because in a way, Evan and I were on trial, too."

"I don't understand."

"If Mountain Davis had been found guilty of murdering his ex and the parking valet, that would have been the end of the case. As it is, the murders remain unsolved. True, almost everyone assumes Mountain's guilt, but an unsolved homicide case is never closed. The police might reactivate the investigation at any time. Because of the not guilty verdict, I became a potential liability to the people who hired me. Do you understand what I'm saying? Why I'm hiding in this place at the end of the earth?"

Rondo shifted his weight on his chair. Martin studied him and thought he saw a glitter of fear in the tiny, pale eyes. Maybe he'd gotten more of a story than he wanted.

"I'm leaving this place soon, anyway," Martin assured him. "It doesn't matter to me if you believe what I'm saying."

Rondo tilted back his head and sipped his beer, all the time watching Martin from the corner of his eye. "The question is, if I believe your story, do I also believe you about leaving this place?"

"Do you?"

"I'll have to think about it."

"You will, won't you," Martin said. He stood up. "Thanks for the drinks." Taking his half-full bottle with him, he made his way into the crowd, avoiding the dancers as he crossed the square toward the cathedral.

He would sit on the cathedral's stone steps and listen to the music, watching the dancers as he finished his beer.

MARTIN awoke about midnight with an aching back and a numb left arm. It took him a few seconds before he realized he'd fallen asleep on the cathedral steps.

Groaning, deploring the mosslike coating on his teeth, the sour taste beneath his tongue, he fought his way up to a sitting position. Something cracked along his spine, not relieving the pain at all. But his arm was beginning to tingle. A good sign. He rubbed it with his right hand to help bring back circulation. His flesh felt clammy despite the heat that permeated the night, even this late.

There was no music now, or lights. The tables around the fountain were unoccupied. On the opposite side of the shadowed, littered square, a group of revelers staggered and jostled, playfully punching each other and laughing. They sounded drunk, Martin thought, but who was he to pass judgment?

He fished his well-worn pocket watch from his wrinkled pants and stared at the face. The crystal was fogged from the humidity, but the hands were visible enough. It was almost one-thirty. El Palacio might still be open. Surely some of the revelers had made their way there to cap off their evening.

Martin was right. As he approached El Palacio, he saw that the place must be crowded. Several men were even standing outside with their drinks, or sitting on chairs they'd dragged out into the night where it might at least be somewhat cooler than inside. But as Martin got closer, it did strike him as odd that these men were unusually quiet, talking calmly or gazing at the ground.

Curious, Martin quickened his pace. He'd been noticed. All the men stopped what they were doing to stare at him.

"Someone inside wants to see you," a maker of leather goods, whose name was Ignacio, said to Martin. He had never before spoken to Martin.

When Martin stepped through the old swinging doors, conversation ceased as if he were a gunslinger in an old Western movie. Enrico, behind the bar, saw him and beckoned with a forefinger. "Martin! Come here!"

Everyone watched as Martin made his way through the crowded saloon to the bar. Enrico waved an arm, exposing a dark crescent of perspiration beneath his shirt sleeve. Slowly conversation regained its momentum.

"Someone wants to talk with you, Martin."

"A drink first," Martin said. "I need some Scotch to wash the night from my tongue."

"Later, Martin. Over there at the back table. Chief Rodriguez has been waiting for you."

"Waiting? For me? How could he know I'd come here when I awakened?"

Enrico shook his head. "Martin, Martin . . ."

"I'm a drunk," Martin said miserably.

"Many of my customers are, Martin. They drink to forget, or because they have nothing to forget."

Martin decided not to think about that until later. He edged through the crowd to a table near the rear exit, off by itself so conversation could be made in private. At the table sat the solid, grim form of Police Chief Hector Rodriguez, a man who had always tolerated Martin but who frightened him. Rodriguez's brown policeman's cap sat next to a bottle of beer on the table. There were three chairs: the one occupied by Rodriguez, an empty one, and one with a filthy and stained white piece of fabric draped over its wooden back.

Rodriguez, dark and somber and with a blunt haircut and bangs that made him look like a dusky Caesar, motioned for Martin to sit in the empty chair.

"Something has happened," he said, when Martin was seated.

"I was drinking with a friend in the square," Martin said. "Then I sat outside the cathedral and fell asleep. I just woke up." Whatever had happened, an alibi couldn't hurt. That it was true was a bonus.

"Yes, many people saw you," Rodriguez said. "Luckily

for you, you went to church and took a nap rather than accompany your friend Mr. Rondo."

Martin licked his lips and wiped his arm across his mouth, staring at Rodriguez's beer. "Something happened to Rondo?"

"Did you know him well?"

Careful here! "I didn't know him at all. I mean, I barely knew him. Just met him earlier tonight right here in El Palacio."

"What did he tell you about himself?"

"Why, nothing!"

"You talked here and then later in the square, and he revealed nothing about himself? Did he have a first name?"

"Rondo. I assumed that was his first name. I didn't know his last."

"What did he say? I mean, what sort of things did you talk about?"

"He said he collected stories."

"And you told him yours?"

Martin felt his heart go cold. "I told him a story, because that was what he wanted to hear. He was interested in baseball, so I told him I used to play minor league ball for the Detroit Tigers. I said I would have been a great pitcher, only I injured my arm."

Rodriguez stared at him with new interest. His unblinking dark eyes made Martin uncomfortable. "Is any of that true?"

"Of course not."

"You can tell me the truth, Martin. You're not suspected of a crime, and we have a very lenient attitude toward drifters like you here in Port Lios. You spend money that doesn't appear to have been stolen here. You and people like you are about the only kind of tourist trade we have."

"That is sad," Martin said.

"And now you're trying to change the subject."

"I was never a ballplayer, I swear! I could never throw a baseball accurately even before I began to drink."

"I don't wonder so much about you and your pitching ability as I do about Mr. Rondo."

"You mentioned a crime."

"You are not so unaware as you pretend." Rodriguez motioned with his hand toward the tattered and stained white cloth draped over the back of the chair next to him. "This is what remains of Mr. Rondo's coat. The stains you see are blood. There are two pockets in what we have here. One contains a dirty white handkerchief, the other is empty."

"He was always wiping his forehead with a handkerchief."

"There is no doubt this is his coat, Martin. Mr. Rondo was the only man for miles who wore a white suit coat in this heat, or possibly who even owns a white suit coat. Revelers on the way home from the celebration found it on the trail near dense jungle."

"Guerrillas," Martin said. "Undoubtedly the guerrillas ambushed him and dragged the body back into the jungle. It's happening more and more often."

"What you say is most likely, Martin. Our problem is that we have no way even to know who he was, or who we might notify of his death. Was he an American?"

"He said he was, but I doubt it. He liked to be mysterious."

Rodriguez shrugged. "Well, like some others who've died here, he will be mysterious even in death. Thank you for talking with me, Martin. If you happen to remember anything . . ."

"Of course, of course. I'll come to you immediately." Martin stood.

"May I buy you a drink?"

"Thanks, but I don't want one now." Martin started toward the door.

"The guerrillas," Rodriguez reminded him. "They are down from the hills in numbers. Remember what happened to Mr. Rondo. Be careful where you walk."

MARTIN did take a jungle trail behind the village, but only a short distance, to the shack where his friend and frequent drinking companion Graham Firling lived. Graham would be asleep, probably deeply, but Martin would wake him. Graham would want to know about this.

Martin didn't knock, as there was only an old sheet of sail canvas nailed to hang over the shack's entrance. Light shone at its edges. It appeared that Graham was awake or had fallen asleep and forgotten to snuff out the old camping lantern he used as his light source in the dilapidated structure. The shack's corrugated steel roof kept the rain out, and its plank siding blocked most of the wind. On hot, sultry nights like this one, Graham usually had the canvas rolled up over the door and a window open so a breeze flowed between. But not tonight, which should have struck Martin as odd.

The first and only thing Martin saw when he pulled away the canvas and stepped into the stifling shack was Graham sitting up in bed, propped on a pillow as if he'd been reading. Graham's upper body was black—no, red. His head was cocked unnaturally to the side, and there was a wound in his throat that looked like an ax slice. Martin swallowed. The coppery scent of fresh blood that hung in the air became taste.

"Graham . . ." Martin uttered in shock. The name was like a burr in his throat.

But the fatal wound had been caused not by an ax but by a machete. It was gripped in the right hand of a large man with a dark mustache and wearing a straw peasant's hat with a broad, tattered brim. He had on a loose-fitting blue shirt and the rope-belted pants favored by local farmers.

"If you stand well back and just so," the man said in Rondo's softly insinuating voice, "you can easily avoid the spray of blood. I thought that might interest you, Martin."

Martin couldn't move. Tried but couldn't. "You're dead," he said. "The guerrillas killed you."

"I'm dressed like this to keep it that way, Martin. All part of the plan. You see, there really are no coincidences. I followed you here to Port Lios because I suspected you might be one of the men my employers hired me to erase." The peasant who was Rondo smiled widely beneath the mustache, showing no teeth. "*Your* previous employers."

Martin was astounded. "You think I killed—you actually *believed* my story?"

"Sure did. And it was a bonus that you and Evan were traveling together, or that you rendezvoued here."

"But that isn't Evan. He's—he was—Graham Firling! You've got this all completely wrong!"

Rondo shook his head firmly. "Isn't that just what you'd tell me if you were the real killers?"

"Or if we *weren't!*"

"Either way, Martin, you can see why I can't afford to take chances. And personally, I believed every word of your story. And the fact that you told it to me means my employers are right: they won't be entirely safe as long as you are alive. Loose ends must be tied. As a fellow professional, you surely understand that. It's the basis of our business. The guerillas are about to take their third life of the night, and I will hardly be a suspect, being one of the victims."

Martin knew he could never make the door. He took a step forward so he could beg convincingly. "Listen! Please! You've got to at least listen!"

The machete flashed dully in the yellow lamplight.

*   *   *

BEFORE leaving the shack, Rondo wiped the weapon clean of prints and dropped it on the dirt floor. The machete, designed for cutting sugar cane, was the favorite weapon of the guerrillas, who probably were miles away from Port Lios and safe in the high hills.

Outside in the steaming night, he set out on the trail that led along the coast, to where a boat was hidden.

The verdict that had been announced in a courtroom and on millions of TVs around the world so many years ago had finally resulted in punishment, though not in a way that any of those watching and listening might have imagined.

Rondo had been the executioner.

He was grinning broadly as he strode along the trail, a big man throwing out long legs and covering ground fast. His mission accomplished, he felt grand. And he'd had plenty of motivation for his mission. If he failed to accomplish it before the killers of Cynthia Davis and Brad Leonard were found by the law, he knew what would have happened to him. Which in a perverse way was why he felt so marvelous and free tonight after executing two men. He himself had escaped their fate.

If Martin had been simply another drunk braggart and teller of tall tales, he'd been among the best Rondo ever encountered. And his accomplice Evan had begged convincingly himself, clinging to his denials right up to the moment of his death. But Martin had been much more convincing with his story than had Evan with his desperate and pleading denials. Both had talked too much, as was the way of such men. Talked themselves to death, in fact.

This movie was over, and with a satisfactory ending.

Yet there might be one other matter Rondo should look into. He'd heard rumors about an American living in San

Mariano who'd made some suspicious utterings in several bars.

Rondo's pace along the trail slowed. His smile was not so broad now.

He decided he owed it to himself to investigate.

HEAT LIGHTNING

Gary Brandner

Gary Brandner, born in the Midwest and much traveled during his formative years, has 30-odd published novels, more than 100 short stories, and a handful of screenplays on his résumé. After surviving the University of Washington, he followed such diverse career paths as bartender, surveyor, loan company investigator, advertising copywriter, bounty hunter, and technical writer before turning to fiction. Since his breakthrough novel, *The Howling*, he has settled into a relatively respectable life with wife and cats in California's San Fernando Valley.

I GRABBED the last lonely bottle of Blatz out of the icebox and rolled it along my forehead. It didn't help much. Neither did the three-dollar fan I bought in July at Kresge's. The blades barely pushed the wet, heavy air across my kitchen table. I sat there in my shorts and undershirt sweating and swearing. The sun was down, but there was no moon, no stars, no cooling breeze. It was a late August evening in Allford, Indiana.

I uncorked the Blatz and poured about a quarter of it down my throat. I belched. The rumbling, satisfying belch of a man who lives alone. The window on my landlady's backyard was open, but nothing stirred out there. Mrs. Kinsella didn't mind the heat. She brewed up a gallon of Kool-Aid and rocked happily on the front porch with the window open so she could hear *Amos 'n' Andy* from the front room radio. Even the June bugs were disabled by the heat. I wondered if I should have stayed at my office downtown, where the door reads Matthew Drumm—Confidential Investigations. There the ceiling fan provided minimal air movement. But Norm, the building manager, likes to lock everything up at six. He gets cranky if anybody stays overtime, and I didn't have a legitimate excuse.

A drop of sweat rolled off my nose and splattered on the front page of the *Allford Courier*. It left a damp spot the size of a dime in the middle of President Roosevelt's forehead. The story under the picture said FDR demanded assurance from Hitler and Mussolini that they would not attack anybody. Yeah, good luck on that.

I flipped to the sports page. Joe Louis was going to fight another Bum of the Month, Bob Pastor. The Cubs continued to spin their wheels in fourth place. It looked like the Reds would be this year's sacrifice to the rotten Yankees in the World Series. When I lived in Chicago, I'd make it to Wrigley twenty times a year. Now I'd get up there maybe once a month, hoping to see signs of life in the Cubbies. Oh, yeah, we have a local team, the class B Allford Aces. They play something akin to baseball, but when you've watched Jimmy Dykes, Gabby Hartnett, and Lon Warneke, it's hard to get excited about Ed Petrowski, Aces star shortstop, who clerked during the winter at Haversack's Hardware.

I drained the Blatz, chipped a hunk of ice off the block, and sucked on that. I paged on through the *Courier* and stopped at the movie page with Louella Parsons's column and ads for the three theaters in Allford. The Liberty had *Now Voyager*, a Bette Davis movie you would have to break my legs and drag me into. At the Grand was *Angels with Dirty Faces*, which I'd seen last week. The Capitol was showing *Stagecoach*. It had John Wayne, which made it worth seeing right there. Even better, the second feature was *Charlie Chan at Treasure Island*. I was a sucker for the Oriental sleuth. But what really got my attention was the little row of icicles at the top of the ad and the legend, "It's cool inside!"

I showered, changed my underwear, and put on a pair of cotton pants and a polo shirt. Starting out the door, I automatically reached for the drawer where I kept my S&W .38 Terrier. Why, I asked myself, would I need a gun in a movie theater? I left the revolver where it was and walked out into the sodden night.

A low ceiling of clouds shut out anything in the sky. Far off there was a mutter of thunder and a slice of the horizon lightened for a moment. Maybe a cooling rain was falling over toward Lafayette. More likely it was heat lightning. My tired '37 Plymouth coupe waited at the curb, badly in need of a wash job. I piled in and headed downtown, trying not to sweat through my shorts to the seat covers.

Downtown Allford was not going to see any traffic jams. There was a Penney's store, Kresge's, Haversack's, the Rexall, a couple of restaurants, half a dozen taverns, and the James Whitcomb Riley Hotel. The tallest structure in town was the Brickman Building, where I had my office. Six towering stories. Allford was a far cry from big-shouldered Chicago, where I worked seven years as a cop until I collared a councilman's kid for beating up a whore and got bounced off the force.

I parked on Main Street half a block from the Capitol theater. The word was they were going to put meters in along here, actually charge money to park your car. Pretty soon nothing would be free.

By the time I walked to the theater, my shirt was stuck to me and my underwear didn't feel fresh anymore. A blue banner with painted white icicles like in the ad hung below the marquee. I laid out a dollar at the ticket window, the fleshy girl behind the glass gave me my ticket, my change, and an unconvincing smile. She had a small rubber-bladed fan blowing in her face.

"That thing help much?" I asked.

"It's better than nothing, but I'd rather be inside."

"I don't blame you."

I pulled the shirt loose where it had stuck to my back and gave my ticket to the freckled young guy at the door. Fred Bland was a likable enough kid who took correspondence courses and supported his widowed mother. He wore his customary white shirt, red bow tie, and black pants. I hadn't seen him taking tickets before.

"What're you doing out here, Fred? Too cold for you inside?"

"My assistant called in sick—hungover, probably. I'm everybody's relief tonight." He sniffed; his eyes were reddened.

"Summer cold?" I asked.

"Huh? Oh, no, hay fever, maybe."

It was not what I thought of as hay fever weather, but what do I know?

Fred ripped the ticket, gave me my half. I walked into the small lobby where, as advertised, it was blessedly cool. The regular ticket taker came out of the men's room, and Fred hustled across to the concession stand. "Popcorn, Mr. Drumm? Coke? Milk Duds?"

I told him no thanks and walked up the crimson-carpeted stairs to the balcony, where I figured I'd get the full benefit of the air-conditioning. Apparently other people had the same idea, since most of the seats were filled, and not just with the usual teenage couples. I found an empty aisle seat and settled in. Up on the screen, my favorite Chinese detective was talking in epigrams to Cesar

Romero, who I immediately tabbed as the killer. The Drumm movie detection system says pick the biggest name in a mystery cast who is not the detective or the detective's foil, and you've got the murderer.

I leaned back and let the cool air seep through my polo shirt. I half dozed through the comfortable rhythms of Charlie Chan as he exposed the bad guy—Cesar Romero, who else?

There followed a short Pete Smith special about a jerk who gets into all kinds of dumb predicaments. Then a newsreel showing scenes of the New York World's Fair, the attempts to raise a sunken submarine off New England, Franco celebrating victory in Spain. Mickey Mouse followed, and the audience stirred happily. Next a preview of *Gunga Din*, which looked good. I have always identified with Cary Grant, though people say I'm more Victor McLaglen. Finally *Stagecoach* came on for its second showing of the night. Almost nobody got up to leave. Why go home to a sweltering house when you could sit another couple hours in cool comfort?

The stage, with Andy Devine driving, rumbled into town, and I let myself flow into the action. We met the passengers one by one: the upper-class lady, the drunken doctor, the sharp-eyed gambler, the liquor salesman, the thieving banker, and Claire Trevor, the hooker with the heart of gold. The story picked up steam when this group was joined by the wandering gunfighter, John Wayne. The stage rattled on with tangled alliances and conflicts among the passengers.

After an hour or so and the delivery of a baby, the Apaches came whooping over a hill and attacked. There was loud gunfire and shouting and galloping hoofbeats. The stage passengers were amazing marksmen, and the Indians dropped like ducks in a shooting gallery. Amid all the noise and confusion there was a single *bang* that was wrong. It did not match the tone of the soundtrack and seemed to come from behind me in the balcony. I swiveled around, but the rest of the audience was transfixed by the action on-screen. Maybe they didn't hear the offbeat sound, or maybe their ears didn't register real-life gunshots the way mine did.

Then somebody up there screamed. There was a flurry of movement at the center rear of the theater. While the Indians continued to drop on-screen, the commotion in the theater spread. I lurched out of my seat and headed back there.

People in the top three rows were ignoring the movie now, standing and craning inward. The beam from the projector flickered just above their heads. John Wayne brought down another redskin. The house lights came on suddenly. The screen went white with a burp from the soundtrack as the projector died. Now I saw what the people were looking at. A young woman was slumped forward, her forehead against the back of the seat in front of her. Her hair was a buttery bleached blonde, except for the crown where there was a spreading wet crimson stain.

While a growing crowd milled around the blonde, several people made for the stairs. I had a brief inner debate. The old cop Drumm said hang around, see if I can help. The realistic Drumm of today said get the hell out of here. It was not my problem, and Lieutenant Driscoll of the Allford PD already didn't like me. Debate over. I headed toward the exit.

"Matt!" It was a female voice with a musical lilt that was vaguely familiar. Now it was edged with panic.

I looked over to see a thirtyish woman with shiny brown hair working her way out of the last row of seats toward the aisle. She wore a flowery summer dress that did not hide her figure. She carried a box of popcorn in one hand and a gun in the other.

"Matt, help me, please."

"Amy?"

She nodded.

I jerked my head toward the gun, a bluesteel .38-caliber revolver. "What the hell is that?"

Amy Reardon looked down and recoiled. She dropped the pistol and the popcorn like they were poisonous lizards. "I didn't do it, Matt! I didn't shoot her. The gun fell into my popcorn."

"You know the blonde?"

"She's Coralee Beaudine. We share a house. We work at the same place."

"The dancing school," I said. It was called Marianne's Studio of Dance, but it was rumored that a lot more than the big apple and the lindy hop went on there.

"How did you know that?"

"I heard."

"Matt, I have to get out of here. Help me, please."

"Why not wait for the cops? Explain to them."

"They'd arrest me. They'd take my fingerprints, and I'd be in trouble."

"What kind of trouble?"

"Do we have to talk about this now?"

"We do if you want any help from me."

"There's a warrant out for me in California. It was nothing big, but embarrassing, you know. I don't want to be locked up, Matt."

"Nobody does. Did you see who shot your girlfriend?"

"No, but I have an idea. Get me out of here, and I can help you find him."

"Why me?"

"You're a detective, Matt. You and I were pretty close once, remember?"

"I remember."

"Leaving you and Allford was the biggest mistake of my life."

"Amy, that was high school. Twenty years ago. If you want me to stick my neck out for old times' sake, forget it."

"I'll make it worth your while."

"It's way too late for that, Amy."

"I mean I'll pay you. Whatever your rate is, I'll pay."

"Exactly what do you expect me to do?"

"You're a detective. Catch the killer."

"Amy, I follow people, I peek through windows, I take pictures of people doing naughty things. I am not Dick Tracy."

A siren wailed in the distance.

"Please help me, Matt. I don't have anybody else."

What the hell, I wasn't going to sleep in this heat anyway. "I'll do what I can, but just for tonight. Tomorrow we go to the police."

Amy started to shake. I grabbed her arm and steered her toward the stairs. As we started down, Fred Bland, the young manager, hurried in past us, looking like he was about to be sick.

We got through the lobby and outside, where the night air smacked us like a soggy, hot towel. My shirt, which had pretty well dried out, started soaking up sweat. Summer thunder muttered again far away. Two Allford police cars wheeled into Main Street, lights flashing, sirens screaming. I stuffed Amy into the Plymouth and walked around to get in the driver's side. I hit the starter button, shifted into low, and pulled away from the curb, trying to look casual. None of the cops piling out of their vehicles looked in our direction.

"Where do you live?" I asked.

"You didn't bother to find that out?"

I answered her with a look. She gave me an address on

the other side of town, not far from the high school where we had once been a hot couple.

"I wanted to call you when I came back," she said, "but I was afraid."

"Of what?"

"That you wouldn't want to talk to me."

I did not deny it.

"You knew I was here. You could have come to see me at the dance studio."

"I suppose so."

"Why didn't you?"

I shrugged, concentrating on the dark street ahead of me.

"Is it what happened to me in California?"

"The warrant? I didn't know about that."

"I mean about the whole thing out there. Fifteen years of crap. Weren't you ever curious?"

"I heard you got married."

"Twice. That was two more mistakes. Everything that happened to me from the time I left Allford was wrong."

"Tough."

"I'm not looking for sympathy, Matt. Well, maybe I am. It's such a corny story, I can't blame you. Small-town girl wins contest, goes to Hollywood, meets some fast-talking hustlers on the fringe of the movie business, gets messed around, screws up her life real good. All I needed to do to make headlines was to die a flashy death. Jump off the Hollywood sign. It all shows on me, doesn't it, Matt. Those years?"

I looked over at her as we passed under a streetlight. It showed, all right, but not too bad. The facial skin was still tight over good bones, the body was a little fuller, but I always thought she was too skinny. The change was mostly in the eyes. They were tired and wise but not happy. "You look fine," I told her.

"Thanks for that." She fiddled with the radio, came up with a station playing Bing Crosby singing "What's New?"

I reached down and snapped it off.

"I really do teach dancing, you know," she said.

"Sure you do."

"And that's all."

"Uh-huh. So what's the story with the roommate?"

Amy took her time answering. "Like I said, we worked together at the dance studio. She was younger than me. I tried to be kind of a big sister to her. But Coralee had big ideas. She was into . . . other stuff."

"Like what?"

"Like screwing guys for money."

"I'm shocked."

"Believe me, Matt, I didn't like it. I warned her she was heading for trouble. She said she was sitting on a gold mine and she intended to work it. She had an important man on the string who was going to pay off big-time."

"Who's the guy?"

"I promised not to tell."

"Promises to the dead don't count."

Amy leaned forward to point at a white clapboard bungalow with green shutters and flowers lining the short path from sidewalk to front door. "That's our house." The blinds were down, and most of the lights were on.

"Nice place."

Amy caught my inflection. "Coralee never did any of her business here. I wouldn't go for that. The men would come and pick her up, or she'd meet them somewhere else."

"Like the Capitol theater? Seems a little public for hanky-panky."

"Tonight was different. She was looking for the big payoff."

"From her important friend?"

"Yeah. He was—"

I had to stomp on the brake as a Packard sedan peeled away from the curb, heading back the way we had come. While I was swearing at the Packard, I almost banged into a Buick parked in front of the house.

"Lotta traffic," I said.

Amy stared at the house. "Hey, I didn't leave the lights on."

"Did you lock the door?"

"No. Why would I?"

I parked in front of the Buick and got out. A shadow moved behind an orange window shade.

"Stay here," I told Amy. I climbed out of the Plymouth and crept up to the front door. The shadow had moved away from the window. I put my ear to the panel and heard rustling and thumping from inside. I twisted the knob and pushed.

The front room revealed little about the people who lived here. Sears Roebuck couch, a couple of easy chairs with flowered covers. Cheap prints on the walls. Card table with a game of solitaire laid out. Zenith console radio-phonograph. I stepped inside. Through an archway I could see the dark kitchen. Two open doors apparently led into bedrooms. Through one of them came a tall, graying man in a rumpled business suit. In his hand was a German Luger pointed in the vicinity of my breastbone. I acutely felt the absence of my Terrier.

I held my hands palms out to show him I was no threat. "Hold it, mister."

The gun wobbled in his hand. Clearly he was not comfortable handling a weapon. That didn't make me feel better. A lot of people are killed by amateurs with guns.

"You bastard," he said.

"You have me mixed up with somebody else. Name's Matthew Drumm. Identification's in my pants."

"You're not the bastard who's been messing with my daughter?"

"I don't even know your daughter."

The hand with the Luger wavered, and dropped to his side. His face crumpled. I thought the guy was going to cry.

Amy, having ignored my order to stay put, stepped into the room and moved up beside me.

"Who is she?" the gray-haired guy asked.

"I live here," Amy said. "Who are *you*?"

All the air went out of his balloon. "I'm Frazier Beaudine. Coralee is my daughter."

"Maybe you could put away the gun," I suggested.

He looked down, surprised to see the Luger, and shoved it into a coat pocket. "I'm sorry," he said. "I thought you were the one who . . . I got a letter today telling me what Coralee was doing. I had no idea. The last we heard from her, she was engaged to a nice young man. Now I learn she's no better than a . . . a . . ." He couldn't bring himself to say the word. "I came to take her home."

I walked past Frazier Beaudine to look into the bedroom. Frilly pillows, stuffed panda bear, girl clutter on the bureau. Pictures propped on the night table of Coralee with a football player, a boy in a bow tie, a ukelele picker, and her father in happier times. A half-filled suitcase lay open on the bed.

"I think you'd better leave her stuff here," I said. "And stick around town for now."

"Why? Is something wrong? Is Coralee in trouble?"

"Somebody is. She's dead."

Beaudine wobbled backward and dropped into one of the flowered chairs. "Oh my God! My little baby!" He put his head down into his hands, and this time he really did cry.

I grabbed Amy and steered her back out the door. Beaudine was sunk into the chair, alone with his misery. When we got outside, I spun Amy around to face me.

"Okay, who's the important bozo your roommate's diddling?"

"His name is Howell. H. Gordon Howell."

"The judge?"

"That's him."

I didn't have to ask who Judge H. Gordon Howell was. His picture was in the *Courier* at least once a week shaking hands with some company president or powerful politician. People in the know were saying he would be the next governor.

"Let's go see him." I drove off with the windows rolled all the way down, but I felt like I was sunk in tepid bathwater.

The judge's house was the showplace home of Allford, the one you took out-of-town relatives to see. Three stories of ivy-covered brick with leaded windows, lots of chimneys, a front lawn like a park. There was a garage wide enough for three cars, a long glassed-in porch on one side, and a service entrance in the back.

"You haven't told me why you were at the show tonight," I said to Amy.

"It was Coralee's idea. She wanted me to come and sit where I could watch her. I think she was a little uneasy about Howell."

"Then why was she still doing him?"

"She wasn't that uneasy. She figured he would set her up in her own place. You know, take care of her. She was going to put it to him tonight."

"And you think he put it to her instead?"

"Maybe."

"Did you see him do it?"

"Not exactly."

"What, exactly, *did* you see?"

"I came in right after Coralee, while the newsreel was on, and sat two rows behind her, up against the back wall. Howell came in a little after the feature started and sat next to her. I could see them kind of whispering to each other, but I couldn't hear what they said. Their heads were close together, and her hand was in his lap, if you know what I mean. It looked like everything was all right. Then . . . well, the picture got exciting, and I started watching. Next thing I knew, Coralee kind of grunted and her head fell forward and there was a lot of blood. Then the gun dropped into my popcorn. I started for the aisle, and that's when I saw you."

"Where were you going?"

"I just wanted to get away from there."

"That was not real smart."

"I know."

"What did the judge do?"

"I think he was heading for the aisle on the other side."

I tried to piece the scene together in my head. There were big chunks missing, like a mixed-up jigsaw puzzle.

I tooled into the neighborhood where Judge Howell lived. The streets were wide and lined with elm trees. The houses were set well back with rolling green lawns. The air here was just as sticky as it was downtown, but it smelled different. It smelled of money. A long, curving driveway led past sculpted cedar trees to the front door. The house was ablaze with electric lights, inside and out. Two cars stood out front: a black LaSalle and a dark blue Packard.

"Do you want me to come with you?" Amy asked.

"Does the judge know you by sight?"

"Probably. I was there one time when he picked up Coralee."

"Then come along. If he gets a gander at you, it can save me some explaining."

As we walked along the flagstone drive, I tested the hoods of the Packard and LaSalle. Both were warmer than the night.

The entrance was in an elaborate portico with white pillars and a steepled roof. As we reached the inlaid oak front door, I could hear angry voices barking inside. They were too muffled for me to make out the words, but the tone was unmistakable. I pushed the pearly bell button, and a four-chime melody bonged inside. The voices went silent. There was no response, so I bonged the bell again. Then a third time.

The door finally inched open. An angular woman with high cheekbones and a long, pointed nose peered out. I caught a flash of movement in the room behind her. There was no welcome in her eyes.

"Yes?"

"I'd like to see Judge Howell."

"He's not here."

I laid the flat of my hand against the panel to keep the door open. "I think he is."

The woman's eyes hardened. "And who are you?"

"My name is Drumm. I'm a private investigator."

"May I ask what you are investigating?"

"A young woman died tonight."

"Died?"

I moved aside so she could see Amy. "She was killed. This is Amy Reardon. The dead girl's roommate."

"How does this involve my husband?"

"Can I talk to him?"

The skin whitened around the woman's mouth. "I told you he's not here."

The judge loomed behind her, a big-bodied man with a flowing white pompadour and the rosy nose of a drinker. "You can let them in, Leona. It doesn't matter anymore."

Mrs. Howell dropped her gloved hand from the door

and glared at her husband. "Do you know what he's talking about?"

Amy and I walked into a front room twice as big as my whole apartment. The furniture was dark and heavy and deeply polished. There was a stone fireplace you could walk into. Real oil paintings on the walls. The air was cool. They actually had air-conditioning in the house. The rich really are different.

The woman shot a look at her husband. "Your career is finished, you know that. You'll be lucky if you're not dragged off the bench. And you can forget all about Indianapolis."

"I did not kill anyone, Leona."

"I suppose you're not an adulterer, either."

Judge Howell turned to me. I thought he might be the second grown man I'd see cry tonight. "What is it you want?"

"Confirmation. I think I got that. I have a feeling the police will want to talk to you."

Amy and I started back out the door. I said to Mrs. Howell, "By the way, where did you go tonight?"

"What makes you think I went anywhere?"

"Both cars are warm. You still have your gloves on."

She drew herself up. "I went to the woman's house to confront her. An anonymous letter told me what was going on."

"You didn't stop by the Capitol theater by any chance?"

"No. Why would I?"

"I don't think you should say any more, Leona," the judge told her.

I left it at that and walked out with Amy. From the tension in the room, I figured Judge Howell would rather be facing a battery of cops than his furious wife.

Back outside, the heat swallowed us again. I cranked up the Plymouth, and we headed back downtown.

"Do you think he did it?" Amy said.

"Hard to say."

"What about the wife?"

"Same answer."

"Some detective."

"You should have hired Charlie Chan."

"Where are we going now?"

"Back to the scene of the crime."

"Why?"

I touched my nose in a wise detective manner. "Fish in sea like fleas on dog, always present, but difficult to catch." I had no idea what that meant, but I liked the sound of it, and it kept Amy quiet while I drove back to the theater.

A couple of uniformed cops were out front taking names as people left, and telling them to go home. Naturally, people were ignoring the advice and standing around in little groups talking excitedly. It wasn't often you got to be on the scene of a murder.

I said hello to one of the cops.

"Lieutenant Driscoll's inside," he said with a smirk. "He'll be glad to see you."

Amy and I went in through the lobby and up the stairs to the balcony. With the house lights on high, all the little flaws were visible: the worn carpet, the rips in the seat fabric, the peeling paint on the walls. Blessedly, the air conditioner was still pumping in refrigerated air.

A sheet now covered the body of Coralee Beaudine. A big patch of red stained the head area. Lieutenant Clarence Driscoll, stocky and red-faced, gray fedora on the back of his bullet head, stood with a couple of uniformed cops in the aisle while a small knot of people sat under his habitual angry gaze. Despite the heat outside, Driscoll wore a double-breasted suit and severely knotted necktie. He was concentrating on a husky blond collegiate type perched in an aisle seat. One of the cops nudged the lieutenant, and he looked up at me.

"Well, well, look who's here, Allford's leading gumshoe. And if I am not mistaken, he is bringing with him an eyewitness to the crime. So nice of you to come back."

"Back?"

Fred Bland, sitting next to the collegian, coughed apologetically. "I told him, Mr. Drumm. He asked who'd been here and left."

"It's OK, Fred."

Driscoll focused on Amy. "You would be the babe with the gun?" A cop handed him the revolver he held with a pencil through the trigger guard. "Recognize this?"

"It's not mine. It fell in my popcorn."

"Dropped out of the sky."

"Like from the ceiling," Amy said.

Instinctively, we all looked toward the high theater ceiling, where faded angels definitely not painted by Michelangelo cavorted among clouds of tattletale gray.

Driscoll returned to me. "And you walked out of here with the main witness."

"I also brought her back."

"What's your stake in this, Drumm?"

"I'm just a working stiff."

"Stick around, I'll want to talk to both of you."

He returned the gun to the uniformed cop. I had a look around the theater. On the back wall, a couple of feet over our heads, were two square windows into the projection booth.

"You know, Driscoll—" I began.

"I already thought of that, shamus. The gun didn't fall from the sky or from the ceiling, either. More than likely it was pitched through one of those holes."

"There's no getting ahead of you, Lieutenant."

He exhaled through his teeth and returned to the college

boy. Then, as though he just remembered his manners, "Oh, yeah, Drumm, this is Wesley Kopay. He's the projectionist. Have you met Mr. Drumm, the famous private eye?"

The blond young man looked confused.

I said, "Hi. Go right ahead, Clarence, just as though I'm not here."

Driscoll forced his normally scowling features into something like a smile. "OK if I call you Wes, son?"

The boy shrugged. "Sure."

"How long have you worked here, Wes?"

"Just for the summer. I go back to college next month."

"Good for you. It's important to get an education. Tell me, Wes, how long has this picture been playing here?"

"This was the seventh and last day. Tomorrow we get *Gunga Din*."

"I guess you know *Stagecoach* pretty well by now."

"I ought to."

"Got it all timed and everything."

"That's part of my job."

Abruptly Driscoll stopped playing Mr. Nice. "And you didn't hear a gunshot?"

"No, I—"

"Seems like nobody heard a gunshot."

I spoke up. "I think it happened when there was a lot of shooting going on in the picture. The Indians were attacking the stagecoach."

"Exactly what I was thinking. Wes, from the projection booth you should be able to tell real gunshots from the sound track."

"I guess so, but—"

Driscoll switched directions in a typical cop maneuver. "How well did you know the dead girl?"

"Huh?"

"Coralee Beaudine. Don't bother to lie, I've been told you were . . . intimate with her."

"Well, yes, I knew her. But, hey, a lot of guys did. I mean . . . no disrespect to the dead, but—"

Driscoll saw that we were all listening. "Maybe we better continue this at the station."

I said, "Wait a minute, Clarence."

"Are you still here?"

To young Kopay I said, "Why didn't you hear any gunshot?"

"I was trying to tell him—"

"Tell me what?" Driscoll barked.

"I was on my break when it happened. Grabbing a smoke in the men's room. You can't light up in the booth, not with all that film. It would explode."

"Is it your habit to leave the booth while the feature is on?" I asked.

"No. Usually I go during the previews or the newsreel, so if the film breaks or something, it's no big deal."

"But not tonight?"

"Sure, tonight, too. But it's so hot, there's no air in the booth. Fred came up and told me to take a few extra minutes to cool off before I had to shut everything down. Said he'd take care of the projector."

Driscoll thrust his chin at me. "Who's asking the questions here, gumshoe?"

"Indulge me, Clarence."

The lieutenant rumbled like a volcano getting ready to erupt, but he let me continue.

"And that was in the middle of the picture?"

"Closer to the end."

"During the part where the Indians attack." I looked past him to Fred Bland. "So I guess it was you in the booth then, right, Fred?"

There was no answer from the young manager.

"You knew Coralee, too, didn't you?"

He looked at each of us as though hoping somebody would deny it.

"I saw your picture at her place, Fred. In fact, I'll bet you were the nice young man she was supposed to be engaged to?"

Fred looked down at his lap for a moment, then raised teary eyes and spoke. "That's what I thought, until . . ."

"Until?"

"I got the letter about Coralee and Judge Howell. I asked her about it, and she laughed at me. Said she had bigger plans than marrying a small-town theater manager. It ripped me apart."

"You saw her come in tonight, and you saw the judge take the seat next to her."

He nodded. A study in anguish. "I went a little crazy. I got the gun we keep in the office. I knew the Indian attack scene was coming. I told Wes to take a break. I could look down from the booth and see them. They were . . . touching each other."

"And you shot her."

"I swear I didn't know I'd done it until I saw the blood spurt. I really lost it then. I threw the gun away."

Driscoll: "That's enough. We'll hear the rest of it at the station. Let's go, boy."

No thanks were delivered by the lieutenant to me for handing him the killer, but I didn't expect any.

I DIDN'T have much to say while I drove Amy home. She kept looking sidelong at me. I kept looking straight ahead.

As we turned into her street, she said, "Thanks, Matt."

"Sure."

"I don't know what else to say. I meant it about paying your fee."

"Forget it."

"Want to come in for a beer?"

"No."

"What's the matter, Matt?"

I pulled to a stop and set the hand brake, but I didn't kill the engine.

"The letters, Amy."

"Letters?"

"The anonymous letters that tipped Coralee's father, the judge's wife, and Fred Bland. Nobody but you could have written them."

"Well, what if I did? What Coralee was doing was wrong. She was messing up people's lives. I thought people ought to know. Wouldn't you?"

I reached across her and opened the door.

"Good-bye, Amy."

She looked at me for a long five seconds and got out of the car. As I drove away, I could see her in the mirror standing at the curb, watching.

Something wet smacked the windshield. Then another. Then a whole spatter of fat raindrops. Lightning brightened the neighborhood for an instant. Thunder boomed like an explosion overhead. The heat wave was ended.

I leaned my face toward the open window and drove home slowly, drinking in the cool, sweet air.

TOO HOT TO DIE

Mat Coward

Mat Coward is a British writer of crime, science fiction, horror, children's and humorous fiction, whose stories have been broadcast on BBC Radio and published in numerous anthologies, magazines, and e-zines in the United Kingdom, United States, Japan, and Europe. He has received short story nominations for the Dagger and Edgar Awards. According to Ian Rankin, "Mat Coward's stories resemble distilled novels." His first nondistilled novel, a murder mystery called *Up and Down*, was published in the USA in 2000 to rave reviews. Short stories have recently appeared in *Ellery Queen's Mystery Magazine*, *The World's Finest Crime and Mystery Stories*, *Felonious Felines*, and *Murder Through the Ages*.

***

"**To** be honest with you, I'm not sure precisely what *sultry* means," I said, because I'd never seen a gun before, and I felt like I wanted to say something.

The man who'd shown me the gun said, "Maybe they keep a dictionary behind the bar. For the crossword fans."

"Well, maybe," I said, but I didn't take it any further. I didn't actually give a shit what *sultry* meant. More importantly, I was worried that if I stood up, he'd show me the gun again. It was a small one, tucked into the back of his trousers, underneath his linen jacket. "Anyway, I know roughly what it means, and you're right; it is a sultry night."

"It is," he said. "Too warm a night to die."

I had *no* idea what that meant.

*   *   *

IN high summer, in this part of the world, you can sit outside at ten o'clock at night and read the small print of the stocks and shares listing in a newspaper without artificial light. Not that I've ever had any stocks or shares, but it's comforting to know that if I ever do have any, I won't need a torch to see how they're doing.

The long evenings of the British summer have had a significant influence on the development of many aspects of our culture. It's why most of our cricket grounds still don't have floodlights, and it's also why the best apples in the world are grown in southern England. Hot days, long evenings, and cool nights. Except when the night goes all sultry on you, shocking and unexpected and paralyzing, like a teenage niece wearing makeup in public for the first time.

A few years ago, before I moved to this town, a friend visited me from America, and as I drove him around, he was highly amused to see that almost every country pub had a sign outside advertising a "beer garden." It was early spring, and he wanted to know what kind of crazy people would sit outside a pub in a country where, as he put it, "Even the hot dogs are cold."

"If it was summertime, you'd understand," I told him. "You should come back in summer." But he never did.

That last, gradual hour of daylight, at the end of a salt-skin day, sitting in the garden of a pub where you know just about everyone well enough to nod to, feeling the sweat on your skin drying out at last, smelling the booze and the tobacco smoke and the flesh, tasting the beer as it cuts through the grit in your throat . . . your thoughts slow down to match the slowness of the hour, your heartbeat steadies, no matter what the day has done to it, and the knots in your muscles ease themselves free. It's *cool,* turned from a word into an experience.

It's something you probably have to experience in order to understand. But then, I suppose everything is, really. Seeing a gun for the first time, that certainly is.

Besides, that was a sultry night. No cool to be had anywhere.

I DIDN'T think I knew the man with the gun, but I didn't want to say, "I don't think I know you, do I?" in case he thought I was trying to place him or memorize his features or—

"You don't know me, do you?" His accent was northern, maybe Manchester.

"I—well, no. I don't think so. Sorry—should I?"

He pulled on his pint and looked around him at the beer garden. We were sitting in a corner, a fair bit from the pub itself, partly hidden by a conker tree. That is, *I'd* been sitting there when he'd appeared, beer in hand, smile on face, and sat across the table from me. Gun in waistband. "This place doesn't change much."

"You know the pub, then?"

He wiped an arm across his forehead. Didn't make any difference; there was as much sweat on the arm as on the forehead. "You been coming here long?"

"Two or three years, I suppose. Moved down from near London."

"You picked a nice spot," he said.

"It's a friendly little town," I agreed. "Or did you mean the pub?"

Even if someone did come over—the potman collecting glasses, or an acquaintance wanting to exchange long sighs and swelter stories over the night's final beer—what would

I do? If I said anything or tried to leave, maybe he'd start shooting. Just start shooting, like a spotty kid in an American high school.

"You live local, then?" he said.

He was a bit older than me, pushing sixty maybe, about my height and weight—both average—with light-colored, thinning hair. Big nose and glasses. Big hands, smart clothes. Cigar in his top pocket. Gun in his waistband. I definitely wasn't going to tell him where I lived. "My name's Dave," I said. I didn't mind him having my first name, plenty of Daves in even the smallest town, and I was thinking: would it be harder to shoot someone if you knew their name? Possibly.

"Dave," he said. He took the cigar out of his top pocket, removed the cellophane, and lit up with a match. "I'm Ed. Just down here on business."

"Nice to meet you, Ed." I didn't offer my hand for shaking, because he had the cigar in his left and the matches in his right. "You work, do you, Dave?"

Perhaps he'd shown me the gun by accident. Perhaps the reason his subsequent conversation seemed so weird to me was because it was so normal. "Not doing much at the moment, no. Not lately."

He took out a big, red handkerchief and mopped beneath his glasses, the back of his neck, and under his chin. "You'd not want to be a waxwork on a night like tonight."

"No, indeed." Speaking of which, my glass was empty. It was one of those nights when no matter how much you drank, you'd never be anything but thirsty, but even so, no sense surrendering without a fight. I pointed at his pint, three-quarters empty. "Get you another, Ed?"

He looked at me and smiled. "No, you're all right. I'll get these. What's that you're on?"

"Lemonade and orange. Saint Clement's, they call it."

"Pint of Saint Clement's, right you are. You're not

drinking then? Funny, I'd have had you down as a drinking man."

"You'd have been right, once upon a time." A cider would have done the job on a night like that. I could feel my shirt, stuck to my back on one side and stuck to the chair on the other, and my pants would need surgery to remove them from my bum. But cider is a tricky drink: sweet and seductive, with hidden powers. Great stuff if you can handle it. Like most of life's pleasures.

Ed stood up, gathered the glasses. "You stop there, then. I won't be long."

How did he know I wouldn't leg it, to coin a phrase, as soon as he was out of sight? Maybe he didn't know, I thought, if he'd shown me the gun by accident. Whatever, I stayed where I was. I wouldn't have got far. I never was much of a one for running, even in the old days. And anyway, I wanted to know who the gun was for.

"Look," said Ed, his big nose pointing up at the aubergine sky.

"What?" I couldn't look upwards for long; it made my neck ache.

"Bats."

"Oh, yeah." I did hear a passing flitter, now that he mentioned it. I couldn't have sworn I'd *seen* a bat, as such—it was more an impression of swoop.

"The swifts go off, the bats come on. I sometimes wonder," said Ed, "if they queue up to wait their turn, at the edge of the sky."

I was wondering what would happen at closing time. Would the man with the gun have gone by then? If not, would he at least have finished with me? Was his target someone who was in the pub right now? I also wondered why it didn't seem to worry him that he was spending the evening sitting chatting with a potential witness.

I hoped he'd shown me the gun by accident. But I couldn't quite believe it. My joints were aching even more than usual. It must have been the heat, a day of heavy sweating sucking the salts out of my tissues. I was dehydrated. I wasn't looking forward to the walk home; maybe I'd get a taxi. Or maybe, depending on Ed's plans, that was something I didn't have to worry about tonight.

"What do you like best," Ed asked, "about living round here?"

Up until then, I'd thought he was just making conversation, just killing time, for whatever reasons of his own, presumably reasons linked to the bulge at the back of his waistband. But he was looking at me now with an intensity that suggested that his question and my answer were of some importance. I thought for a while—if this was an exam, I wanted to pass it—and eventually said: "Knowing people."

"Oh, aye," said Ed.

"Knowing your neighbors. In cities, you know the people you work with, the people you socialize with, old friends from elsewhere, but everybody's scattered across the whole metropolis. Your community, such as it is, is dispersed, each member living a tube journey from the next."

"True," said Ed, and he looked pleased.

"In London, you only meet your neighbors when the water main bursts."

"I know just what you mean." Ed nodded, sipped his icy lager. "Small town . . . it's nice, isn't it? You feel the people around you will look out for you in bad times."

"Yes, I suppose so."

"Because we all have bad times, don't we?"

I looked at him, trying to read his expression, but the

light was going, and he had his face turned away from me, looking for bats perhaps. "Well, yes, I suppose so."

"I was born in the country, moved to a city when I was a young man. But I've spent most of the last thirty years in small towns, and you can't beat 'em in my book. An old market town like this. Self-contained but never insular. New blood arriving all the time, keeping the old place fresh. You've got everything you need here, haven't you? Shops, factories, cinema, theater, sports facilities, medical facilities. Beautiful countryside on the doorstep. Great place. And such a mixture of folk, too: all sorts, all different types. Different classes, if you'll forgive an old-fashioned word. All fitting together like a bloody great jigsaw."

"I have to ask the obvious question: if you love it so much, why did you leave?"

He put his pint down and sighed. "Ah well, simple enough. Marriage broke up. The way they do. My wife had family connections here, so I thought it better if she stayed and I moved. You know, easier for all concerned."

"I'm sorry."

"Well, we've all stayed on good enough terms. In fact, do you happen to know a guy called Chris Eastman? Big fellow, big beard, runs the cricket club?"

"Yes, I know who you mean. Ex-copper, from Bristol? Nice bloke."

Ed looked delighted. "You know him, do you? That's my brother-in-law. Former, I mean. Great bloke. Do anything for a friend or neighbor, that one."

"And is that who you're here to—" I choked, took a sip of Saint Clement's to clear my throat. "Is that who you're here to see?"

He laughed. "Well, I expect I shall see him while I'm here, yes. I imagine so."

"Actually, I've got to know him quite well these last few months. Like you say, he's a very helpful guy. Very kind." I wasn't sure who I was speaking up for: the ex-brother-in-law or me. Or whether I was just showing the man with the gun in his waistband that I didn't only talk about small town life, I really meant it. Really lived it. "He roped me in to do some scoring for them this season."

"For the cricket team? Good for you, mate! You're another cricket nut, then?"

"Not particularly, no. It's just—"

"You want to get involved. Exactly! Just what we were talking about before, isn't it? You get involved, you meet people. You build walls around your life. I don't mean walls to keep people out, mind. I mean—"

"Walls of protection." Yes, I knew what he meant. Was that what I was doing? Building fortifications? If so, it hadn't been conscious. But now I thought about it, that was certainly something my old life had lacked: a human wall to lean on when things went wobbly.

"So, you're getting into the life of the town, are you? That's good."

"Well, yes," I said and tapped my leg. "As much as I can, you know."

"Ah, yes. I couldn't help noticing the leg was a bit buggered. Accident, was it?"

"Yes."

"Back in London?"

"Yes."

He laughed. "Not your favorite topic of conversation?"

"If you don't mind. It's just that, you know . . ."

He leaned over and patted me on the arm. "No, not to worry. We all have bad times in life, don't we? Like I said. It's what you do afterwards that counts, isn't it?"

"I suppose so."

"Course it is. So what brought you to this particular town? Do you have connections here yourself?"

"No," I said.

"Ah! Quite the opposite, in fact? I get you. A clean break can be good. If you're trying to change your life, you know, moving somewhere new can be good."

"I suppose so." His conversation had distracted me for a while—perhaps intentionally—but now my mind was back where you'd expect to find it, under the circumstances: on the gun in this friendly man's waistband.

"One of the things I like about small towns," said Ed, "not the most important thing, but it's illustrative. Plumbers can't rip you off so easily."

I used to be a plumber. "How do you mean?"

"Not just plumbers, I'm not having a go at plumbers. Electricians, roofers, whatever. In a big city, there's a never-ending supply of victims. All you need is a listing in the Yellow Pages. But in a place like this, word of mouth is everything. Population this size, you won't last for long if your work isn't up to scratch. Apart from anything, the guy only lives over the other side of town. If your pipes start leaking the day after he's fixed them, you go round and thump on his door! Am I right?"

"I suppose so."

"I'm not having a go at plumbers particularly, you understand. Just an example."

I used to be a plumber. I felt as cold in my guts as I was hot on my skin. I couldn't look at him. Suppose he had the gun out now? Had it in his hand. Smiling behind it. Suppose he *had* meant to show it to me, and suppose he had meant me to know that he knew things about my old life?

A bell sounded from the pub. "Last orders," said Ed. "You fancy another?"

"No. No thanks. I'm . . . I'm all right, thanks."

"In that case," said Ed, "I think we'll just sit here quietly for a while. Watch the stars come out. All right?"

Twenty minutes passed, half an hour. He sat back in his

chair, with his hands linked behind his head, and watched the stars and the bats. I just watched the darkness. The beer garden lights went off. The small car park emptied.

The landlord of the pub appeared in his back doorway and shouted up the garden. He couldn't see us from where he stood; we were too far away, sheltered by the conker tree and the dark. "Anyone still out there?"

"No," said Ed. He spoke much too quietly for the landlord to hear. But then, of course, he wasn't talking to the landlord.

WE watched the lights go out in the pub, we listened to the bangs and rattles of bottling up and locking up. When all was quiet and had been for a while, Ed stood up, stretched, and said, "I'll walk you home."

I stood and didn't stretch. Somehow, being upright after sitting for so long made me hot all over again; hot and chafing and drained in areas of my body that I hadn't noticed when I was sitting down. Cold sweat followed gravity down my back and the back of my neck and the back of my legs, to be replaced at its point of origin by hot sweat. Nothing like being sober to make you suffer in the heat.

"I wouldn't want to take you out of your way," I said.

"No, you're all right. Dubb's Rise isn't out of my way."

He had shown me his gun on purpose. I gave up arguing with myself about that.

"OK," I said, because in that heat I couldn't find the energy to say anything else. All that had happened in my life, all, that I'd lost or thrown away, I could feel it all sliding down my back, pooling around my ankles, soaking me through and weighing me down. I wondered if they'd be able to get anyone to score the cricket next Sunday. Yes, they would; plenty of volunteers. It was that sort of town.

"OK," I said and set off across the garden towards the car park and the road.

"You're not going that way, are you?" said Ed. "You use the shortcut, don't you?"

I did, of course. Ever since it'd been pointed out to me, I'd always used the old beast track through the woods that led from the beer garden into a twitten that came out halfway along my road. Even though it was dark and too bumpy for me to walk on comfortably, I always used it to get home from the pub. It made me feel like a real local. If you weren't local, you wouldn't know about it.

"Right," I said. I turned round and limped back towards him. I wondered if he'd kill me along the way or whether he'd wait until we got home.

I used his arm for support over the more uneven parts of the track. It was so hot, and I was so tired, and the puddles had dried out into treacherous craters. Even with Ed's help, though, it was hard going.

"You want to take a moment, Dave? You're not looking so good. We'll stop for a breather, if you like."

"What's it about?" I said, because I didn't have the salt left in me to be brave. "What have I actually done?"

Ed fished another cigar out of another pocket and lit it. "Oh, you saw the gun, then? I wasn't sure."

"I saw the gun." I'd packed up smoking years before. Couldn't remember why, now.

"Someone from before," he said, "from London, still harbors a grudge. On account of what happened. A big grudge, you might say, which you can't blame him for, I suppose."

"Big enough to want me dead?"

Ed's cigar nodded in the dark. "Oh, yes."

I must have been mad to think I'd got away with it— got away *from* it. You can change your life all you want, change your future, but that doesn't change the past. I lowered myself down onto a tree stump. "How did you get into this line of work?"

"No, no," he said. "You've got me wrong. I'm like you, don't do much these days. Play a bit of golf, which is almost the definition of not doing much. Game for dead folk, golf is."

The cigar smelled good. I wondered if he'd got another one. "So, what—you're doing this as a favor, are you? Favor for a friend?"

"That's it. That's it exactly." He sounded pleased, happy that I understood.

"Am I allowed to know the name of this friend?"

"Oh, it's more of a syndicate, you could say. Several friends."

I rolled off the stump onto my side, and threw up into the undergrowth. I hadn't been sure which end it was going to come out of, in all honesty, so I was relieved when everything that was inside me emerged as vomit. A man doesn't lose his fear of humiliation just because he's about to die.

"You all right, Dave?" He threw the cigar onto the path, stomped it, and leaned over me. "You all right there?"

I had to laugh at that. "Yeah, I'm fine, thanks. Better now."

"Too much of that Saint Clement's, that's what that'll be."

"I expect so."

"Drop of brandy would settle that. Good for gut ache, brandy."

I struggled to my feet. I wanted to say this standing up. "I don't drink alcohol anymore, Ed." Even then, in that situation, I needed to get that straight. I didn't have much to boast about, but I had that.

"What, not even a drop for medicinal purposes?"

"Not even a drop."

"Fair enough. You know your own business. Very acid, though, all that orange juice; you'd be better off with something less acidic."

"Not even a drop," I said, and this time I walked unaided.

ED had the gun in his hand as I unlocked the front door of my bungalow. I could smell it.

Dehydration, exhaustion, and that other thing: I was feeling light-headed. "Shall I put the kettle on?" I said. "Nice cup of tea?"

Ed was opening the doors, looking into the rooms, his gun pointed at the ground in front of him. "You don't have anything stronger, I suppose? For unexpected guests?"

"I don't keep any in the house."

"No, of course. Sorry. I won't bother with the tea, thanks. Glass of water wouldn't be bad, though."

He was right, it wasn't bad. It was wonderful. I drank a pint of water straight down, felt it refilling my cells, then drank another. I couldn't remember when I'd ever enjoyed a moment so much in my life.

"Ah, that hits the spot," said Ed. "You got one of those filters fitted, have you?"

"Yes."

"Who fitted that for you, then?"

"Bloke along the road. He got me a special rate. I look after his house when they're on holiday."

"What, Mal Hunter? Yeah, I know him. Good kid." He rinsed his glass and set it on the draining board. "Right then, Dave, you get along to bed."

I thought I was going to throw up again. He was going to make it look like a suicide, I thought, or a burglary. I clenched my mouth shut; I wasn't going to lose all that beautiful water.

We went through to the bedroom. Ed brought a dining room chair with him and sat just inside the door, gun on his lap.

"Shall I get undressed?"

He laughed. "What, on a night like this? Up to you, pal, but I'd say it's too hot to sleep with your kecks on tonight!"

I got undressed. Ed turned the light out. I lay there on my back, naked, stinking, listening, waiting. I couldn't hear him breathing, but I knew he was there. When he moved, when he finally came for me, would I hear him?

I pushed back the sheet and put my feet on the floor as quietly as I could.

"You all right there, Dave?"

"Can I open a window? I usually have the window open in this weather."

He swore under his breath. Had I made him angry? But next moment he said, in his usual, affable voice, "It is like an oven in here, isn't it? Sure, good idea."

I opened the window and looked out, and thought about it. How things had come to this, and how there must have been a time when it was in my hands to prevent this. I looked through the window for a while, and even tested my leg against the sill, but in the end I decided I'd done enough running over the years. Or maybe I was just too hot.

I got back into bed. "What shall I do now?"

"What do you usually do?"

"Think about Kylie Minogue," I said, because the water had made me feel that much better, had given me that much more fortitude.

He chuckled. "Yeah, well, you can do that tomorrow! I

should just get some sleep, if I were you. Getting late after all, isn't it? Past your usual bedtime."

I started to laugh at the idea of sleeping, but it hurt my throat, so I stopped.

A noise woke me, even though I don't think I was really asleep. I think it's more that I was somewhere else. Nowhere very pleasant, as it happened, so that I was almost glad to be back.

A noise.

Ed was crouching over me, staring down at me. I could see him by the moonlight, and I thought, *Well—*

The moonlight vanished as the overhead light came on.

I couldn't figure that out. The light switch was over by the door. I looked over, and there was Ed, still sitting on his chair, gun in raised hand. I looked back at the man by my bed, and it was a kid, a teenager, someone I didn't know. He had a knife in his hand.

An accomplice. I opened my mouth to tell Ed that was unfair, that wasn't right, after everything we'd said to each other tonight, this should just be between the two of us. But my throat wouldn't work, and anyway, the kid wasn't looking at me anymore. He was looking at Ed.

"Look at the gun, young man," said Ed, "and think about it."

The kid said, "What the hell—"

"Put the knife down. Think about it."

The stranger looked at the knife in his hand and started crying. He hurled it away from him. It bounced and stuck into the wardrobe the other side of the window. "I might have known," he said. "I might have bloody known."

"Well, now you do know," said Ed. "This man is protected. Think about that, son. I'm giving you a chance to turn around, walk away, forget about it. Live your life."

The teenager rubbed his hands against his face. "After what he did? Do you know what he did?"

"I know what he did. And I'm telling you I'm doing you a big favor here, because if you ever come to this town again, you will be shot dead. That is what will happen to you. You're getting this one chance because of what he did to you. Now go back out the way you came in."

"After what he did?"

Ed raised the gun and pointed it right at the boy's chest, but the boy turned his back on Ed, looked down at me, and raised his fist as if he still had the knife. Then he scrambled out of the window, and I heard his howls and sobs trail off into the night.

"DON'T worry," said Ed, pouring boiling water into two tea mugs in the kitchen. "He won't be back; he's done what he needed to do. That'll be enough for him. He tried. He can get on with his life now."

I pulled my dressing gown around me, glad of the warmth, glad of the sweat. "I don't know him. I've never met him. Why did he want to kill me?"

"No, daresay you wouldn't recognize him. He was a fair bit younger last time you saw him—in court, in the public gallery. His father died when you got that." He pointed at my leg.

"Oh God."

"He'd been around town the last couple of weeks, that poor kid had, sniffing about. Asking questions, showing a photo of you from the report in the paper. Anyway, Chris Eastman, being an ex-cop, he checked you out. Made a couple of phone calls, found out what brought you down here, how you did your leg in, why someone might go looking for you."

"You can't blame him," I said, and I meant it.

"For trying? No, you can't blame a kid for that. He's got his mother to think of. They called me up—Chris,

Mal Hunter, a few others—because I'm the only one who knows a bit about guns. They were as sure as they could be that *he* didn't have a gun, so he'd have to get close to you. When you were alone. The lad disappeared for a few days, then he turned up again this morning. Chris, with his training, you know, he'd noticed you always sleep with your windows open when it's hot like this, so he assumed the kid would have noticed, too. There was that vicious hot night last Saturday, you remember? That's why we reckoned it'd be tonight. If he had the guts to go through with it."

"Which he did."

Ed shrugged. "Maybe, maybe not. Give the kid the benefit of the doubt."

I didn't know how to say this to a man who'd just saved my life, but I had to say it anyway. "Ed, I don't see why—"

"No, you're right. I could have told you from the start what was going on. I could have."

"If it was because you didn't want to worry me, I've got to tell you—"

"Aye! Good one, lad, good one." He rubbed a knuckle against the end of his big nose for a moment. "No, it wasn't that. Do you remember at school, they used to make you copy poems out in your best handwriting? Did in my day, anyway. And those poems, you remember them all your life. I could recite one now."

"You were . . . teaching me a lesson?"

"Because, Dave, when you learn a lesson, it shouldn't be easy. If it's easy, it won't stick. Now, you—I know that you haven't had a drink and you haven't driven a car in almost three years. Have you? So you learned that lesson. Learned it hard and learned it forever. Didn't you?"

"I suppose so." I hadn't been aware I was learning anything. As far as I knew, all I was doing was trying to put a ship back into a broken bottle.

"And if by any chance you hadn't, well, you bloody have now, haven't you?"

We drank our tea. The sweat it produced on our brows was new and refreshing. "If you'd been here not long ago," I said, "there'd have been a bottle of Scotch to go with that. I never touched it, but I kept it around because . . . well, you know."

"Oh, aye. We all have hard times."

"I got rid of it in the end." Smashed it in the bath, scoured the smell away. Blind panic; not resolution. "Because some days are longer than others."

"Oh well," said Ed. "Some days my timing's off, and some days it's on."

He left after breakfast, when Chris Eastman came round to see how we were doing. I walked him to his car, parked a few yards down my street, outside Mal Hunter's house. We shook hands, and he wrote his address down on a piece torn from a matchbox.

"I'm up in West Yorkshire these days," he said. "If you ever find yourself up that way, make sure you drop in."

"I will. Thanks."

"You'd like it," said Ed. "It's a pleasant little spot."

GREEN HEAT

Angela Zeman

Angela Zeman's new book, *The Witch and the Borscht Pearl*, features Mrs. Risk, the "witch" of a long-running short story series published mostly in *Alfred Hitchcock's Mystery Magazine*. One story was chosen for last year's MWA anthology edited by Mary Higgins Clark, still selling in several countries and languages. Nancy Pickard chose one of Angela's suspense/thriller stories for her 1999 anthology, *Mom, Apple Pie, and Murder*, which *Publishers Weekly* reviewed as "magical." Both anthologies are still in print. A full-time writer, Angela has begun three new short story series and is presently working on a suspense novel. She also coauthors nonfiction articles about the mystery field with her husband, Barry Zeman, an authority on the history of the mystery and book collecting. One book using two of their articles as chapters won an Anthony Award and an Edgar nomination in the Best Critical/Biographical category.

___

TYREE Garcia arrived late in the afternoon. For the last twenty miles he'd ridden State Highway 6 all alone and so felt free to indulge in a leisurely survey of Rushing River Hollow by riding the brakes of his black Cherokee van down the final hill. At a Mobil station, by all appearances the official western border of the town, he pulled over and rolled to a stop next to a gas pump. According to tattered and faded ads pasted across the office's windows, the Mobil supplied repair services, gas, tires, beer, sodas, cigarettes, and tobacco in chewable form. Tyree guessed the strips of paper served to shade the Mobil's glass-walled office from the merciless sun as much as to list the services offered.

The narrow asphalt highway flattened out and disappeared into the town's main street, which was as neatly obscured beneath a layer of dirt as if deliberately coated. While he sat massaging sleep-deprived eyes, he noticed the occasional pedestrian scuff down the middle of the street, raising dust that obscured his or her feet in little dun-colored clouds.

He wondered if avoiding the sidewalks was a local habit. His was the only vehicle in sight. For all he knew, the tourist trade infused the Hollow with bustling life in spring and fall, and maybe even winter, but the intense summer heat drove them away—if this was a normal summer. Was this brain-sizzling heat unusual for the Hollow? Like a drought? He didn't know that either. Country, especially genuine country like Rushing River Hollow, baffled him, was beyond his experience. Heat waves shimmered up from the concrete slab sidewalks bordering each side of the road. Maybe the thick layer of dirt was kinder to tender feet than roasted cement. He just didn't know.

To a Chicago kid born, raised, and devoted to its crowded neighborhoods, West Virginia looked like a foreign kingdom of crystalline creeks and river rapids and green, softly rounded mountains. An occasional ramshackle cabin propped up on a webbing of raw, unpainted four-by-fours dotted the steep slopes. A paradise—unspoiled, vast, and rich—which accounted for the sprawling luxury resort hotel he knew from his AAA map occupied the other end of this dirt-crusted road. Pinebrook Resort offered, if one paid outrageous fees, hunting, golf, tennis, skeet and trap shooting, river rafting, nature hikes, even lessons in falconry. He'd picked up a travel agency brochure before driving all the way down here. He wondered if the privileged lives of the guests—outsiders—invited jealousy and comparison to the obvious scratch-scrabble lives of the residents.

Tyree finally swung his long, stiffened legs to the ground and began a series of stretches. He was a tall man, heavily muscled, and moved without haste.

As he reached for the fuel pump handle, he noticed a small sign propped against the second of the Mobil station's two pumps (one for diesel fuel, but he'd happened to park beside the one dispensing gas: a sign he interpreted as a favorable omen; in his profession, he constantly looked for favorable omens). The sign, weatherbeaten almost to illegibility, said Rushin River Hollow, Population: the 421 was crossed out, 303 crossed out, 112 crossed out, then 427. A graph of the town's fortunes. Had the millennium brought about a baby boom here?

Suddenly, a short, thick man with roughened skin so red his neck and face resembled a turkey's wattle rushed up and grabbed the pump handle from Tyree's grasp and inserted the nozzle into the Cherokee. "High test, I'd say, right?" He moved fast but talked slow.

Tyree nodded. The man punched a square plastic button on the pump, then turned on the juice. He apologized that he'd been "out back," his slight flinch telling Tyree that "out back" meant the men's rest room, then introduced himself as Emil Powers.

"Tyree Garcia," Tyree said politely, nodding down at the top of the little man's head. He saw no reason to lie about his name; nobody would've heard of him in this wilderness.

For no reason other than to open a conversation, Tyree asked what had happened to the *g* in *Rushing* on the population sign. The gap from its loss was obvious.

"Aw," said Emil, sounding deeply distressed, "if'n you don't mind a long story?"

Tyree shook his head, eyebrows lifted.

"Ya see, it ain't in truth Rush-*ing* River. It's *Rooshion* River. Like the Rooshions that come from Moscow. And somehow, 'cause we do a lot of business river rafting, y'know from the hotel, it got mangled over the years inta Rush-*ing* River. By the tourists, I guess." He shrugged his narrow shoulders, jiggling the gas pump handle. "We need them tourists. So we jes' didn't know, should we change it legally or what, or did it even matter? So when the sun bleached the *g* off'n the sign, we left it. I got maps in the office, legal ones from the gov'ment, *they* even call us Rushing River Hollow now. How they got aholt of the wrong name, nobody knows, or gives a hoot. Well, except for the Rooshions what established the town. They's pissed. But," he waved his free hand, dismissing them, "just Joey and Eban left, and they's ninety something. Be gone by the time we decide anything. So we're kind of relaxed about it. Now the sign itself, though—"

To Tyree's amazement, he took a deep breath. Then, with a stiff dignity obviously meant to disguise personal embarrassment, confessed that he'd promised the Chamber of Commerce last spring he'd make a new sign, but jes' hadn't got to it. But he will. He will! He promised Tyree as fervently as if Tyree were an important Chamber member to be placated, a color-blind attitude that amazed Tyree. He'd anticipated some anxiety or even obstruction because of the color of his skin. After all, West Virginia was not known for high standards of education, an aspect that usually coincided with prejudice. Suddenly Tyree thought of the extreme heat and the deserted street. Possibly the color blindness meant only that in a roasting August barren of tourists, his color was green: income on the hoof.

A companionable silence set in between the two men as

the gas slowly filled the Cherokee's immense tank. Tyree
nearly grinned as he watched Emil struggle not to peer too
obviously into the darkened side and back windows, curious about what might be in there. He would see nothing,
Tyree knew, of his altered shotgun, his semiautomatic
9mm and .357 Magnum with extra clips, a red-dot laser
scope on the .357, and the Archangel holster Tyree favored
for its fast-draw design. His laptop, connected wireless
phone, and portable printer were packed neatly in shock-
proof canvas carriers. His monocular night-vision headgear, an air taser (stun gun), and a Dazer he used for
protection against guard dogs; mace in various sizes and
canister shapes; and a digital camera with special lenses
were all nested, like the laptop, in specially designed carriers. As was his Game Finder scope for detecting body
heat behind walls. Tyree's Cherokee was also designed with
special features, one of which kept his equipment from
prying eyes. And just as well. No need to panic the pop-
ulace. Yet.

Emil sighed and gave up his covert peeking without
resorting to the rudeness of trying to pry info from Tyree.
Tyree liked him for that sigh; it revealed an easygoing
nature. Tyree liked laid-back attitudes. They worked so
much better for him when he was on a job.

Soot-blackened buildings dotted both sides of the street,
reminders of the town's coal mining history. Edna's Gift
Shop leaned, bricks crumbling, against the timbered
stones of Willem's Pizza, which looked sturdy. The tall-
pillared, red brick U.S. Post Office, which despite its
height was about as wide as a cubicle, shared a wall with
Mick's rakish wood-paneled Railroader's Pub. Across the
road, Janna's Coal Miner's Daughter Clothing Boutique
had been a similar wooden shack before being amateurishly
slathered with a coating of infelicitous yellow stucco now
flaking into a blotchy mess. A cracked cement sidewalk

fronted these places of business, tilting along with the fortunes of those who'd hung on through both good and bad years.

"Where ya from?" asked Emil.

"Chicago," murmured Tyree absently, studying the town. "Tourist trade the big industry here?" he asked his new friend Emil.

"Only industry, now the coal's played out." Emil tossed a hand to direct Tyree's gaze down the length of the street. "They do what they can to brighten up the storefronts." Emil shook his head sadly. "Order stuff from Sears catalogues or haul fancy goods in from Richmond or from Charleston, our capital, and then tell people it's local handicraft. That's big here, handicrafts. Not to criticize."

Tyree nodded.

Elaborate Victorian wood lace and railings festooned porches that hadn't worn such finery since their birth at the turn of the century. Log cabin–style benches had been sprinkled about, nestled near cedar tubs that Tyree guessed normally overflowed with pansies or geraniums or whatever grew here in cooler weather. He was no gardener, either. Flowers, in his experience, were just bright things hung in great lush balls from light poles lining Lake Shore Drive or the Miracle Mile. The tubs here were barren, filled only with tangles of sun-roasted brown moss. The stables near some derelict railroad tracks had been transformed into a hardware store, but the owner had scattered old horse tack and hay bales around to contribute to the desirable "charm."

Suddenly Emil volunteered, "Talk's going around about making a public park on the east end, just afore you get to the hotel grounds. Everybody hopes Miz Doree Zendall will donate her family's Civil War iron cannons and cannonballs, now she's widowed and no kids. Three generations of her husband's family owned 'em. What good're

they to Doree? They'd make a center of interest for the
park. Half rust, but still, it's history. Lotta history here.
And *that's* genuine!"

Tyree nodded, tiring of his new friend. He checked the
revolving numbers on the pump. He breathed deeply for
patience and prepared to ask if there was a place to stay
here other than the hotel, but Emil jumped in again.

"That woman! City council tried to bribe her with a
white-painted gazebo, her name on it on a brass plaque.
Only Doree's cannons and the streetlamps on Main Street
here are for real; ever'thing else is like I said, from a Sears
catalogue or hauled in. But Doree thinks her cannons
ought to fetch her more 'n' a plaque."

Tyree jumped in as Emil took a breath. "You know a
place I could stay? That hotel of yours is too rich for my
wallet."

Emil shrugged a bony shoulder. "We gots a couple B
and Bs, if you don't mind sharing bathrooms."

Tyree frowned. He did mind. "No."

"Oh, wait now. Doree's place is huge. One of the rooms
she rents gots its own bath. I'm sure it's empty. Hell,
whole damn town's empty lately. Except she talks a lot, if
you can stand it. What'd you say you here for?"

Tyree understood and didn't hold it against the little
man. Curiosity was a tough urge to control. "Vacation. No
hunting yet, right?"

"Out of season right now."

"Good. I don't care for shooting." It was true. He didn't.
"I'll need directions."

Tyree got the directions, climbed back into his Cherokee, and devoutly wished for a soft bed. If Rushing River
aimed for historical accuracy, then the bed should sport a
feather mattress. Of course, the blacks all slept out back
in those historical days, too. He hoped Ms. Doree Zendall

would be greedy enough to see his color as green, as Emil had.

He rolled slowly down the street, still taking in the sights, noticing a few side roads, unpaved paths, really, not visible from Emil's station. He also noted a small, slightly built old man sweeping the sidewalk in front of a store. Suddenly the man looked straight at Tyree, shouted, "Ho! What's up?" Tyree looked again, taken aback. The man hastily ducked inside the Little Bear Market's screen door, banging his broom on the stone steps as he dragged it in behind him.

Later. First get a place to park his car and his aching body.

Ms. Doree Zendall's tiny raisin eyes narrowed, taking a long, silent moment to catalog the price of his black tee belted neatly within his black silk-and-linen-blend slacks, and the subtly expensive sleek black sneakers. Tyree congratulated himself for leaving behind his gold chain, bracelet, ear stud, and rings; he didn't like to fit into a cliché of a typical big city black. The word *hood* usually attached itself to the end of that description. No he was gold-free, and his watch stainless steel, although it included a few features he doubted Ms. Zendall would understand. Finally, she nodded. She tucked a stray strand of coarse hair into the ratty gray ball that rested on the roll of fat behind her neck and led the way to his new home for the next few days. As she hauled herself up the stairs, she began a rambling stream-of-consciousness monologue that Tyree listened to carefully in case he could use any of the info.

She was short and very heavy, a fireplug of a woman. Huffs appeared between her words as she struggled to talk and climb stairs simultaneously. *Emil had it right,* Tyree thought. Her house was massive and empty. The winding stair seemed endless. Her face reddened until sweat coursed down her round cheeks to plop like rain on her heaving bosom. When they finally gained the top landing of the wide, curving stairs, painted white but carpeted thickly in plush deep maroon, she abruptly finished with, "Breakfast is extra, how do you like your eggs?" The sudden cessation of sound as she waited for his answer woke Tyree from the mesmerizing flow of words. He'd almost fallen asleep on the stairway behind her.

He blinked, then registered the question. "Four eggs, easy over medium. You got whole wheat toast?"

"Muffins are better."

"Toast," he said firmly. "Whole wheat. No butter. And fresh juice?"

"Well sure, fresh!" she bristled. "Seven sharp."

Tyree nodded, then handed her the agreed in-advance fee in cash. One shrewd glance at the interior of his exposed wallet, and she wheeled smartly and plodded downstairs to leave him standing before the open door of a room more appropriate for a debutante than Tyree Garcia. The bed was a double, with an overlarge white lace coverlet that drifted to the varnished wood floor all around, the corners puddled like piles of snowflakes. It felt scratchy to his skin. He bundled it onto an overstuffed boudoir chair and dropped onto the crisp sheets, careful to let his feet hang off the side, too tired to remove his sneakers. The two corner windows were open, but no breeze stirred the sheer white curtains to cool the stagnant air.

The next hour passed in a luxurious haze of drifting between sleep and a blissful physical consciousness of the soft mattress cradling his weary body. When his conscience demanded he pull himself erect to get to work, it was a wrench. He wasn't here to laze away the day after driving eighteen straight hours, racing newspaper or TV reports that might complicate his errand.

An early dinner, he decided. Coffee with sugar for the jolt, although he rarely drank coffee. Then get to it.

With little trouble he found a diner, the only source of food within sight, which helped narrow his choice, slid into the red plastic covered bench seat, and just avoided propping his elbows in a pool of syrup left by a former customer. A battered window AC unit manfully refrigerated the air, although it hampered conversation with its metallic death rattles. Tyree basked in the chill.

After an agonizing attempt to swallow the larded slab of meatloaf floating in a lake of ketchup, he gave it up and asked for the freshest pie in the place. The waitress, a moonfaced teen, studied him like a science specimen, then brought him a large plate of banana cream pie. It was fresh, fragrant, and tasted like heaven. He got a second piece, making a mental note to ask for her recommendations if his job lasted long enough to force him to eat here again, swilled down the burnt coffee, and left her a 50 percent tip.

He strolled back towards the main part of town, suddenly aware that he, like the others he'd watched, was walking down the middle of the dirt-covered asphalt. After a small laugh at himself, he focused on looking for more conversationalists like Emil and Ms. Zendall. A small group had gathered in front of Edna's Gift Shop, so he shifted his direction to end up there, but he moved slowly.

Give them all a chance to look him over, take in the details, like Ms. Zendall. He hoped his color would again be judged green. Helped a hell of a lot.

Again a good omen: Emil was there, holding court, telling the saga of Tyree's arrival. Tyree stepped up on the sidewalk and smiled warmly at Emil, nodded hello. Bristling with pride, Emil greeted Tyree like a cousin, made introductions. Told his name and that he had come from Chicago, and didn't have any interest in hunting. Just liked the peace of the area, "That right Tyree?" he asked. Tyree nodded.

The nervous sidewalk sweeper was there, head bobbing. Again he declared in a booming voice, "Ho, what's up!" then shyly backed away, tangling his broom between his own legs, nearly falling. His head hung as if ashamed of himself.

Emil said, "That's Frankie. Says that to everybody. Sweeps sidewalks for the town. Gotta do something. 'Sides, it's awful dusty this time o' year. Good thing to do."

Tyree nodded. Close up, he could see that Frankie was much younger than his wizened features indicated. An impaired young man who looked sixty. "Good job, Frankie," he said. He held out his hand to him. Frankie went totally still. Despite his lowered head, his eyes went up to Tyree's, holding there for a second. Then he grasped Tyree's hand and squeezed, grinning. "Hey!" he said.

"Hey," Tyree answered. Frankie's hand was bony and fragile, with skin like leather. Then Emil introduced him to an older woman, nearly as fat as Ms. Zendall but taller. "This is Mrs. Barstow. Lisle. And her beautiful Wendy-girl. Wendy married Rudy Stern a whiles back. Rudy's on late duty today. At the hotel," he confided. "Desk clerk. Good future!"

Tyree nodded, smiling. "Congratulations," he said. The girl could not possibly be older than seventeen or eighteen and looked many months pregnant, although Tyree was careful not to mention this in case he was wrong. The women he'd met so far in this town had a tendency to corpulence, and he couldn't afford to offend quite yet.

He turned to the girl's mother and tipped his head. "You couldn't possibly be old enough to be this young lady's mother!" *An oldie but goodie*, he sighed to himself. Women. But to his surprise, Mrs. Barstow didn't do the normal simper and denial that usually followed the compliment. She just gazed at him with a puzzled look on her face.

She blurted, "You rent that car? Don't look like no rental. Rentals don't normally black out their windows like that. But it's got a West Virginia plate on it."

Tyree nodded. "Yeah, I thought that odd myself, the dark windows. But I'm fond of vans. Roomy. I'm a big guy, long legs." He shrugged at the mysteries of rental car companies, put an earnest but puzzled expression on his face. But Mrs. Barstow's eyes chilled as she took in his explanation, studied his face. Calculating. *Shit,* he thought. He habitually changed the plates every time he crossed state lines to stay inconspicuous, but weariness had led him to reveal to the town crier, Emil, that he'd come from Chicago. Might as well've put a blue chicken on the roof for Mrs. Barstow to point out.

"You drive here from the airport?" she asked.

He nodded.

"Which one?"

"Well, hell, Lisle. Give the man a vacation, will ya?" Emil rescued Tyree, who silently blessed the man. "Obviously he drove in from the capital. Look at the dust on the thing."

"He could've flown in to the Greenville airport," she said defensively. "It's closer. And lotsa straight flights come there from big cities, 'cause of the hotel."

"C'mon, Lisle. Then he woulda driv in from the opposite direction. I saw him myself hit town back thataway," Emil exclaimed in exasperation, pointing towards the Mobil station. "Obviously he came by way of Charleston!"

"Well his car's so filthy looks like he drove here all the way from Chicago!" she demanded. "And where's the rental car sticker?"

Tyree rapidly reassessed the intelligence of Rushing River's population. No detail too small to notice. "They don't mark rental cars anymore, since the tourist shootings in Florida," he said, crossing mental fingers that West Virginia had subscribed to that policy, too. He groaned, wondering what else he'd screwed up. Better get in, do it, get out. This is what allowing himself too little sleep got him.

"There now, happy, Lisle?" started Emil, gathering wind to begin a good long rebuke.

"You know what made me think of coming here?" Tyree said to divert attention from his car. "I had a buddy. Moved to this area, around, oh, twenty years ago."

"Colored like you?" asked Mrs. Barstow innocently.

He distrusted her innocence. "No. White like you," he said, trying to restrain his annoyance.

"What's his name? You been in touch, know where he lives exactly?"

"Not exactly."

She tilted her head, looking up at him with opaque pale eyes, same color as a blued gun barrel, he thought. She continued, full of attitude: "But twenty years pass, you think, hell, he probably hasn't moved in all those years. I'll just look up my old buddy an see how the fish'er jumpin', is that it? What's his name? You didn't say."

"Jeeze, Lisle. What's your britches in a hitch for?" asked Emil plaintively.

Yeah, Lisle, Tyree asked himself, his interest in her sharpening with each passing second. "My friend's mother died. And he didn't come to the funeral, her only child. Didn't seem natural. Wonderful woman, awfully good to me over the years, and she mentioned he was still here shortly before she died. That's what brought me. I'd been working hard, had some time off coming to me. Thought, well, I'd see what was up with him and get some R and R same time." *Don't explain so much,* he reminded himself. *Too much detail could trap a man like a web of steel.* He shrugged. "No big deal if he's not here anymore." He gazed around the green mountains surrounding the dusty town and said, "Beautiful," his voice quiet with appreciation. Sunset had begun, streaks of brilliant coral and mauve tinting the rows of small shops and even his new friends' faces a reddish gold. He figured the time to be about eight or eight-thirty. Darkness might not come until nine-thirty or after, this late in the summer. He sighed inwardly. He was tired, but no rest waited for him tonight.

"Whatcha do for a livin', Mr. Tyree?" asked a new voice softly. "In Chicago?"

He looked down at the area near his right elbow. A pixie stood there in baggy overalls, yellow work boots, and a white sleeveless man's ribbed undershirt.

"Hey, Tyree, this's one o' our Master Wilderness Guides. Miss Amy Bearclaw." Emil's voice lifted with pride.

The dusky-skinned pixie smiled, but like Mrs. Lisle Barstow, her greenish eyes had a metallic glint. With the experience of a lifetime of observation, he saw she was the product of some sort of mixed marriage. Bearclaw? Sounded Indian. Her dark hair was cut like a boy's, and she obviously ignored makeup, but nothing could make this little woman look like a boy.

"Master Wilderness Guide?" he repeated.

She nodded. "My pa and I have an exclusive contract with Pinebrook, because we're the best. And the hotel believes in maintaining the highest standards."

Obviously she had no objection to self-promotion, thought Tyree, amused. "Do you ever take on outsiders, people not guests at the resort? I wouldn't mind a tour of a mountain or two. Maybe a river ride."

Her eyelashes lowered to half-mast as she considered him. "Your city ways shine through you like a lamp, although you'd be good in a fight, I'd bet."

"It's been said," he agreed, wondering why she didn't talk as much like a hick as the others in the group. "Fights happen in a city. In the country, too?"

She ignored this query, her expression labeling it stupid, as it was, he admitted to himself, and asked him if he'd had his dinner.

"At the diner," said Mrs. Barstow. He looked at her. "I saw you in the window," she said, shrugging.

"The pie was fantastic," he said.

"That was the banana cream, right?" asked Emil with authority.

Tyree nodded, beginning to feel hemmed in.

The pixie said, "My mom made it. She bakes for the hotel, too. And grows vegetables so they can offer organic dishes. You couldn't a liked anything else there, though. Somebody big as you needs to eat. Want to come home with me for dinner?"

Dazed, Tyree threw all plans to the wind and just nodded yes. The pixie wheeled to tromp down the middle of the street. Automatically, he hastened to follow. She would've made a natural military drill sergeant, was his first thought. It took a stunned second before he remembered his manners and turned to wave good-bye to Emil and the others. Frankie boomed out, "Ho, what's up?" but also waved good-bye. Mrs. Barstow just turned and strode away, pulling her daughter along by her plump arm as if otherwise the girl might run off. To Tyree's amusement, all moved to the middle of the deserted street before taking to their individual directions.

Dinner took on dimensions he hadn't expected, but by now he'd learned not to let anything surprise him. This place was too far beyond his experience.

Mrs. Bearclaw was a beautiful woman, slender and graceful and tall, her hair silky and pale and twisted back out of her face. And she was blind. Probably not completely, he judged. Legally blind. Although he'd offered to help, at Amy's command he instead sat quietly on a small painted wooden chair in the kitchen and watched as

Mrs. Bearclaw kept track of several operations going on simultaneously on a modern commercial stove with three ovens that took up at least half the space in the kitchen. The smells seductively drove away all memory of the diner's meatloaf. As if drawn home by the aromas, Mr. Bearclaw soon arrived, a small lanky man with ropy muscles, obviously Amy's father and the source of her miniature dusky version of her mother's beauty. They shook hands, and he was invited to call Amy's father David, her mother Lydia. When the food finally reached the table, Amy nodded he could start eating.

He tried to restrain himself, knowing a belly too full of food would work against him that night, but Lydia Bearclaw's talents overcame him. When he finally sat back with a sated sigh, Lydia spoke. In a cultured East Coast voice, she asked who he was after.

Tyree lowered his head and shook it. "Is every person in this Hollow psychic?"

Amy tilted back on the hind two legs of her wooden chair, thumbs hooked in her overalls pockets. She grinned. "You think we're so danged dumb we ain't never ran up against bounty hunters before?"

"Don't say *ain't*," reproved her mother.

Amy ignored her. "Look around. Are we overflowing with cops, DEA? Feds? We got no sheriff, even. Half the world has tried to hide here: Colombian drug dealers, punks from Atlanta, kneecap men from New Orleans. I mean, we're so nowheres, we're ripe for disappearances— or so these types think before they get to know the locals. Besides, it's pretty here. People like it."

Tyree stared at her.

As if patiently explaining the obvious to a halfwit, Amy finished, "You saw our town's population numbers if you was at the Mobil. You know how in each others' pockets neighbors get in a place this size? Nothin' else to do." She held up her hands as if to say, *Well duh!*

She finished, "So who you after?"

He stared at her father, who just shrugged, then her mother. Lydia sat quietly, just sipping her coffee.

Tyree squirmed, which is what he suspected Amy had intended him to do. "What's with the jump in population, then? From 112 to 427 in the last year. Or did I read it wrong?"

David Bearclaw nodded, his mouth screwed tight as if suppressing anger. "You read right. The hotel. Sells plots now, fancy houses all squashed together like fleas, in sections tucked between the three golf courses they got. Word is they're building another golf course just for the residents. Pools, all that."

Tyree asked, "Vacation homes or permanent?"

David eyed him. "What's the difference?"

"Permanent means schools," said Tyree. "Post offices, restaurants, sewers, service roads. And eventually some type of industry to employ them. Lotta extras come with permanent residents. Money for the Hollow, though." He lifted an eyebrow in question.

David shook his head. "Don't need, don't want that kind of prosperity."

Tyree frowned. "You got no police at all?"

Amy grinned. "Didn't say that. We got Kizzy."

David said quietly, "My mother. One of the remaining full-blooded Cherokees from the Trail of Tears. Descended from those who hid so the soldiers missed them in the roundup."

Tyree considered. "Didn't I read that about a third of the Indians force-marched to the reservations out West died on the trail?"

David nodded, looked aside.

Amy grunted. "That's why the name, Trail of Tears."

Tyree folded his arms, said to David, "So your ma, Amy's grandma, is the law here?"

Lydia smiled.

Amy grinned. "She's a Wise Woman. She sees and knows it all. Nobody can get away with a dang thing. She nails somebody, they're nailed for good. Who needs a pushy cop shooting up innocent bystanders? She's teaching me to take her place someday. She can't die until I take over from her."

Tyree slid his eyes sideways to examine the half pint size girl so smug, so *big* for such a pixie. Tried to keep the flummoxed look off his face. He finally sighed. "I believe you. You asked about my mark: don't know his name. I know what *used* to be his name. Edgar Fallon."

Silence.

"What'd he do?" rumbled David Bearclaw at last. "In Chicago, was it?"

"Oh, Dad. Drugs and beatin' up women, you can guess that much."

Tyree lifted his hands. "Holy shit. You sure Captain Sabinski didn't just mail you the guy's jacket?"

Lydia Bearclaw smiled. "It's hard to get used to, I know. Like jungle drums. Kizzy is a . . . a natural force, like a tornado. Amy, too. *She's* just not as disciplined or schooled. Yet."

"And where'd *you* come from?" Tyree asked. "The Upper East Side of Manhattan?"

"Very good," she said, still smiling.

He thought a minute. "So you were running, too, when you got here. From what?" He studied her, brow furrowed in thought. "Were you blind before you got here? From birth. Or from—"

"Not nice, Mr. Tyree," said Lydia Bearclaw. "Mind your manners. I know you have some. And I know you're used to minding them, because you've restrained yourself amazingly ever since you arrived in Rushing River."

Tyree nodded. "You read me right. Sorry, ma'am. Sir," he said to her husband, who just faintly smiled and shrugged. *Not a talker,* thought Tyree.

"So now what?" he said, more to himself than to his hosts.

"Tell us the whole thing," insisted Amy. "I don't get the twenty years ago part."

Tyree looked at her ruefully. "Twenty-*four* years ago, to be exact. This kid lied about his age—he was seventeen then—so he could marry a twenty-year-old dumb Polack girl in Chicago. He'd knocked—he'd gotten her pregnant. Too innocent, no family. A pretty blonde. So she works hard in a local diner while he's supposedly driving a cab, and she thinks they're socking away every penny so they can escape the projects with their baby, but he's depositing it all into his veins. But she trusts him. The sweet little girl has her beautiful baby boy, goes right back to work, he switches to nights to watch the kid during the day. Next thing she knows, stuff starts missing from the apartment. See, his addiction's growing beyond their joint income. So she reports the thefts to the precinct, but they're all petty. I mean, what do they have to steal? The local beat cop, after one look at the husband, guesses the truth, tries to tell her, but she won't listen. Until one day she catches hubby snitching her paycheck from her purse. Big fight, lots of screaming, and then silence. Some hours pass, but the silence bothers one neighbor who really cares about the poor girl, who finally decides to check on her. He pushes open the door, finds the girl in the kitchen, bloody and out cold on the floor next to her baby. Baby's head is smashed flat on one side. The woman's physically OK. The blood is all the baby's."

"Jesus wept," murmured David Bearclaw.

"The cops went for the husband at his place of work, found out he'd been fired a few weeks before. His former dispatcher confirmed Eddie was supporting a monster habit and unable to hold a job. He had to be getting desperate for cash. Dealers don't extend credit." His mouth twisted wryly. "Cops figured, with nerves raggedy from too long off the juice, his wife catching him in his theft—screaming wife, screaming baby—he popped. Then either he slam-dunked the child to shut it up, an accidental murder, or he just flat murdered it. Luckily a chop to his wife's head knocked her cold, or the cops figured she'd be dead, too. No Eddie. And when she woke up, she'd lost herself. Catatonic."

Mrs. Bearclaw asked gently, "That makes it twenty-three years ago, then. So why are you here? And why now?"

"Because after twenty-three years of institutionalization, therapy, and whatever they do to help poor souls like that sweet girl—woman now—she regained her mind and memory. The doctors say she not only recovered, although still frail, but can be believed. And she told what happened. The cops had the story nailed pretty much correctly."

"But you're no cop," said Amy. "Doesn't sound like there's a bounty on the guy. Why are *you* here?"

Tyree sighed. " 'Cause I had the misfortune of going through elementary, then junior high, then high school with a good buddy who's now Captain Lee Sabinski of Homicide in Chicago. And over the years, he's kept track of our running balance of favors. I owe him big right now, and bounty hunters don't suffer from a need for search warrants, extradition paperwork, and that stuff." He looked Amy in the eye, man to man, so to speak. His sharp cheekbones bunched up into his own grin. "Plus, I'm good at my job. The cops had nothing then, and Sabinski's men found the same nothing now. They aren't even sure he ever left Illinois. But I work with a rather special computer information expert—a genius in his own way. Probably should meet your Grandma Kizzy. He decided to start with Eddie's car. Even if he ditched it fast, in that first flight away from his own house, we figure he used his own car. In the projects, he was one of the few who *had* a car.

"So my man patiently traced from car to car to car, all but a few of them stolen, natch, but the ones that he didn't steal: he changed his name just a little with each transaction. And two patterns emerged: a trail that never went beyond West Virginia, and a name that by now we figure might somewhat resemble Roy Barso."

Amy settled her chair back down on all four of its feet and gazed levelly at her father. Her father shook his head, then stood to take the used dishes from the table to the sink.

Tyree jumped to his feet, grabbed his dirty dishes. Lydia patted the air. "Never mind, Tyree. Amy, better lead Mr. Tryee back to his car."

"If it's still there," Amy agreed. David nodded and started squirting dish soap in a large metal sink.

"Better run on," David said, taking the dishes Tyree held.

"What?" said Tyree.

"C'mon," said Amy. "Gotta chore to help you with, then you can bed down in comfort until tomorrow."

"No, not tomorrow. Tonight. Sabinski and I both know the newspapers're onto this. We have to nail him before he's warned. He could run again and be smarter about it by now."

Lydia shrugged, her back turned to him.

Tyree let out the breath he'd been holding, and a puzzled anger started to rise. Amy grabbed his large hand and tugged. "C'mon, we might be too late as it is."

Tyree went.

When they reached the car, pulled into the deep shadow beneath a golden rain tree, Amy chided, "You parked under a rain tree? You've got crap all over your car from the tree droppings now. Worse than sitting under a caged polecat."

She was right. Yellowish green bits covered his black car all over. "I bet your mom wouldn't like you to say *crap*."

"I know. I do my best around her."

Tyree felt like saying worse than *crap* as he tried to brush the sticky yellow stuff off and it only rolled in the dust already coating his Cherokee.

"There." She pointed at the back window of his car. Or actually, at the black hole where the window had been. He didn't need his key to open the door. Swearing fluently but as quietly as possible under his breath to keep from corrupting his accomplice, he stuck his head inside the Cherokee to view—nothing.

He swung in fury to face Amy. "You knew!"

Amy shrugged, absolutely unintimidated. "Guessed. Might as well go on in and get a night's sleep."

He glared at the pixie, his eyes slits. Then he relaxed. "Good advice. See you in the morning." He wheeled and strode his way up the broad white stairs to Ms. Doree's back door. Finding it unlocked, he let himself in. As soon as he reached his room, he turned on the light, moved around here and there, sure Amy must still be down there watching, then extinguished the light. He rolled around on the bed for a few seconds, pulling back the covers, ruffling the sheets. For an instant, his body sank into fatigue like a warm bath, but he didn't allow himself to stay there. He rolled sideways off the bed, crawled to the window, looked down. No sign of Amy. He couldn't even see his car in the darkness, and he noticed the moon cast hardly any shadow. A good night for hunting. A frail sliver of moon slid from behind a cloud, confirming his assessment. He sat down and thought. Hunt with what? He held up his hands. Well-trained weapons. He preferred them to guns anyway. He hadn't lost everything after all.

He let his back rest against the wall under the window. An hour's rest. Sitting up. He didn't trust the soft bed he longed for. One hour. Then go.

The hour passed, he lunged to his feet, did a few limbering stretches, then like a black cat crept down the stairs to let himself out the back door. It still wasn't locked, at which he tsked, until he remembered he was in the land of Kizzy and Amy.

He took the side paths one by one, figuring that with many of the four hundred population tucked cozily up by the hotel, he could scan from house to house for a forty-year-old man without it taking all night. He had a detail he hadn't shared with Amy. The man had a tattoo of a knife etched onto the back of his left hand. A jailhouse tattoo, which meant it was blue and homemade fuzzy, probably nearly invisible after so many years. The point of the knife aimed at the fugitive's left middle finger, recording a knifing he'd done in Juvenile many years ago, his way of refusing a jailhouse romance. A matter of pride for a punk kid, to have killed an enemy and gotten away with it. For no proof had ever pointed to Edgar Fallon except that he'd never shown up in the clinic with a torn-up ass, and then the sudden appearance of the tattoo. Health and a tattoo were proof of nothing in court, although crystal clear evidence inside. And Edgar was left-handed.

Keeping his head down and low, wishing fervently for his monocular night-vision headgear and the Game Finder scope, he made do with his own eyes and crept through the Hollow. At both cabins and houses, going slow, he found that the Hollow residents had an uncommon love for dogs. One cabin even had pigs roaming free. He'd read that pigs were smarter and even more vicious than dogs, and he skirted this place nervously. Finally, the sky lightened and made his stealth ineffective. Not having gotten even close to one cabin, one bedroom window, or one man of the right age, he turned to creep home, then said, "Fuck it," and straightening himself, scuffed like a native directly down the middle of the street.

In his room, he threw himself onto the soft bed and totally disgusted, fell into an intense, dreamless sleep. As the sun moved high enough to enter his window, he woke long enough to remember breakfast, then fell asleep again.

In the early evening he finally came to. His dusty sweat had dirtied the sheets, a detail he knew would anger the formidable Ms. Doree Zendall. He peeled himself off the hot bed and climbed naked into the curvy tub with legs and a shower nozzle like a sunflower. The shower curtain, a daisy-covered film of plastic, glued itself to his thighs as he stood in the hot downflow of water. Washing away his sins, he thought to himself with a snort. His stupidity in thinking all people were the same, all methods would work the same everywhere. He should've farmed out this chore to a fellow skip tracer from a nearby area, one used to country ways.

He put on clean clothes and descended the stairs. Ms. Zendall stood waiting, a stony expression on her flushed face as she watched him descend. He felt like he was approaching doom, not a landlady. He wondered if the glistening coat of sweat on her brow was from the heat or anger at him for missing breakfast.

"I'll pay for—" he started, but she chopped off his words with a jab of a fat hand.

"Ms. Bearclaw is waiting to talk to you. Her and Amy." She wheeled and marched away, her errand fulfilled.

Eyebrows high, Tyree whistled away the ghosts of last

night's failure as he strode easily down the middle of the road again, aimed for the path to the Bearclaw home.

Again seated in the kitchen, Tyree waited. Amy clearly had some things to say. Eyeing him with amusement, Amy asked, "Any luck last night?"

"You know the answer to that."

She tapped her foot on the linoleum floor. "Ready to meet Kizzy now?"

He thought about it. "Whyn't you offer this meeting last night?"

" 'Cause you weren't in any mind to listen to anybody. You knew what you wanted, and what you wanted was no interference. Now. Ready to meet Kizzy?"

He sighed. "Sure."

In minutes he found himself climbing a hill along a path he doubted he'd have found without Amy's guidance. A small, square cabin sat up high, tucked among the treetops and wedged into the hillside. With no knock, Amy opened the screen door and waved him through. The front door was in direct line with a back screen door, and as a result, a slight breeze cooled the small house, and the air felt pleasant to his baked skin. Amy pointed to a scoop-shaped bench of a sofa, padded with patterned Indian blankets, so he sat. The blankets smelled of sweet chamomile.

An old woman of an age he couldn't guess, using a stick to lean on, was ushered into the room by Amy and helped to lower herself into a rocking chair padded so thickly it looked like a catcher's mitt. Her balding head was outlined against the sun coming through the back door, and her hair looked like wiry fuzz in shadow. He stood to be polite, but she patted the air, motioning him to sit down.

"I'm Kizzy, hon. Amy's told me about you and said she told you about me, so that starts us both off square."

Tyree blinked. "Yes, ma'am."

"Amy told you to rest yourself last night; you shoulda taken her advice. But you didn't."

"Ah, no ma'am."

"Wasted yourself, din'tcha, son."

Tyree settled back into the sofa with a sigh.

"I understand your feelings," nodded Kizzy. "Now fill me in about this boy you're after."

Tyree told her all he knew. And this time included the tattoo and the left-handedness.

Amy frowned. "You held back on me."

Tyree shrugged. "Sorry."

Kizzy tapped her stick on the floor twice, turned to Amy, said, "Fetch 'im, hon. Hurry up afore he takes off."

Amy said, "I kept watch on Elroy all night. He's still here, but not much longer."

Kizzy nodded and waved Amy away. "So run, then." Amy darted for the door and was soon out of sight.

"You tellin' me this little girl is going to fetch my perpetrator to me while I sit here?"

"Rather be bit by a pig?"

Tyree shut his mouth, shifted his broad shoulders within his T-shirt.

Kizzy smiled.

DESPITE slamming the flimsy screen door of Barstow's Dry Goods store in her haste, then her boots tromping loudly on the wood slat floor, Amy composed her face in a pleasant, hopefully sociable smile. "How ya doin', Mrs. Barstow?"

Mrs. Barstow nervously fingered a bolt of flowered cotton material still draped across her counter from some earlier customer. "Just fine, Amy. 'N' you?"

"Oh, good, good." Amy lounged against the counter to show her worry-free state.

Mrs. Barstow tugged the material from beneath Amy's forearm. "You're dusty, hon," she said apologetically.

"Your hubby round back like usual?" asked Amy.

Mrs. Barstow firmly eyed the material as she wound it back onto the bolt. "I 'spect. Always doin' the books, don't know why it takes him so long. Why?"

"Got a question for him, ma'am. You mind?"

Mrs. Barstow looked at Amy for a long moment. Then she looked again at the bolt of material and took a deep breath. She shook her head and turned her back on Amy.

Amy pulled reluctantly away from the counter. "Gonna be OK?" she asked.

Mrs. Barstow glanced over her shoulder at Amy, eyes glistening. "Was fine before. Got Wendy now. 'N' the grandbaby's comin' soon. I'll be fine again." Amy squeezed the woman's round arm quickly, then rushed for the back door. Mr. Barstow wasn't there, but the outside door stood ajar, so she pulled it open. Mr. Barstow was in his old brown Buick, slowly edging it backwards, spinning the big steering wheel to back and turn the huge car down the alley towards the road.

Amy just walked over and stood in front of the old car's front bumper. He turned his head to put the gear into forward, then saw her. Mr. Barstow slammed on the brakes. They looked at each other. Amy could see his left hand, high on the steering wheel, illumined in a glare of sun through the windshield. A big scar disfigured the hand. A scar that ended in a point over his middle finger. Amy'd known about the scar for years, never thought a thing about it before. Lots of people have scars. Of all kinds.

Amy pointed. Mr. Barstow, without a word or nod, rolled the car back into its parking place. The backseat was piled with boxes and clothes wadded into bundles. *Not a good packer,* Amy thought. A black, rectangular nylon case poked up through some shirts. Tyree's goods might've pawned into enough to stake a man to a modest new start in life.

When he opened the Buick's door, it creaked. Dust and old age had worn down the hinges. He slowly emerged from behind the wheel. Amy took his right hand in hers. "Kizzy wants to see you."

He nodded.

No Lie

Robert Lee Hall

Robert Lee Hall is a San Francisco native. He has exhibited his paintings in galleries, he has taught art and English, and he has published several historical mystery novels featuring detectives as varied as Dr. John Watson and William Randolph Hearst. Currently he writes the Benjamin Franklin mystery series and is drama and dance critic for a Bay Area newspaper.

RUTH Stark hated lies, but it was not a lie that made her tremble as six P.M. drew near.

Truth. She clenched her fists. Let truth finish the bloody thing.

And blind, stupid fury.

First she had to make sure the gun was ready.

She walked down the hall toward the low teak cabinet. The gun was hidden there; Charlie had tucked it in the right-hand top drawer. Ruth was a small woman with soft brown eyes and shingled hair. She had been impetuous once, loving, giving, but eight years of marriage had stifled those feelings, forcing them to retreat to secret spaces deep inside. How she hated denying herself to make Charlie happy! But her husband's mind always twisted truth into something shameful, dirty.

She sucked a rasping breath. She would give him a truth that would end all that today.

She listened for the sound of the lawn mower. There it was, on time. Good. As its clatter cut the afternoon, she pictured the monotonous green scallops of suburban conformity that made up Valley View. How shocked the town would be when it heard about the murder. But (her fingernails bit her palms) there would be pockets of hope. Behind the curtains of low, ranch-style houses, women would smile in silent glee.

She pictured a particular house, number twenty-three, just across the street, where the mower was cutting the grass: tan stucco, shake shingles, forest green shutters, and in its master bedroom a queen-sized bed where she had cried out in bliss: "My love!"

I'll spend all the time I want in that bed after today, Ruth thought.

She jerked open the top right-hand drawer of the cabinet. Flatware clattered, and moving cloth napkins, she uncovered the gun, just where her husband had hidden it. A faint, cold smell of steel came off it. There were two others: a Smith & Wesson .44 in Charlie's nightstand drawer and an old but well-oiled Browning in the kitchen behind the cereal boxes, but this was his Walther .38. The guns were for burglars. "Just let one of those bastards break in *my* house!" Charlie liked to brag. He practiced at the Green Hill Range every Saturday, waving shredded paper targets in Ruth's face when he got home. "Just gimme a reason to shoot somebody! Just gimme a reason!"

Ruth's mouth flattened. *I'll give you a reason, Charlie, dear.*

She picked up the gun. She hated it, but though Charlie usually kept all three loaded, she had to make sure, so she checked the magazine. A dozen hard, tiny cylinders nestled there. Good. She inserted the magazine, replaced the gun, left the drawer open.

Leaving the hall door open, too, so the cabinet with the gun would be in plain sight, Ruth took the three steps down into the garage.

It was a two-car garage, concrete-floored. Its door was up, letting summer light in from the broad, curving street. The mower clattered louder, and she saw Ben Stillman pushing the machine back and forth over his manicured green grass across the way. So predictable, but predictability was what she counted on. Children yelled in happy play at the Silberts' next door, while a Volvo station wagon purred by carrying three girls in purple soccer shirts. Alice McKean sat at the wheel of the car, and Ruth felt a pang. Lucky Alice! Ruth had always wanted a baby, but Charlie said no.

But could she have planned murder if she had a child?

August's heat pulsed in suffocating waves as she leaned against the big white freezer to steady herself. *I'm thirty-two, still young. I want love.* But she had love; the trick was to keep it, and the memory of tender arms and quickening breath stirred her. *For you, dear, as well as me!* But could she really kill a man?

She girded herself. *I won't have to, the truth will do it for me.*

The mower kept clacking, and she glanced at her watch. Nearly six. In sudden panic, she flung open the freezer and began rearranging icy packages. Charlie was predictable, too, and she wanted to be doing something when her husband got home.

Then he was there. Ruth heard the long white pickup growl up the drive, felt its bulk slide like a dangerously purring animal into the garage behind her. Frantically, she rearranged frozen peas around a leg of lamb. The motor died, and the driver's door creaked. Then she heard a heavy scrape of boots, and bright flashes seemed to explode behind her eyes as she made herself turn. "Hot today, mm?" she got out.

Charlie Stark stood by the truck. He made a face. "You figure that out all by yourself?" Dragging his leather tool belt from the seat, he clattered it on the workbench, then he slammed the door. Ruth jumped at the sound, but she made her eyes stay on him. She tried to smile. Charlie was a short, blunt man, five six, with brush-cut hair on a squarish head. Sweat trickled from his sideburns, and he looked pissed off. *Why do I get all this shit dumped on me?* his bleak eyes whined. That was Charlie for you. Once Ruth had thought she could gentle him, make him happy, when he had courted her, when her Samaritan's heart had made her say yes to his proposal of marriage. But all the midnight calls he had made before they were married hadn't meant he loved her; they had meant he suspected her. *He's the opposite of Ben Stillman,* Ruth thought. *Ben never worries about his wife. Why should he? Who would cheat on Ben Stillman?*

Ben's mower kept whirring while Charlie dragged off his coveralls. He hung them on a hook. A sign on his truck said A-1 Building, and Ruth wanted to laugh. Didn't he know the name was a joke? Charlie's business should have gotten bigger—times were good—but it never went anywhere, so year after year he pounded nails, strung electrical wire, plumbed toilets himself. "Godammit, I'm better than toilets!" he would yell.

His mean look found her. He always blamed her when things went bad, and jamming a hip against the workbench, he folded his beefy arms. "So . . . what'd you do today?" he demanded.

It was the familiar catechism, and Ruth's stomach knotted. He opened cans of paint with a forked tool, working its tines around the rims until the lids popped off, and she felt just like one of those cans. For a second she thought she heard a siren, but the police couldn't be here yet. She pressed against the freezer to keep her knees from buckling. "Well, I talked to the insurance man——" she began.

"Bill Sikorski?" Charlie's eyes narrowed. "He come to the house?"

"No."

"Whatta you mean?"

"I talked to him on the *phone,* Charlie," Ruth pleaded.

Charlie's look said no. It said Bill Sikorski had probably come over and she'd let him screw her. *Did you?* the look asked. He might even check. He might ask the neighbors what they'd seen——though if he did, he'd find out his wife had told the truth. She always told the truth.

And when you learn the real truth, what will you do? Ruth wondered. *Will you kill?*

She licked dry lips. "I did some shopping, too."

"Where?"

"Market Fare."

"You see anybody?"

"Chloe." Ben Stillman's wife. "For coffee."

Charlie's face twisted. "That bitch? What a nothing! Her husband's a piece of shit, too."

Ruth flinched. *Because he's a Jew?* Charlie was always muttering about Jews, but she knew the real reason he hated Ben Stillman: Ben was handsome, successful. Why shouldn't he be successful? He was charming, he could make you believe anything, even that he was faithful.

He was quick, too. People on the block had often seen him make a fool of Charlie when Charlie went off on one of his paranoid rants.

Ruth peered past her husband into the summer day. She wished Chloe Stillman were at her kitchen window so she could wave to her, but she had to check on Ben. There he was, mowing his lawn like he did every Thursday, barechested in tight-fitting shorts. She watched his lean, brown body crisscross under the sycamores, brutally handsome, with thick black hair above lazy eyes that said he knew what any woman wanted. Just mowing the lawn he appeared sexual, predatory, and her lips compressed.

How many women had he lured into that queen-sized bed when Chloe was off selling real estate?

Ruth recalled when she had first met both of them. It had been at that evening swim party at the Conants a year ago, just after the Stillmans moved in. Frogs had cricked in the dusk while she stood with her gin and tonic in the shadows beside Ben's wife. She and Chloe had watched Ben in the lights by the pool. He wore skimpy black Speedos, and other women watched, too. He flexed, dove, cut the water, and Ruth had started. "He's handsome," she had murmured, standing close to Chloe, so close.

Chloe's hand had gripped her arm. "Oh, much worse than handsome," she had replied. "Much, much worse."

Betrayal, Ruth thought in sudden fury. *How good it will be to tell the truth at last!*

She blinked. Charlie wasn't leaning against the workbench anymore. He had seen her watching Ben, but that was just what she wanted, so she was glad to see his I-know-you're-a-slut expression.

He wiped a hand across his mouth. "Like the way Ben Stillman looks, huh?" he snarled.

You deserve anything you get! Ruth thought as she drew herself up. Now was the time. "I'm going to tell you the truth," she gave him back.

Charlie stared. "Wha-at?" She saw his surprise. Fear, too? Where was the wife who always turned herself inside out to deny everything? *Does he know he's about to be hurt?* Ruth wondered, but she hardened herself. He had made her into a whore too many times for pity.

"I've been having an affair," she flung across the space between them.

Charlie flinched. He tried to smile, but his mouth wouldn't work. He turned to stare at the house across the way, turned back. He gaped. "With . . . with . . . ?" He couldn't even say the name, so Ruth just nodded.

In a sudden lurch, Charlie made for her.

Darting sideways, she slipped through the door that led into the house. She halted by the cabinet, by the drawer with the gun. She stood there, trembling. This was where it might not work, where he might shoot her instead. Crashing after her, Charlie stopped so near she could smell him: the sweat, the anguish. Ruth hadn't known it would be so horrible. He was making strangled sounds in his throat, his hands worked wildly at his sides. He needed something to do with those hands—but not beating, that was not like Charlie. He had never hit Ruth. She counted on that.

It was for another man, Ben Stillman, to beat a helpless woman.

Then Charlie had the Walther in his hand. He didn't ask why the drawer was open, he just scooped the gun up. "How . . . how could you?" he sputtered.

Ruth lifted her chin. "I wanted a good lover! I needed love!"

The whole truth at last.

Charlie's eyes shimmered. His lips shrank back, and he began to shake. Beyond the garage door, in the dying afternoon, Ben Stillman's back gleamed with sweat. Charlie still might not do what she wanted, so Ruth fixed her eyes on that powerful back, on the handsome man who owned it. *Look, Charlie, look!* she willed from the bottom of her heart.

He did. He followed her gaze. "I'll kill the bastard!" Whirling, he lurched out of the house. A red Ford Taurus barely missed him as he dashed across the street.

Ruth closed her eyes. She heard the mower stop, heard

Charlie's screaming accusations. "You're crazy!" she heard Ben Stillman yell back before she shut the door. She sank against it. Things were out of her hands; she had done all she could. Now it was up to Charlie. Oh, where was the bang of his gun? She listened, but it did not come. *Don't fail me, Charlie! Shoot the son of a bitch!*

She heard a frantic tapping. Opening her eyes, she saw someone outside the sliding glass door of the kitchen just down the hall. Somehow she got there.

It was Chloe Stillman in a green print dress.

Ruth opened the door, and Chloe slipped in, pale and frightened. "I ran across the street when I heard it start. What's going on, Ruth? Charlie is yelling *crazy* things."

Ruth calmed. Chloe was here. "I told Charlie the truth," she said.

Fear swam up behind Chloe's eyes. "The truth?"

Ruth nodded. "About the affair."

"The . . . affair?"

"I couldn't keep quiet anymore." Through the open kitchen door, Ruth heard Ben Stillman's patronizing laugh, followed by—at last!—the sharp slam of Charlie's gun.

How stupid men were.

But Charlie was a good shot; he would not have missed. Chloe gripped Ruth's arm. "But, why . . . why?"

Because one of us had to end it, Ruth thought. Gently, she stroked Chloe's cheek. The bruise where Ben had punched her last week was fading; with tender hands she would soon soothe Chloe's less visible wounds. "Listen," she said as she heard the sirens coming (some neighbor must have called when the shouting began), "when they take Charlie away for murder—" But screeching tires cut her off. Bull-horn warnings crackled: "Drop the gun!" Then more shots, a rattling fusillade.

Charlie.

Ruth sighed. So he had chosen to have it out with the police. But it was better this way. His misery was over, and though she hadn't planned it, a dead Charlie would make things considerably simpler; she wouldn't have to sit through a trial.

Taking Chloe in her arms, she stroked her hair. "It's out of our hands." She kissed her lover passionately on the lips. "I couldn't let the abuse go on. Yours. Mine. But we're both free now. I didn't lie. Couldn't. I had to tell the truth, and I told it today. I told Charlie I was having an affair." She clasped Chloe near. "I just didn't tell him who I was having it with."

THE STAY-AT-HOME THIEF

Tim Myers

Tim Myers is the author of Berkley Prime Crime's Lighthouse Inn Mystery series, featuring innkeeper Alex Winston and his replica of the Cape Hatteras Lighthouse nestled in the foothills of the Blue Ridge Mountains. Mr. Myers is the award-winning author of over seventy short stories as well, drawing upon personal experience for his contribution to this volume, hastening to add that his research concerned being a stay-at-home dad, and not a thief. To learn more about Mr. Myers and his work, go to **www.timmyers.net**.

I **LOVE** alarm systems, the more sophisticated the better. Well, that's not strictly true. What I really love is getting around them. For me, part of the thrill of stealing is outsmarting the alarm companies and their laughable guarantees to keep people like me out.

As I worked my magic on the Watchdog 2010, a drop of sweat raced down my nose. Even though it was late, the humidity of summer was still thick in the air. I'd have to take Anna swimming tomorrow. I knew if I did, she'd want to invite one of her friends. She liked to do that more and more lately, and I'd been fighting the growing twinges of jealousy.

A light started flashing on the control panel in front of me that should have been dark, the rhythm speeding faster and faster. *Okay, Chuck, focus on the task at hand. What happened?* My mind raced over the schematics I'd pulled off the Internet, struggling to find out how I'd tripped the system. I could almost see the circuitry in my mind as I traced the path in my head.

Moving a few color-coded wires aside, I quickly saw the problem. I'd accidentally nicked one of the wires when I'd clipped in. From the look of it, I didn't have long to fix the problem, or I was about to have an explosion of lights and sirens I couldn't afford. Gently easing the split wire back together, I wrapped the break with a small bit of electrical tape. The light went off just as I did it! Whew, that had been too close.

Driving Anna from my mind, I concentrated on the task at hand.

There would be plenty of time for my daughter tomorrow.

EARLIER that evening, I'd tucked her in, just as I'd done every night for the past seven years. Alone. Jenny had died in childbirth, and I'd buried my wife the day after I brought Anna home. Stealing was all I'd ever known, the only thing I'd ever been good at, and we always managed to get by, just the two of us.

"Do you *have* to go out tonight, Daddy?"

I brushed the long blonde hair out of my daughter's face. "Don't worry, sweetheart, Cindy's just in the other room. I'll be back before you wake up."

"Sing to me again before you go," she said.

I leaned forward and whispered a song. "You're stalling again, you're stalling again, good night my sweet Anna, good night my dear child."

"Come on, Dad, I want a real song."

I laughed as I tucked the covers under her chin. "You'll just have to wait until tomorrow night. Now go to sleep."

SHE was asleep before I got out of her room. Cindy was hitting the books at the dining room table when I walked in. "Chuck, I need to be home by midnight. I've got a huge final tomorrow."

"I'll be back in plenty of time," I said as I started to walk out.

"If I have to sleep on the couch again, I'm going to double my rates," she said with a smile.

"You're a thief, you know that, don't you," I said with a smile.

"Hey, college isn't cheap," she said. "Besides, this is the end of my senior year. I've got bills to pay."

AS I got into my car, I felt the thrill of the hunt rush through me. Stealing wasn't just a profession with me; it was an avocation.

My hands started to sweat as I grabbed the wheel, and it had nothing to do with the summer heat. I always got that way before a score, no matter what time of year it was.

AFTER I coaxed the alarm into submission, I took a deep breath before I headed for the safe. Stolen air smelled somehow better to me, as if I could taste the sweet oxygen around me. There was a richness that couldn't be explained any other way.

THE homeowner should have put less money in the alarm system and more into the type of safe he had. It was a

Claxton 150, one of the first safes I'd learned to crack starting out. In just a little more time than it probably took
him to open it, I was transferring the cash and jewelry
from the heart of it into my fanny pack. I love fanny packs;
they are absolutely perfect for the kinds of things I steal,
tucked close in case I need to get away fast.

It was time to go, but I have one weakness that I can't
seem to break. Creeping into the library, I scanned the
titles, searching for a book small enough to fit into my
pouch. Every house I visit, I take a little token from their
shelves for my own.

As I raced through the titles, something caught my eye.
I pushed the light back, and sure enough, there it was. A
first edition Poe! What was it doing hiding in the stacks
though? I chuckled as I pulled the book down, smelling
the richness of the old leather binding. This particular pur-
loined letter was going home with me.

As I zipped my pack shut, I caught a glimpse of a stuffed
animal, a copy of the original Winnie-the-Pooh used to
illustrate the books. I'd read about the battle between
countries for the original, but I thought Anna might like
it, so I grabbed it, too. No room in my pouch, so I tucked
Pooh under my arm.

That's when the overhead lights came on.

CINDY and I have a nice working relationship, and Anna has
a dream that someday we'll all be together. How do you
explain to your child that even though Cindy appears to
be old enough to her, she's just a child herself to me? I
dated enough, but the women rarely made it to the point
where they got to meet Anna. It was just too hard for her
to say good-bye. A part of me knew my daughter needed
a mother, but I couldn't get serious about anyone. For me,
Jenny was it, and I had just about accepted the fact that I

was one of those odd birds, a swan mated for life whose spouse was gone.

But it was tough telling Anna all that without sounding like a real sap.

HE was holding a revolver right at my heart. Why do these guys always have weapons? Is it some kind of inferiority complex?

"What do you want?" he asked, his hand shaking more than I liked.

"Listen, stay calm. Nobody's going to get hurt." Brave words indeed, since I didn't trust him not to pull the trigger. I never robbed a place armed. In the first place, I hated guns. That's what happens after you've been shot a couple of times. Okay, some people say it's an expected risk from the business I'm in, but even a nick hurts like the devil. Too, armed robbery is a whole different ball game.

His voice shaking, he said, "Who sent you? You can tell Bruno he'll get his share of the money."

Was this guy on drugs? Clearly he was shaken about something, but what? I had nothing to lose, so I decided to play along. "Yeah, well Bruno's not so sure. He wants a little collateral."

"More," the man said, almost crying. "The bastard's got my dog. What else does he want?"

So Bruno was a dogknapper. I didn't even want to know what was going on between them. I hid Pooh's body with my arm. I didn't want this guy to know I'd stolen it. I was kind of embarrassed about it, to be honest.

Then I remembered the book. I started to unzip the bag, and I saw the guy's finger go white on the trigger. "Hold on," I shouted. "You asked me what he was after, and I'm going to show you."

I gently pulled the book out and showed him the Poe.

The relief on his face was obvious. "You don't seem too upset about it," I said.

"It's insured," the guy said, and his finger eased off the trigger. "No big deal. What else do you have in that bag?"

As he asked it, he eased up on the trigger, and the gun moved to one side. We were making real progress now. Funny thing, though. As he lowered the gun, I could see the safety was still on. Believe me, all it takes are a couple of hits to learn when another one might be coming.

I jammed the book back into my pouch and headed for the door.

Was I right, though? Could the safety have been off after all? I braced myself for an explosion as I hurried off, but thankfully, none came.

"Bruno isn't going to like this," I said as I took off into the night.

I was almost to my car when the alarm went off. At least he'd given me time to get away. But boy, he and Bruno were going to be at a whole new level of pissed when they found out what I'd done. Not that it mattered to me. I'd be out of their lives forever.

CINDY was asleep on the couch when I got home. I thought about waking her, but I really didn't mind the double time, not with the score I'd just made. She *was* pretty, especially when she slept, but she was still just a kid, nearly ten years younger than me. I covered her with a blanket, looked in on Anna and tucked Pooh in beside her, then stuffed my bag in a better safe than that of the guy I'd just robbed, before I went to bed.

"COME on, Dad, wake up." I looked up blearily to find Anna at the foot of my bed. She had Pooh in one hand.

As I rubbed the sleep out of my eyes, I said, "Morning, sunshine. You like your present?"

She threw Pooh on the bed. "Please, Dad, I outgrew Pooh ages ago. He can sleep with you if you want."

I pulled on a robe as I said, "We're both offended."

Cindy popped in the door. "Are you decent?" she called.

"Come on in," I said.

"It's double time again, Chuck," she said with a smile. Then her eyes caught Pooh. "How precious," she squealed. That alone told me Cindy was way too young for me.

"Miss Anna doesn't like him. Why don't you consider him a bonus?"

"I'd love to have him," she said as I got my wallet and paid her. Still clutching Pooh, Cindy said, "Would you like me to drop Anna off at school? It's not a problem; it's on my way."

"No thanks. Good luck on your final."

She grinned. "I'm going to ace it. After all, I've got my good luck bear now."

After Cindy was gone, Anna asked, "So, did you like your note?"

I asked, "What note?"

"The one I tucked in your pocket last night. I was pretty sly, wasn't I?"

I grabbed for my pants, but there wasn't any note there. "Which pocket did you put it in, sweetheart?"

"The one on your shirt," she said. "You couldn't tell?"

"No, babe, you fooled me." I grabbed my shirt with relief, but it was quickly gone. There was no note there, either.

I had a sinking feeling I knew exactly where the note was.

"Honey, I lost it. Can you tell me what it said? Exactly word-for-word?"

I tried to keep the creeping fear out of my voice as I

asked. I hadn't touched it, so there couldn't be fingerprints, at least not any the cops could trace. So that left the words.

She thought a minute, then said, "It said, 'Dad, I love you. Kiss me good night.' You didn't, did you?"

I kissed her again. "I didn't need a note to remind me. I kissed you anyway." There was no way I could be traced back to it.

I glanced at the alarm clock. "You need to get ready for school."

"Come on, Dad, let me play hooky. School's almost over."

I said, "You have a test today, young lady. Now scoot. I'll be ready in a minute to drive you."

I grabbed a quick cup of coffee from the auto-set coffeepot and managed to get Anna to school two minutes before the bell rang.

As I drove back home, the flutterings came back in the pit of my stomach. Stealing was one of the best parts, but I loved going through my take the next day nearly as much.

I opened the door and walked in. A thug was standing just inside, and I noted quickly that he had no confusion about the safety at all.

So Bruno had managed to track me down after all.

I HELD up my hands. "Can I help you?" I said as calmly as I could. "I don't have much, but you're welcome to what I've got."

The thug said, "Cute, real cute. Give it to me, smart guy."

I said, "I take it you are Bruno."

"Who I am isn't all that important. Just grab the stuff you took from Jenkins, and we'll be done here."

"I don't suppose playing dumb is going to work, is it?"

He held up a piece of paper and said, "It was mighty nice of you to leave a calling card behind."

With a sinking feeling in the pit of my stomach, I saw that Anna had used my stationery to write me the note. A woman I'd been dating around Christmas one year had thought it was cute to give me fancy stationery. The only problem was that it had my name and address at the top of it. I'd given it to Anna to draw on.

"Okay, it's all in the other room."

We went to my safe in the floor, and I started to work the combination. Bruno crept up beside me and said, "Not so fast. You have a gun in there, you're never going to get it out in time."

It took me twice to open my own safe, but in my defense, there *was* a gun jammed in the back of my neck. I was still embarrassed about it, professional standards and all.

I carefully handed Bruno the swag I'd worked so hard for. He didn't even care about the book, tossing it aside onto the bed. As the money floated down beside it and the jewelry landed in a noisy clunk, Bruno said, "Very funny. Now where is it?"

Now I was the one in shock. "It's all there, everything I took last night."

The gun jammed harder into my skin. "You'd better be lying. Jenkins told me you had it."

"I'm not in the habit of lying to men with guns in their hands. Jenkins is trying to double-cross you."

"Listen, I've had enough of this, Charles. Give me the bear."

"You want Pooh?" I said incredulously.

"That's where the diamonds are," Bruno said. "I already wrecked your kid's room, and it wasn't there. Are we going to have to go to school for show-and-tell?"

My daughter had never been a part of what I did. She

only knew that her old man slipped out at night now and then. And now this thug wanted to go to her school.

"She doesn't have it," I said earnestly.

"Charles, you've just told your last lie."

Not by a long shot. "I didn't grab Pooh for her. I gave it to my girlfriend."

"You're a busy guy, Charles."

"It's Chuck," I said, annoyed by him using my real name.

"So where is this mysterious girlfriend?"

"She lives off campus; she's in college. I can take you to her."

"Like 'em young, do you? Let's go."

I grabbed for the telephone first. "I'd better call ahead."

Bruno knocked the telephone out of my hand. "I don't think so. Let's surprise her."

I just prayed that Cindy and her roommates would be gone. The faster I got Bruno off my back, the better the chances for my survival.

JUST my luck. Cindy was still there.

"Chuck, what's going on?" She eyed Bruno suspiciously as he stood behind me.

"Anna changed her mind. She'd like Pooh after all."

"Ask us in," Bruno said.

Cindy didn't catch the menace in his voice. She couldn't have, not by the way she blew him off.

"In your dreams," she said. "Taffy's not dressed. Hang on a second, I'll go get Pooh."

As we stood in the hallway, Bruno said, "I don't like this, Charles."

"It's Chuck," I said again automatically.

"It's going to be 'dead' if she doesn't bring me that bear."

Less than a minute later, Cindy came to the door carrying Pooh. "Sorry, I got a phone call. Here's the bear."

I reached for it, but Bruno grabbed Pooh before I could. "Thanks," he said.

"Everything all right, Chuck?" Cindy asked.

"Yeah, it'll be fine. Sorry about this."

"Not a problem," she said.

As soon as the door closed, Bruno tore Pooh's head off. "The diamonds aren't here," he snarled.

"Then Jenkins ripped you off, and he's blaming me. I grabbed the bear for my kid. When she didn't want it, I gave it to Cindy."

Bruno scowled a second, then said, "I thought this whole bear thing was a load of crap. I'm going to kill Jenkins."

"I don't blame you a bit," I said. "I'd go after him, too."

"Not so fast. I just can't—"

"What am I going to do, call the cops? He's the one you want."

Bruno nodded. "Yeah, you're right." He grinned. "Tell you what. Why don't you keep all that other crap you stole from him? The mook deserves it."

"Thanks, Bruno," I said as sincerely as I could.

He started down the stairs, Pooh's body in one hand and his head in the other.

As soon as he was gone, Cindy opened the door and pulled me inside.

"That was close," she said. "I thought you'd had it."

"You heard what happened?" My cover was blown. There was no way Cindy would keep baby-sitting for me after finding out I was a thief. Anna was going to kill me.

"Chuck, the walls are so thin around here you can hear yourself think."

"Listen, I'm sorry about all this," I tried to explain as she put a finger to my lips.

"You don't have to apologize. I just have one question for you. How are we going to fence these?"

Then she showed me a handful of glittering stones. "That's what took me so long. I knew something was wrong, and it only took a second to find the diamonds sewn in Pooh's head. I had a devil of a time finding a needle and thread to sew him back up, though."

"So you don't mind what I do?" I said, staring unbelieving at the diamonds.

"Mind? I've been trying to tell you for the past year. I'd like to join you. What do you say, partner?"

"I'd say you've got yourself a deal, my friend."

Then she slid into my arms, and it felt like the most natural thing in the world. "That's another thing I've been meaning to talk to you about."

After we kissed, I almost forgot about the diamonds still clutched in her hand.

Almost.

WAR CRIMES

G. Miki Hayden

A member and board member of Mystery Writers of America, G. Miki Hayden has had a steady stream of short mystery fiction in print. Miki's novel, *Pacific Empire*, lauded by the *New York Times*, was well received by readers, as was her psychiatric mystery, *By Reason of Insanity*. Miki, the author of *Writing the Mystery: A Start-to-Finish Guide for Both Novice and Professional*, a Writers Digest Book Club selection, is the immediate past president of the Short Mystery Fiction Society, which presents the yearly Derringer Awards. She teaches, coaches, and book doctors from her home in Manhattan.

———

"**Do** you have a case that you consider most memorable, Your Honor?" the young man asked benignly, with a smile.

On the occasion of my retirement after forty years on the bench, the boy was interviewing me for the following Sunday morning's *Herald*. The photographer was gone, but the cakes and coffee that my wife Madelyn had put out still sat on the glass-topped trolley in my den. I inclined my head toward the gleaming silver serving pot and gestured to refill the reporter's cup.

"No, sir, thank you," he declined agreeably, covering gold rim on bone china with his hand.

I smiled in turn, considering the boy—he was a boy to me—substantially naive. Twenty-five years as a criminal

court judge even in this rural county of Indiana still had
before me innumerable and inutterable instances of man
killing man; cold-blooded and brutal sexual violation; felonious, self-centered disregard for the welfare of others—a
virtual devil's litany of ill intent and rabid villainy. Most
could not be wiped away from mind, remaining forever a
stain on my memory.

But I related the story I told on social occasions to someone curious about what a judge faced—a rather nice story,
too, embellished only slightly over all these years. I
sketched in the anecdote of a youngster caught with a car
stolen for a joyride. Then I recounted the leniency I had
shown the offender, with a sentence of 100 hours of community service and repayment to the victim for damages
done.

"And was it worth it, Judge? Did that turn out to be
the right thing to do?" Having prompted me to the recital
of my coda, the journalist, at last, poured himself a little
more coffee from the pot and sipped at it, his tape revolving in the recorder, working in his stead. The young knew
so little and these days seemed to *do* so little, too.

But I was old now and severe. When his age, I had been
more ignorant and bullheaded than any of these boys in
the present, without a doubt.

"Oh yes, well worth it," I remarked, settling back. "The
car thief was Frank Johnson. And he tells that story on
himself to remind others of the road he could have taken
and was saved from."

"Johnson Chevrolet—the dealership," the reporter observed, his eyebrows rising, glad, no doubt, for some spice
to sprinkle in his pro forma article.

I nodded in an agreement of delight. The tale was an
easy one to tell. So little pain remained. Everyone had recovered from the incident almost as quickly as it had oc-

curred, a happy conclusion. As for the fraud accusations against Frank two years ago for the sale of used cars as new, those charges had been worked out quietly between his attorney, the prosecutor, and a passel of civil litigants.

Madelyn entered to take away her lovely service and as a prompt to the boy that he should leave, that the judge's time was valuable.

And so it was. I got in my car afterward and drove to the new putting green past Slocum's farm, to put in an hour of preparation for retirement.

It's funny how you can think better sometimes when in motion, and while hitting those balls with my new stainless steel putting iron, I contemplated the most memorable case I'd really ever been involved with. But that, of course, had been long before I'd gone in for the law, had been a real-life prosecutor, and had consequently been elected to hear the trials and tribulations that poured forth endlessly from Baxter County. The circumstance I meditated on, as I often did, was something that had happened during the war while I was a prisoner of the Japanese, held under unimaginable conditions among a pack of wretched, starving, disease-ridden soldiers deserted by their country on the Philippine island of Panay.

Someone had kept a calendar. God, now I don't recall the man's name—but his face, surely. A young face, an unwashed, oily, sweat-streaked, miserably thin face, missing a couple of teeth on the bottom of his jaw, teeth that had been loosened by malnutrition and then knocked out by a rifle butt. I honestly could not now remember if he—whatever that soldier's name was—had survived the war. So many, many had not made it through. Twenty-five percent of the POWs held in the Pacific Theater had died by the time MacArthur and the others returned for us, as had 5 percent of those in the Nazi and Italian Fascist camps. But, of course, we didn't know all that until much later.

I'd had a good disposition in those days and even the extreme deprivation during the first six months at Camp Mabuchi didn't entirely knock the stuffing out of me. I had been an idealist when I'd gone to war, and I still was at that point, a clean boy, a Christian from the Midwest, trained up to all the virtues a mother wanted to stuff into her son and that he would, despite stubbornness, allow.

For some reason, then, while I still had my belief in divine-given justice, I befriended Buster after he was brought from the caves up in the hills. Anyone, though, with the slimmest of instincts for doing "right" would have chosen Buster as an object of good works.

The boy had been blinded in both eyes by shrapnel from a tossed grenade and had lain in the caverns, dying, when one of the Filipino natives found him and brought some food, water, and bandages. But those caught harboring an American soldier would have been shot—or tortured and shot, a more likely outcome. Therefore Buster had been left, eventually, to his fate, and his fate had been to be "arrested."

The minute I saw him, I took Buster under my wing for pity's sake. And the moment I heard his Arkansas accent, I felt gratified that I had made him my charitable pick. Here was a young man my own age—we were teenagers, eighteen years old in fact—to whom I could play the guide (literal and physical) and mentor. He was greener than even the green boy I myself was and though not younger than I, he was more rural, which made me somehow the elder. I led him where he needed to go, protected him from the bullies who would steal the blind boy's food, and gave him small portions of my own gruel when I felt less desperate.

The men in Camp Mabuchi were a mixed bunch, from not only various services of the armed forces, but nationals enlisted under different flags. In our hut, suited to fourteen but which held about twenty-three, we were mostly Americans with a few Brits attached to a captured American unit.

Supremely patriotic though I was in those days, I was pleased with the British lieutenant in our midst, thinking that he brought a touch of class to a classless assembly of privates and our one noncom, Corporal Webb. In addition to having a crisp, exotic accent that spoke to a little country boy like me of royalty and lineage, Lieutenant Hightower was what they called in England a solicitor. He was a lawyer, and although before the war I'd thought to be a doctor like my father, hanging around in the vicinity of Hightower made me think of the law as a possible profession.

While we marched off in our rags each morning to build an airfield for the Japanese, Hightower would talk about Blackstone and the concepts on which English, and thus American, law was founded. I forgot the hunger that perpetually knotted my gut as hard as hickories. I admired the man. He set a good tone for the hut, I felt—would inspire us to survival if anyone could—and I tried to emulate his actions and maintain his example of cleanliness and civility. In short, I was a boy seeking a model to base myself on. I had not yet formed a center of my own, and the normal development I would have gone through was thwarted by our situation.

Anyone who has been in that small section of the world—a few square miles of land somewhere between the Philippine and Sulu Seas—will understand that, even had all treatment of us been reasonable, conditions were not comfortable for the average person from the West. During the day, the sun blazed intently, the sand fleas bit, and those on labor detail often dropped in their tracks and simply died. The nights were sultry and malarial. Not a breeze stirred inside the hut, and those who sat outside in the humid but at least occasionally moving air risked a capricious beating from a passing guard.

Still, reasons existed to hazard sitting out alongside the building. The latrine, a trench dug behind the hut two barracks down, was closer—a necessity for those weak with stomach cramps and diarrhea. This was the spot also to access gossip exchanged from hut to hut.

From here, too, one could sometimes sneak to the barbed wire fence and pass out what of one's treasures had not been stolen by the Japs—a ring, a watch, an extra shirt—in exchange for a blessed bit of food—a chicken, an egg, a few root vegetables—handed in by some courageous Filipino. Courageous because those caught were beheaded on the spot and because many did it solely out of sympathy for the prisoners, coming with their gifts long after we had not a single shred left to deliver in recompense. That is so much the truth that I sometimes still cry over the men who befriended us, much oftener than I shed bitter tears due to the traitorous withdrawal of MacArthur and the top brass. Or over the mindlessly brutal men who imprisoned us.

That night, I tucked Buster into his spot on the loose-dirt floor and paused in concern. The boy had a terribly bad fever again. But bringing Buster to the infirmary to get him out of work the next day would guarantee an early and pain-racked death. The report down the line was that injections given to the ill were of substances not meant to go into the human bloodstream.

Not all the Japanese there were exactly evil. How can I explain? They behaved in a manner we could never have imagined, but many did so in fear of their superiors and because, while Buster and I were ignorant country boys, these soldiers were peasants with many times less learning then we. The background of some of our guards made them rough but made them vulnerable as well to the occasional decent act. One in particular I called Herman, because his name began with an *H* and I couldn't begin to repeat how it was pronounced. Inexplicably, he took a liking to me, showed me a photo of an old farm couple in their Sunday best, while I shared a glimpse of my dad in his three-piece suit and pocket watch, my lovely mother with a set of genuine pearls around her neck, and my bright-eyed, ten-year-old brother John. After that, Herman would sometimes bring me a few grains of rice rolled together so not a grain would be lost. And yet I knew the guards themselves got little to eat, supplies not being plentiful for the Japanese forces.

Saying good night to Buster then, I wavered. My friend wasn't likely to live until morning, but if he could, he might recover and live on. I sat back down and fetched the last two bites of a rice ball out of my pocket. "I'll sit you up so you can eat this," I suggested. I had weighed the possibility of my survival against the improbability of his; yet here I was again, sharing what I so sorely needed myself.

Buster shook his head, too fatigued to rise and probably too weak to swallow. I placed the remaining rice down on that photo of my family and showed his fingers where it was. "Try to eat," I urged him and, staring at the small portion of dirty rice, I swallowed in restored appetite. "I'll come back in a while."

I left the fetid chamber to sit with the lieutenant and his men outside the hut. We watched the shadow of a buddy patrol pass in the moonlight and then were free to whisper among ourselves. Or rather, I listened to stories of England, a place as exotic to me as the Philippines were. I, too, longed for the countryside of Cornwall, the lanes of Yorkshire—anyplace where a man could have a shower and shave and change one shirt in for another, cleaner one.

Maybe that night my turn had come to stick my neck

out by the wire fence and see if any of our Filipino bene-
factors had made it through. Perhaps that night I lay flat
against the ground for half an hour or more, sitting up
every few minutes to make a soft bird call to no response.
At such times I imagined the whole world dead, the native
villages mowed down with machine gun fire. Tokyo burning with more Doolittle raids. Indiana itself with Mitsub-
ishi bombers overhead, dropping their loads. The only
living reminders of our species were here, in this place, and
slowly giving up our life force ourselves.

Back in the hut, I checked on Buster. The rice was gone,
and I pocketed my photo and smiled. The sacrifice had
been worthwhile. He had eaten. If man was dead, God still
reigned.

My friend woke slightly, his fingers fluttering as if to
pat the food, now gone. My face lit up. "You ate it, Buster,
ate the rice," I whispered assuredly.

He came to consciousness more fully now and shook his
head slightly. "No," he denied. "I didn't have it."

To say I was stunned at that pronouncement would be
to put the matter mildly. If you informed me today that
my retirement savings had all been embezzled, that our
two-story Tudor was sold for back taxes, and that our lake-
side home had gone at auction, I would not be more
astonished and enraged than by those few words telling
me that what I'd surrendered for the sake of another had
been plundered. A terrible wrath was ignited within me,
and plenty of fodder would keep this fire burning. I was a
youth turned ancient by war and by betrayal. Until that
moment, I had perhaps not known just how angry I was.
My head and nerves smoldered, and sweat poured off my
brow in the confinement of the prison camp, the constraint
of the hut, the bonds of my overwhelming emotions. Helpless tears streamed down my face. I soothed Buster's fore-

head, and he fell back to a fitful sleep. Then I sought out Hightower and wet his bent ear with my story.

I couldn't sleep, but that, I suppose, was just as well. Buster needed my murmured words of comfort through the night, up until the hour when he looked me clear in the eyes, seeing something, someone else, and died. And then I sat watch over his corpse, divided between prayer and my refusal to pray, just as God had cruelly declined to give the body next to me a mouthful of succor his last night on earth.

The following day during our work detail at the airfield, Hightower and a few of us puzzled over these events while we cleared the ground, picking up stones and loading them into baskets woven from fronds to carry away. I was too worn out to grieve over Buster's passing but not too tired to grunt in recognition when Tom King's name came up.

In withdrawing from the Philippines, MacArthur had left behind 56,000 men under his command but had taken with him (aside from General Wainwright) as many of the officers who could be evacuated. The remaining American army was virtually leaderless. Men like King who had been forced to obey by threat of their superiors' actions came into their own in the POW camps. Their depraved agenda was twofold: to collaborate with our captors, the Imperial Army, and to get whatever they could for themselves, no matter the cost to other Americans. King, if not the first type, was at least the second.

My instincts told me that King was the only one among us who would have had the lack of scruples to steal a morsel from a dying man. "I'll kill him," I muttered, and I meant that; indeed, I intended to.

Fights break out at the slightest insult when soldiers are starving and their minds no longer function as they should. I was at the point at which emotions and lack of judgment met, capable of doing anything that occurred to my swollen, hungry brain.

Hightower calmed me and coaxed me to continue with clearing the land. I went down on my knees in the dirt and dust, searching for pebbles. A great sobbing arose from my rib-thin chest as I worked, and the men circling around me, busy with their chores, began to sing "The White Cliffs of Dover" to drown my cries. In a while, too fatigued to continue, I gathered myself and went quiet as if all were well. I still had in mind to kill King though—in any way I could and at any cost to me. Any.

When night began to fall and we marched back to the camp, my eyes scanned the lines of men for King. I expected to see a look of satisfaction on his face, I suppose, and his belly bulging with his theft—the murderous robbery of two bites of rice, the outer grains gray from several filthy hands, that food intended to save Buster's fragile life. And, before long, I spotted King, but he was somber, like one who had spent his day working in the broiling sun, head bent like all the other heads beside him, those who still lived at the end of just another day.

I churned with passion, spooning the gruel into myself in front of the hut. Automatically, I stopped eating three-quarters through that meager meal, setting aside the last portion in my mind for Buster. But Buster wasn't there, and after a second, I swallowed down the rest, feeling as bloated as if I had stolen that last meal from Buster myself.

Later, we rested outside as long as we were generally allowed, talking and catching up on the day's gossip. One of the Filipinos had brought news of fighting at Guadalcanal, the battle reported on the illegal radio as indecisive. Not having any maps, we speculated wildly as to where Guadalcanal was located, the optimistic putting it at the door of the Philippines, the pessimistic assuring us that Guadalcanal was one of the islands closer to Hawaii. Even the educated men among us didn't know much about the geography of the Pacific. Any maps we had owned had been taken from us as dangerous tools of insurrection.

In the end, a few fell back to contemplating the mystery of the theft of the rice and Buster's death. The arguments ranged from whether the one could be attributed to the other, to who had done the murderous deed. The name King was mentioned by several on that occasion, again. Most of the men plainly disliked him, having been taken advantage of in a trade or by a suspected theft, one time or another.

Corporal Webb, the leader of the American contingent at that end of the camp, a slow-speaking and reserved fellow of somewhere in his thirties (or sixty-something, if you went by his looks after eight months in Mabuchi), was the only one to counter the general accusations against King. Seeming uneasy at the degree to which the men were stirred up, Webb suggested in a word or two that "just as likely" a rat had made off with the bits of rice. This led to a controversy so strenuous that we had to shush ourselves at several points, seeing the guards staring in our direction.

I got up and went inside, realizing when I got there that I really hadn't any task at hand. Other nights I might have taken Buster to the latrine, then tried to make him comfortable on the floor with a rolled-up pair of pants for a pillow. Tonight, I sat in silence and stewed, listening to the hushed conversations around me. Men talked more about food than they did about women here. Food at least seemed somehow possible—though it wasn't.

A little while later, Hightower came in. Despite the inside of the hut being dark already, I could tell it was he by the shape etched in the doorway against the moonlight. Knowing where I was, he came and sank down and from time to time I could make out his features when he turned and his eyes glistened in my direction.

"What is it?" I asked. I could feel a strangeness in his presence, and that he had something to say that would be momentous.

He shook his head, staying quiet until I asked again.

"I hate to tell you, old boy, but you'll hear the news sooner or later." He still shook his head in the negative, and I supposed his information was something bad, very bad, that he had just heard we had been beaten at Guadalcanal, too.

The whisper came so low I had to strain at first to hear him, though Hightower wasn't one to shirk from a duty.

"They used his body for bayonet practice, the bloody swine."

I tried to register what he had said and make sense of the words. First, I had to realize the news had nothing to do with the fight in the Solomon Islands. Second, I had to understand that the body he referred to was my dead charge, Buster.

I gripped Hightower's arm, that's all, just grabbed and hung on, all the feelings that remained in any part of me channeling through the strength of my fingers. I hadn't anticipated this dimension of the nightmare we were caught in. Most of the time those generally sick enough or stupid enough to remain in camp during the day attended to tasks such as burying the dead. Abuse of Buster's lifeless form was beyond my wildest imaginings.

"Hang on, old boy," Hightower counseled. His hand went on top of the fingers that pinched at him. I relaxed the hold I had on his weak flesh and, worn out, lay back on the pile formed by my only set of clothes. Although I recollect that Hightower spoke to me again, I didn't rise until the morning.

The next day when we lined up for our march to the airfield, I revealed to Hightower my intention to kill King. I was resolute, determined, and unshakable, and Hightower cast worried glances in my direction throughout the morning. Meanwhile, our hands tugged recalcitrant rocks from the mud into which an overnight rain had turned the surface of the land.

Sometimes I still dream about that undistinguished landscape: the palm trees along the far perimeter, fronds shredded by mortar shells; a lifeless sandy soil, littered with rocks and remnants of the ocean floor. I can only recall that vista as brown, the smell a salt tang with an occasional waft of the odor of carrion. I had always been there, before I had arrived. And, thereafter, I had never left.

That afternoon, Hightower began to talk up a new idea of his with great ebullience. His sense of the matter was that King should be placed on trial for theft and the murder of Buster. I could prosecute. Corporal Webb would defend, and Hightower would judge. He'd make sure that the absolute strictest courtroom protocol was applied. His enthusiasm for this business was palpable, and the others discussed how we could enforce our will over the whole camp. Hightower made it his job to petition the ranking officer in camp, an American lieutenant—Logan—to hold the hearing. I didn't say anything, thinking it over, but at last gave in.

Hightower was right, as usual, I decided. He was a man of principle, and a fair hearing was an honorable act. Although I was still eager to be King's executioner—almost madly zealous toward that end—I managed to rein in the power of my insane rage. I could wait a few days until King's sentence was declared. The virtue of my position made me feel strong.

Hightower and I went to Logan with our request and were turned down. Logan told us he had "no authority to empower a kangaroo court." He said that anyone violating the ordinary laws of human conduct and military law would be subject to a court-martial at the end of the war, including anyone carrying out an illegal trial of an enlisted man.

I have to admit that I was shocked by his response. I was so swayed by Hightower's reasoning in proposing the prosecution that I was confident we would be given the go-ahead by Logan. Still, in my eyes, the theft of the rice was tantamount to murder, and I was absolutely positive that the thief was King.

The logic underlying my certainty was the single missing ingredient. Although I wasn't ill, exactly, the stress and deprivation we were subject to produced strange results in all our thinking. But I don't use this fact in my defense. I have never encouraged this type of argument in my courtroom, and I won't excuse myself from full responsibility in this instance, either. I suppose, in terms of alleviating my ego—lest anyone aside from myself think me a downright idiot—I would merely provide this information as a footnote. If anyone cared.

The question I would ask myself, now, that I didn't ask then, is a simple one: How did King know that I had put down some rice for Buster that night? King wasn't even living in our hut. My illogic stands out to me today in gigantic proportions, yet no one even suggested this brief rebuttal to me at the time. We were all carried along by the idea that King was guilty. The trial was to be fair, and being fair, would prove his culpability.

The probable explanation for the missing rice, I now see, was exactly as Corporal Webb laid out: A rat had darted in and carried it away. Or, sometimes I am able to persuade myself that Buster did, after all, consume the mouthful of nourishment, that in his fog, he then forgot. But while eating those few grains of food, he had experienced a surge of hope. I imagine his feeling of optimism at that moment and the picture of home that formed in his mind. Certainly he would live to see Arkansas again.

I never understood at the time that I was compensating for my sense of guilt in letting Buster die. I had made myself responsible for him, and he was dead. Worse still was the fact that I myself remained alive and reasonably functional, never mind a few loose teeth, stiffness of joints, or an occasional bout of parasitic infestation.

While I plotted King's murder, saving sharp-edged rocks from the field in my shirt, word got out quickly enough that several of us planned to place King on trial. As he was disliked, our dead-end idea was generally supported. Moreover, while concocting various schemes for how I would kill King—and, in some of the scenarios, get away with it—every time I saw the man, I conveyed my intentions through my eyes. King, despite his reputation as a happy-go-lucky type even under our conditions of imprisonment, could not remain oblivious of the rumors or my hard, cold stares. I was in such a manic state, in fact, that I was transformed from a generally likable, wholesome Midwesterner into a persona that my own mother would not recognize. My intractable *idée fixe* that King had to die gave me the first hint I'd ever had in my life that my personality had a power to it (a power that I later realized needed to be curbed).

I could tell that King was aware of what I had in mind. His reaction to me was an increasingly nervous one, despite the fact that I was stick thin while he had the muscle tone of a man who daily ate a normal calorie intake. He continued to try to appear self-confident, but I watched his eyes. The expression in them became wary soon enough. Then wariness turned quite quickly into fear.

In the meantime, Hightower both distanced himself from me and tried to talk some sense into that thick head of mine. We had heard about the Americans winning control of Guadalcanal, and broadcasts were beamed at the Filipinos in their own language, encouraging them to believe that MacArthur would, without fail, return. Of course this promise was quite a bit premature, but Hightower assured me that we wouldn't remain in the camp too long and that King would reap his just reward after our release. Hightower begged me not to place myself in a position of jeopardy.

In all those weeks, one might imagine that I would take definitive steps toward such a well-defined objective. Yet I didn't. I continued to dither as to how to accomplish my goal. I discarded the idea of the rocks and hid them under the hut. I had no other weapon, no poison, no means to carry out my intent—other than my clear physical inferiority. If I attacked King, not only could he defend himself without a great deal of effort, but others would plainly intervene, even disliking him as they did. Any fuss would draw the attention of the Japanese guards, and any focus on the prisoners was not to the good.

I was frustrated all right, but I hadn't given up. I began to sneak into King's barrack during meals to leave threatening notes. I went out of my way to pass behind him on the walk to the latrine or as we lined up in the morning. "You're dead meat," I whispered. Or, "Remember Buster." I did my utmost to master the art of psychological terror. I dreamed of enlisting others in the warfare, although by then, I had no real confederates. Maybe I didn't even notice.

But I was a fool in every respect. In my mind, things would continue on the way they were. King would grow thin, like the rest of us, but with anxiety. He, as the rest of us—one by one—would sicken and die. Just as I saw so clearly the guilt for Buster's death as being King's, so, too, I viewed this little scene in my head as being played out in actuality, without room for any other possible outcome.

We were building an airfield, yet even a boy such as

myself, unused to the construction trades, knew full well that the job required more than a mere few hundred hands. We had labored magnificently as far as we could. The ground in front of us was free of obstruction and knocked perfectly flat. Nonetheless, the earth was friable, subject to both the monsoons and the nonrain periods during which the land dried up under the flaming tropical sun. So either the field would wash away in days or blow away as soon as it returned to sand. Packing the soil down with a steamroller might help, but the obvious solution was to cover the level surface with macadam, creating a tarmac.

But that was the American way. We had supplies. We had suppliers. The Japanese had suffered since before the war under blockades against the import of raw materials; the war had only increased consumption but not their available resources. So we had built an airstrip on this island except for the most important ingredient. Panay was not a priority in terms of paving. Luzon, the island of the capital, Manila, might have been. The efforts of our group would not pay off.

We were glad, of course, that all our work had come to nothing. The Japs would not benefit from our slave labor. At the same time, men prefer to perform meaningful work, and we muttered among ourselves about the stupidity of the waste. But the Japanese, though cruel, had some ingenuity, and work groups were taken up a little way into the hills to the line of pine forests where, oddly, we were shown how to insert spigots to collect tree sap. Naturally, we surreptitiously experimented with the taste, but this was not for our nourishment. One of the boys from North Carolina explained that we were going to make tar—something his home state was quite famous for and the reason they called the population there Tarheels.

At any rate, soon after that, the camp commander, Captain Ichioka, began his scorched earth policy. The airfield finally denuded of every hard pebble, our work was now to render the entire island free of any growing thing other than the pines. I exaggerate, but not overly. First we knocked down the palms, then worked our way to higher elevations and softer woods, logging skill-lessly as we went. We hacked the hapless trees down with much burning of calories, a matter that concerned us, and wrecking of Imperial-issue bayonets, which did not.

As nonproductive as this work was—we thought—by the end of a week or two, our band of around 249 men had dragged a pile of rubble to the near edge of our previously neat and tidy landing spot for bombers and their Zero escorts. We learned through the grapevine that we were in the process of creating coal, an appropriate thickener and stabilizer for the boiled sap, a bituminous binder.

All the while during this new period of greatly efforted destruction, my own personal campaign had not been ignored. I had sent the word out to everyone I met that I was going to get King, that the trial was still on, that he would be convicted and executed without mercy. I continued to go out of my way to harass the man, and others began to pester or shun him. I enjoyed the process. In a world in which a boy is rendered impotent by circumstance, the finding of one means of having an effect is a heady brew. I had no awareness that the illusion of control was what I sought or that anything I might have done was morally objectionable. King had killed Buster, and he was my enemy.

One relatively dry and unbearably sizzling morning, under the watchful and curious eyes of our guards, we started a bonfire, which soon raged in a wild hunger to consume our work of many hours, many days. We had actually amassed quite a bundle of trees of various sorts, and the smoke that arose from the conflagration was thick and choking. Why we had stood in such proximity to the pyre is another mystery of fate.

Eyes tearing, guards and soldiers alike, we coughed our way back away from the monster we had evoked. My eyes were so stung by the smoke that I didn't even see the event—more or less the culmination of my crusade.

King, no doubt driven to some far reach of desperation by my attacks, chose this seemingly opportune moment to make an escape. Where he thought he would go (up through the pines?) or how he intended to turn the Filipinos to his own use, I have no idea. His move was a stupid one, and he might have tried regardless of my pitiful daily annoyances, but I'm not convinced. I have remained more or less certain that I was the cause behind his trying to run . . . and the reason my Japanese friend Herman dutifully shot King in the back.

At the sound of the rifle crack, my eyes came open, and I saw King lying dead—or nearly—on the ground. The blood continued to flow out of him as we backed away, the blackening smoke concealing his body.

King was dead, and at once I felt a vacuum much greater than the loss of Buster himself. King was dead, long live— what? Without King, without my living hatred, I was nothing.

I've heard from other veterans, POWs, or just plain combatants, of singular moments that defined not only the rest of the war for them, but the rest of their lives. This was that instant of change or epiphany for me, but it wasn't a realization that took place on the spot. Many years were required to digest this point of world-shattering truth. And maybe I'm still in the process of integrating it. As to what the meaning of all that was, I can't say I'm certain. The essence of what I received from the incident on Panay when I was eighteen and a prisoner of war had something to do with how I had to live my life. I stood hitting golf balls from a bucket, wondering.

We were probably among the last of the Philippine islands to be liberated by the returning MacArthur. But as the American forces came closer in the Pacific, our treatment grew somewhat less severe. We still didn't have much food, but the beatings became less frequent and with less conviction. When the American troops arrived, our guards took to the hills, where we could hear the pounding of mortar for a couple of days. Finally, we were saved by soldiers from our homeland, big men, a species alien to us though we had once been as they.

Our eyes dripped saline and water, but we were not jubilant. We were famished. We were numb. We were leaderless. Lieutenant Logan had died of dysentery, and Hightower, being a Brit, had not been accepted by the men.

I was shipped home to Indiana, eventually, fed along the way and fattened up. Still, when I arrived at my parents' door, uncertain whether I might have to knock or not, my mother, who opened the door to me before I made up my mind, was horrified at my skeletal appearance.

I lay in my house two years more, bringing various foodstuffs into my room at night, and otherwise not expressing much lively motivation. At length, I went to Indiana State, graduated, and went to law school there. I had been demobilized. I had regained my place in society. All was well.

I only told my wife Madelyn once about King, wanting to share with her my sense of guilt and how it had become a primary foundation for me. Madelyn is an intelligent and sensitive woman, down to earth. "That was the war," she responded straight out. "Now it's over."

"But he's dead. Dead forever. And it's my fault." I waited, breath bated, for her to see my terrible point.

"Yes, he's dead," she agreed. "And that's that. There's no going back. The war is done with."

But does that make any sense to anyone else? We still blame the war on the Japanese people, on the Germans. And most of those we condemn for these actions weren't even there. The Germans have paid reparations for decades, and recently the Japanese have begun to apologize to those they harmed. Those who pay and those who apologize know little of the war. I was there when King was killed. I was directly responsible. Yet I'm not reproached.

When a guilty defendant comes into my courtroom, I hand out a punishment. I alone have gone without repercussion for my crime.

I served four years in the worst hell on earth, I tell myself in consolation. But that doesn't console me.

I tracked down King's family and wrote them a nice letter after the war, saying what a fine young man he had been and how proud I was to have served with him. I described how he had met his heroic end. I suppose his father wouldn't have believed me, knowing his son. But his mother would have. I wrote the letter for her, the mother. The mothers are always willing to believe the best.

I also kept in touch with Hightower, writing him when I went to college, then to law school, and when I finally became a judge. He had been a great friend to me before the King incident. Then, after King's death, he often paused to bring me some cheer. He was a fine man and died about fifteen years ago of prostate cancer, leaving two sons.

On my way home from the putting range (a later arrival at Mabuchi taught me to putt with a stick of bamboo), I stopped outside of Johnson Chevy, idling and gazing at the place. Frank Johnson had, from the first, put me in mind of King. I'm always careful sentencing a man to prison, since I've been in one, but I could never have borne to see Johnson locked up. I couldn't have stood any possible consequences to him. To me, Johnson was King.

The mind is a funny, willful, and capricious instrument. No telling what it will come up with next. I have tried since the war not to be subject to its direction but to stick to principle—the reason why, even more than Hightower's influence, I chose the law. Somehow the law seemed to offer a certainty.

Still, when Johnson came to me two years ago, begging me to help him with the fraud charges, I called in a couple of favors from the district attorney's office, as if Johnson were my own son and I had to protect him. Almost as if Johnson were Buster. The logic of our thoughts, the logic of our emotions is utterly unreliable.

I do my utmost to keep Frank Johnson in line, however, and I hoped the reporter would put the story I'd told him in the paper as a reminder to Frank. Probably, though, the *Herald* won't want to risk a libel suit.

Have I made peace with my war, my crimes, and the crimes committed by everyone else? I doubt if I have. But I live my life as if all that was completely in the past. And when they talk on television about prisoners of war in Vietnam or Iraq, I can't watch. When hostages are taken in the Middle East and shown on the news, I leave the room. So long as no one is hurt, every man is allowed his quirks. Those are mine.

———

AUTHOR'S NOTE: Although no prison camp on Panay was named Camp Mabuchi, Maasaki Mabuchi was a defendant in the Tokyo War Crimes Trials and was executed in September 1946. All the atrocities depicted are well-documented. Further, the story is not meant to be anti-Japanese but merely historic in nature; elsewhere, I write from the viewpoint of Japanese protagonists.

THE SLOW BLINK
A Rory Calhoun Story

Jeremiah Healy

Jeremiah Healy was a professor at the New England School of Law when the release of his debut novel about private detective John Francis Cuddy, *Blunt Darts,* announced that there was a wise new kid on the block. Since then he has written more than a dozen novels featuring his melancholy PI. His books and stories have done nothing but enhance his reputation as an important and sage writer whose work has taken the private eye form to an exciting new level. Winner of the Shamus award in 1986 for *The Staked Goat,* he is one of those writers who packs the poise and depth of a good mainstream novel into an even better genre novel. Recent books include *The Stalking of Sheilah Quinn* and the latest Cuddy mystery, *Spiral.*

IT wasn't supposed to be this hot during March. Not in south Florida in general, and not at the Lauderdale Tennis Club in particular. Even at four in the afternoon, just blinking made you sweat.

I was lying on my back in the swimming pool by the tennis center and tiki bar, my weight supported by a couple of those Styrofoam noodles left by some kids from Green Bay, Wisconsin. The kids had visited for a few days the prior week before their parents decided the snow back home wasn't so bad after all.

I was beginning to agree with them.

I'd found the club back when I was still on the professional satellite tour. The place sprawls over ten acres, but it's also four miles from the beach, making the rents reasonable. So, when I injured my left knee, I returned to lease a condo while doing some rehab on the leg. Only the cartilage didn't seem to be getting any better, meaning I'd really begun to use the private investigator's license I'd acquired as a way to earn "day-labor" money from an established security firm downtown. But not when August appeared during the Ides of March.

By keeping one of the noodles under my shoulders and wrapping my arms around the top, and the other noodle under my knees, I probably looked from above as though I'd been crucified on the surface of the pool. But in that contortion, my head stayed mercifully half-submerged, to the point that I remained at a reasonable body temperature, the only outside sensation being a rhythmic vibration from the bass in the bar's sound system.

Until somebody tugged on my right foot.

It was an effort, but I lifted my head enough to bring my ears into the air. The person apparently doing the tugging was Reg Devonshire, a retired police officer from Toronto, even in the pool wearing a white ball cap with a bright red maple leaf on its crown.

"Rory," he said. "Could I have a word with you?"

Oh, I probably should explain my name, too. Back in the early sixties, my mom had such a crush on a certain movie and television actor that she eventually married a man named Calhoun, just so that any son she bore could carry on the actor's name, if not his genes. I suppose there are worse fates, but try fighting your way home from school the first couple of days each year because the other students made fun of—

"Rory, my lad. Your eyes are open, but have you achieved full consciousness?"

"Uh, sorry, Reg." I slid my legs off the bottom noodle. "What's up?"

Devonshire looked around the pool apron. I did, too, but no one in their right mind, even vacationers, were out sunning themselves just then.

He said, "Maybe if we just sat down in the shallow end?"

"Sure."

I let go of the other noodle and swam behind him. As we both reached standing depth, Devonshire began to walk. At six three, he was about my height, but stick thin, and his somewhat professorial manner would make you think he might have been a teacher at one time. However, the ropy forearms and steady eye still projected—as he pushed his seventieth birthday—a "don't-mess" aura that probably served him well back in uniform.

When we both were on our rumps and facing each other, Devonshire took one more look around the apron before saying, "It's about my niece, Marion."

I'd met the pretty, twentyish woman briefly at our club's Christmas party. "From back North?"

"Yes. She flies down from Toronto every school vacation during the academic year. I warned her about this absurd heat wave, but Marion insisted. So I told her, come ahead."

When Devonshire didn't continue, I said, "And?"

"And," the normally steady eyes squinching shut for just a moment, "I'm afraid she's gone missing."

"Before or after she arrived in Florida, Reg?"

"Sort of in between."

"What, on the airplane?"

"Let me elaborate." Devonshire resettled himself on the pool bottom, as though some invisible stone had gotten under his saddle. "Marion is my sister's daughter. My brother-in-law, Tom, hasn't been well for quite some time now. Coming down here was Marion's way of getting a bit of a respite from helping care for her dad." This time the eyes went off somewhere. "Canada has a wonderful social medicine program, but occasionally the priority system it creates makes for long waits on some procedures. Longer than Tom believed he had, so they began looking to get the operation done here in the States."

"Where our system *doesn't* cover the cost."

A grin, like a sergeant being pleased by his recruit's response to an officer's not-yet-asked question. "Precisely so." Then the grin disappeared. "Well, none of the family's exactly rich, but somehow the money was raised, and the operation performed. And Tom's much the better for it, which meant that this trip should have been a true vacation for Marion."

"Probably why she didn't get put off by the heat."

"My thought, too. But while she boarded the aircraft in Toronto, she never arrived here."

The Fort Lauderdale/Hollywood International Airport is only about five miles from the tennis club, and residents are always taking someone to it or picking up someone from it. "Reg, you were at the arrival gate?"

"No. No, Marion always let us take her to the airport at the end of her stay. Poor girl would arrive back in Toronto chronically airsick, perhaps anticipating getting 'snow sick.' But she also insisted on using a taxi when she landed in Lauderdale."

Meaning about twenty-five dollars American, or almost forty Canadian. "Why, though?"

"Said she didn't want me waiting around for her if the flight was delayed by weather, which would happen, so her system made some sense. And we'd never had a problem with it."

"Till now."

"Correct. I have a friend with the airline back in To-

ronto, and he confirmed that Marion boarded the plane."
Devonshire reeled off the company, flight number, and
arrival time. "But she never showed up here last night."

"Have you done any other checking?"

"I called the taxi companies that service the airport.
None of the dispatchers had someone from the right terminal slated to be brought to the club."

I thought it through. "Busy time at the airport, Reg.
Not very likely that somebody could have taken a young
adult against her will."

"And Marion's a spunky one. She would have put up
quite a fuss if they'd tried."

"Police?"

"I called them, too. Both Fort Lauderdale municipal and
the Broward County Sheriff. No reports of any problems
logged with either."

It seemed to me Devonshire had taken things as far as
he could on his own. Dreading leaving the pool, I nevertheless said, "You'd like me to look into it?"

"I would, indeed. My sister's beside herself back in Toronto, and apparently Tom's ranting on about the
Quebecois."

"The French Canadians?"

"Yes. Tom's always been very conservative on hot-
button issues like crime, sexual orientation, and so forth.
And that extends to his being utterly profederal and an-
tiseparatist. Thinks Quebec Libre is a terrible influence on
the rest of the country."

A lot of people from Montreal and elsewhere in the
province vacationed in Hollywood, the town to our south
sharing the airport with Fort Lauderdale. "Any reason to
think someone from Quebec is involved?"

"None, Rory. But the only person here who might know
something about Marion that I wouldn't is a young woman

that a handsome lad like you might have better luck contacting."

"And which young woman is that?"

A smile before Reg Devonshire told me.

"Yes," said Deirdre, "Marion and I talked, we did."

The lass from Ireland's air conditioner—an old window unit—rattled loudly enough that I could barely hear her. While all the residential units at the Lauderdale Tennis Club have central air, some owners of two-bedroom, two-bath flats can close off one of each, creating a studio apartment that can be rented during the season for probably what it costs to carry the entire unit for the year. Only problem is, the central system doesn't always cool down the studio enough during the summer, and certainly not enough for the deadly heat wave we'd been in lately.

So Deirdre, a pretty redhead from Dublin with eyes to match her green card, worked in one of Lauderdale's many Irish pubs and rented a studio at the club, thus causing us to be sitting together in her single room on the one large piece of furniture that doubled as couch and bed.

Though strictly couch at that moment.

I said, "Have you heard from Marion lately?"

"Not since she was down over Christmas." Deirdre reached behind her to a suspended shelf for a photo of the two of them in Santa hats, mugging for the camera. Then Deirdre's lovely eyes clouded. "There's no trouble, is there?"

I hadn't mentioned Marion being missing. "You have reason to think there might be?"

A pause, as though Deirdre was gauging whether or not she could trust me with something. "Rory, if something's happened, tell me, please?"

"Reg Devonshire asked me to check around. It seems

Niece Marion got on a plane in Toronto to come visit him, but she never arrived here at the tennis club."

Deirdre's expression turned to relief. "Oh, is that all?"

"You know where she is?"

Now relief to suspicion. I sensed that Deirdre, who hadn't been renting a unit much longer than I had, would be a tough one to keep pace with, emotionally speaking.

"Deirdre?"

"Marion swore me to secrecy, she did. I'm not at all sure she'd want me to be sharing that with the likes of you, Rory. Or her uncle." Deirdre's attitude had morphed again, to playful now.

"Look, if you know something that would let us both stop worrying about her, you—"

"I don't seem to be the one with the worry, do I?"

"Deirdre, what if something really has happened to Marion? If you keep dancing around my questions, she might be running out of time."

Suddenly, Deirdre *did* seem the one with the worry. "Do you really think so?"

I was losing my usual patience. "Look, how about this? You tell me where you think Marion is, and I promise not to tell her uncle."

A little nibbling on her lower lip, which, under any other circumstances . . . "Nor her father, now?"

Uh-oh, but I saw myself as committed. "Not her father, either."

More nibbling. "You seem a man of your word, Rory. And I've always loved your first name."

First time I could remember counting it as an asset. "So?"

An abrupt nod. "So, Marion met someone here."

"At the tennis club?"

"No. No, down in Hollywood."

I was beginning to see where this might be leading. "Somebody from . . . Quebec?"

Now a smile that my mother probably would have called "saucy." Deirdre said, "I wonder, Rory: can you read my mind?"

A short story, at best. "So, the guy was French-Canadian?"

Disappointment, as though I'd missed the next question on her mind-reading test. "No."

"Okay, then. He's from Quebec, only—"

"You don't understand. The French-Canadian part's on the mark, but it's not a *he*, Rory. Marion's friend is a she."

I closed my eyes for a minute. Reg had said his brother-in-law was a conservative on the issue of sexual orientation as well as Quebecois separatism. "Deirdre, do you have a name for this woman?"

"Just a first one."

"Which is?"

"Yvonne."

"Ever meet her?"

"No. In fact, when Marion told me she'd been at this bar last year and met 'a divine vision named Yvonne,' I said, 'I thought you were straight?' Marion just laughed and replied, 'Deirdre, a rose is a rose.' "

Which didn't seem to fit the context of the conversation. "Could that be the woman's last name?"

"What? Rose, now?"

"Yes."

"Maybe. After Marion told me that Yvonne called her 'my little rabbit,' I didn't exactly feel I wanted to hear very much more about their relationship."

Couldn't blame Deirdre there, I guess, but it sparked another connection to something Reg had told me. "Would this Yvonne pick Marion up at the airport?"

The saucy smile again. "Rory, can you read my mind only on every *other* thought?"

"So the answer is yes?"

More disappointment, though I didn't think it related directly to any telepathic ability of mine other than the obvious. "It is."

I took a minute to go over in my head what I'd learned so far before asking, "Deirdre, what's the name of that bar?"

She told me, even let me take the Christmas photo. Standing up, I thanked her.

"Rory," Deirdre still sitting on the daybed and kind of leaning back now on an elbow, doing a hair flip with her other hand. "Can you read my mind this instant?"

"If I find out anything about Marion, you'd like me to tell you."

"In person, if you please," hooding those emerald eyes.

Now Deirdre was the one who had pretty successfully read my mind, and I turned for the door before she could divert it from the task at hand.

ON the ride to Hollywood, I kept the top on my Chrysler Sebring convertible up and the air on full blast. However, my shirt had barely dried out from walking to the car in the tennis club's parking lot thirty minutes before. Slewing to the curb outside the bar, I opened my door and got slapped in the face by a smothering blanket of heat and humidity.

Maybe because it was still early evening, the place just off the boulevard wasn't very crowded. The bar itself was elliptical in shape, and the proprietor kept the place dark. Some ancient ceiling fans wafted the fetid, tobacco-tainted air around a little, but about all you could say for the interior was that it managed to be five degrees cooler than the exterior.

I took a stool in the middle of the bar on the door side, two middle-aged guys appearing to share a bottle of red wine across from me. The bartender came over, a towel around his neck instead of over his shoulder. Even in the heat, though, he had a lit cigarette dangling from the corner of his mouth.

"Get you something?"

A French lilt on the words, which I found encouraging.

"Beer?"

"And what kind?"

"Whichever is coldest."

One of the guys across the bar said, "When it is so hot, you should drink the red wine, not the beer. It is already warm, so it makes love to your body, eh?"

His friend laughed, and they exchanged some further bon mots in machine-gun French that my menu-level mastery of the language couldn't catch. But the 'tender came back to me with a Budweiser long-neck, and I swallowed about half of its contents before setting the bottle back down.

My new friend across the bar said, "You make love so quick like that, the woman will not be so happy."

More laughter, and I began to wonder how Marion ever had found this place. Despite the criticism of my drinking style, I finished off the Bud and waved for another.

When the bartender brought it, I figured I'd established myself as enough of a patron to bring out the photo of Marion and Deirdre. He squinted as I rotated the shot in the available light.

"I'm looking for this woman on the left."

The guy's cigarette did a push-up, a reaction that made me think he recognized her. "Pretty girl."

"Know her?"

The 'tender looked at me evenly. "It is the season. Many come in, stay for a while."

"She's from Toronto."

"Then what would she be looking for here?" from my friend across the way, both him and his friend getting another charge out of that remark.

The bartender said, "Pay no attention to them."

Which made me want to. "What are they drinking?"

"Wine."

"I meant, what kind?"

"Red."

Rather than give him the satisfaction of pulling his teeth, I called over myself. "What are you guys having?"

The word "chateau" with a French name to follow.

I got up and carried both my second Bud and the Christmas photo around the bar to them. "Another round for my new friends, please."

The 'tender didn't say anything, I imagine measuring profit against discretion. But by the time I reached the two guys, I could hear a cork popping.

"My friend," said the guy who'd been heckling me. "That is very kind, but too generous, since we make fun of you a little."

"Yes," the second guy speaking English for the first time.

We introduced ourselves, all using just first names.

The new bottle arrived. "Please," said Charles, the more talkative of the two. "Try with us some of this wine, so you know we tell you the truth before, eh?"

The bartender grudgingly came up with a third glass, and I tried what he poured. On top of the beer, it tasted like engine oil, but I smiled and agreed with Charles and his friend, Jean-Louis the Quiet.

Charles said, "What did we tell you?" but Jean-Louis just nodded and took a sip of his own.

"I wonder," squaring the photo between them. "Have you guys ever seen this woman on the left?"

Charles squinted, Jean-Louis barely glancing at it before saying what seemed one word in French to the bartender, who answered the same way, received a torrent back, and reluctantly produced a flashlight from under the bar.

Charles clicked its button, the bulb's glare bouncing off the glossy print. "Ah, yes. The hair is a little more long, but she is the one."

Jean-Louis just nodded again.

I said, "The one what?"

Charles shrugged. "The girl we saw with Yvonne from the marina."

A third nod from Jean-Louis, but my first real lead.

I said, "Can you describe her?"

Charles raised his eyebrows, and even Jean-Louis shot me a sidelong glance.

Charles said, "But why, Rory? You already have the photograph, no?"

"I meant the other woman, Yvonne."

Now Charles's eyebrows knit, and Jean-Louis grunted. It wasn't until Charles laughed hard enough to spill his wine that I realized his friend's grunt was a laugh, too.

I waited until the surge had passed before saying, "I don't get the joke."

"The joke," said Jean-Louis, "is upon you."

"You're going to have to explain it, then."

Charles wiped his eyes with the soggy cocktail napkin under his glass. "Rory, the joke is that the person from the marina is not a woman."

I felt my day shift one-eighty again. "Not?"

"No. In French, we pronounce the name the same, but the spelling is Y-V-O-N. Like Yvon Corn-why-ay."

"Yvon . . . ?"

"C-O-U-R-N-E-Y-E-R."

"Now," put in Jean-Louis, "there was a hockey player. Not like the corps de ballet Montreal sends out on skates now."

I had the feeling I'd just been privy to Jean-Louis's longest speech of the new millenium. "So, the woman in this photo met a man named Yvon here?"

"Yes. Last year sometime it was."

"And his last name?"

Two expressive but unhelpful shrugs.

I said, "Any idea where I can find him?" ·

Charles shrugged again. "I have not seen Yvon for a while, but maybe you should try the marina in Dania."

"Which one?"

My new friends debated that in French before agreeing on a location, at least.

Charles said, "Yvon, he works sometimes for the Devereaux brothers. On their boat for charter?"

THE airport was a little closer than the marina, and at eight P.M. a little more open. I also thought that before I risked any teeth rousting guys who worked on docks, I should make at least some inquiries on Marion's flight. Sometimes things happen even in public places that wouldn't necessarily be reported to a police or sheriff's department.

And if Deirdre thought I had telepathy, what happened shortly thereafter might have convinced me of clairvoyance.

I'd parked the Chrysler in the hourly garage and made the rounds of the skycaps and gate agents. None of them working the night before—when the flight in question had arrived—remembered the woman on the left of the photo, even when I told them Marion's hair might have been cut differently. After exhausting the apparent supply of janitors and rent-a-car people, too, I decided the marina would have been the better route.

Then, leaving the terminal, I spotted a short and chubby skycap that I hadn't tried as yet. When I walked up to him, he smiled, a gold front tooth standing out against the perspiring black complexion around it.

"Help you, sir?"

A singsong lilt from the Caribbean. "This woman on the left came in last night. Did you by any chance see her?"

He stared at the photo as I wondered how the hell anyone could survive eight hours a day in the scorching, motor-fumed air under the pedestrian bridge between the terminal and the garage. "The hair does not look right."

I snapped back to him. "You recognize her, then?"

"Yes. The young lady came out from Baggage Claim and looked around. I asked her the same as you, if I can help. She said, 'No, thank you,' and then a car honked its horn several times, which I did not like very much."

"Why not?"

"It was not a 'Tap-tap-we-are-here.' It was more 'Hey-mon-get-yourself-over-to-us,' you know?"

"Can you describe the car?"

"It had four doors, not two. I am not good with American automobiles made before I came to the States, but . . ." The gold tooth again. "Do you know what a 'Keys cruiser' is?"

In the Florida Keys, a lot of the native-born—called even by themselves, and defiantly proudly, Conchs—drove their cars into the ground, with primered fenders and bungee-corded trunk lids and exhaust pipes. "I know what you mean."

"Well, it was a car like that, which did not seem to suit the young lady. But then someone called out to her from inside it, and I noticed there were three men."

"Called out to her by name?"

"Yes. 'Mary Anne,' I think it was, but with a French accent, so I am not sure."

I was starting to be. "What did the woman do then?"

"She looked inside the car, but from the curb, here where we stand now. Then one of the men called out to her again, and she smiled and went over to the car, but still a bit . . . uncertain?"

"What did the man say?"

"The second time?"

"Yes?"

"I would not know, but for my own father being from Haiti. It was 'Come, get in with us, my *peh-teet lah-pahn*.' "

Even a tennis pro's menu French could handle that one. *Petit lapin* meant "little rabbit."

I PARKED the convertible a few blocks from the marina and began walking through the parking lot. At that hour, there were only four vehicles, and two were a pickup and a spiffy new sport ute, I assumed owned by charter captains who lived aboard their boats. Slumped next to the high-rise Pathfinder was an old, low-slung Buick: a four-door that came pretty close to Keys-cruiser status. I touched the hood of it. Warm, thanks to the still oppressive heat, but not like the car had been driven recently.

I made my way down to the dock area, bathed in that sour smell of dead fish. At the wide, chain-link gates onto the even wider wharf, I stayed in shadows near a pile of nautical junk, my sweat dripping onto jagged scraps of fiberglass and discarded lengths of pipe and rope. After a while, I began to notice that all the boats I could see had only security lights on them.

All except one, that is.

About eight slips down the wharf, three guys were sitting and swigging straight from the bottle on the fantail of a motor trawler around forty feet in length. Their conversation carried, partly due to lack of breeze, but mostly due to raised voices. I couldn't understand much of what they were saying, because it was in French.

One of them, however—the biggest and the loudest—motioned with his hand toward the hatch leading belowdecks and pitched his voice sarcastically to end a short speech with *"petit lapin."*

Badly outnumbered, and by definition outgunned if they had any firearms at all, I decided to find the Dania Police Department as quickly as I could get back to the Chrysler.

But the biggest guy chose that moment to rise and turn his bottle upside down. I couldn't see anything pouring forth, then realized that was his point as he pushed the smallest guy out of a chair and onto the deck, now waving the bottle back toward the parking lot. When the little guy struggled to his feet, the biggest one put the base of his bottle in his own crotch and pelvic-thrusted a few times, making the neck of the bottle rise. Then he motioned toward the hatch again, and the middle-sized guy laughed with him. As the smallest guy climbed over the gunwale and began walking unsteadily up the wharf toward me, the middle one handed an apparently *not* empty bottle to the biggest guy, who took a slug from it before sitting back down himself.

It didn't take a linguistic genius to figure out that Reg Devonshire's niece might not have time for me to find the Dania police.

I picked up a two-foot hunk of three-inch pipe from the junk pile and drew out some pieces of braided nylon rope, one nearly twice as long as I am tall. Then I made my way back to the Pathfinder. Hunkered down on its rear bumper, I soon heard stumbling steps and muttering in French, both sounds getting closer.

I waited until I heard a door handle engage without my sensing any motion through the sport ute. I came around and behind the driver's side of the Buick, just as the smallest guy crouched down to get behind the wheel for his booze run. Holding the pipe up like a backhand volley at the net, I rapped him over his left ear hard enough to make my forearm ring.

ABOVE the incessant whine of countless mosquitoes on the rim of the access canal, I could hear something in drunken French from the bottom of the steep, slippery slope to the water.

Calling down, I said, "If you can't speak English, we're going to be here awhile."

The man beneath me shook his head and twisted at the end of the longest piece of rope. I'd used two shorter lengths to bind his feet together and his elbows against his rib cage on each side. The longest piece ran from between his shoulder blades back up to me. It's not likely he could see the rope on his feet, as he was up to his waist in the murky water.

"What . . . what do you do here?"

Good enough for conversational purposes. "First, your name."

"Why do you want—"

I let about a foot of the long rope slip through my hands.

"Hey, what do you do?"

Another foot, and the rope binding his arms was underwater.

"No, no! My name is Pierre. Pierre Devereaux."

"Okay, Pierre. Here's the drill. I ask you questions, and you answer them. If you don't . . ." I let the rope slip another six inches.

"No! *Oui,* I understand you."

"Okay. Why are you guys holding Marion belowdecks on that boat?"

A pause, but since he was speaking in his second language, I gave him the benefit of the doubt.

Pierre said, "It is because of that pig, Yvon."

"Her boyfriend."

"Yvon, he meet this Toronto one at the bar in Hollywood. She is . . . I do not know your English for when she go to the place of lower class for her."

"She was slumming?"

"Slumming, *oui,* like bad houses. So, Yvon take this Marion to his bed, and they have the idea to use her for the mule."

Great. "You mean to smuggle drugs?"

"*Oui.* My brothers and me, we get the drugs on our boat from the supplier in the Bahamas, when we go there for charter. We use Yvon sometimes for the mule, flying back to Montreal. But now, he say to us, we can use her for Toronto."

"And Marion agrees?"

"She want to do it! Her father is sick with something, and he need the operation in the States."

The money that Reg Devonshire said the family had to come up with. "So Marion carries the drugs back on the flight."

A grunted laugh, like Jean-Louis the Quiet back in the Hollywood bar. "*Oui,* but not in her bags. In her stomach."

I should have guessed. Stuff condoms with drugs, and swallow them, which would also explain Marion's "chronic airsickness" at the Toronto end of each flight back. "So what happened this time?"

"Her father need the operation, like I tell you. This time, she bring our drugs to the dealer up there, but the bitch keep the money for the hospital."

"And you can't pressure her in Toronto?"

"We have the dealer there, but he get our drugs, so what should he care? Only we do not have our drugs *or* the money from them. Then . . ."

Pierre might have realized he was telling me a little too much by that time.

I said, "And then . . . ?"

When I still didn't get an answer, I let him slide far enough that all I could see of the thrashing man was the hair on top of his head. I hauled on the rope, but, given the sweat on my hands, it was a lot harder bringing him back up.

Pierre hadn't stopped sputtering when I said, "This kind of heat and that kind of kicking, we could attract a bull gator, don't you think?"

Pierre whipped his head from side to side, canting it wildly as he scanned the water for logs with eyes.

"So," I said. "Cooperate?"

"*Oui*. I . . . cooperate." A little more hacking, then, "My brothers take Yvon . . . and we make him tell us about . . . this Marion, his '*petit lapin*.' Then we have him call to her . . . on the telephone to Toronto, tell her she come down with our money . . . or we make him do—I think in English, you say, 'the slow blink.' "

"The slow blink?"

"*Oui*. When a man die, and the last thing you see is the slow blink of his skin over the eye."

Lovely image. "Pierre, did you kill him?"

"No," he maintained. "My brothers do it, though, once we have Marion from the airport. So she know we are serious, they choke the life from Yvon in front of her and say, 'Make your father send us the money.' But she tell us it is all gone, and my most old brother, he decide . . ." Now laughing, kind of man-to-man. "He decide we make her swallow something more than our drugs."

I dunked Pierre again, left him down there a little longer this time, the thrashing more chaotic.

I yanked him back up.

"Hey," sputtering and hacking worse now. "You said that . . . if I tell you . . . your questions——"

"Chalk that one up to general principles, Pierre. Now, how many of your brothers are on the boat?"

"How many? Just . . . the two I have. . . . There is only the three of us."

Since I didn't know how much time the others would think it should have taken Pierre to get their booze, I pulled him all the way up to his butt on the bank, then took the pipe down with me.

DRIVING the old Buick back from the canal toward the marina, I said over my shoulder, "This car handles pretty well for a clunker."

Little Brother, lying across the rear seat, didn't see fit to answer. Or maybe he just wasn't awake yet. And the breeze through the windows—the humidity stultifying even at forty miles an hour—wasn't doing much to dissipate the swamp smell coming off him.

As I approached the parking lot, I tried to figure the best way to handle things, just like the strategic planning you go through before a tennis match. If the opponent serves predominantly down the tee, do I shift my stance to compensate? If he favors slice returns, do I angle the ball cross-court or send it up the line?

However, driving the Buick was less *before* the match, and more *during* it, so I decided to go tactically with whatever felt natural when I arrived.

And "whatever" turned out to be barreling into the parking lot, using the car's momentum to crash through the chain-link gates and onto the wharf itself. The Buick's tires beat a rumbling staccato as we careened over some looser boards.

Middle Brother, probably the more spry of the two still on their boat, vaulted over its gunwale and put his hands up, as if to ward Pierre off a terribly wrong turn.

Which felt "natural" right then, too.

When I veered toward the boat, Middle Brother almost got free of the Buick's right fender, probably missing his timing by about half a bottle. I'd once hit a deer on a country road, and the impact felt pretty similar as this Devereaux flew through the air, folding into a ball and hitting the water on the other side of the wharf.

The car's encounter with the charter boat went a bit differently.

The nose of the Buick punched a hole in the stern from headlight to headlight, the front wheels riding up and onto the fantail over the crushed frame. Big Brother Devereaux was already up and roaring in French as I pushed open the driver's-side door and came out with my pipe.

From under a gunwale, he snatched a broom-handle gaff. The hook of it spanned only about six inches, but more than enough to do the job.

Even drunk as Big Brother must have been, he jabbed at my throat and torso efficiently with the butt end of his gaff, keeping me nearly pinned against the hood of the Buick. I parried his thrusts with my pipe, but I'd carried a club into a spear fight, and the sweat from my scalp and forehead made matters worse by cascading blindingly into my eyes.

Big Brother finally caught me in the solar plexus, and I went down to my knees, gagging. He deftly reversed his grip on the gaff, and I ducked just in time to have the sweeping hook miss my throat. Driving up off the deck and feeling the lack of oxygen from Big Brother's prior jab about to put me out, I grabbed the handle of the gaff and wrenched it as hard as I could toward his face, hoping to catch an eye.

Instead, he turned the wrong way at the wrong time, and the sharp point of the hook went through the left side of his neck, tearing out a hunk of flesh.

And, I guessed from the blood, severing his carotid artery as well.

Big Brother Devereaux let go of the gaff handle and clamped first one hand, then the other on the wound without much effect. He was gushing blood between his fingers like a fire truck pumps water, all the alcohol he'd consumed probably not helping him any.

Then Big Brother staggered back, taking one hand away long enough to point at his neck wound and gasp, "Please . . . my . . . Please . . . doctor."

As that last word faded into the sultry night air, I began to regain my own breathing, and I registered Middle Brother screaming in pain from the water on the other side of the wharf. He needed medical attention, but I also knew that the man bleeding out before me would never last long enough to be treated.

Then Big Brother sagged down into his chair, which wasn't fixed to the deck, and he carried it over backward, his head lolling toward the hatch and the interior stairway leading to the cabin below. There was already enough blood flowing over the planks to make them slippery, so I carefully inched my way toward the steps that I hoped would lead to Marion.

Turning at the hatchway to climb down more easily, I suddenly realized the eldest Devereaux was showing me his version of the slow blink.

Hot Days, Cold Nights

Alan Cook

Alan Cook spent one lifetime in the computer industry before deciding to spend his second lifetime as a writer. He is the author of two mystery novels featuring Lillian Morgan, a retired math professor turned detective. *Thirteen Diamonds* starts off with a thump when a resident of Lillian's North Carolina retirement community drops dead at the bridge table while holding a perfect hand. *Catch a Falling Knife* addresses sexual harassment at the college level and features a coed who moonlights as a stripper. Alan's first novel, *Walking to Denver,* is about people who are crazy enough to walk from Los Angeles to Denver for shoes (and the hope that they can resolve their personal "issues"). Alan can be reached at **alcook@sprintmail.com**. His Internet address is **alancook. 50megs.com**.

———

A SLIVER of moon rose just inches in front of the still-hidden sun as Connie O'Connor came down her driveway and started along the sidewalk with the easy stride of an experienced runner. It was already too warm for the T-shirt she usually wore over her athletic bra, and the day would be a scorcher before long. Her ponytail tickled her back as it pendulumed from side to side with each step.

As she turned the corner onto Main Street, the only car on the road was some distance in front of her, a bright red SUV. It caught her attention because of its color and because it was moving very slowly. Then it stopped. Two objects came flying out of the passenger-side window before it sped off.

"Damn litterbug!" Connie sputtered. As she approached the scene of the crime, she saw two white trash bags, which had come to rest among the weeds in a vacant lot.

Ordinarily, she would have picked them up, but trash collection wasn't until the next day, so there wouldn't be any cans sitting along the street to dump them in. *I'll get them tomorrow*, she thought as she ran by.

She took an unusually long run. She had to exorcise some demons connected with her live-in boyfriend, who had taken off to "find himself," leaving her with a lease on the house they shared and not much money. Her route took her in a circle; she returned almost two hours later from the opposite direction along Main Street. A river of sweat poured down her hot body. However, as she turned into her block, a chill went through her. A paramedic truck, an ambulance, and several other vehicles were parked near her house.

She had seen ambulances often enough in her job as a nurse, but to see one in her own neighborhood made it personal. They were centered in front of the home of old Mr. Wilson, who lived just two doors from the house she rented. He had recently suffered a stroke.

"What happened?" she asked a paramedic, who was returning to his truck.

"You a neighbor?"

Connie nodded.

"Poor guy. He died in his bathtub."

She didn't wait to hear any more, but ran up the driveway to the open front door and into the house. She knew the layout and ran directly to the bathroom. The doorway to the bathroom was inhabited by a large man in a white shirt and a loose tie, with beads of sweat on his upper lip, talking on a cell phone.

Connie tried to squeeze past him, but he abruptly blocked her way. To the phone he said, "Call you back," and to Connie, "Where do you think you're going?"

She didn't like his attitude and the way he stared at her chest, especially since it occurred to her that her sweat-soaked bra was a poor excuse for a cover-up. "He was a friend of mine," she said, icicles coating her words.

"Well, little lady, this is no sight for you. He's naked, and his skin has turned blue, just like he was frozen in a meat locker."

Strange. The temperature had stayed above seventy last night. "Well, little man, I'm an emergency-room nurse, and I've seen my share of dead bodies." This time she made it by him, then gave an involuntary gasp. She'd never seen a body quite so blue before.

"Gets to you, doesn't it?" the man said.

Connie wasn't about to admit it. She took a deep breath and turned toward him. "What did he die of?"

The man shrugged as he mopped his forehead with a large white handkerchief. "Old guy. Natural causes."

On a hunch Connie asked, "Are you a detective?"

The man nodded. "Detective Fixx." He flashed an official-looking badge at her.

She ignored it and was also careful not to look at Mr. Wilson. "If it was natural causes, what are you doing here?"

"I'll ask the questions. You said you're a nurse and you knew him. Tell me about the state of his health."

He sounded like a detective. "He had a stroke about two months ago. Since then he's used a walker. His left side is weak—was weak. He talks in a whisper."

Detective Fixx referred to a tan spiral notebook. "House-keeper said about the same thing."

Then why did he ask her? "She took care of *him*, not the house."

"Caregiver then—whatever. Did you see him recently?"

"I . . ." Connie had an urge not to tell this jerk anything—to stay out of it. But Shirley would tell him if she didn't—may have already told him. "I take . . . I took care of him on Shirley's day off." Sacrificing one of her own precious days off to earn extra money. To repay her college loans.

He wrote in his notebook. When he looked at her again, she noticed that he had green eyes. She'd never seen a man with green eyes before.

"Were you in this house at all, yesterday or last night?"

Connie hesitated. Should she say any more? Shouldn't she demand to speak to a lawyer or something? But that was ridiculous. Mr. Wilson's death had to be from natural causes. Whether or not she liked Detective Fixx, his questions were routine. "Yesterday was Shirley's day off, so I was here yesterday."

Detective Fixx raised his eyebrows. "But Shirley slept here last night."

"She always sleeps here."

"Even on her day off?"

Her day off is part of always. Connie didn't say that. Instead, she nodded.

"What time did you leave here yesterday?"

"When Shirley arrived. About six."

As Detective Fixx wrote more notes, Connie became conscious of Mr. Wilson's body beside her, even though she wasn't looking at it. It wasn't just any body but the body of a friend. She and the detective and the walker standing beside the bathtub filled up the available space in the small bathroom. And it was so hot. In addition, she needed to sit or move around after a hard run or she would feel wobbly. She had to get out of the bathroom. But Detective Fixx blocked the door from the inside, just as he had previously blocked it from the outside.

She said in what she hoped was an offhand manner, "Can we go out in the hall?"

Detective Fixx gave her a little smile—a superior smile?—and let her pass. She walked out into the hallway and took a drink from the water bottle she carried. She immediately felt better.

He followed her and said, "One more question."

Now what?

"What's your name?"

Feeling one up because she had managed to avoid giving it before now, she said, "Connie O'Connor."

"Well, Connie O'Connor, I think that's all I need from you at the moment. It's lucky you came along."

So you could grill me. Her turn. Connie asked, "How did Mr. Wilson get in the bathtub? He usually doesn't get up until eight. And he doesn't take baths. He takes showers. He has a stool he sits on in the shower for support." The shower was in the other bathroom.

Detective Fixx was writing again and ignored her. Connie turned to leave in a huff. As she took the first step, he said to her back, "Shirley pretty much explained that. He must have gotten up in the night to go to the bathroom. Sleeps in the nude, she says. Must be a thrill for you *care-givers* to take care of an old guy who won't wear clothes. His walker was beside the toilet. When he tried to turn it around, he must have fallen into the tub and couldn't get out. He couldn't yell because of the stroke. Couldn't reach his call button—it's attached to the walker. Shirley says she's a sound sleeper and didn't hear anything. Found him this morning. Probably been dead several hours. In short, the trauma plus his existing condition did him in."

"Did he hit his head when he fell?" Connie asked.

"We couldn't find any sign of an injury."

"Are you going to do an autopsy?"

Detective Fixx contemplated her chest. "Does that story square with what you know about him?"

"Yeah, I guess." She wasn't about to call Shirley a liar, if that's what he wanted.

"Coroner's sending somebody out. Should be here soon." He gave her a card. "If that pretty red head comes up with any ideas, give me a call."

AFTER her shift at the hospital, Connie drove home in the heat. She didn't turn on her air conditioner because she had been having chills all day—possibly the aftermath of seeing the blue body of Mr. Wilson. She hadn't been able to get his image out of her mind. As she drove along Main Street, approaching her neighborhood, she remembered the car she had seen that morning whose occupant had thrown the trash bags out the window.

She stopped at the field containing the bags and walked across the street. Might as well do her good deed for the day. At first she thought the bags were gone. For once somebody had picked up litter. No, they were there, but they were lying flat and empty. Why would somebody take the contents and leave the bags? She picked one up; it was still sealed at the top with a twist-tie, but there was a small hole in the bottom. A few drops of clear liquid dripped out. She sniffed—no odor. She put a finger on a drop and touched her tongue with it. No taste—it must be water.

Connie took the bags with her, wondering why anybody would throw out bags of water. The world teemed with peculiar people. As she drove by Mr. Wilson's house, she saw the yellow police tape blocking the front door. Detective Fixx was taking Mr. Wilson's death seriously. And Shirley must have left. She was probably staying with her sister.

*   *   *

IT was at dinnertime when Connie missed her boyfriend's presence most. He was a good conversationalist, and they had had some stimulating discussions on many and varied topics. Varied enough so that she had thought of him as an open-minded individual. Her mistake.

She ate and washed the few dishes she had dirtied and wondered what to do next. She was restless—because she was alone, because of the heat, because of Mr. Wilson. She couldn't stand it in the house.

She walked outside. The sun was low in the west, casting a giant shadow of her body. It wasn't going to cool off much tonight. Prickles of sweat tickled her skin, even though she wore only a tank top and shorts. She glanced at the police tape in front of Mr. Wilson's house and strolled in that direction.

When she arrived at the house, Connie remembered something. Something she should have remembered before. She had to get inside the house. Now. She looked around. Nobody was about on the residential street. The neighbors were sealed up in their houses with the air-conditioning on. Escaping the elements. She ran around to the back of Mr. Wilson's house. No police tape here. Fortunately, the key Mr. Wilson had given her opened the back door. She let herself in.

It was stifling and eerily dark in the house. Trees blocked the remaining rays of the sun so they didn't reach the windows. She decided not to turn on any lights. She knew her way around the single-story plan. She went to the bathroom first. Of course Mr. Wilson was gone, as was any evidence that his body had lain in the bathtub. Even his walker was gone.

No surprises, but one had to make sure. A faint odor lingered, but Connie couldn't place it. She stared at the bathtub. She had been in that bathtub, herself. Perhaps that's why it had been such a shock to see Mr. Wilson's body there.

She walked into the room Mr. Wilson used as a study. An ancient wooden cabinet dominated one wall. It had two doors that opened out from the center and locked with the same key. Mr. Wilson wore the key on a chain around his neck. Connie tried to remember whether the key had still been around his neck in the bathtub. She couldn't picture it. Of course, Detective Fixx would have removed it.

Her heart beat faster as she knelt down and felt underneath the cabinet for the spare key. Mr. Wilson kept it in a small hollow behind one of the legs. She had never been so thankful to feel anything metallic. She stood up and unlocked the left-hand door. She could just see the outlines of several boxes on the shelves, but not the box she was looking for. Somebody had taken it. Still, she picked up each box and frantically opened it. Only papers—documents of some sort.

In despair, Connie closed the door and locked it. Now what? She could try the other door, but she knew what she would find behind it. She unlocked it anyway. The box she expected to see was there, but she was surprised when she opened it and saw the neat piles of twenty-dollar bills. Why had the intruder not taken these? Something was wrong. She quickly replaced the box, shut, and locked the door. She had to get out of here.

"Is this what you're looking for?"

Connie jumped out of her skin. In midjump she recognized the voice. She whirled around as the door to the closet opened, and the outline of Detective Fixx emerged.

"Do you get a thrill out of giving people heart attacks?" Connie asked in what was meant to be an imperious voice, but the quaver in it gave her away. She shook all over.

"Sorry," Detective Fixx said, but he didn't sound sorry. He groped along the wall and light flooded the room.

The detective looked as if he had just come out of a steam bath. His shirt was soaked with perspiration. His tie was gone. Sweat rolled down his forehead and even glistened on his head beneath his short hair. In his hands Connie saw what he had been referring to: her box. She wanted to snatch it from him, but when she took a step toward him, he pulled it away and smiled a wicked smile.

"So Ms. Connie O'Connor—runner, nurse—now we find out about your secret life." He opened the box and pulled out a photograph. "Here's Connie in her under-wear." Another. "Here's Connie out of her underwear." A third. "Here's Connie in the bathtub, dressed the same way Wilson was. I will say this: your body's a helluva lot sexier than Wilson's."

Connie was livid, more so because he was taunting her. She had an overwhelming desire to attack him, rip the photos out of his hands, and scratch his eyes out. What stopped her was the feeling that perhaps that's what he wanted her to do. Assaulting a police officer. Didn't they lock you up and throw away the key for that?

She mustered all the dignity she could and said, "May I please have those?"

Still leafing through the photos, Detective Fixx raised his eyebrows and said in an offended tone, "Evidence. My dear, I can't let evidence get out of my hands." And then with a leer, "I assume your friend Wilson took these. So how does it feel to give an *old man* his jollies?"

"At what age does a guy cease to be a normal libidinous male like yourself and become a dirty old man?"

"Ouch!" He pulled an imaginary knife out of his chest. "The lady can hurt you." And then in his police interrogation voice, "Did he pay you?"

"Yes. He paid very well." *And helped me make payments on my college loans.*

"And you didn't mind taking his money?"

Remain calm. "It was his idea. And he was loaded—as you must know by now."

"You don't give an inch, do you?" He finally put the photos back in the box and closed it. Reluctantly.

Her turn. "If you think Mr. Wilson's death is in any way connected to those photos, you're wrong. As you must have seen from your hiding place, I know where the spare key to the cabinet is. He told me that if anything happened to him, I should take them. Since his stroke I've been meaning to do just that because I think he's lost interest in them."

In an almost civil voice Detective Fixx said, "I had to make sure. And you didn't take the money, either."

"How did you know I would come?"

"Just a hunch. I knew you wouldn't if you thought I was here, so I parked my car in the garage. But I needed to get the feel of the place anyway. Without a lot of other people running around. When I heard you at the back door, I had just time to lock the cabinet and hide in the closet."

"And scare the hell out of me."

"Listen, because of you I couldn't even turn on the air-conditioning. I should charge you to get these pants pressed."

Indeed, their creases had disappeared. Connie thought of what had nagged at her since Detective Fixx had shown himself. "You're still treating this as a murder case, aren't you?"

The detective focused his green eyes on her for several moments before he spoke. Then he said, "There's no reason not to tell you. Remember this morning, I said Wilson's body was cold? In fact, the paramedics found it was colder than the room temperature. Now, as a nurse, doesn't that strike you as odd?"

"You mean he died of hypothermia?"

"Strange thing to happen during a heat wave, isn't it?"

"What could have caused it?"

"That's what I'm trying to figure out."

"Do you think Shirley did it?"

"Well, if it wasn't you, or some combination of you and Shirley, Shirley working alone is the best bet."

"But why? She didn't take the money. In fact, I don't think she even knew it was there. And I know she didn't know about the spare key. Although she could have used the key around his neck."

Detective Fixx grinned and said, "Now you're thinking like a detective. I checked on some of the people she took care of before Wilson. The last several died suddenly."

"Old people sometimes do."

"I'm sure that's what everybody thought. Probably why there were no investigations. But one died in a bathtub, like Wilson. What if she pictures herself as some sort of . . . angel or something?"

"You mean an angel of mercy?"

"Exactly. It's happened before. In addition, she lied to me."

"Oh?" Connie didn't know Shirley very well. She wasn't talkative. Even when their paths crossed as they had last night, they usually just said hello and exchanged information about Mr. Wilson's condition. And Shirley had been even less verbose than usual—as if something was on her mind.

"She told me she hadn't been out of the house this morning. As part of my investigation, I went into the garage where her car was parked—or rather, her sister's car. Apparently, hers is in the shop. The engine was warm. It had been driven not long before I got there."

"What kind of a car does her sister have?" Shirley drove a beat-up old Nissan.

"A fancy red British car. A Range Rover."

"Bright red?"

Detective Fixx's eyebrows went up. "Yes, ma'am. The kind you can't miss."

Connie flashed back to that morning and the bright red SUV moving slowly along the street. The trash bags being thrown out the window. "I think I know how Mr. Wilson died."

"Tell me."

Connie enjoyed being in the driver's seat. "Shirley froze him with ice cubes. The refrigerator has an icemaker. That's probably where she got them. Come with me." She led the way to the kitchen, turning on lights as she went. She went to the refrigerator and opened the freezer door. Ice cubes spilled out of the plastic tray. "The ice-making machine has been going all day. Looks like Shirley forgot to turn it off."

"Interesting theory," Detective Fixx said. "How do we prove it?"

"This morning, when I started out on my run, somebody driving a bright red SUV threw two white trash bags out the window into the vacant lot on Main Street not far from here. Trash bags just like these." Connie lifted a box from the pantry shelf and pulled out a white trash bag. "Being a compulsive cleaner-upper, I stopped to pick them up this afternoon on my way home from work. By then they were empty—except for a few drops of—"

"Water." Detective Fixx looked at Connie with new respect. "She must have made so much ice she figured she'd better get rid of some before she called the paramedics. And she had to dry out the bathtub since her story was that he fell in."

Hot Days, Cold Nights

"Of course, hot water in the sink might have worked just as well to melt the ice."

"But when you're committing murder, you don't always think rationally. And the passenger seat of the Range Rover was damp this morning. It looked wet, and the window was open, so I poked my hand in and felt it."

He opened the box and started flipping through her photographs again. Connie didn't know how long she could suppress the urge to grab them. He pulled out a bathtub shot, stuck it in his notebook, then closed the box and placed it on the counter. He asked, "Where are those trash bags now?"

"At my place, two doors from here."

"The lab should be able to test the bags and verify your ice/water theory. Tell you what. I'll get my car out of the garage and meet you there in three minutes."

He headed for the door to the garage. As soon as he was out of sight, Connie picked up the box of photos from the counter, went out the back door, closed and locked it, and ran around to the street. The sun had set, and the temperature was slightly cooler outside than inside. But it was still sticky. Connie needed a cold beer, and she had some bottles in her refrigerator. Detective Fixx could use a cold beer, too. She wondered if he drank on duty. His decision—beer or lemonade. For herself, she would stick to beer.

PROM NIGHT

David Bart

David Bart is a writer and consultant living in New Mexico. His work has appeared in *Alfred Hitchcock's Mystery Magazine* many times, one of the stories reprinted in a French anthology, *Histoires d'homicides à domicile*, published in Paris. He says, "I enjoy writing from a woman's point of view because they have more accessible sensibilities than men and can be believably portrayed as intelligent and resourceful even while displaying inadequacies many of us share. 'Prom Night' has its origins in an aggregation of overheard conversations and private exchanges with women on the edge who eventually came to terms with difficult circumstances and bravely moved on."

———

KYLIE frowned at the ghostly reflection in the fogged mirror, shaking her head at her own thoughts: *Figures . . . air-conditioning's broke, weather guy's going off on how it's the hottest damn day in a decade, perfect night for a date . . . be all hot and sweaty. Very attractive.*

She wiped the steamy glass with a washcloth, her slowly clearing image reminding her of some teenybopper primping for the prom: starry-eyed young thing wondering if that study hall note from Sally or Pam about Bobby giving her his class ring was really true, and would he get his father's car so they could go to the dance in style? Would he try to get fresh? Would she let him?

Would you just shut up?

The woman looking back at Kylie from the mirror was well past high school; wrinkles fanning out from the corners of her green eyes, another collection at the corners of the mouth: a topography of her life, representing every disappointment, hurt feeling, betrayal, broken promise, shattered dream, and cruel intent she'd endured in her thirty-eight years. As a matter of fact, she remembered, it had started on a prom night; persuasiveness of backseat promises ultimately resulting in her being a teenage mother, her baby girl in college now, though—dean's list, eye on the prize. Hopefully staying out of backseats.

Kylie stared at her streaked reflection. Managed not to weep.

Everything sagged; perky breasts were a vague memory, though ample enough to attract more attention from men at the office than she really wanted . . . hips so wide they had separate area codes, though she knew they weren't as bad as they looked to her. Kylie was aware she was like a lot of women, quick to trivialize her good points and even quicker to find defect in some feature less than extraordinary.

Was that the doorbell?

Kylie Baumer turned away from her pathetically hopeful stare, ran barefoot and nearly naked out of the bathroom and across the hall, hands covering and holding her breasts secure as she jogged across the darkened living room to the draped window next to her front door. Peeked through a tiny opening.

Nobody out there, nothing in the glowing patch of yellow light from the porch lamp other than a few moths doing what moths do; it had just been performance anxiety evoking the sound of doorbells. Because that's what a date is, a performance.

God, it's hot. Why in hell do we girls put ourselves through all this? she wondered as she headed back toward the bathroom, noticing that even the invigorating chill of the tile floor had abandoned her, the floor warm beneath her bare soles.

She shivered anyway, though she figured the trembling to be a kind of middle-age angst, a sort of pregeriatric apprehension. That would be Tracy's fault; because just that morning by the copy machine Tracy'd been telling her, "He's just what you've been looking for, girl—and time's a-wastin', we ain't gettin' any younger—hey, if he'd come onto me a month ago, I'd keep him for myself, but Alec and I are getting along, so this guy is all yours."

"No way," Kylie'd told her frizzy-haired friend while taking her turn at the copier, duplicating and collating the report Crapnoggin wanted by three o'clock. Craig Nugent was her boss's name; Crapnoggin was just her label for him.

No modern-day sexual harassment from Nugent; he made his subordinates' lives hell the old-fashioned way: yelling, screaming, threatening termination, and tectonic mood shifts.

"Yes, 'way,' " Tracy had insisted. "I know you like the intellectual type, and this guy's a real brain," glancing at the two other girls waiting to use the copier, a gleam in her eye.

Kylie knew that Tracy was putting her on; around the office they believed her a little slow, but it was just that she was always so uptight worrying about what people thought of her that sometimes she'd get confused. Her dad had told her on a daily basis how stupid she was, saying, "If brains were free, you'd be too dumb to get any." It took her until all the way through high school and two years community college to realize it was her dad who was not too swift, that she was much smarter than he. Still, his mocking tone followed her around even today, presenting as self-doubt.

Her mirrored reflection sternly admonished as she turned on the tap, "Just have a good time, Baumer, don't get all worked up, imagining this is going to be Mr. Right or some knight in shining armor or something. Anyway; been there, saw that, got the black eyes to prove it—and divorce papers, bruised ribs, broken heart." Need she go on?

Her reflection shook its head.

Kylie bent forward and washed makeup off her hands. Noticed a chip in the polish on her left thumbnail; it's what she gets for being so damn nervous. *But every little flaw adds up,* she thought, reaching for the cabinet knob to get at the polish.

Doorbell again?

No, the phone. She picked up the remote handset. It was on no-ring; she'd heard the one in the kitchen. "Hello."

"Is he good looking or what?" the female voice inquired. Her daughter, Sarah, calling from her dorm, no doubt.

Kylie pictured her red-haired daughter fingering the silver antique cross she'd given her for high school graduation, something Sarah always did when on the phone. "Not here yet, honey. What time's your game?" Kylie asked, cradling the phone on her shoulder and holding it there with her chin.

A sigh. "Boys can be such boys," her daughter replied.

"What happened, Sarah?"

"The *effect*? He didn't show up. The *cause*? Hell, who knows. Maybe he finally noticed I'm a little light in the boob department or decided he didn't like smart girls or redheads or someone who uses utensils when they eat. Since he didn't call to cancel, I didn't even get an excuse."

"Did you like him?" Kylie asked.

"Just met him . . . but I sure don't like the shithead now."

The bitterness in her daughter's voice disturbed her. A little concern wouldn't hurt right now, she thought, plus it might be a way out of this damn anxiety. "Why not drive up here? I'll beg off this date," she said.

"No way, José. You need to get out. Anyway, I don't feel like anything but maybe some Austen and the heavily laden pizza that's about to arrive."

Kylie'd never been able to get all the way through one of Jane Austen's stories, though she enjoyed the romantic aspects. She liked crime novels better. "You sure you're all right?"

Her daughter snorted softly. "Mother, if I got upset every time some guy disappointed me, I'd be gulping Prozac instead of pizza and beer. I'm fine, just wanted to see what this dude looked like, but you can call me in the morning—after ten though, I plan to eat a large, triple-cheese pizza all by myself, and the narcotic effect of all that mozzarella marinated in beer might keep me unconscious till nine or after."

"Honey, I think that's the door. Call you in the morning. Love you!"

"Me, too, Mom. Have a blast, but don't elope; I know you can be impulsive."

Laughing, Kylie punched the power button on the handset and put it on the counter . . . listened harder. Nothing—imagination again. Dried her hands, thinking, *Hell, girl, the only dingdong in this house is right here in that fogged mirror. Kylie Baumer, getting ready for prom night. Yeah, right.*

But after hanging the towel on the rack, she glanced over at her reflection, which seemed to be frowning contentiously, something inside her saying, *Wait a minute, dammit, so I want this to be prom night, what in holy hell's wrong with that?*

Kylie sighed, wishing just once in her life, inside her mind, she could be in agreement with herself.

She thought back to that morning and how Tracy hadn't stopped at just telling her this dude was just what Kylie was looking for; no way, she had to describe him, for Christ's sake. Dark blond hair and mustache. Dark blue eyes. "Kinda like Robert Redford as Sundance," her friend had promised, adding, "a lopsided smile lets you know he's interested, but maybe a little craz—"

This time it is the bell.

Flitting across the ceramic floor, bare feet slapping the warm tile like tentative applause, quickly over the soft living room carpet to right up beside the window, hand reaching for the drapes—*her mother's voice coming from somewhere behind other mildly unpleasant memories, telling her not to be seen like that, looked like she was eager, for heaven's sake.*

Kylie peered out through an opening in the drapes. *Yep, somebody's there.* The porch light illuminated a tall, thin man, looking around like he's lost, tiny beads of perspiration on his forehead.

Had to be a really hot night. Christ, I'll be sweating like a pig, too, she thought, sighing.

Don't use the lord's name in vain, Kylie, her mother's voice admonished as Kylie continued to look at her guest through the opening. *Brown* hair, not dark blond . . . couldn't make out the eyes, could be blue, could be chartreuse for all she could see. And he must have shaved the mustache; she was sure Tracy'd said he had a "cool" mustache. But damn, are those work clothes, for Christ's sake? (*Blasphemy, daughter!*)

Kylie ignored her mother's nagging, wondering, *Doesn't anybody dress up anymore?* Jeez, her black cocktail dress will look silly next to Mr. Green Jeans out there.

She took a breath before speaking loudly. "Just a minute, I'm running late—be just a second," watching the guy flinch, head jerked around to face the door, flinging a drop of sweat off the tip of his nose. Staring at the peep-hole.

And Kylie projected into her suitor's mind as she headed back to the bathroom: *Well, bitch, which is it, a minute or a second? Goddamn hot out here.* Yeah, rudeness wouldn't surprise her either—been there, done tha—

Back in front of the mirror, a quick check after applying lipstick . . . smoothed out the pancake glop a little more (*Too much, honey, you'll look like poor, white trash*) and running across the hall, through the living room and into her gorgeously humongous bedroom, over to her four-poster with canopy, thinking how she always knew she'd someday have a huge bedroom to make up for that square closet she shared with two sisters as a kid.

On the bed lay the little black dress, low-cut and sexy: cleavage city. Smiling as she thought, *Good thing about having a few extra pounds on the ol' frame is it can fill you out in places that matter.*

Course, Mr. Green Jeans out there will probably drool, say something crude about her boobs—Jesus, blind dates—and hell, the way he's dressed, maybe she should wear chinos and a sweatshirt and tell him in a starry-eyed way how fascinating his recitation of baseball statistics is. Great cologne; didn't know Kmart carried it, blah, blah, blah.

But old habits and battered self-esteem compelled her to shimmy the slinky black dress down over her head, letting it fall silently in place—glanced at the little Sony sitting on the armoire. Its sound was off, but the picture glowed colorfully: patches of pale green in the beige savanna, impossibly blue African sky. *National Geographic Special*; female lion lunging from high tan grass, soundlessly bringing down and killing a small gazelle. Poor thing.

Turn the TV off before you leave, goddammit; I'm not made of money. Her father's whiny voice. Long dead now.

"Just one second—I'm sorry!" she shouted in the general direction of the front door, slipping on hateful high heels. (*Don't shout, honey, not ladylike.*) Mom again.

All these voices careening around in her mind, even Tracy getting in on the act, Kylie remembering her saying this morning, "We like the same kind of guy; you'll love him." They were the same age, just a month apart. Tracy's birthday was today, September 24. Tracy telling her, "He's my gift to you for your next birthday. What'd you get me for mine?"

Kylie grabbed the thin strap of her silver purse, but it slipped through her fingers and fell to the floor. She scooped it up on the move, jogged to the front door, and leaned forward to look through the peephole. (*Don't do that, Kylie, he'll see you being rude. Don't worry about him; he's a fine, handsome young man.*)

No argument there, Mom, she thought, her mind racing ahead through the evening, deciding that if this guy was decent and even a little fun and she found him marginally human, then what the hell, it's been a long time.

Swinging the door wide open, she gave him a high-voltage smile just in case he's deserving of it—could always take it back. Damp feeling of perspiration had gathered in mutinous patches of moistness under her arms, at the small of her back and—

Well, hell, first impression was certainly an OK deal, though his hair was dull brown, not dark blond with sun streaks and—hazel eyes? Goddamn good-looking though, and she smiled openly, gratefully. (*Not the Lord's name, Kylie—please.*)

Smiling even wider, she took in his handsome face—every detail—and told her guest that she's Kylie, Tracy's friend, and he must be Adam and my, he sure looked familiar. . . .

She chastised herself, *Oh, yeah, right—now ask him his*

horoscope sign, goofy. Something in her mind collided with something emotional, and before she could quell the confusion she blurted, "What's your si—?" cutting herself off, face reddening and a champagne feeling of bubbling embarrassment rising through her nose into her—

—*empty goddamn head, what's wrong with you, Baumer?*

Her guest moved as though to enter—jerkily, the semblance of a smile on his face, but not really a smile.

(*He's just shy, Kylie, you be nice, or the boys won't like you.*) She frowned, wishing her mother would shut up and a tad startled by his sudden proximity—so surprised she stepped out of the way, teetering on the high heels, stumbled on the footstool, lost her balance, and fell over the ottoman to the floor—scalding embarrassment of galactic proportions washed over her as a self-destructive wish flashed through her mind . . . then an image of her ex-husband laughing and pointing.

Blinking, her face feeling as if she was looking in a furnace door, Kylie struggled to reorient herself . . . became peripherally aware of the little Sony in her bedroom—a stabilizing, familiar object—she turned to look at the same ol' screen she'd watched a million times, the picture glowing brightly. *National Geographic* was over, and it was the Channel 13 news, some talking head giving viewers the skinny.

Damn, you forgot to turn it off. Are you as stupid as you look? Her father, posthumously worried about electricity bills. Hell, even if he'd been there, still alive, he wouldn't notice his oldest daughter had just fallen to the floor, suffering bruised pride and a slightly twisted ankle.

Her attention was wholly captured by the tiny screen— reporter's face was gone, and there's that serial killer the cops are looking for—murdered nine girls the past two years in and around the Twin Cities. Stabbed and mutilated. They call him the Slasher. God, just like Bundy:

handsome and well-groomed. At least in that police sketch.

Kylie turned her head at a noise—her suitor noisily twisting the doorknob as he closed the front door from the inside—she glanced back at the TV, then quickly back to her handsome guest. Christ, was her date for the evening that guy on the screen? It's a police drawing, not a photo, hard to tell for sure. But that's why he'd looked familiar earlier—she'd pretty much thought her remark to him about seeing him before had been just her own insecurities voiced as nervous banter.

Sudden as a predator's attack, a prescient chill had its way with her spine, skittering upward on clawed little feet, creating twitching waves of icy apprehension in their wake. *I've let a killer in the house! I'm going to die right here in my own—*

Kylie felt disoriented, dizzy, as though hurtling through a dark tunnel of charred perceptions, her self-image crumbling into black, brittle remnants of some indefinable substance, her essence filtering to ground in what seemed to be the future. . . .

It's the office copy room with Tracy, her boss, and the other girls talking in hushed tones, not noticing the amorphous pile of dark debris on the floor that was once their coworker, Kylie Baumer. "She let the guy in without knowing him," Tracy's telling them, trying to hide the fact that she'd vouched for Kylie's blind date, said she knew him and that he was a nice guy. Nugent, her boss, nodding his crappy noggin and saying, "She was wound too tight, too needy; woman like that is just asking for trouble."

Kylie felt her feelings magnetize suddenly, gathering around her in an ever-tightening vortex, plucking her from the copy room floor and whirling her from that imminent future back to her house.

Deposited softly, like cold ashes, on the living room carpet and just inches from where a killer was standing; dark, cruel eyes staring down at her.

Another noise outside. Someone's footsteps on the porch. *Doorbell ringing, thank God!*

Her visitor quickly bent down to her, roughly lifting her to her feet beside him, Kylie feeling a sharp twinge of pain in her ankle, the guy pulling something metallic from his coat—(knight in shining armor?) she couldn't see what it was—put his incredibly strong hand over her mouth, flicking the metal object close to her face, the menacing movement causing her to close her eyes tight. *Oh, God, is it a knife?*

He put his lips close to her ear, whispered something that might as well have been in another language—heard him clearly, but her mind wouldn't process the words. Gibberish, uttered in a sibilant stream of mint-flavored breath; she could catch just a couple phrases: ". . . kill you . . . your friend, Tracy."

Felt a slight pinch on her arm—opened her eyes to see her "suitor" for the evening putting his finger to his lips— hard, cold eyes telling her that to speak would not be good. Then he nodded, looked out through the little opening in the drapes.

After a couple beats, he glanced back down into her eyes and shook his head calmly, whispering, "Not a sound, OK?"

The doorbell rang again.

Kylie blinked a couple times, her eyes stinging, thinking: *Last date . . . ever.*

Sudden scuffling sounds from outside as if someone was running down the stairs—shouts, gunfire. More shots from off a ways.

And then silence arrived so suddenly it seemed to roar.

The front door burst open, and someone rushed inside, stopped, looked at her and the man with his hand over her mouth. Kylie peered out toward the darkened yard, the body lying on her sidewalk in a sliver of yellow from the porch light. She gazed directly into the dead stare sightlessly fixed on some meaningless point in the night sky, tiny glint of orange streetlight reflecting. Police officers moved in and formed a blue forest of legs around him, and she couldn't see his face anymore.

The dead man had dark blond hair, though, and a Sundance mustache. Just like the drawing on TV, which also matched the description of her blind date Tracy had given her that very morning.

A shiny badge flickered in Mr. Green Jeans's hand as he put it away and gently removed his hand from her mouth. "Sorry, but I needed to keep you quiet. We had to get this guy." Introducing himself as Detective Dylan Keegan, continuing, "Twin City Task Force has been watching your friend Tracy and other girls in the Minneapolis–Saint Paul area ever since the Quantico profiler gave us a match on victims. All had birthdays on the twenty-fourth of the month they were killed, blonde hair, in their thirties."

Kylie heard him, but the words weren't making a lot of sense. She tried to focus, tried to slow the whirling sensation in her head. Something snapped, and she could finally get what he was saying.

"Incredible luck really—the operative following Tracy lost contact, and we were going around to all her friends to see if anybody knew where she'd been heading or where she was now. I spotted that guy in a van around the corner whose description matched our police sketch. Called for backup and waited. Wanted to get him on private property attempting entry so we'd have intent, though DNA would've probably clinched it. Course, courts being the way they are, you can't be too thorough."

Kylie just stared at him. Some goddamn suitor. A tad verbose.

"You all right, Ms. Baumer?" the detective asked, tilting his head in a way to indicate concern, like he really cared or something . . . and then, of course, he reached out and brushed away some perspiration from her chin with his left hand, giving her a really intriguing smile. No wedding ring.

She sighed, crossed the living room, went into her bedroom, and turned off the TV. Her thoughts were basic, wondering whether she should call Sarah tonight or wait till after ten in the morning. She'd call tonight—make her daughter feel better to know getting stood up isn't the worst thing that can happen to you.

Kylie slowed her breathing, calming herself for a few beats more, trying to put the last few minutes into some kind of perspective, something you could explain. Gave it up . . . looked out at the detective, his intriguing smile reasserting itself. She again saw his ringless finger. But she was too tired to flirt. Way too tired.

Noticing he was about to speak, Kylie cut him off, saying, "Some goddamn *prom night*," headed for her closet, saw out the corner of her eye he was frowning at her remark, maybe thinking she was odd or ditsy, going off on prom nights.

Whatever. So damn hot tonight. She'd hang up the dress, put on something relaxing, cool. Maybe shorts and a halter. He wants to watch, that's his business.

NIGHT ROSE

Ana Rainwater

Ana Rainwater lives with her husband in Texas. She has a Ph.D. in literature, teaches university literature and writing courses, and has published a number of essays and scholarly articles. "Night Rose" is her first foray into fiction. Ana wishes to note that in real life her mother is a very nice woman, although she did in fact present Ana with a crowbar and super-size coffee can on the day Ana got her driver's license.

ON the August day I turned sixteen and got my driver's license, my mother presented me with an empty Folger's can and a crowbar, right there in the DPS parking lot.

"If the car breaks down, lock the doors and wait for me to come find you," she said in the clear, carrying, Southern aristocrat voice she so carefully cultivated. "Don't get out, no matter what. If you have to pee, use the coffee can."

Teenage self-consciousness was as alien to my mother as any other form of self-doubt. I glanced around surreptitiously. Except for an elderly woman trying to negotiate the curb with her walker, we were alone with the flagpoles, cars, and warning signs reminding the public what not to do on government property.

Peremptory as always, my mother held out the coffee can.

"It even has a lid," she said.

"Aw, Mother," I began, eyeing it with distaste as she forced it into my hands. She cut me off with a flick of her wrist, the silk sleeve of her elegant blouse making the motion imperious instead of just bossy.

"No arguments," she said. "Remember what happened to Sandy Bontke."

Sandy Bontke got pregnant on the high school chorus trip to Wichita Falls, according to the school grapevine, or else maybe behind the gym during the last basketball game of the school year, but my mother pooh-poohed such mundane theories. As the Bontkes' nearest neighbor, she felt she had a right to an opinion, never mind that her shadow never once had darkened the Bontkes' door.

"It was the night she got that flat tire," Mother insisted. "Some man stopped to help her, and he raped her in the dark."

No one else, not even Sandy's own mother, had ever put forth a rape theory, but my mother was adamant. "It had to be rape in the dark," she said. "What man in his right mind would sleep with Sandy if he could see her?"

"That isn't very nice, Mother," I replied uncomfortably, again scanning the parking lot now that she'd moved from bodily functions to sex. Secretly, I liked Sandy Bontke and was sorry for her troubles, though certainly Sandy was a bit unfinished by my mother's standards. Then again, wasn't everyone?

My mother put her hand on her slender hip—the hand not holding the crowbar—and fixed me with her cool blue gaze.

"Nice has nothing to do with it," she retorted calmly, then with her own particular brand of logic began to elaborate. "Sandy Bontke is young enough to know better. When a girl that age goes out of her way to look frumpy, she's obviously a lesbian, or worse. Any man who got a good look at her would know immediately."

Her eyes ran slowly down my own less-than-spectacular figure, and she nodded shortly. "You'll do," she said. "You look like you mean to be a woman one day. Sandy Bontke looks as if she means to be a mule. As I'm sure you know, mules are asexual, unable to reproduce. Biologically speaking, it's amazing she got pregnant."

My upbringing was rather short on the milk of human kindness.

"Stop thinking about Sandy Bontke," my mother said then, impatiently, as if she weren't the one who had introduced the subject. Her glance rested on the DPS sign set in the pavement near us, and she smiled as a pleasing thought occurred to her.

"Sandy Bontke is carrying the seed of a criminal," she said. "It would be a blessing if she lost that baby."

Horrified, I stared at my mother. She shifted her hips in their fashionably thin skirt and waved cheerfully to a trooper leaving the building, then turned her attention back to me.

"Perhaps I'll take her some flowers," she said brightly. "Now, pay attention. This is important highway safety."

With a snakelike twist, my mother swung the crowbar, still in its protective blue plastic wrap, up between my legs. I shrieked and jumped back just in time, feeling the pointed teeth of the crowbar almost catch on the thick crotch seam of my faded jeans. For a moment I was speechless with indignation.

"Mother," I finally said, almost stuttering. "You could hurt somebody!"

This was a feeble response even for me, but actual physical assault was a novelty. Did this mean I could hit her back? The disgraceful thought flitted through my head and instantly was gone. This was, after all, my mother.

She tilted her head and regarded me as if I weren't quite bright. "Exactly," she replied, exaggerated patience dripping from every word. "Hurting someone is exactly the point. If you'd been a boy, I'd have got you. See, you've got to start low and swing upwards, fast. Don't hesitate, and don't you ever raise that crowbar up above your head and swing it down—a newborn baby could block that move. Go ahead. Block it."

With that, she brought the crowbar down on my head.

THE night wanderings began a few days later. They started because of the headaches, which led to nightmares, which led to insomnia. One night I stared for hours at the breeze-blown curtain, afraid to turn on the light or pace the floor lest I wake my mother and deprive her of her beauty sleep. From the open window, wafted on the night air, came the scent of my mother's flowers, and claustrophobia over-whelmed me. As silently as a vapor, I pulled on clothes and sneakers and swung a leg out my second-story window.

The fact that we lived thirty miles from town and I bought my own gas took some of the initial thrill out of the escapade, and besides, I couldn't figure out how to start the car without waking my brothers or my ever-vigilant mother. But hours of silence persuaded me that the night had value of its own, separate and apart from whatever I might do in it. I grew accustomed to the black-and-white world of moonlight, a world washed clean of the gaudy colors of day.

After that first night alone in the velvety darkness, I was hooked.

Soon I perfected my Indian walk, one foot placed sound-lessly in front of the other, rolling smoothly heel to toe. Without disturbing a rabbit or silencing the crickets, I haunted the cowless cow pastures, looking for arrowheads in the moonlight. We had only a handful of near neighbors, none of them kids my age except for Sandy Bontke, who was pregnant and by summer's end gone, so for a long time I ignored the potential of other people's houses. Shadows came and went with the rising and falling of the moon, and I was just another shadow, quieter and less noticeable than most.

Until the night I found a use for the coffee can.

It had been almost two years since my mother hit me with the crowbar, and my hair had grown back out to shoulder length, more than sufficiently hiding the scars from twelve stitches in my scalp. In the two-inch-long gash where the crowbar had hit, the hair came back a whitish blonde, startling against the dark brown of my natural hair. Mother assured me it looked very chic.

By that time, she and I weren't speaking much. I was seventeen; she was menopausal. The Hormone Zone, my younger brother called our house, and I thought it was a credit to his ten-year-old intelligence that he noticed the unspoken tensions during the marginal hours before Mother went to work and after she came home. Mother divided the stress nicely: the mornings were devoted to criticizing my appearance, the evenings to fixing it. My rebellion took less direct forms.

Some evenings Mother would insist on rolling my damp hair on those pink sponge rollers, standing behind me, staring balefully at my youthful reflection in the mirror, gripping the comb and brush like weapons. Later at night I'd unroll my hair, sometimes all of it, sometimes just part of it, pleased the next morning by the resulting vagaries.

"Your head looks like a rat's nest," she'd say as I hurried out the door for school.

"It came undone during the night," I'd reply, the picture of teenage innocence.

Then it was June, full summer, the summer before my senior year. Somebody had to stay with my little brother during the summer break, so I couldn't get a job in town where all my friends from school were minding counters, flipping burgers, or mowing yards. Instead, I worked at home tending our large garden, which meant weeding, fertilizing, thinning, staking, tying up, watering, harvesting, canning, and freezing. Benjy helped some, but he was easily distracted, and I didn't begrudge him his free time. Besides, I felt a sort of affinity for the poor mundane vegetables and tended them with dedication, growing browner and browner in the Texas sun despite my care with hats and sunscreen.

One day the wind got up, and though it was windy, it was still hot, as if someone had turned a heater on during a hundred-degree day. It kept blowing all day long as I worked, antagonizing my restless blood, and in a moment of abandon I severed the neck of my mother's prized cherry tomato plant with a single neat stroke of my hoe.

Standing there in the heat, I knew I'd pay for my recklessness later. Sure enough, upon her arrival home, Mother stared me down over the top of her designer sunglasses and remarked haughtily, "You treat my garden like a hired hand would, so I shouldn't be surprised that you look like one."

By evening when I went indoors, the wind's whistling cadence seemed as taunting as a demon's laughter, and my very blood felt hot from the long day in the sun. Hours before my mother and brother went to bed, I knew I'd be going out that night. I knew it was time.

At midnight I slipped out my second-floor window, shimmied down the rose trellis, and carefully stepped over my mother's beautifully manicured border of daylilies. The full moon seemed to give as much heat as the sun, and under my plain white men's T-shirt I had already begun to sweat.

This was the night I'd been waiting for since the day I

was too stupid, too distracted by whispers of evil, to duck my mother's blow.

"Weren't you listening?" was the first thing she said to me when I regained consciousness in the ambulance. Then she turned to the state trooper who was riding along with us, giving him the full benefit of her dark-lashed gaze. "I told her even a baby could protect herself from what I was going to do!"

But I had been listening too well.

In the shadowed darkness I gazed around the yard, noting every bank of flowers, each tended by my mother's own manicured hands. Lavender, blue monkshood, foxglove, bleeding hearts, lupine, delphinium. So many to choose from, so many odd flowers belonging to milder climates, coaxed along like puny children, pampered and prompted to grow. But these held only a cursory, reminiscent interest for me tonight. My purpose lay behind me, whence I'd come.

The white of the house was blinding in the moonlight, and the scent of the roses was nauseatingly strong. Perhaps the excessive heat drew out their fragrance; perhaps they sweated it out like blood. I stared at their disgusting domesticity, at the way they clung to the house. Pretty little roses, the flower everybody loved. The world's most popular flower, or so my mother claimed.

Standing there by the defenseless roses, I considered the demands of my plan. Any noise inside the house my mother would hear; the contents of the tiny garden shed held nothing of use. Then I remembered the survival supplies my mother had placed in my ancient Plymouth Duster, and I smiled.

Silently I crept around the house to my car and collected the coffee can. Returning to the rose trellis, I carefully stripped each and every sweet little bloodred bloom from the thorny, climbing branches. Climbing roses don't have thick stems, so I could manage easily without the garden shears, but still, my fingers were bleeding from a score of small wounds before I'd finished.

The coffee can was giant-sized—either my mother severely overestimated the capacity of my bladder or else she planned to wait a good long time before coming to find me—but though I packed the roses down tight, crushing their petals against the silvery metal, I had to make three trips before the trellis housed only desolate, prickly canes.

Three quarter-mile trips up the asphalt road, walking in the windswept, sultry darkness. Three trips ready to climb down into the bar ditch and scurry under the barbed wire fence at the sight of headlights, which never came. Three trips keeping an eye out for cover in the fields, a cactus patch, a scraggly mesquite. But the trips were uneventful.

The Bontkes' house was silent as a womb deprived of life, was perhaps as empty. I'd heard that Mr. Bontke's drinking problem had worsened after Sandy's trouble, that he drove out to Impact and sat in front of the liquor store until dawn. It's tough being a drunk when the nearest town is dry.

Where Mrs. Bontke went in the evenings, nobody was saying. Maybe she visited Sandy. Or maybe she had a friend in town, someone to keep her company on long, hot nights like this one. Maybe they played cards, I thought as I strode down the deserted farm-to-market road, or maybe they shot pool. Maybe they made virgin daiquiris and danced on the back porch. Mrs. Bontke had frowsy blondish hair, just like Sandy's, and eyes that accepted what they saw. She looked like she wouldn't object to company, even less-than-perfect company, maybe somebody who smoked or chewed tobacco, or who forgot and took the Lord's name in vain when he blackened a thumbnail.

Unlike my own mother.

I took each can of crushed roses, guiltily thankful that the Bontkes' dog had got hit by a pickup last winter, and I spread the blooms around the house, lining the perimeter of Sandy's home with bloodred blossoms.

Then I went home, climbed up the beautifully denuded rose trellis, and went to bed.

It wasn't until late the next day that my mother noticed the vandalism.

"I declare!" she said, coming into the kitchen where I was fixing supper. "My roses are all gone!"

Busily stirring gravy on the stove, I kept my eyes down and remarked nonchalantly, "That's odd. Maybe the heat got to them. It's an awful hot summer."

"No," my mother said impatiently. "I mean gone, really gone. My roses have simply disappeared."

My little brother walked into the kitchen as she spoke and began humming the theme to *The Twilight Zone*.

"Aliens abduct Texas roses," he said in what he thought was a sinister voice. Poor kid wouldn't sound more sinister than a mouse for a good three years, and even then I bet he'd have to go through all that squeaking first. Benjy, like me, wouldn't be the sort to coast through adolescence gracefully. At least I didn't have a gorgeous older sister to live up to, whereas poor Benjy would always be in my older brother Mark's shadow, at least if my mother had anything to say about it.

"Shut your mouth, Benjamin," my mother said, irritated. I felt sorry for Benjy, so I laughed at him and continued his game.

"Scientists yesterday were stunned to note the deflowering of every red climber in the state—" I paused. "What are your roses called? Blaze?"

"Don Juan," she said absently. "As you well know. Stop being silly, you two. Come see what I mean."

"Can't, unless you want to stand here and stir the gravy."

She took the slotted spoon from me. "Go on," she said, turning up the heat. That would make lumps in the gravy, but I supposed it was the price I'd have to pay for my fun last night. Benjy and I shoved open the screen door and went out back.

"Wow!" he said, gazing at the white trellis with awe. "They really are gone. What do you suppose happened?"

"Hmm. I don't know. Do rabbits eat roses?"

"Dumbbell," he said, shoving me affectionately. "Rabbits sure don't climb trellises. Even the roses up top are gone."

"You're right," I replied. "What do you think happened?"

He shrugged, already losing interest. "Mom probably went whacko and deadheaded them all without noticing," he said. "You know how she gets when she's on a tear."

Then his eyes lit up. "But if they weren't dead when she did it, it wasn't deadheading. It was liveheading."

"Beheading," I offered.

FOR the rest of the summer, every time that rose produced so much as a bud, I'd pinch it off and carry it up the road to the Bontkes'. Once I let the bush produce a good crop of blossoms, and Mom was thrilled. She'd decided some mysterious pest was to blame, perhaps grasshoppers or birds, and never seemed to notice that the flowers always disappeared during the night. Then I cropped the blooms again, carried them petal-light up the road in my coffee can, and poured them across the hood of the Bontkes' station wagon.

All the night walking firmed up my figure some, and Mom started making approving noises.

"You keep this up, maybe Mark will bring some of his friends home from college to meet you," she said one Saturday evening, back from her work at the Dillards' cosmetic counter.

"I don't think I'd like any of Mark's friends," I replied, though really I had nothing against my brother save for his genetic inability to stand up to my mother. I would save Benjy from that disintegration of personality, that gradual paralysis in the face of my mother's gale-force will.

My mother snorted. "That's what girls always say when they think they don't stand a chance," she said. "Here. I've bought some extra eggs. Every morning I want you to separate one and use the yolk on your face. It'll clear up your complexion. Egg yolks are high in vitamin A. Leave it on ten minutes and rinse with warm water, and don't scrub dry with the towel. Just pat gently, and then put on some light moisturizer. Don't use regular hand lotion. I'll get you some Oil of Olay with my employee discount."

She was proud of that discount, of that job, of the fact that the other "enhancement consultants" were twenty years younger than she. It gave her a kick to try her beauty treatments on poor little me, hoping aloud that I'd improve enough to appeal to some rising young man, someone like my brother, who had been shipped off to college despite all obstacles. Nothing would prevent her son from attaining an education, she said to all and sundry—nothing and no one, not even Mark himself. She and she alone was the mother, and she knew best.

That night, for good measure, I stripped her irises and carried them to Sandy's house.

The summer got longer, and hotter, and the more my mother tried to prepare me for what she was pleased to call "a woman's life," the more I walked the sweltering night. During the day I was too tired to do anything but manual labor; if I sat down, I directly fell asleep.

So I worked slowly, half in a stupor, unable to take long naps for fear that Benjy would say something about my lethargy in front of Mother. In a daze I worked, and sweated, and thought about my perfectionist mother and her influence on my brothers, my father, myself, those of us who weren't perfect and could never hope to be.

Finally my birthday drew near, and with pleasure I planned the present I would give myself to celebrate my freedom from minority status. At long last, it was time to use the crowbar.

The very moment when the fifth day of August became the sixth, when I was eighteen years of age and legally able to be guardian rather than guarded, I crept out of bed and out the window. Another hot night, and I welcomed the heat, let it strengthen the blood in my veins. I glided silently across the grass to the garden plot, picked up my heavy gardening gloves from the shelf in the tiny shed. Opening my car door, I bent low and removed the crowbar from where my mother had stowed it two years before, deep beneath the driver's seat. It was the first time I'd touched the thing.

The walk to the Bontkes' house was the most enjoyable of the entire summer. The asphalt breathed out waves of heat stored up during the day, and the stars above twinkled merrily, bright eyes that had seen everything that wasn't seen under the sun. The stars knew, and the moon knew, and I knew. We knew who sneaked out of my mother's house, how long ago, how often, and why. We had seen the shadow, every time.

They say that sweltering summer brings crime waves, but I was a one-woman wave of honor. My birthday present was justice.

The Bontkes' house was, as usual, dark and silent. Both cars were gone tonight. I hoped Mrs. Bontke was at the cemetery that backed onto the Quick-Stop gas station, visiting her only child, and the beginnings of her only grandchild. It would be fitting if she were there tonight with Sandy.

Just to be safe, I rang the doorbell. It echoed in the lonely house, and I pounded on the door. When I was certain the place was deserted, I pulled a shower cap from my pocket and fitted it snugly over my hair, tucking in every single wayward strand. Then I walked around to Sandy's window and, raising the crowbar high, brought it down with a crash through the glass. Reaching in carefully with my gloved fingers, I undid the latch and shoved the window up.

I climbed in, ever so carefully.

Then I trashed the place. I smashed mirrors, overturned furniture, dumped dresser drawers across the floor. In less than ten minutes, you'd have thought a tornado had hit. Back in Sandy's room I gently laid the crowbar in the middle of the bed, along with one red rose. Its petals spilled across the coverlet like drops of blood. I reached in my pocket and pulled out the hairs I'd removed from my mother's brush, dropping one, two, three of them randomly across the floor.

Task completed, I climbed out the window, brushed my clothes off carefully to make sure no shards of glass clung to them, and stepped deliberately in the broken glass, embedding tiny pieces in the soles of my mother's tennis shoes.

The sheriff took longer than I'd expected, but in the end he came, after supper on my eighteenth birthday. Mother was dying her hair when he arrived, a bit of serendipity I've always enjoyed. He took her fingerprints and as an afterthought mine, and asked where we'd been the night before.

"Your neighbor says you've been trespassing on her property all summer now," he said to my mother, when she demanded to know what was happening. Uneasy, he shifted his tan cowboy hat from one hand to the other, glancing at me from beneath grizzled brows. He'd heard about us.

Mother stared at him, pointedly waiting for him to explain. He opened his mouth to speak, then stopped and cleared his throat. Still Mother waited, and eventually, as all men did, he gave in.

"Miz Bontke thinks you resented her daughter," he said, setting his hat on the table and crossing his arms across his chest. It was a defensive posture, but I saw that his gaze was fixed on Mother like a hawk watching its prey. He wasn't quite the harmless old country gent he pretended.

"She says that during the course of this summer you seem to have developed some sort of unhealthy fixation—she used the word *obsession*—with the family in general. Even claims you had something to do with Sandy's death, though I don't see how that could be. Even a child could tell that was suicide."

My mother snorted.

"How dare she attempt to psychoanalyze me. Tell Mrs. Bontke she should have psychoanalyzed her daughter," she retorted, then cast a dark glance at me. "Sounds to me like she's the one who's obsessed."

"Be that as it may, ma'am, we'll need to ask you some more questions," the sheriff said, getting up to leave. "Especially if these prints match, and Mrs. Bontke seems sure they will. And you'd best be prepared for them newspaper reporters to be knocking on your door."

Mother smiled grimly. "I'm prepared for anything. Come back tomorrow morning, Sheriff, and you'll get all the answers you need, tied up neatly with a bow on top. I have no intention of living with this scandal hanging over me."

Even I couldn't have planned such a perfect little speech.

The sheriff shot a swift look at my mother, then put his hat on his head and turned toward me and the door. His eyes lingered on my oddly streaked hair, and I felt him hesitate, so I smiled brightly at him, willing him to believe I wasn't afraid of my mother. For the first time in my recollection, I wasn't.

The sheriff nodded, opened the door, and walked down the caliche path toward his car, winding his way through my mother's flowerbeds. Tactful man, the sheriff. Only his glance at my skunk-striped hair had revealed that he remembered the crowbar incident, and not even a glance to the left or the right as he walked to his car suggested that he remembered anything else. But of course he did. I certainly did.

I would always remember watching my mother walk the caliche path among the flowers, touching gently those blossoms whose beauty, like all beauty, hides only death. From my bedroom window I saw her gather certain blooms with her own hands, and I crept down the stairs and peered out from behind the kitchen curtains. Feeling eerily like a mouse watching the cat pursue other prey, I sneaked behind her as she walked the road to our nearest neighbors' house, a house she had never once deigned to enter.

Sandy, not yet half through her pregnancy, was home alone.

From the shadows I watched, helpless and frightened, my stubbly hair hiding a still-aching scalp, as my mother pretended friendship. I heard her bright, joking warnings as she stood on the porch and presented her goodwill offering.

"I know you've been having a hard time, darling, and you've got far more troubles ahead, believe you me. Single parenting, no more dates or dances, and all for the baby of a man who despises you, who only wanted to see you hurt, who impregnated you in darkness and then disappeared forever. That's what you're carrying in your womb, sweetheart, the seeds of hatred and darkness.

"So I picked these especially for you, Sandra dear, especially and only for you. They're pretty enough to eat, don't you think? But you mustn't. Are you a gardener? No? But you have heard that sometimes pregnant women get odd cravings, for tree bark or soap or whatnot. You must be sure to remember that these flowers must not be eaten. They would be very, very bad for your baby."

Then she winked slowly and deliberately at Sandy.

That's how close I was, close enough to see Sandy's eyes widen, her mouth open in understanding.

"Mother Nature has answers to all a girl's problems," Mother said as she turned away. "There's no reason to suffer through female trouble."

I heard, and I understood, and I should have warned Sandy, but God help me, I was afraid of my mother and I didn't. And only I had heard, no one else was near, no one else could tell why Sandy locked herself in the bathroom that night and ate death. Everyone knew, or pretended to know, that of course foxglove was fatal, and not just for fetuses. Sandy must have known it, too. So they assumed.

Poor Sandy, so depressed, humiliated, taking her own life. She was raped, you know.

Raped by the shadow who repeatedly stole down the road through the night, raped without a scream or a cry or a struggle, raped in pleasure and with pleasure and not raped, not raped, not raped at all, sowing the seeds of life with love and hope and pleasure. Not raped. All that long summer, not raped.

Until the second shadow came and tricked her into eating the seeds of death.

To my surprise, my mother said nothing after the sheriff left. Silently she went to bed, and after some thought, I followed suit. There could be no wandering tonight.

In the morning we sat opposite each other at the sun-drenched kitchen table, eating toast and marmalade and drinking tea—mine plain, my mother's as usual strongly honeyed. Benjy, only moments away from freedom, was still asleep.

"I don't understand how they knew the crowbar came from this house," my mother said quietly, leaning back in her chair and tightening the belt of her floral silk bathrobe. "Why did they think to come fingerprint me, of all people?"

I shrugged.

But I knew, and so did Mrs. Bontke, who once had loved my mother's flowers. And now, staring out the window at her flowerbeds, my mother knew as well. She eyed me, stretched out one perfectly manicured finger, and stroked the silken petals of the freshly picked bouquet on the table. Then she opened her mouth to speak but stopped at the crunching sound of tires on the drive.

"My, the sheriff is prompt," she said, pushing back her chair and standing up. "And me not even dressed yet. Well, it won't take us long to straighten this mess out."

Her breakfast was all but finished. She picked up her cup of tea, glanced into it, and drained the last few drops.

"I don't know what you were thinking, missy, but you know better than to cross me," she said. Then her hand went to her breast. Startled, she tried to set her cup down on the edge of the table but missed, and it fell to the floor with a crash.

There was a knock at the door. For an instant, I shut my eyes, readying myself to face the sheriff with the terrible news. It shouldn't be too difficult, given her fortuitously phrased speech of the previous night. He wouldn't be surprised that an unstable woman had chosen not to face the consequences of her increasingly irrational actions.

When I looked back at my mother, her face had paled,

leaving her makeup as garish as a clown's. She pressed one arm tightly against her stomach, held the other hand against her chest. She staggered slightly, only slightly. Then she raised her head and looked at me with a gleam in her eye. In any other woman it would have been a tear, but in my mother it was a glint of satisfaction. She would have the last word, and say it as sweetly as if she were conferring a blessing rather than a curse.

"You're stronger than your brothers, child of my heart," she said. "Good-bye, Rose."

Neighborhood Watch

Sinclair Browning

Sinclair Browning is the author of the award-nominated mystery series featuring Trade Ellis, a woman who is part Apache, part rancher, and all private eye, against the backdrop of the modern Southwest. The books include *The Last Song Dogs*, *The Sporting Club*, *Rode Hard, Put Away Dead*, and *Crack Shot*. One of five nominees for the 2000 Arizona Arts Award, she has also published two historical novels: *Enju, the Life and Times of an Aravaipa Apache Chief from the Little Running Water* and *America's Best*, a World War II story. She is the editor of *Feathers Brush My Heart* and is the coauthor of the best-selling horse-training book, *Lyons on Horses*. She lives in southern Arizona, where she still breaks her own horses, team pens, rounds up cattle, and struggles with her web site: **sinclairbrowning.com**.

———

I **WAS** sweating pretty good, but July in Tucson will do that to you. Nerves will, too.

My name is Trade Ellis, and answering personal ads is definitely out of my bailiwick. I'm a rancher and a private eye. Cows and cases, that's pretty much my life.

But I'd answered that damned newspaper ad, and now here I was sitting in the bar at Stewart Anderson's Restaurant, staring at my Canadian Club and water while my date was trying to see if we could slip into the dining room for a quiet dinner. We'd started out agreeing to just meet for a drink, and now he'd moved into food gathering. Apparently our first encounter was going swimmingly.

I studied the wet glass rings left on the table and tried to figure out just how far I would go with him on our first date. Doing *it* of course was out of the question. I mean, there's just so far I'm willing to go in the line of duty. But a hug, a lingering kiss, maybe even if he wanted to cop a quick feel, yeah, I could probably go along with all that if it meant a second date.

And I had to have that second date.

Not only did my fee depend on it, but so did an old friend. Marisal Valdez had been missing since last Valentine's Day. She'd disappeared from her university-area town house a day after she'd answered a personal ad. Not a lot like the one that had brought me here, but close enough that her family had called me and asked if I'd look into it. They'd been scouring the Arizona newspapers for months in the hopes that her last date would run his ad again, the same one that had run in the *Tucson Weekly*, an alternative newspaper here.

While the ad wasn't the same at all, a phrase from the original ad—the one that Marisal had tucked into her bedroom dresser mirror—had appeared, and that was enough to give a heads up to the vigilant Valdez family.

"Loves curling up with a good Disney movie." That was the tip, for that particular phrase was identical to the one that had run months earlier.

And while the police had tried to run the earlier advertiser to ground, they had little to show for their efforts other than an abandoned post office box with no forwarding address.

The Valdezes had also shared the new information with the Tucson Police Department. I had no idea if they were also monitoring my date's ad, but he'd answered my response, so I figured I'd go for it.

The ad had all the other usual abbreviations: SWM. I'd already noticed there was no *D* for divorced. Curious, since most guys who are forty-five—the age he'd advertised—had been married before. But then maybe he was waiting until we became better acquainted before he shared his marital history. Besides, just because he'd neglected that *D* didn't make him an ax murderer.

Marisal's parents were desperate. The Tucson police were doing what they could, but it was not enough. It never is. Their daughter's disappearance was compounded by the fact that she had answered quite a few of these ads, enough so that she had been teased unmercifully by her family. The result was that she had unfortunately quit sharing the particulars of each of her blind dates. Big particulars. Like names and telephone numbers.

"Uh, I think they can give us dinner," my date pulled me out of my reverie.

"Great," I said with an enthusiasm I didn't feel. What I was feeling was guilty. John Wistrich had already told me he was a bricklayer, so I suspected that he wasn't shot in the ass with bucks, and here he was about to unload a pile of money for a nice dinner that in all likelihood was going nowhere. Still, I'd promised the Valdez family I'd see it through.

That bricklayer thing didn't sit well with me, either. Not that I have anything against masons, just that it seemed like a stretch from the "successful businessman" that had run in the ad. The one tucked in Marisal's mirror had touted "professional." I'd already determined that Wistrich didn't own the company. Still, if there were many more whoppers like that one, I'd need to get out my hip boots.

Dinner was one of those hunt-and-peck attempts as each of us tried to feel the other out. It was difficult with John because he seemed to be sorely lacking in social skills.

He wasn't a bad-looking guy. Sort of a Harry Potter grown up. Tall, with thick glasses that shrank what looked like could be interesting eyes, and an oversized Adam's apple that bobbed up and down right before he answered any question I tossed his way. Even the most innocuous query I lobbed seemed to embarrass him, for a slow red burn would creep up his neck to his face.

I did manage to learn that he had never been married and was very fond of his Tibetan terrier. In spite of being overly keen on four-legged creatures, I had to confess I'd never heard of a Tibetan terrier.

"He's great," John assured me. "Fluffy hair and a tail that curls over his back. We watch movies together."

Wow. Could a guy who was that enthusiastic about his dog really have done away with the thirty-year-old Marisal?

Sure. In a heartbeat.

But the dog lover opposite me was shy and lacking in self-confidence. I noticed his hands were shaking when he held the menu, and the few times I'd caught him staring at me, he had abruptly dropped his eyes to the salt and pepper shakers as a telltale rash crept up his neck and threatened to oxidize him. Definitely not my type and I suspected not Marisal's, either.

But I couldn't overlook that he had perhaps been the last person who had seen my friend. Her car had been found in the Tucson Community Center parking lot. No one had seen her there, and there were no strange prints in the car, although, if I was to believe Uncle C, my closest relative in the Pima County Sheriff's Department, there had been a number of interesting rug fibers and strands of hair that didn't match anything known to have been connected with Marisal Valdez. So far, unfortunately, they hadn't been connected to anyone else, either. Had a body turned up, the police probably would have been a teeny bit more interested in my friend's disappearance.

The one clue the cops had to go on was *Main.* Just *Main.* The word, written in Marisal's handwriting, had been found on a scratch pad near her kitchen telephone. I imagine they had, like me, wrestled with its significance. Street, was of course, the obvious connection. And Tucson had a Main Street all right, blocks and blocks of it. I'd already checked out the other Mains: Main Glass Company, Main Street Billiards, Main Meat Market, Main Supply, Main Water Company, even a Main Street Market in Mammoth.

I attacked my fillet, tempering it with healthy doses of Merlot as I tried to draw a mental portrait of Wistrich with Marisal. I'd always thought that Marisal was one of the most striking women I'd ever seen. Her big brown eyes were shaded with thick black eyelashes, and her straight black hair fell to her waist. She was tiny, less than five feet, and not much bigger than a bag of horse pellets. Although she'd recently been trying to get a handle on it, she'd been bulimic since high school. We're talking a top contender for a major Puke-o-rama.

In spite of being very thin, she still had a knockout figure. I'm no dog, but I imagine if John was nervous in my presence, he must have been a real basket case in hers.

"Do you do these often?" I asked.

"Steak?" He looked flustered.

"No. These blind dates. I mean, with that great ad and all, I imagine your post office box is overflowing."

"Uh, I have to confess something."

I was all ears.

"That ad?"

I nodded.

"My mom wrote it."

I tried to get behind his thick lenses to see if he was

putting me on, but there was no guile there, just an innocence that I hadn't seen in a man since fourth grade.

"Your mom wrote the ad?"

He nodded and refused to look me in the eye. "She puts them in occasionally, and then I answer them. Sometimes she gets a little carried away."

I didn't want to hurt his feelings with the "successful businessman," and I couldn't mention the "professional" without tipping my hand, so I said nothing.

"She thinks I'm getting old and would like to see me married."

I nodded. "Well, do you get a lot of answers?"

I was rewarded with watching a crimson tsunami creep up his neck and flood his face.

He looked around us to make sure that no one was listening. "Do you ever listen to G. Gordon Liddy?"

I had to confess I didn't.

"Well, women from all over the country somehow see fit to send him pictures of themselves in their, uh, intimate apparel."

"You're getting those?"

"No, just doilies, a few pictures of Mickey Mouse, and a tin of chocolate chip cookies."

"Well, there's always hope." I said.

After dinner, he walked me to Priscilla, my Dodge truck I'd left in the restaurant lot. On the way, I stumbled deliberately, letting one of my boobs brush against his arm. He helped me with my balance and said nothing.

At the truck we lingered a bit, remarked on the starlit night (although that was a real stretch given the light pollution and the traffic) and how beautiful it was. The night was beautiful. And hot. Probably a degree or two cooler than hell, but just barely.

I tried to look as fetching as I possibly could, given the

fact that sweat was rolling down the center of my back, and my thin cotton dress was soaked.

Leaning in close to him, I thought maybe the mood was building and he was coming out of his shell. But then the damned Tucson Police Department helicopter flew over, and it was quickly shattered.

If John Wistrich had any thought of moving on me, it seemed to evaporate with the fading light from the bird.

I opened the truck door, feeling totally inadequate. Hell, if the guy wasn't going to ask me for a second date, how would I ever find out anything?

Still, he lingered, so I hit the power window button. I was dying to turn on the engine and get the air-conditioning going, but I didn't. The diesel would drown out any sweet nothings he might whisper in my ear.

"Say, do you eat fish?" He leaned toward the open space.

"Everything but crab."

"I know how to barbecue fish," he said.

He sounded like a little kid saying, "Watch me ride my bike."

I waited.

"Would you, uh, like to come over sometime and try it?"

"Sounds great!" I said with real gusto. "What can I bring?"

He looked startled, as though he hadn't really expected me to say yes.

"Uh, na-na-nothing. I can fix dinner."

"When would be a good time?" I pressed.

He rubbed his shiny forehead with the fingers of his right hand as though he was trying to find the answer there. "Tomorrow? Tomorrow night would be good. Is seven o'clock all right?"

"That's super." I fumbled for a pen and a piece of paper. "What's your address?"

This time there was no hesitation in his voice. "1234 Main Street."

Could this be bingo?

BY dawn the next morning, I sat in my cousin Bea's Honda drinking a cup of lukewarm McDonald's coffee. Still sweating. It was going to be 102 today, and although the sun hadn't been awake long, it was on the job.

I was parked on the curb a block or so from John Wistrich's house, armed with a pair of small binoculars and the newspaper. So far, in spite of the Neighborhood Watch signs I'd seen, no one had asked me what I was doing there. Bea's car hardly looked like something a burglar would drive. She'd been my backup plan the night before since I'd arranged to call her at a certain time, told her where I was headed, and asked her to call out the cavalry in the event that I didn't call her in time. Of course I had.

At 6:43 A.M., John Wistrich came out of his house and got into his pickup. I watched him drive down the block, thankfully the same direction I was facing so I didn't have to cover my face with the newspaper.

I waited another thirty minutes to make sure that he wasn't returning and then, after grabbing a dog leash and a picture of Mrs. Fierce, my cock-a-Schnauz, I got to work.

My first step was to ring his doorbell. I rang and rang, and no one answered. Of course I knew he wouldn't since I'd seen him leave. This was all for show. I made a big pretense of trying to look in the windows. Impossible to see anything, since his blinds were drawn. I called out his name, although as far as I knew, no one was listening.

Finally, I quickly stepped around the side of his house. His backyard was fenced with that old redwood slat fencing. I peeked through the crack between the gate and the fence, scouting for a watchdog. After making catlike sounds and getting nothing in return, I decided the coast was clear.

It was no trick to reach over the top of the gate and unlatch it.

The yard was neat and clean and bricked. Not surprising, I guess, since John was a mason. No sign of a recently dug grave. There were a few struggling oleanders along the far fence and a built-in barbecue on his masonry deck. Probably the scene of tonight's crime against fish.

I went to the back door and tried it. Locked. It was a good one, too. I'm not the best lockpicker in the universe, but I'm good enough to know that I'm no match for a Schlage.

I peeked through the window in the top part of the door. It was the kitchen. Wall telephone, gas stove, and what looked like the morning newspaper sprawled across yellow tile countertops. Very cheery. John appeared fairly organized, as the small Formica table was set. I assumed for our dinner tonight. In my assessment there was nothing extraordinary in what I was seeing.

The drapes were drawn on the second window facing the backyard.

I was disappointed. I don't know what I'd expected, but there was nothing suspicious here. Short of breaking in, there weren't any clues. Sure, I was on Main Street and *Main* is what Marisal had written down on her scratch pad. But there were a lot of other houses on Main, too. If in fact the clue had meant Main Street.

Besides, I go a lot on gut instinct, and none of my antennae had been up on this guy. He was a nerd, but that didn't make him a murderer or the David Copperfield of disappearing women. Besides, it was too damned hot to be playing Nancy Drew.

I had just pulled the gate behind me when I heard her.

"Who on earth are you, and what are you doing in Johnny's yard?"

I jumped and faced my inquisitor, a small elderly woman with a face like one of those shriveled apple dolls. She was wearing an apron frosted with flour and armed with a rolling pin.

"I, uh, I'm looking for my dog." I pulled the leash out of my hip pocket and dangled it in front of her, I hoped convincingly.

"Well that gate was closed. Mrs. Murphy saw you open it," she said suspiciously.

"Mrs. Murphy?"

She pointed to herself.

"I heard a noise in there." I pointed to the backyard. "I thought it might be Ginger." I fumbled in my Levi's again and pulled out the picture of Mrs. Fierce and handed it to her.

She squinted, I suppose in an effort to make out what she was looking at.

"Humph." Her faint gray eyes looked me up and down. "Snooping is what you're doing, miss."

"No, really, I lost my dog." I threw my hands up in supplication and tried to look sincere.

"We got us a Neighborhood Watch program here and don't take kindly to strange people snooping around."

"I'm really sorry. Obviously, I made a mistake."

"You sure did, missy. John's got his own dog. Now, be on your way."

I retrieved Mrs. Fierce's picture and got the hell out of there, fervently hoping that Mrs. Murphy would not see fit to tell John Wistrich that she'd caught a stranger trespassing in his yard.

*　　*　　*

"**HOW** long have you lived here?" I asked in an effort to keep the conversation going. It was like pulling hen's teeth. If anything, John was even quieter on his home turf than he'd been in the restaurant. The few times we'd gotten a conversation going this evening, he seemed to get easily distracted, changing the subject abruptly.

"Two years." He aimed a lemon wedge at his salmon and ended up squirting me. If he noticed that his aim was a bit off, he said nothing as I wiped my face with the paper napkin I'd been issued.

Tinkerbell, the Tibetan terrier, was under the table. Although the TV was blaring in the living room, the terrier was sound asleep, his head on my boot.

I'd already complimented Wistrich on the fish—a mild lie since it was the driest piece of salmon I'd ever eaten.

In the living room I could hear scenes from *The Lion King*. It had been playing since my arrival.

"What was your favorite part?"

"Pardon me?" I had no clue what he was talking about.

"In this one." He waved a fork vaguely in the direction of the living room.

"Ah . . ." Boy, I was in medium trouble now. I hadn't had enough time to study all the Disney movies, although of course I'd professed to be an aficionado when I'd answered Wistrich's ad. I'd sort of passed a pop quiz given to me by Ginny Eske's kids. Fortunately, I'd crammed on *The Lion King*. "The part where Mufasa, king of the lions, tells Simba he'll always be with him."

He beamed, his mouth full of fish. "Me, too."

I *had* liked *The Lion King*. Its themes of guilt and redemption reminded me a lot of *Hamlet*. Somehow, I suspected that was not a discussion I was going to have this evening.

I was beginning to think that Marisal had disappeared *after* her date with Mr. Wonderful.

I helped him clear the table, and then he said, "I've got a surprise for you."

My hand instinctively reached around to my back. I could feel the butt of my .38 holstered there, hidden by my overshirt.

He returned with two pieces of mud pie. They looked great, covered with what looked like chocolate fudge topping and pieces of pecans. The perfect dessert for a hot, sultry night.

"You didn't make these, did you?" I had to ask, for they really did look homemade.

He shook his head. "My mom. She loves to cook."

Mud pie hardly qualified as cooking, but I wasn't going to mention that.

We finished the rich dessert, and then I helped him with the dishes. It worked out great because he was washing and I was drying, a responsibility I take seriously since a good dish dryer can always get the dishes clean.

It was finally time for me to chum a little. When he wasn't looking, I dropped the dishrag on the floor.

"Oh dear," I said in an effort to get his attention.

I bent over to retrieve it, thankful that I'd worn a blowsy shirt so he couldn't make out the .38. As I bent over to retrieve the wet towel, I made sure he had a good look at my butt. Like using nymph flies for trout, this usually works. It's been my experience that most men when faced with a bent-over woman see this as a sexual invitation. Hell, when I accidentally dropped towels in the kitchen with my ex-husband, I was usually rewarded with getting dry humped against the kitchen sink.

John Wistrich wasn't quite that blatant. He waited until I retrieved the towel and then turned to me and quickly made his move. I turned my head and felt his wet tongue slide across my cheek. Yuck.

Remembering I was doing this for work, not pleasure,

I turned back to him and let him kiss me. There was nothing tentative as he grabbed me in a bear hug and pressed his lips to mine. Foreplay apparently wasn't much of an issue, as his right hand moved quickly up my side. I clenched my arm tight against my ribs to stop his campaign.

We'd just gone from zero to sixty in fifteen seconds flat.

"Whoa," I muttered.

"Let's go somewhere comfortable," he muttered into my hair.

I tried to push him away, but he held me tight. He was a lot stronger than I'd thought. "John."

Still, he held me as he whispered crazy love-type things in my hair.

I squirmed. I was beginning to get worried. I needed my hands free for my gun in case I needed it.

He was kissing my neck, which under normal conditions would have been very fruitful. But right now all I could think of was my gun.

He was walking me across the kitchen floor now, toward the hallway.

I didn't need my investigative skills to know where we were headed.

"John, really, no," I said as firmly as I could with my arms pinned. I was really getting worried. Is this what had happened to Marisal? I stomped down hard with my boot, catching him on his instep. Suddenly I was free.

I took a deep breath and stepped away from him.

"Oh." He seemed startled, his eyes glassy. "Gosh. I'm sorry."

I took a quick peek. His pants were bulging with something that I suspected was not a pickle.

Had I been on the way to being date raped? I wasn't sure, since I'd never felt threatened enough to really fight him. On the cusp, sure. But not quite there. I didn't want to push it.

"I think I'd better be going."

"Oh, please, please stay. I'm sorry I got carried away. Say, I could put on *The Little Mermaid*. I've got the Disney remake. Have you seen it?"

"Dozens of times," I lied. "But it's late, and I have to be at the hospital early in the morning." I'd told him I was a nurse. Another lie. They were beginning to stack up.

He opened the front door for me and flipped on the porch light. A blast of hot air greeted me. I could barely make out the walkway.

I held out my hand. "Thank you for a wonderful evening." *And thank you, Jesus, for giving me those words to tumble out of my mouth.*

"Say, would you consider going to a movie with me sometime soon?"

I glanced downstairs and noticed that his friend had calmed down.

"Sure. I'd like that," I said as I skipped down his front porch steps, leaving him in the light of the porch.

I was almost at Priscilla when his porch lights went out. I fumbled in my purse for my truck keys, cranky with the heat and the evening. Just as I unlocked my truck door and the light from the cab spilled out, I felt something.

I jumped when I saw Mrs. Murphy, the nosy neighbor standing next to me.

This time the rolling pin had been replaced with a gun. A major gun. Like a double-barreled sawed-off shotgun.

"Close the door quietly, missy," she said.

HER house was not dissimilar to the one I'd just left two doors down, other than the prominent Neighborhood

Watch sticker in the front window. It was as neat and tidy as John Wistrich's was, but this one was filled with the smell of fresh bread baking. Not too comforting, given the shotgun.

"Back there. I don't want to burn my bread."

We ended up in the kitchen.

"Good thing Johnny didn't walk you to your car," Mrs. Murphy said as she leaned over and squinted at her kitchen timer. I could hear the steady tick-tick-tick of the mechanism. "But then I knew he wouldn't. Scared of the dark, he is."

I thought she was taking this Neighborhood Watch thing to extremes.

"You should have left well enough alone, missy."

"Look, I'm not a prowler. I was supposed to be there tonight. John invited me to dinner. Call him; he'll tell you."

"That's one of the things I was talking about."

One? What in the hell *was* she talking about?

"No one likes a snooper."

"I can explain that."

"And Mrs. Murphy saw you kiss him."

Jesus, the old hag had been spying on us.

"He's married, you know."

"I'm sorry. I didn't know that." Where had she gotten an illegal sawed-off shotgun? It didn't much matter if she knew how to use it or not. At this range, she could hardly miss.

The good news, if there was any, was that I still had my .38 tucked in the back of my belt.

"He has a beautiful bride. Stupid boy, I don't know why he ran that ad again. It just got you snooping around, stirring up his lust."

I thought I was beginning to get the picture.

"Come, you can meet her."

My mouth went dry and my stomach plummeted.

She nodded to an enclosed porch attached to the kitchen. Herding me into the enclosure, she prodded me with the barrel of the shotgun as she pulled the chain for the overhead lightbulb. The porch was hot and still, without the benefit of the refrigeration from the house.

As the light snapped on, I saw a door to the outside. It had a deadbolt on it. I couldn't make a run for it. She'd still nail me with the shotgun.

Although there were windows looking out on her dark yard, I still felt terribly confined in the small space occupied by me, Mrs. Murphy, and a chest-type freezer.

"Go ahead, open it."

In spite of the heat, there was no way I wanted to open the cold, white chest.

She prodded me with the shotgun barrel. "Go ahead."

Looking at Mrs. Murphy, I slowly lifted the lid to the freezer, pushing the top back against the wall.

And then I looked.

Deep in the freezer, Marisal Valdez was curled in a fetal position, faceup. Her beautiful, big brown eyes had shriveled as the fluid in them had dried up. Dull and flat, they were framed with eyebrows resembling arctic caterpillars.

She looked browner than I remembered, and her skin was splotched with random patches of a greenish mold. Her lips were pulled back from her small, shiny teeth in an unbecoming grimace, and her long black hair was stiff and encrusted with ice crystals.

My stomach lurched as the salmon threatened to reappear.

Marisal's hands were folded over her chest. Her beautiful long fingernails that had always been a source of pride to her were ragged and broken, with the skin peeled back from the tips of her fingers. Her nails were covered with glacial blood.

My eyes drifted to the inside of the freezer lid that was scarred with deep scratches and blood where she had tried to claw her way out of her frozen grave.

"Jesus Christ," I said, fighting tears.

"Isn't she lovely?"

Balanced on Marisal's bent knees was a wedding cake topper of a bride and groom. The figures were ancient, faded and cracked.

I pointed to it and took a deep breath. "That was yours, wasn't it?"

"Oh yes," she said.

Next to Marisal's head was half a tin of frozen mud pie. I fought the bile rising in my throat.

"He'll never be afraid of the dark as long as his bride is with him."

"What's that?" I said, pointing above Marisal's head. It was a ruse. I was hoping if I could get her close to me that maybe I could grab the barrel of the shotgun and deflect it from me.

"I don't think so, missy." The little old lady was very cagey.

Suddenly there was a loud *ping* as the kitchen timer went off.

Mrs. Murphy glanced for a fraction of a second toward the kitchen.

It was enough for me. Probably as good a chance as I'd ever get. I slammed into her while at the same time pushing the barrel of the shotgun toward the floor.

There was a deafening explosion as the pelleted load shattered the wood beneath us. I was vaguely aware of a smattering of pressure against my feet, but I held on for dear life, pushing Mrs. Murphy backward into the kitchen.

I pressed the barrel hard into her stomach, and the force of my action was enough to let the air out of her. She stumbled against the kitchen counter, all the while trying to hang onto the weapon.

I hit her hard in the stomach with my right elbow, and she started slipping to the ground. As she struggled to regain her balance, I pulled up hard on the stock of the shotgun and wrested it from her grasp.

She hit the floor hard as I turned the gun on her. She floundered around on the linoleum for a minute, grabbing her side.

"My hip!" She wailed. "My hip! I think I broke it."

"So sue me," I said, feeling not at all kindly toward her.

I reached across the counter for her wall phone and dialed 911.

A few minutes later, I heard a police siren in the distance.

And then I heard the front door open.

"Hello?" The voice was tentative and familiar. I stepped over Mrs. Murphy so the shotgun could cover her and the kitchen entrance.

"Hi, Johnny." Mrs. Murphy was holding her hip, and she fluttered the fingers of one hand at her neighbor from two doors down.

John Wistrich looked on in amazement. "Oh, Mom, what have you done this time?"

SPLITTING

Marilyn Wallace

Marilyn Wallace, daughter of a former New York City policeman, has written three books featuring Oakland, California, homicide detectives Jay Goldstein and Carlos Cruz (*A Case of Loyalties*, a Macavity winner, and *Primary Target* and *A Single Stone*, Anthony nominees) and four suspense novels (*Shall You Reap*, *The Seduction*, *Lost Angel*, and *Current Danger*). She is a founding member of Sisters in Crime, has served Mystery Writers of America as the NorCal chapter president, as National Board member, and as General Awards chair for the 1999 Edgar Awards. Editor of the five-volume award-winning *Sisters in Crime* short story anthologies and coeditor with Robert J. Randisi of *Deadly Allies*, she has led numerous writing workshops and classes across the country.

LIKE that single taste of Proust's madeleine that set off all those remembrances, midsummer heat has the power to evoke memories, detailed and important and otherwise unavailable. But I didn't realize that when the Thursday night group therapy session started last week. I was only aware of preparing to start work. As a therapist, my goal is to help the women I work with escape the confines of their altered realities. They come to me wanting to play a more productive, positive role in society, and I want to help them reach that place.

The work, always interesting, is always demanding.

Every member of the group I lead on Thursday evenings had exhibited varying degrees of antisocial behavior in the past. They were making strides, but we still had a lot to do.

And so even though the heat threatened to dull my energies, I practiced mindfulness, a kind of hyperalertness that allowed me to listen acutely. If you spend too much energy anticipating a group's mood, you're likely to miss the real signals they're sending. I learned that in my group therapy practicum in the third year of my doctorate studies. I had worked too hard to establish this group to let one oppressively hot night ruin everything.

First, I'd battled the unenlightened bureaucracy to convince them that I could offer more to these troubled women than the ineffective, terminally boring gripe sessions that had been run by a staff member for decades. Gradually, I earned the trust of the higher-ups. Then I had to lobby hard for the freedom to experiment, albeit under supervision, with different treatment modalities. My final task was to create a climate of safety in which the women could share with me and with each other any thought, any impulse, any behavior, all the self-destructive and antisocial patterns that had brought them here in the first place.

In retrospect, my early awareness of the heat last week should have been a clue to the potential for trouble, but like everyone else, I was moving and even thinking slowly. Not the kind of delicious, languid slow that you experience when the sun pours down a golden, healing light as you sit on the beach with a pretty and deceptively lethal umbrella drink in your hand, but the slow simmer that keeps you stuck in the same place from lack of energy.

The day had started out damp and warm, but by evening the heat had become a shroud swaddling us in the misery of a malfunctioning air-conditioning system. An odd combination of edgy restlessness and lassitude seemed to have afflicted the five women sitting in the circle with an inability to focus.

Except, I noticed, for Caroline.

Caroline Clemants was attending her next-to-last session with this group. She tapped her knee, wiped a drop of sweat that made its way from her forehead toward her green eyes, and moved closer to the edge of her hard plastic chair. Her gaze no longer darted toward the corners of the room in search of spiders. After a program of systematic desensitization to cure her primary phobia, she had joined the group sessions and had become an articulate, perceptive contributor. Now, a teasing smile lifted the corner of her mouth as she watched the ceiling fan push the damp, still air in desultory circles.

Marte Johnson raised a plump hand and lifted her hair off her neck, twisted it into a thick brown coil, and then fixed it in place with a clip. Debra Fischer fanned herself with a limp paper napkin that looked like it had been used for too many meals before being pressed into service as a cooling device. Only Elizabeth Holley and Andrea Shime maintained their normal posture: joined not only at the hip but also at the shoulder and knee, chairs pulled close to create a self-contained universe, a simultaneous breached individuality that was very nearly a classic folie à deux.

"Sorry about the air-conditioning not working," I said. "Maintenance promised it would be fixed by seven o'clock but—"

"Sure, why bother for *us?* You coulda got them to fix it if you really wanted to. You got some say around here, right?" Debra high-fived Marte and then pressed the napkin to the side of her face and crossed her arms over the buds of her breasts.

Regression.

Debra was clinging to her role as middle child in a family of nine, assigning to somebody else the power to make all the perceived injustices of her world right again. Her anger was directed toward the Depriving Mother, and I was the designated recipient.

I knew better than to rise to the bait. I glanced over to the camera's eye above the red Exit sign beside the door, wondering whether Debra's outburst would be interpreted as hostile or merely assertive.

"Who can think when it's this stinking hot?" Andrea slumped in her chair.

Elizabeth's spine curved to echo Andrea's posture as she exhaled noisily. "Man, all I want is to take off all my clothes and lie in a tub of cool water."

A nervous giggle bounced around the circle.

"If you all think it's too warm, we can call off the session and come back on Thursday for our next regular meeting." I kept my face neutral to show that I had no personal stake in the outcome.

Finally, Marte jumped out of her chair, one plump hand resting on her broad hip. "Hey, Elizabeth, don't be a little baby weather wimp. So it's hot. So what? We can take it."

Projection.

She was projecting her own vulnerable feelings onto another member of the group and deriding them, because admitting to being affected by the heat would be dissonant with her need to be tough.

Sweat glistened on her cheeks as Marte's generous mouth widened into a grin. Her red polished finger punched the air. "We here, we stay. We been working on the idea of empowerment, right? Well, I am empowering myself to say we got work to do in this group, so let's go, ladies."

My pleasure was too immediate, too deep for me to hide it behind any mask of neutrality. I let my satisfaction show in my smile. I asked, "Does everyone agree with Marte?"

Caroline ran her fingers through her short, blonde hair.

The tips of each piece of pixie spike had darkened with perspiration. "Okay, but do we have to talk about what we were talking about last time?"

Resistance.

With her chin jutted out, Caroline was the very picture of a patient trying to derail her own progress, daring the therapist to keep her on track. She looked different this evening, a little more tentative, her eyes a little more eva-sive. I wondered if she was about to retreat into old pat-terns of defensiveness. Maybe she was just hot. Or maybe her flush and the tenseness in her normally animated face heralded an impending breakthrough.

I'd have to feel my way through the session carefully. Tonight was Caroline's show. She had one more session before she'd leave the group, and I was doing my best to make sure she'd do well without us. She needed the tools to examine her patterned responses and change them to more appropriate behavior.

"What do you mean, Caroline?" I asked.

What was she doing beyond mere resistance? Was there something I'd missed in our previous sessions? She didn't often speak with such vehemence. Other members of the group might try to use her situation as a sounding board for their own separation anxieties, but I wanted to keep the focus on Caroline. She had worked hard in these ses-sions, and she deserved a proper send-off.

"It's boring, you know, same old same old," Caroline said finally. "Men don't give women nothing but trouble, nothing but meanness and babies and pain. So why do we have to sit here in this oven and talk about men when we could talk about something useful? Like how I'm going to figure out a way to pay all my bills. Like what kind of decent job I can get after being out of the workforce for so long. I'm too old to go to school, you know."

It's never too late to get what you want, I wanted to tell

her. I'm living proof. I'd dutifully sat through all those hours of postgraduate classes, studying theories, learning the biology, the sociology, ology after ology of human behavior. Then I'd done more endless hours of supervised therapy, exploring maladaptive coping mechanisms and self-destructive constructs. I'd participated in years of weekly sessions on the other side of the couch, so to speak, and now I was aware of the process and also constantly vigilant about my own tricks and games.

There's probably more preparation for my job than there is to become a nuclear physicist, but Caroline's resistance might not let her see the rewards of following through on her dreams.

As though they'd been listening in on my thoughts, Elizabeth and Andrea nodded in unison, puppets controlled by the same string.

"Anyone have a reaction to what Caroline said?" I sat straight in my chair.

"I told you. I'm in meltdown here. I can't think to save myself. Just, I know you have to try if you want your life to be better." Another precinct heard from: it was unusual for Elizabeth to play the bratty spoiler, and I waited to see if one of the other girls would notice. A pout pushed out her lower lip.

Caroline tightened her arms around her slender ribs and rocked in her chair. "Elizabeth doesn't know how to handle her life; nobody here does. What's the point of trying to do better if my daughter won't see me or won't even talk to me? I'm afraid I'm never gonna see her again. She hates me. I don't get it. I don't get why she feels that way."

Don't think about never, I wanted to tell her. It's possible for people to change. Everyone wants forgiveness, and they want to forgive.

"Your child don't want to see you right now, that's not

the end of the world." Marte pulled her chair closer to Caroline's and laid a pudgy brown hand on Caroline's thin, pale arm. "You got to earn her trust and her respect a little at a time. You got all sorts of things to give the world. And, baby, lots of things to get. Don't you go pinning your hopes and your happiness on just one thing."

I couldn't have said it better myself.

Even if it takes you years and years to get what you've always wanted. Maybe all you want is a chance to do the work you've trained for. You know in your heart that you'll be good at your chosen calling, that you'll help people maneuver the shoals of their complicated lives, so if you don't get to do the actual work, that's a cause for concern. Eventually, the appropriate response becomes anger. The question then is whether you ultimately accept your own part in creating or abetting the circumstances that shape your life so that you can move on.

I could tell Caroline a thing or two about patience and planning. Now, seventeen years after getting my degree, I was finally counseling on a regular basis.

"You better do for yourself. Not for anybody else." Debra clutched her napkin as she scraped her chair back, retreating from the circle.

She needed just a little more space around her than most of the other women in the group. Despite special individual sessions of cognitive therapy, her panic disorder still surfaced unpredictably, although less often than before.

"Doing things for yourself. Ah, there's something we've heard before." Not as often as they might have, I knew. I'd never mentioned that Alan forbade me to start a practice or even work in the office where I did my clinical internship. He'd never provide such an opening for an argument. Arguments represented an assault on the fortress of control he'd so carefully built. Instead, he saw to it that I had too much to do. We moved six times in seven years, until he found the right situation. Joining the infectious disease practice at Mount Mercy Hospital was just the ticket. He was heading for the chair of medicine, while I was left to scurry around with realtors. All the duties of a good doctor's wife—furnishing our home, making dinner parties to court the hospital board, raising our two children—were burdens that fell to me.

I dabbed at the sweat on my upper lip. "So, does anyone have anything to say to Caroline about her apprehensions?"

I was hoping that Marte would offer up one of her insights. Early on, I'd caught myself underestimating her because she was sixty, round everywhere, and brown-skinned. Now I welcomed her wisdom. When Marte was cooking, I could step back from my leadership role. At those times, the group seemed to do quite well on its own.

"Well, she better think about a lot of things. Work. Men. Keeping a lid on her anger." Andrea nodded to emphasize her point.

Elizabeth nodded, too, and took the ball from Andrea. "It's gonna be plain damn hard, after all these years, after having this group to prop you up, to go off and be on your own."

I brushed a trickle of sweat from my eyes and waited in the silence. Andrea and Elizabeth leaned forward. Debra fanned her napkin in the air. The second hand on the clock seemed to move through sludge.

Caroline spoke first.

"Yeah, it'll be hard. Like you said, Elizabeth, damn plain hard. But better than sitting here with all of you for year after frigging year, putting up with your bullshit." Her eyes blazed, and she pointed at each person in turn. "You want to trade places with me, don't you? You'd give up five years of your life to be in my position, wouldn't you?"

She stopped before she got to me. "I don't mean you, Leah. We all know you're exactly where you want to be."

And she was right. I wouldn't trade places with Caroline Clemants for anything. My work was satisfying. I loved tending my rosebushes. My life was simple, a routine that suited my need for peace and contemplation. Caroline would confront challenges that I didn't envy in the least.

"Tell us some more about what you don't want to talk about, Caroline." I smiled at the group groan. We'd followed the same procedures for five years. Gradually, they'd come to understand that exploring the very issues they tried to avoid was the key to making lasting changes in their perceptions and their behavior. Finally, they were beginning to recognize their own mechanisms. The others turned their sweat-slicked faces toward Caroline, encouraging her without providing inappropriate coaxing.

"Why do I have to say this again? All right, all right. After next week, I won't ever have to talk about this again. You all heard me a million times, but OK. James Hoover played me for my money. Eddie DeFranco played me for my money. And T. R. Boswell . . ." Her voice trailed off, and she shrugged.

An electric sizzle leaped around our little group. T. R. Boswell—that was a new name.

Caroline had talked about her first husband most often. She'd married James when she was a student. He'd built a successful business with her help, using her ideas, her energy, her support to help him become rich. He'd disappeared one morning fifteen years earlier and phoned her from an island in the Caribbean to say he wanted a divorce. He'd managed to hide well over a million dollars of funds from joint accounts and investments, so that she got nothing in the divorce.

Not unlike my own Alan . . . Caroline's stories had helped me break through my forays into denial. I'd worked through a tangle of feelings, accepted my anger as well placed. I saw that my shame at not getting out of a bad situation sooner was unproductive. With that experience behind me, I was much better able to help Caroline.

She'd also mentioned Eddie before. He was the private investigator she'd hired to help find her husband's hidden assets. But somehow all he'd ever turned up was a sheaf of invoices for his services, to the tune of $15,000. When she refused to pay him, he'd sued her.

Ironic that I should end up leading this particular group. Alan was the embodiment of every miserable manipulative man each of these women had suffered by knowing.

I struggled with a moment of self-censure. Had I pushed Caroline for premature closure? And then I laughed to myself. Her timing in leaving the group was beyond my control. Still, it was my job as therapist to absorb the group's anxiety only enough to allow the session to continue. A certain tension could be helpful. In the silence, I felt my annoyance rise. I managed to put it into a bubble and let it float up, up, up on the hot air, to the ceiling.

Caroline no longer needed her denial, I'd thought. But now here was someone called T. R. I didn't want to scare her back into resistance by pressing her for details. Her behavior was an interesting phenomenon I'd observed more than once in the past five years. Just as someone was about to leave the group, something that hadn't been raised before drifted up to the surface. Sometimes a trigger—a dream, a memory, a story told by someone else—opened the lid of repression. But more often, as in Caroline's case, it seemed that the new information was proffered as a parting gift. A mystery. Something we couldn't help her with because she'd no longer be here.

When I tried to make eye contact again, I realized that Elizabeth and Andrea were staring past Caroline to the door at the far end of the room. I looked over, saw a face framed in the window glass, waved a thumbs up.

"Building security. Just doing their job." I waited until the face turned to profile, then disappeared out of sight. At exactly the midway point of our Thursday evening sessions, the same face always appeared in the same window, yet tonight Elizabeth and Andrea seemed unsettled by the routine. Maybe it was the heat, which had a way of turning everyone's brains to mush. I smiled. What would my clinically oriented colleagues make of *that* astute psychological observation?

"I never wanted to hurt him, you know, but he kind of left me no choice." Caroline's denial was typical of the repertoire of responses she'd displayed when she first joined the group. For a moment, I thought she might be teasing us.

Did she say she hurt him? I reined in my self-congratulations. This was news, real news. This was the revelation she needed to share with this group; I was sure of it. She had done something to hurt a man who had hurt her. Fair play, turnabout, simple justice—I wondered how she justified her behavior to herself?

"You always got a choice, Caroline. You got to remember that when hard decisions come your way. And, baby, you know that's gonna happen. You got to be strong. You got to remember your own beauty. Your goodness." Debra's maternal side was suddenly evident, as it had been every time someone came close to leaving the group. I could see her working hard to be liked, to be remembered as a caring, loving person by the women who wouldn't be showing up in our little room anymore. If she could see her Good Self reflected in another person's eyes, she might learn to believe in it.

"You think you know so much?" Caroline's breath came hard and fast as she plucked at the seam of her pants with tiny, agitated movements. "You can't make up the shit I've been through. You can't know. He made me believe up was down and left was right."

Hid things from her. Assets that should have been in both their names, bank accounts, foreign properties, equities traded in the name of a holding company registered in Zaire. Prevented her from getting what was rightfully hers through trickery and deception and just plain coldness, and then sat back with his arms folded across his big, fat belly and lied to the whole world that she was crazy.

"And how did you feel about that at the time, Caroline?" I kept my voice neutral and waited.

"We don't have time to go into all that. I just needed to say that sometimes you end up here, and it's not your fault. You get . . . you know, temporarily insane. But it's not who you'd be if some pure jerk didn't play you for his own benefit."

More resistance. More denial. More feelings split off to protect her Good Self.

She was right that we didn't have time to go deeply into this issue, but I wanted her to acknowledge her current feelings.

"I see what you mean about the time. What about now, Caroline? What do you feel about the situation now?"

I looked around the circle to see if anyone was reacting to all the attention I was giving Caroline. I'd encouraged the group to give a member attending her last couple of sessions as much time as she needed. I worked hard the rest of the time to make sure everyone, especially the more reluctant attendees, had time in the spotlight.

"I'm glad he's gone. Makes it much easier for me to build a life." She nodded as though to convince herself. "I just wish I could figure out how to get my daughter to understand."

Glad he's gone? Of course she is. Living without the

man who had mistreated her was the only way she could make strides toward health, toward reclaiming her place in the world. How could she get better if the source of all her troubles was still able to affect her, to reach out from his high ivory tower and pull down the foundation of everything she'd ever worked for? She was still denying her responsibility for righting her own world, and I wanted desperately to help her make the transition to doing that without the group.

"So, without T. R. around, what difference will that make to you?" I bit my lip to keep back the rush of my own answers.

I did not say: I will be free to work without someone else claiming my time. I will sleep like a baby at night because I can breathe now that he's not sucking the air out of my lungs and the life out of my days. I will write checks without worrying that they'll bounce because he sent huge amounts of money to his offshore accounts and then lied to my attorneys when I filed for divorce.

She said, "I'll miss him. Isn't that stupid? He was mean to me, but only sometimes. The rest of the time he treated me like a princess, especially when we went on trips. He would come home with presents for me. Little things, like a crossword puzzle book. Big things, like a gold necklace because he heard me say I never had one in my entire life. I guess I'll miss him. But I'll get by without him. That's fine. He's in California."

Split off.

"In order to split off your Bad Self," I said, "you had to first deny T. R.'s death."

T. R. was dead, and she was distancing herself from that fact to mask her own unacceptable guilt. A pertinent bit of information, but she had suppressed her acceptance that he had died, a painful, ugly death that had, in the end, isolated him. I couldn't break down that myth tonight, not when this was her next-to-last session. Unless she came back. That was always a bit disheartening, to me and to the members of the group. When someone left, we wished them well. When they returned, it only signaled that acting out had once again become the standard way of coping with difficulties.

I blinked the sweat out of my eyes, overcome by the heat. *Heat. Steamy and thick. The jungle hospital is not air-conditioned. Alan makes the rounds on the Ebola ward, preening for the potential investors who trail behind him taking notes. People lie on thin mattresses and moan, bleeding onto the sheets. But Africa will be saved. Alan will be the instrument. His research only needs an infusion of cash. His hand rests on the shoulder of the Belgian woman, a banker looking for a philanthropic write-off.*

As I watch them walk away together, I understand that I cannot let him do to these poor, sick people what he has done to me. A rape of the spirit. A murder of the soul.

"When you split off your Bad Self, you are disowning your role in his death. Until you can see that, you're living in a reality that no one else shares. You . . ." I could hardly breathe. It had become so hot and still, the air so damp with our exhalations, that it felt as though we were drowning in steam. I longed for the shock of something cool, the fragrance of a breeze that has traveled through lilacs. I knew the window couldn't be opened, that we couldn't leave yet.

It's difficult to breathe the damp air. The Clean Room key is unattended. Seconds, that's all I need. Gloves and mask on. Swab into culture, culture into spray bottle.

"You have to acknowledge you killed him." I shivered and looked at Caroline. The room was quiet as everyone stared at me. Finally, Elizabeth came over and put her cool hand over mine. Startled, I took a deep breath and waited for the rest of the drama to unfold.

"Hey, Leah," she said softly. "That's your story, not Caroline's. Caroline never killed anyone."

As I sat at the desk in my small room, I reviewed the evening's session. Somehow, in the last minutes, I'd managed to steer the discussion away from myself and had regained my objectivity. Now, I worried that my momentary lapse had attracted the attention of the therapy director, and I wondered if I'd be allowed to continue.

My thoughts were interrupted by the familiar sound of the compressor as it groaned into action. A loud cheer rose from all over the building. We would all be calmer, more present, less sensitive by morning.

I wouldn't derail my program by speaking about the incident when I had my own therapy session with Dr. Leland. I wouldn't tell the good doctor how perfect my life has become. Not ever. There is no need for anyone to know how close they've come to granting me everything I need to make up for the past. I have my work, and I have access to good quality paper, sable brushes, and the watercolors Alan thought frivolous and dilettantish. There is no need to disillusion them, no need to deprive them of the notion that they are punishing me. Their God is vengeful, and their behavior allows them to feel closer to Him.

And the setting is beautiful, the grounds well kept. That was one of my jobs in my first year, although they gave me no sharp tools, no hoe or trowel or pruning shears until I'd proved myself responsible. I weeded. I knelt in the soft dirt around the thorny rosebushes and pulled out blades of grass, one at a time, until the circle around the base of the bush was perfectly clean. Like the underarm of a ten-year-old girl, I thought the first time I yanked the last of the hairlike tendrils from the soft earth. I have graduated through the years so that now I have access to all the forbidden tools.

That was a silly restriction, anyway. Alan wasn't stabbed or even hit over the head with the proverbial blunt instrument. No, that wouldn't have had a bit of elegance, and above all, Alan cherished elegance. He died after contracting Ebola. The disease he was studying so he could find its cure. The disease growing in the blood agar I managed to remove from the Clean Room of his lab so that I could slip the culture into the nasal spray he used for a chronic sinus condition.

I smiled at how I'd split off that Bad Self and attributed my actions to Caroline. I would miss her. Her twelve years for forgery had been reduced to eight, and now she would take all the insights and skills we'd worked on with her into a new life. I allowed myself a moment of self-congratulation. She'd made great progress in our little group, and she'd do fine on the outside. It was a source of pride for me that I had prepared my girls well.

After all, leaving prison isn't exactly like graduating from Vassar.

What the Dormouse Said

Carolyn Wheat

Carolyn Wheat was a New York legal aid attorney for twenty-three years and later an administrative law judge. When she introduced Brooklyn lawyer Cass Jameson in 1983 in the novel *Dead Men's Thoughts*, the torrent of lawyer novelists (male and female) that would be unleashed by the success of Scott Turow and John Grisham had not yet begun. That first novel was well received, earning an Edgar nomination, but Wheat proved the opposite of prolific, the second Jameson novel appearing three years later, the third not for another eleven. When she stepped up production with books like *Mean Streak* (1996) and *Troubled Waters* (1997), a novel that looked back on radical 1960s activism more briefly but just as effectively as Scott Turow's *The Laws of Our Fathers*, it became obvious that Wheat ranks near the top not just among lawyer novelists but contemporary crime writers generally. After leaving the practice of law, she became a valued teacher of writing, including a stint as Writer in Residence at the University of Central Oklahoma. She has won the Agatha, Anthony, Shamus, and Macavity Awards for her short stories, and her single-author collection, *Tales Out of School*, was nominated for the Anthony Award in 2001.

———

August 1970: The Freaks

I WISH I were dead.

Sweat pours from Bobbie Tate's face onto her tie-dyed

tank top as she climbs, positioning one exhausted booted foot after another up Slide Mountain and thinks long, hard thoughts about death.

How could love go so wrong so quickly? It's like that song by Janis Joplin, whom Bobbie never used to like all that much, but now it's as if she and Janis are soul sisters in pain and grief. Joplin's raw-liver voice cuts through the haze of sweat and pain, searing itself into Bobbie's brain as she climbs ever closer to the white angels of death.

"Take another little piece of my heart, why don't you? You know you got it, if it makes you feel good."

Enid takes pieces of her heart any time she wants them, and Bobbie, like Janis, dares her to take more, to chew bits of her heart between her even little teeth, and spit them on the ground. The meadow behind the commune, which was once known as the Thompson place, is littered with pieces of Bobbie's sixteen-year-old heart.

One day she and Enid were like two vines intertwining. They couldn't leave the house to go to the barn without holding hands and halfway there starting to kiss and then fondle one another and by the time they were in the barn, the fragrant hay called to them and they gave in. She couldn't get enough of Enid, not the taste of her kisses or her green apple breasts, and she was sure Enid felt the same, the way Enid's slender fingers always went to the zipper of her jeans, the way Enid's soft hand explored under Bobbie's blue cambric work shirt.

Oh, God, she'd never felt like that before, and it was like being in heaven only better, and now—

Now Quinn is here, and all Enid does is follow him around, her hand in the back pocket of his jeans, her naked body draped across his clothed one like a stole, her teasing little smile telling Bobbie how wonderful she thinks Quinn is, and how having sex with Bobbie was just another phase in her development as a woman.

Thinking about it makes Bobbie want to scream.

So she does. Long, howling screams like a dog in pain, punctuated by sobs so gusty they could sink small boats. She has never felt so much pain in her whole life, not even the day Pop told her that Mom was gone for good.

Thinking of Pop only makes it worse. She sinks to her knees halfway up the last rise to the top of the mountain, crouches down like a child, and lets her hair trail in the dust. Moans emanate from her throat, moans so deep, so anguished, she doesn't even notice she's inhaling dirt from the trail.

She's a lost child, lost and alone. First Mom, then Pop, and now Enid—will no one ever love her completely? Will no one ever not leave her?

She is consumed by pain, eaten through with it the way Grandma was eaten through with cancer, and the pain she feels is no less than what Grandma suffered in those last skeleton days.

Pain and hate. Don't forget the hate. It is, she thinks, all that keeps her alive, all that keeps her from going to Kaaterskill Falls and throwing herself off the highest rock into the stream below. Indians did that, according to local legend. Indian maidens died for love, and perhaps Bobbie Tate will, too.

Then Enid will be sorry. Bobbie sees her own corpse in her mind's eye, as she plods steadily, sweatily, up the mountain toward the white death waiting to be picked and used in the final ceremony. Her face will be serene, waxen, beautiful at last. She will wear white gauze, Mandy's Mexican wedding dress, and her hands will be folded on her breast like an angel's, and candles will flank her head and feet. Enid will sob and beg forgiveness; Pop will throw himself on her coffin and tell her he's sorry for all the things he said when he found out about Enid.

She stops suddenly, as if she'd heard a rattle in the lush

growth, but it isn't that. It's another thought, another vision.

Why should hers be the dead body? Why should Quinn remain alive to be with Enid?

She straightens her shoulders and pushes farther up the trail with renewed purpose, visions of little white mushroom caps dancing in her head.

"**If** it wasn't Quinn, it would be someone else," Mandy tells Bobbie, but that doesn't help at all. Not at all. She needs to hear that Enid is temporarily brainwashed, that this thing with Quinn is a passing phase, and Enid will wake up tomorrow and realize that Bobbie is her true love, that Quinn will leave the commune and go back to Taos without Enid.

Is it worse because Quinn's a man?

She isn't sure. Picturing Enid with Patrice doesn't feel any better—worse, maybe, because after all, Quinn does have one thing that she, Bobbie, doesn't have, whereas if it were Patrice or Mandy, then Bobbie would feel even more inadequate, more certain that something wrong within herself is what pushed Enid away.

"*Go home*," Warren tells her. Behind the barn, where she's feeding chickens, he walks up and says the words bluntly, no frills: "Go home. You don't belong here."

As if she didn't know that. As if she had no clue how much Warren resents her—not that Warren's in charge or anything. It's a commune; nobody's in charge, but somehow Warren always acts as if he is, as if he has the right to give orders.

He thinks she doesn't contribute because she doesn't make anything the way the others do. Enid with her stained glass, sharp cutting edges with bright, stabbing colors, whirls and triangles and wavy glass and little round gems that glitter like bug eyes. Leo's wooden bowls, hand-turned, polished to gleaming perfection, the touch of them as soft as silk, Mandy's patchwork quilts, like stained glass you can sleep under, Scott's pottery, so thin, so delicate, they might be made of paper instead of clay. Patrice makes big copper bracelets and brass earrings, just the slightest trace of Africa in their shape and bulk. Warren—Warren isn't the creative one; he manages the money and places the crafts at the consignment shop off Route 28A near the Ashokan Reservoir.

So if Warren contributes because he handles money, why can't she contribute by feeding chickens, cleaning the house, tending Joachim, and minding Katie?

She doesn't say this to Warren, any more than she tells him she has no home to go to. She hasn't told anyone her father threw her out. She's afraid to say the words because if she does, she'll cry forever.

And maybe it won't matter. Maybe no one will care that she has no place else to go.

MANDY sits in the rocker, her long, patchwork skirt catching the firelight. She smiles at the baby sucking her breast with loud smacking noises. She moves her leg, and one patch glares iridescent green. John's old tie. That square is flanked on one side by plum-colored velvet, on the other by a piece of the aqua dress she wore to be invested into Eastern Star.

So long ago, that dress, that life. She and her mother, two peas in a Methodist pod, hair identically teased and sprayed into bouffants as stiff as meringue. Long, pastel formal gowns, stiletto heels, matching clutch purses. Pat Nixon clones in suburban Chicago.

She fingers the black wool, cut from the suit she wore to her mother's tasteful funeral. No tears; Mom wouldn't have wanted them. But, oh, the ache, the gaping hole where her mother had been.

Tears clog her throat; tears that even now her WASP upbringing won't let her shed. She longs to show Joachim to her mother, to point out how Katie has grown, to introduce her to the miracle that is Scott.

Truth: Mom would be horrified at the leaky old farmhouse, at Mandy's black-soled bare feet, her home-sewn clothes, the baby born out of wedlock, Scott. She'd wonder how Mandy could ever have left a man like John, a solid man with a future, for an unemployed hippie who threw pots for a living. More, she'd hate that Mandy dragged Katie into this nomadic life, commune to commune, pad to pad, run-down funky area of town to tie-dyed, psychedelic-painted section of some other town. Milwaukee to Denver to the Haight to Dupont Circle in D.C. to the East Village, and now, at last, to this little farm in the Catskills, the first place she can see herself and her little family growing old.

She smiles at the vision of herself with long white hair, of Scott a white-bearded Merlin, of Joachim grown to manhood in the image of his father, of Katie strong and beautiful in her womanhood, a baby at her own breast.

Joey's fist falls away from her breast and the hungry, milky lips still. She bends down to kiss the top of his downy head, then places him slowly, lovingly, into the cradle Leo made when he was born.

They are so lucky. Home at last, home in the cooperative with friends and comrades, safe at last.

Katie runs into the house, all flying hair and barefoot smiling excitement. "He's putting up a tepee! Like an Indian! Come and see, Mommy."

Mandy rises gracefully from the rocker and follows Katie outside to where Quinn, naked from the waist up, his tanned back oily with sweat, raises the poles for his tent.

Quinn's long, lean, sinewy body is like Dylan's voice made flesh, and a shiver of hunger, deep animal wanting, thrills through Mandy's breasts, sensitive from baby sucking.

"Come on without, come on within, you'll not see nothing like the mighty Quinn."

Quinn's sexuality is like the electrically charged air of the summer Catskills. Always there, always threatening a storm. He looks at Mandy with his avid, promising eyes even as Enid rubs her barely covered breast against his chest. He slides appreciative glances at Patrice's nut-brown skin and talks, talks, talks about open sex and throwing off the shackles of middle-class monogamy, pointedly aiming his remarks at Scott, whom he'd known back in San Francisco.

Will Quinn get to Scott, fan the flames of discontent just under the placid surface of their lives, remind Scott that once he was free?

That she will be the one to succumb to Quinn's siren song doesn't enter her mind.

"REMEMBER that girl, what the hell was her name? The one you were balling back then?"

"Moonstar. She called herself Moonstar." The weight of Joachim in the body sling pulls down on him, weighs more than a baby should.

"Yeah. What a chick. What a free spirit. I saw her in Taos, man. Still zooming out there, still exploring. We did some peyote together, man, it was like the old days in the Haight. Next day she split for California, and I headed east. No baggage, man."

Joachim is baggage. Mandy is baggage. Katie of the blue eyes and dirty little toes, Katie is baggage. Even the tools of his trade, his art, pottery wheel and kiln, root him.

With Moonstar he was air, he was fire. Now he is earth,

solid, packed down, heavy with responsibility for three other people, when once he'd refused to accept responsibility even for himself.

Through Quinn's eyes he sees at once what he has unknowingly become: his own father.

THEY make their own ceremonies, no longer tied to Hallmark cards and ribbons made in Taiwan. The Mushroom Feast becomes a hallowed eve, to be celebrated in song and story. Best clothes are put on, velvet skirts and silk blouses, embroidered shawls with long tendrils of fringe. Leo wears a sarape from Mexico, tinkling Indian earrings dangle from Enid's shapely ears, Patrice is adorned like an African princess, and even Bobbie, who has few clothes of her own, sports borrowed finery in the form of an Indian gauze shirt that shows her braless chest.

The priest, the shaman, Quinn the Eskimo, wears his ceremonial robes in the form of a long-fringed leather vest, a belt with silver *conchas*, a leather headband with an eagle feather dangling from it. Bare feet and a leather thong around his neck, with Enid's handmade glass beads and a cowrie shell from the Bahamas, Patrice's contribution.

They smoke a little grass first. Before that, they eat a fine chickpea and wild mushroom stew Mandy made with Bobbie's help. Bobbie the mushroom expert, who picked the wild fungus on the slopes of the mountains where she trekked herself to exhaustion, trying to forget Enid.

Katie is upstairs in bed; Joachim sleeping in his cradle in the corner, near the black woodstove.

At first, Bobbie feels nothing, just full and content and for once accepted by the circle sitting on the floor around Leo's low maple table. The smell of sandalwood incense romances her nose, and she rocks back with the power of it, the pungency, the taste of exotic lands, the vision of

Marrakesh or Ceylon. Faraway places, gold shot through fabric, the light from the fire catching Mandy's hair, her incredible hair. The colors like wood, like Leo's work, like brass and bronze and leaves in the autumn and maple syrup. She wants to taste Mandy's hair, which looks as rich as the sandalwood smells.

The connection is like a silver thread powered by thousands of watts of electricity. It shoots from Enid to Bobbie, then from Bobbie to Mandy, Mandy to Leo, and so on around the circle, binding them forever in a state of perfect love. Bobbie sees clearly now how silly, how juvenile, her passion for Enid was. The love she felt for Enid isn't special at all; it's just one tiny piece of the global love that fills her now, has her eyes streaming tears of joy, her hand clutching Mandy's with the simple faith of a child. The tears choke her and then dissolve in laughter as spontaneous as butterflies drunk on nectar.

They are all drunk, not with alcohol, not even with magic mushrooms, but with Life Itself. The love of one another, of the human race, of the earth and all living creatures, overwhelms them, and they laugh and laugh at how absurd their old lives used to be and how free they are now. Free to hold anyone's hand, free to look anyone in the eye and hold the glance until true human connection is made, free to take off their clothes if they want to—and suddenly everyone wants to.

Tasting and touching skin soft as powder, tasting of peat and curry, of roses and musk, Scott settles down to a feast of skin and hair, lips and breasts, no longer aware of identity, just knowing this woman, this amazing woman with skin the color of amber, is inside him and enveloping him at the same time. He thrusts and she parries, he kisses and she kisses back, both swept away into a world of sensory pleasure he'd never before dreamed existed.

"Patrice," he says, and the name sounds like an incantation. Her hair, luxurious and oiled, seems to melt in his hands.

Did the baby cry?

Does he have a baby?

Where's Mandy?

Does he care?

MANDY can't keep the voice of Bob Dylan out of her head. That raspy, knowing voice is the way Quinn looks, rough and male and sinewy, eager and detached at the same time, way beyond cool and hot as the devil himself.

"When Quinn the Eskimo gets here, everybody's going to jump for joy."

She wants him so much. Scott is wonderful, a tender lover and a good man, a father to both her children, and the man in whose arms she wants to die someday, but right now she has to have Quinn inside her. She sees herself as a giant black jaguar, a female animal in heat, eager for a male to enter and possess her, then walk away without looking back.

Mushrooms give Quinn to her. Mushrooms take her where she wants to go.

But once it's over, will Scott still be there? Will she still die in his arms?

TOUCHING naked skin is the most beautiful thing Bobbie has ever done. Like velvet—no, velvet is too coarse, silk too earthbound. Like a baby, like Joachim's soft fuzzy head, and now everyone feels baby-soft, baby-innocent. First she strokes Mandy's long hair, lets the hair flow over her face, drinks in the scent of rosemary from her herbal rinse, then allows her lips to wander downward until Mandy's breast is in her mouth.

Everyone tastes everyone until languor and slumber set in.

Screams bring her out of a long, velvet funk, a meditation on skin and hair, lips and—

But whose screams? And why? High-pitched, but male or female?

The crash is inevitable. Bobbie wakes in a tangle of sodden blankets, wet and sticky, smelling of sweet wine. Her head throbs and her hands shake, her stomach feels tender and raw.

Can she move? Is she alive or dead, and whose hands, whose lips, touched her last? Why does she remember blood and screaming?

The sound of retching comes from the bathroom upstairs. Bobbie wonders whether the commune's single toilet will be enough.

EARTH into airy, light, shiny forms, useful things as old as mankind. Shaping wet clay with his fingers, the sensuous feel of it like making love, the hot flame hardening, setting, glazing, taking it to another dimension of existence. All this Scott loves about his work.

The ancient Japanese technique of raku separates his pottery from the clumsy chalices and honey pots turned out by most hippie potters. He creates works of art, delicate yet strong, powerfully shaped yet thin as glass, iridescent colors swirling in metal-based glazes whose formulas were intricate and tricky to produce.

Timing is all. Baking just long enough, cooling just at the right moment in a water bath of the right temperature. Some cracked, some hardened too quickly, some just didn't sing when they were finished, lay there like the mud they were, soulless and dead.

Getting rid of Quinn, saving his family from evil, will

take the same attention to detail, the same precision, the same dispassionate, artistic eye.

ONE week later, alone in his tepee, Quinn dies.

EVERYONE got sick, but while most of them just felt dizzy, Quinn was still seeing visions, ranting about the earth melting and giant spiders coming after us, all kinds of weird shit. Mandy was scared for Katie, listening to all that craziness, so she asked Leo and Warren to get Quinn back into his tepee.

What were they supposed to do? Call the pigs, tell them there was a guy out here stoned out of his gourd and please send an ambulance? Get them all locked up and it was his fucking shit in the first place; none of them would have taken the mushrooms if he hadn't turned it into a fucking ceremony.

The thing is, he really seemed to be getting better. He stopped throwing up—but then he'd stopped eating, so there wasn't anything left to throw up. He slept a lot, and he did seem to have nightmares, but it wasn't until the last day of his life that everyone realized Quinn wasn't going to make it.

It was awful. Convulsions, retching horribly and blood coming out of his mouth, sweating like hell, as if every single drop of fluid in his body had to come out one way or another. The tepee smelled terrible, and Patrice sat outside in lotus position, rocking and sobbing.

The only person who seemed more upset about Quinn than Patrice was Bobbie Tate. Which was weird because if anybody hated the guy, Bobbie did.

*   *   *

MELTING golden coins fluttering in the air, the sound like baby hands clapping. Hot sun boiling her skin, big huge blisters going to pop, flood her with water, skin so hot, so hot, hot like Enid, hot like Quinn with his crazy fever. Quinn dead and gone, could she die out here? Float away like a dry leaf, like the dry leaf suddenly in her hand, the essence of dry, no life, no softness, only decay and brittle falling apart into fragments like the fragments of her heart.

"Take another little piece of my heart, now, baby. You know you got it, if it makes you feel good."

Her heart hurts, she can feel it beating, hear blood whooshing through like water down a flume, like the Esopus when you float in an inner tube and your butt gets cold and your knees gets sunburned. Blood rushes through her veins like the Esopus, loud as a sunset, powerful as a summer storm, red life keeping her from blowing away.

Blowing in the wind, the golden coins hanging from the white birch tree, birchbark like paper, like the dead leaf, peeling like the paint on the outside of the farmhouse. Golden leaf coins from a living tree, bending and swaying. Staying alive. Sap rising in the trunk like the blood in her veins; cut the tree, and it would bleed her own red blood.

She is the tree; the tree is her secret soul made flesh.

She asks the tree for a single leaf and it says yes, bending over her like a mother, like the mother who'd left when she was eight. She cries, soft spring rain tears of relief and joy, and rubs the golden leaf against her cheek and prays to the tree for forgiveness, and when sanity returns, only partly welcome, she is Birch. Birch who bends and does not break, no matter how fierce the pain.

No longer Bobbie, Roberta Susanne, Bobbie Sue Tate— she is Birch, and she will be Birch forever.

AUGUST 1970: THE PIGS

IT was a hot summer, hot as any Ulster County could remember. Corn all but roasted itself on the stalk and tomatoes burst on the vine. Flowers withered unless they were watered daily, and most people knew better than to waste water that way. Some said, better to waste it here than send it down to New York City, but they were in the minority.

A storm was needed. The kind of Catskill thunderstorm old Washington Irving used to write about, the kind where the gods vented their fury on a world gone mad— which it had ever since the rock festival. Lightning and thunder fit to scare the worst sinner back to church, splitting the sky with light so powerful you could read by it. Gully-washing rain, ripping whole sides of mountains, pushing boulders down the hillside for the county to plow off the roads in the fall. Maybe a storm like that would send the hippies back where they came from.

The storm was overdue by a long two weeks when the call came in. Sam Tate, Woodstock's chief of police, took it himself.

"A dead body? You sure, Al? Yeah, of course you are, I just mean, well, hell, we don't get a whole lot of dead bodies around here, so—

"A hippie. A dead hippie out by Wittenburg Pond." Sam wasn't surprised. Ever since the festival, the whole Hudson Valley had become a magnet for dropout kids wearing fringe and headbands. Not to mention that Bobbie was one of them, living in that goddamn commune.

He couldn't think about that now. He turned his attention back to his caller.

"Just off the pond road, mile or so out of Bearsville." He nodded and jotted a note on the pad in front of him. "You're calling from where? The firehouse? You gonna wait there?"

A mental picture of the scene rose in his mind: August foliage, deep, dense, green, shading and blocking the pond from the view of passing drivers on State Route 40. So how had Al—oh, yeah, Al had a prostate the size of a grapefruit, probably stepped out of his pickup to take a piss and stumbled over a dead body.

"Well, yeah, I can see where you need to—but, Al, it would really be a big help if you'd just wait there and take me to the body, OK?

"Al, I owe you one, buddy."

THORSTEN Magnussen, the only detective on Woodstock's tiny police force, grabbed his notebook and walked to the black and white with a heavy heart. A dead body outdoors in August wasn't going to be pretty, and a dead hippie was going to make Sam madder than any other kind of dead body. The whole town wondered why Sam didn't just drive up to that commune and drag Bobbie home, but Thor didn't wonder. If Sam did that, Bobbie would run away to God knew where the next day, and at least this way Sam knew where his daughter was, even though he hated where she was.

"Any idea how long the body's been there?" he asked as Sam headed toward Bearsville.

"No." A man of few words before his daughter was discovered holding hands with Enid in the Tinker Street Cinema, Sam was positively Trappist now.

"Any idea how the—"

"No. I figured we'd wait and see what the coroner had to say." Sam shifted his unlit cigar from one side of his mouth to the other, chewing on the end with a ferocity that told Thor to stop asking stupid questions.

The hippie was dressed in well-worn jeans and had a fringed leather vest over his flannel shirt, moccasins on his feet, and a leather thong around his neck.

"Pretty hot for a long-sleeved shirt," Thor remarked, wiping sweat from his sunburned brow. Big, blond, and Nordic, he suffered every summer, but this one was especially brutal.

The coroner pushed his way through the bystanders with his medical bag in one hand and a fishing rod in the other.

"He didn't die here," Foley said after a cursory glance. "Body was moved."

"Hey, I've seen that guy!" A small, balding man pointed at the body. "He was at the post office about a week ago. Said his name was Quinn, and he was staying out at the old Thompson place on Meads Mountain—you know, where those hippies are. The ones with that purple van."

Sam stood frozen, his face a mask. Thor took a deep breath and let it out in a long sigh.

He knew the Thompson place, all right. It was where Bobbie Tate lived.

AN hour later, Thor flipped on his left-turn signal and waited for traffic to pass before turning left and making his bouncing way up a steep gravel trail off Meads Mountain Road, about four miles before the Buddhist temple at the top.

Eighteen trees later, a rutted, signless dirt road opened; he cut another left and dropped his speed, taking the second and then the third right fork, moving upward until he caught a glimpse of dirty white paint.

"Shit." Doppler ran the window down and tossed out his butt. Thor said nothing, just hoped the damn thing was fully extinguished. "Look at the state of that place. Damn dirty shame, house like that going to hippies."

"It needed a few coats when old man Thompson was alive, as I recall."

"Hey, man had arthritis, he couldn't take care of the place. These kids just don't give a shit, live like animals. No wonder somebody died out here, the shit they get up to. Drugs. Group sex. Never had this garbage till they had that damn rock concert."

This was a litany Thor had been hearing for too long and really didn't want to hear again. He gunned the car up the last stubborn bit of hillside and pulled up sharp, kicking the gearshift into park and slamming on the emergency brake.

"Holy shit!"

Thor's eyes followed Doppler's pointing finger. In the meadow behind the house stood a tall, white tepee.

"Think that's where Tonto lived?" Doppler asked.

The man in the barn looked exactly like Jesus Christ—if Jesus wore jeans and worked a pottery wheel. Hair and beard the color of mahogany, mild brown eyes, bare feet in sandals—put a white robe on this guy and churchgoing Woodstock would say it had seen a vision.

He stopped the wheel, taking his foot off the pedal and cupping the wet clay in his hands until it subsided into a mass ready for reshaping.

"Who are you?" Doppler spoke without removing his cigarette from his lips.

"I'm Scott. Scott Andrews." The Jesus face grew guarded, wary, but Thor had to admit, he'd probably look the same if he'd ended up on the wrong side of Doppler.

"We need to talk to you and your pals," Doppler went on. "Get 'em all together; we'll talk in the kitchen."

Doppler turned without waiting for an answer. He stepped from the barn to the back of the house, swung open the screen door, and walked into the kitchen as if he'd been invited to dinner. Showing that he knew the house, felt at home there, and was going to by God be in charge.

Thor followed. He'd never been inside the old farmhouse but doubted that the hippies had made it any worse than it was when a drunken old man had lived there.

To his surprise, the kitchen sported a new coat of cream-colored paint and had handmade green stenciling on the walls. Mismatched, old-fashioned kitchen tools and canisters sat on the counters: a red-handled pastry cutter like the one his grandmother used, a faded ceramic dog-shaped cookie jar, hand-thrown bowls and pots, a cutting board striped with different shades of wood. It was homey and inviting, cluttered but clean, speaking of careful purchases at junk stores and yard sales coupled with handmade things.

The commune residents made things to sell at the crafts cooperative off Route 28A. Thor, grandson of artists, had pictured crude, shapeless masses of clay, tie-dyed T-shirts, macramé pot hangers—useless objects made by clumsy hands. But the stained glass piece in the window, the glazed pot on the hand-rubbed kitchen table, all spoke of a love of materials and an attention to detail that impressed him.

Scott came into the room followed by a dark-haired woman wearing a long patchwork skirt and a light-skinned black woman with a shiny, oiled Afro. "I told the guys," he said. "They're coming in."

The women were Mandy and Patrice.

Doppler turned to Thor. "Which one's the lezzie?"

"Neither," Thor replied. The girl who'd seduced Bobbie Tate was a light-skinned blonde with a slender figure and an exhibitionist's way of showing it off.

The women looked at one another, naked fear on their faces.

Was the fear because they knew the dead man, or because all hippies hated and feared all pigs? It was too soon to tell.

"We just found a body in the woods," Thor said, carefully moving his eyes from one face to another. "Someone said the man might have belonged to your commune."

"He had on a leather vest," Doppler added, "and it looks like he died of a drug overdose."

Many times in Thor's professional life he'd had the urge to strangle Doppler, and this was one more to add to the list. He glared at the man and added, "Right now we just want to identify the guy, notify any family he might have."

Again, the two women exchanged looks but said nothing. A man with long, curly hair and a lush beard came in, introduced himself as Leo, and told them Enid was in town buying supplies. No one answered the questions Doppler kept peppering them with until Warren entered the room, and all eyes turned to him.

He was pasty-faced and clean-shaven, with long, straight, lank hair and heavy, dark-rimmed glasses. Buddy Holly gone flower child.

"What are the pigs doing here?" His voice was reedy, but his tone expected answers and expected them now.

"They found a body somewhere, and they think we know something about it," Scott replied.

"We don't. So you can leave now," Warren said, challenge in his cool gray eyes. "You can take your kid with you if you want," he added. "We're not keeping her against her will or anything."

"Nobody said you were," Thor replied mildly. "And she isn't my daughter."

"Who lives in that tepee out back?" Doppler jerked his thumb toward the kitchen window, where the tent dominated the view.

"Oh, we take turns using it," Warren said. "It kind of belongs to all of us, like everything else out here."

Thor left the kitchen stonewalled and frustrated.

"Lying sonsabitches," Doppler muttered. Thor cut him

off with a brusque wave. A little girl about six, her hair the same maple syrup color as Mandy's, sat in a tire swing, her bare feet scuffing the ground.

Thor signaled Doppler to stay back and approached the child. He knelt down on the grass near the swing and said, "That looks like fun. Who put it up for you?"

"Scott."

"What's your name?"

"Katie." The child gazed directly up at Thor with candid blue eyes.

"That tepee is pretty neat," Thor said. "Do you sleep in it?"

"No, that's where Quinn sleeps. He's an Eskimo, and he lives in a tepee. My mom makes him soup because he's sick. Really sick, throwing up and everything."

"When's the last time you saw Mr. Quinn?"

"Not for a while, because he's so sick. Mom says I have to be quiet and let him sleep, even in the daytime. He stays in his tepee all the time, and Patrice brings him my mom's soup. He won't let anyone else come in."

"He never slept in the house?"

Katie shook her head. "Not at night. Sometimes in the day."

"He slept inside during the day?"

"Sometimes. He'd go to Enid's room and that's why Bobbie sleeps in my room. Because she didn't like him going to Enid's room."

"Hey, what are you doing talking to her?"

Thor turned; Warren stood on the back porch, an outraged expression on his face. "You get out of here now, and don't come back without a warrant. We know our rights."

For a moment, Thor thought Doppler was going to make a fight out of it, but in the end they had no choice but to leave, to let Warren have his temporary victory.

Back inside the car, Doppler said, "The dead guy didn't look like an Eskimo."

Thor sighed. Sometimes he felt like an interpreter. It wasn't that he was a hippie, just that he did live in the actual twentieth century and listened to WDST on his car radio.

He explained to Doppler what he'd later have to explain to Sam Tate, that Quinn the Eskimo was a character in a Bob Dylan song, and his name came from dealing cocaine.

That was enough for Sam. He got on the phone to the sheriff in Kingston, asked for a full tox screen on the dead man. Then he called the most antidrug judge in Ulster County and got a search warrant.

"Take that place apart," he told Thor, and he didn't seem to mind at all when Doppler's mean little eyes lit up.

And what if they did find drugs? What if they had to arrest Bobbie?

As long as he'd known Sam Tate, he didn't know the answer to that one.

"NO drugs?" Sam couldn't keep the amazement out of his voice. "Nothing, not a marijuana seed?"

Thor shook his head. The old house had four bedrooms. The biggest had a double mattress on the floor, covered with an Indian cloth. In one corner, an old-fashioned cradle on rockers had a handmade quilt tucked into it and a sleeping baby under the quilt. Mandy and Scott.

The second bedroom belonged to the little girl, Katie. The third bedroom was Warren's, the fourth Enid's, and Leo slept in the unfinished attic. Not one of the rooms had a bed in it. Mattresses, sleeping bags, homemade pallets of blanket and quilt lay on the floor like dog beds. They'd searched everything, emptied drawers, dumped clothes onto the floor, shredded sleeping bags.

"You tossed the place hard? I mean, you looked everywhere, right?"

"Nothing taped under the drawers, nothing behind the
toilets, nothing in the heating ducts. We emptied out
the flour barrels and dried beans, dumped spices out of the
spice rack." Thor grinned. "Doppler even went after the
compost heap, raked the whole thing, and came up
empty."

His grin faded as he recalled the assault on the little
girl's room. Dolls were slashed open, plastic toys broken
against rocks, even the child's quilt, obviously handmade
by her mother, was ripped end to end. When he'd protested, Doppler had replied, "Hell, that's where they'd hide
the shit, knowing damn well a bleeding heart like you isn't
gonna rip up a kid's stuff. Well, that's the difference between you and me, buddy."

Difference or no difference, they'd left empty-handed,
both of them knowing full well that the commune used
drugs but finding no evidence, not even a residue-filled
hash pipe. Somewhere on the property, perhaps in a hollow
tree, they might find dope and works, but for now, they
had nothing. No evidence, no reason to suspect the hippies
of anything more than getting an inconveniently dead
guest off their property.

Even the tepee, fetid with the smell of sickness, had no
telltale clues pointing to drug use, no roach clips, no hash
pipe—nothing but sweat-stained blankets and a backpack
filled with extra clothes.

"Did you—did you see Bobbie?"

Thor shook his head. "Mandy said she spends a lot of
time out hiking, I suppose because Enid switched her attention to the dead man. She probably feels uncomfortable
hanging around."

"I never should have named her Roberta," Sam muttered, and it took Thor a minute to realize what he was getting at.

"You think she's the way she is because of her name?"

Sam directs his gaze at the hunting scene on the back wall of his office. "Once her mother was gone, I just—I don't know, I just raised her the way my dad raised me. Took her hunting, taught her to fish, let her go on those Boy Scout hikes with you. She seemed to like it. It never occurred to me she liked it too much, that she'd want to *be* a boy."

A hundred memories fought for dominance in Thor's mind. Bobbie Tate at seven, adamantly refusing to wear a dress to church. Bobbie at ten, baiting her hook, tongue protruding from the corner of her mouth as she poked the metal through a wriggling worm. Bobbie at fourteen, outpacing Eagle Scouts up the slope of Mount Tremper.

Bobbie at sixteen, walking down Tinker Street holding hands with a willowy blonde, her face alight with pride and pleasure and a sexual awakening he'd never seen before, a glow that can only come from crossing the threshold to adulthood.

"She is who she is, Sam," he said, knowing the words were inadequate.

"I want her back the way she was before that bitch got to her."

Thor decided he wasn't going to be the one to tell Sam he might never get that Bobbie back again.

THE first break in the case came two days later. "Guy was on some kinda mushroom shit," Doppler said, the unfiltered cigarette dangling from his lip dancing in tune to his rhythm. "Fuckin' hippies, always lookin' for some new way to get high."

"Yeah, fuckin' hippies," Thor agreed. Backup singer to

Doppler's insistent pounding beat, the theme of which was always fuckin' this and fuckin' that. If it wasn't fuckin' hippies it was fuckin' summer people, fuckin' rich people, fuckin' white trash, fuckin' not-so-white trash, fuckin' bosses—

"They got a song about smokin' bananas, the hippies," Doppler continued. His eyes were flags: red, white, and blue, so raw they made your own eyes hurt just looking at them. "You heard it, Thor? Smokin' fuckin' bananas." He shook his head, and a long block of ash dribbled to the ground, wind blowing it back onto his uniform shirt.

"So we're calling it an accidental overdose," he said, suddenly sick and tired of Doppler's shit.

"Seems like," Doppler said, stifling a yawn. He spat the butt onto the asphalt. Flecks of tobacco stuck to his thin, dry lips. His hand reached automatically for the soft pack in his shirt pocket, pulled out another, and shoved it into his mouth.

"So why are we on our way to see this tox guy? Why not just call it an overdose, close the file, and move on?"

ASSISTANT toxicologist Andy Grossmacher met them at the door. "Damndest thing you ever saw," he said with a wide grin on his freckled face. "Guy got himself high on *Psilocybe,* but what killed him was amanita."

"Wanna try that in English?"

"He was poisoned."

"I THOUGHT you said amanitas were everywhere." Thor hoped he didn't sound as whiny as he felt. Andy thought the use of local mushrooms pointed to the only local in the commune: Bobbie Tate. The thought of Bobbie deliberately giving someone deadly mushrooms had Thor's stomach tied in knots. She couldn't have turned into a killer before her eighteenth birthday.

"Not *these* babies. This is *Amanita verna,* and it doesn't grow west of the Cascades. Now, if they'd been *pantherina,*" Andy goes on, a fanatic's glint in his eye, "then I could tell you what you want to hear. I still say they couldn't have gotten into the guy's stash by accident, but at least he could have brought them with him from the West. But *verna,* no, I'm sorry; those are Eastern mushrooms, they grow under beech trees, and they just happen to be out right now. I saw some myself last weekend on a hike I led up near Phoenicia. You know the trailhead just off—"

"Tell me again about hallucinogenics," Thor said, moving toward the window and gazing out on a perfect summer day that suddenly gave him no pleasure at all.

Andy's freckled face beamed with pleasure, almost as if the dead man had been murdered just to give him added fungus information. "He went for the best, I'll say that for him. You can get high with several species, you know. Not just *Psilocybe.* Around here, there's fly agaric, boletus—"

"Cut to the chase, Andy. What did the guy have, and where did he get it?"

The smile that split his companion's face was the one that earned him his childhood nickname: Raggedy Andy. "He had Mexican, man. The Carlos Castaneda stuff. When I was in Santa Cruz, I turned on with *cubensis.* Not bad, but this was *Psilocybe mexicana,* and you get it in Mexico and nowhere but Mexico. So now you have another reason why those amanitas didn't just wind up in his stomach by accident."

"IF it wasn't an accident, then whoever killed Quinn had to know something about poisonous mushrooms," Thor said for the fifth time. He could barely look at his boss, knowing they were both thinking the same thing and knowing Sam hated thinking it even more than he did.

"Hell, Bobbie's not the only person in this county who knows something about mushrooms, for Christ's sake."

"Right, Sam," Thor said with a nod. "But how many people in that commune know that *Amanita verna* grows on the north side of Slide Mountain during July and August?" He ran his big fingers through sun-lightened blond hair. "Hell, Sam, I *took* Bobbie on that hike with the mushroom guy from New Paltz. I was there when he showed her the destroying angels and told her how poisonous they were. You think anyone else in that commune knows that stuff?"

"They might," Sam replied, but he stared out the window at Tinker Street, not meeting Thor's eyes. "It's up to you to find out what they know. Dig until you get something."

He didn't have to finish the sentence: *Dig until you get something that proves my little girl didn't kill anyone.*

"THERE were two mushroom trips, OK? One was with all of us, like a ceremony," Scott said, taking charge of the gathering once Mandy had served iced herbal tea. "Quinn took his own trip two days later. Didn't offer any to the rest of us, said he had to get his head straight."

"I thought 'straight' meant not taking drugs," Thor was unwise enough to reply. Eyes were rolled.

"Okay," he conceded. "Quinn was the only one who took the mushrooms the second time. And that's when he started getting sick."

"Right," answered Scott. He seemed to have appointed himself spokesman for the group this time, odd since Warren had made such a point of being in charge before. "At first we thought it was normal. Most of us felt kind of weird after the mushroom feast."

"We didn't throw up, though," Mandy said quietly. "We should have known something was wrong."

"After Quinn got sick, what did you do?"

"I made him soup," Mandy said. "Vegetable broth. Sometimes I'd break an egg into it, stir it around, like Chinese egg-drop soup. That's all he ate for—until he died."

"At first we thought he was getting better," Warren said. "He threw up for a day or so, then got up and started walking around like he was OK. Then he had convulsions, went back into the tepee, and died two days later."

Thor nodded. That was precisely the pattern amanita poisoning took, according to Raggedy Andy.

He turned to Bobbie, who sat on the floor at the far end of the room, trying and failing to look invisible. "I know you picked them, Bobbie. You brought them here. Did you deliberately put them in Quinn's stash?"

"No," she said, her voice a sob. "I picked them. I—I don't even know why. I thought about taking them myself," she cried, staring hard at Enid, "but I didn't, and I didn't give them to Quinn, either. They were in my room, that's all."

"In *your* room?" Mandy turned disbelieving eyes on the sixteen-year-old. "In *Katie's* room, you mean. What if she'd found them? Are you crazy?"

"I think I sort of was," Bobbie admitted. "I had them wrapped in a bandanna on the top shelf of the closet, way in the back. I really didn't want Katie to get them."

"Who else would know they were there?"

"You don't mean you believe her?" Warren burst out. "Man, I knew it. Just because her daddy's a cop, you're going to let her off the hook and find a way to blame one of us."

"I didn't say I believe her," Thor replied in an even tone. "I'm considering all the alternatives."

Bobbie looked at him with brimming eyes. "What do you mean, you don't believe me? You think I killed Quinn?"

"Bobbie, please, I have a job to do here. What I believe isn't the question."

"It is to me. You—" She broke down, sobbing and hitting her thigh with an angry fist. "You were my best friend. You have to believe me."

Sam was right; he and Thor both failed the little girl they loved so much. A teenager who called a thirty-year-old detective her best friend wasn't normal. Bobbie was breaking his heart, just as he was breaking hers.

There was police work and there was friendship. He put his notebook on the floor, stood up, and walked over to where Bobbie sat huddled, all her energy consumed by racking sobs. He touched her hair, short, boyish, tomboy hair that curled slightly at the ends.

"I believe you. As Thor your friend, I believe you. As Detective Thorsten Magnussen, I have to consider you a suspect. So let me get back to work, OK?"

She nodded. Incredibly, even as she poured her entire soul into grieving for her lost innocence, she nodded.

"Very nice," Warren said, clapping slowly and ostentatiously. "The pig has a heart after all. Too bad she's guilty."

"You'd better explain that remark."

"I saw her go into the tepee." Warren cocked his head toward Bobbie. "After the mushroom feast and before Quinn went on his own trip. She looked around to see if anyone was watching, and then she crept inside. She was there a few minutes, and then came out."

Thor's heart felt too big for his chest. He'd believed her,

but now—what innocent reason could she possibly have for going into the dead man's tent?

"Bobbie?"

She gasped for breath, sobs still shaking her body, tears still streaming down bright red cheeks. "I didn't put mushrooms in," she said brokenly, "I took some out."

"Why would you do that?"

"Quinn went on a trip to get his head straight, and I really needed to get mine straight, too, so I thought I'd take some and—"

"You stole from Quinn's stash," said Enid. "I can't believe you'd do that."

"I didn't think of it as stealing," Bobbie replied. "But I guess it was."

"Of course it was," said Warren.

"Well, it's easily proved," Patrice said. "Just show the deputy the mushrooms, and he can get them analyzed and tell whether they're magic or poison, right?"

Thor nodded, but Bobbie said in a small voice, "I took them already."

"Oh, that's convenient," Warren replied.

"I went up to the mountain," Bobbie said, her voice growing stronger. "Up near the monastery." The Buddhist monastery, a fixture in Woodstock for many years, was a natural place for soul-searching, drug-enhanced or otherwise.

"I lay under a birch tree and I—I became one with it. I was the birch and the birch was me, and that's why my name is Birch now." She gazed with newfound serenity into Thor's eyes. "Call me Birch."

"Birch." No one on the planet could look less like a slender birch tree than Bobbie Tate, with her volleyball player's body and her Campbell's Soup kid face. "It's perfect."

She smiled a watery smile that had him believing now

for good and all. She did not poison Quinn, she entered his tent to take mushrooms and not leave them—but there was still one more thing.

"Bobbie, I mean Birch, you must have known he was poisoned. Why didn't you get help?"

"I did," she said, giving Leo a quick, apologetic smile. "I asked Leo."

"How could Leo help?"

"He was a medic in Nam. He used to work for the Free Clinic in the East Village. He knows a lot about drugs."

"Not much about mushrooms," Leo replied. "But when Birch told me she thought Quinn might be poisoned, I gave him some ipecac, just to stimulate vomiting. It was all I could think of to do."

"Well, it worked all right," Warren muttered. "Guy was throwing up day and night for a couple days there."

"So you suspected he'd been poisoned," Scott said, "and you didn't tell anyone?" It wasn't clear whether his remarks were directed at Leo or Birch.

"I wasn't sure," she said. "I went to look at the destroying angels, and it didn't look like there were any missing, but they were all dried out so it was hard to tell. I didn't think—I guess I wanted to believe he was sick from something else. But I told Leo, just in case."

"Who else knew there were poison mushrooms in the house?"

"Everybody," Bobbie answered. "I said so when we all got high. Remember?" She looked from one to the other. "I talked about destroying angels and white death and how there were mushrooms and mushrooms. I remember saying it when we were all still in the same room."

"Well, I don't remember that," Warren said loudly.

"Was that what you meant?" Mandy was frowning. "I remember the white angel part, but I didn't know you meant mushrooms."

"Everybody's going to say they didn't understand," Patrice pointed out.

"Who could have gone into the tepee without arousing suspicion?"

"Any of the girls," Leo said with a wry smile. "Quinn was balling every one of them at one time or another. Enid, Patrice, Mandy—"

Thor raised an eyebrow and turned his attention to the woman in the patchwork skirt. "You and Quinn had something going?"

"Not really," Mandy replied, but her face was pink. "It was the mushrooms, that's all. I did something crazy while we were high. I never went into the tepee after that night."

Thor glanced at Scott. Another motive heard from; he doubted that even this placid potter would take Mandy's defection lightly.

"Patrice went in," Enid said, and her little teeth shone in the firelight. Malice charged her voice. "Mandy made broth, and Patrice took it in to the tepee. Quinn wouldn't let anyone else feed him when he got sick."

"Is this true?"

"Yes. I don't know why, but he told me to keep everyone else out," Patrice admitted. "I knew him from before, so I guess he trusted me."

"The real issue is who put poison into the stash, not who went to the tepee after he got sick," Scott pointed out.

"I'm not so sure about that," Bobbie—no, Birch—said in a faraway voice. "What if the mushrooms were OK? The ones Quinn took, I mean. What if the poison was something else instead?"

"That's crazy," someone shouted.

"You think I poisoned him with the soup?" Mandy said, her voice rising.

"Don't be stupid," Warren pronounced.

"She may be right," Thor said thoughtfully. "Getting poison into the kitchen and putting in into the broth would be easier than sneaking into the tepee without being seen."

"The broth was for Quinn," Mandy agreed with a slow nod. "I used it to make vegetable soup for everyone, but I saved the broth for Quinn. No spices, no big chunks—it was in its own special pot in the fridge."

"So anybody could have gone into the kitchen, dropped some amanitas into the soup, strained them out again, and left poison broth to be carried to Quinn?"

"Pretty dangerous," Scott pointed out. "Anyone might have eaten the broth. Katie might have—"

Thor thought Mandy was going to faint. She swayed slightly in her chair, eyes rolling back in her head. Unless she was a powerful actress, Thor decided she hadn't killed Quinn, and neither had Scott.

Who had? If Bob—Birch was telling the truth, the amanitas weren't in the stash of *mexicana*.

What if—Thor looked directly at Leo, who lowered his eyes and gazed into the woodstove's blazing fire.

"You gave him the ipecac because he was vomiting," Thor said. Leo nodded. "And you gave it to him because Bo—I mean Birch told you about the poison mushrooms," he added.

"Yeah," Leo agreed.

"Exactly when was that?"

"I don't remember exactly."

"Birch?" Odd how the name was becoming second nature.

"It was Saturday afternoon," she said in a small voice. "I didn't want to believe it, so I didn't mention it earlier."

Thor turned to Warren. "You said Quinn was throwing up a lot at first. What day of the week would that have been?"

"Thursday, Friday, something in there."

"The mushroom feast was Tuesday," Mandy said. "So Quinn took his own trip on Thursday."

"Here's what I think happened," Thor said, and the spreading red stain on Leo's averted face told him he was close to the truth. Not the world's most adept liar, Leo had committed a murder of opportunity, not executed a well-laid plan.

"Quinn was no more sick the day after his trip than you were. He started throwing up because Leo slipped ipecac into his food. Birch came forward and 'reminded' Leo about the poison mushrooms. That made Leo the unofficial doctor, which meant that Quinn would take anything Leo gave him. So he soaked the amanitas in water and added that to the ipecac. Every day he gave Quinn a little more poison, and every day Quinn got sicker and sicker until he died."

"But why?" Birch turned disappointed eyes on the teddy bear man with the curly hair and beard. Her eyes widened and she whispered, "It was you who screamed. What did Quinn do to you?"

"We were all—everybody was having sex with everybody else," Leo said, his face burning and his voice a strangled cry. "I—I didn't want what Quinn was doing to me, but I couldn't stop him. He—he said later it was something I needed to explore, a side of myself I should—but I didn't want to. I hated him for making me do that!" Leo sobbed like a child, burrowed into the side of the sofa like a wounded bear.

When Thor had Leo handcuffed in the back of the black and white, he turned to Birch and said, "Can I give you a ride home?"

"Did Pop tell you to say that?"

"No, but I know he wants you—"

"He wants me to be something I can't be," she said, her voice steady and her eyes dry. "I love him, but I can't change who I am."

LATER that night, the sky cracked open. Booms so loud babies woke crying, rain falling so hard that looking through the car windshield was like trying to see through a shower curtain, hard, pounding rain that washed away sins.

Sam felt his soul lighten as he rammed his way up Rock City Road, straight the hell up, no switchbacks. Gutting it out, making his Ford Crown Victoria do the work God made a jeep to do. Going after Bobbie come hell or high water, he told himself with a manic grin.

He loved her, loved her no matter what, loved the way she cocked her head to one side and looked skeptically at him, forcing him to defend his position in an argument. Loved the way her short hair curled at the nape of her neck, loved the stubby little fingers with bitten nails, loved the husky tomboy voice, the shy, eager smile. He wasn't at all sure he could handle her sexuality, but he was goddamn going to try.

Making the turn spat gobs of mud into the bushes at the side of the dirt road and had his wheels spinning madly. He rocked back, then pushed ahead and plowed up the hill toward the lights of the Thompson place.

Making the dash from car to front door had him soaked to the skin. The tepee, battered by the fierce winds, had fallen in the backyard like a downed hot air balloon. He pounded on the door, water streaming from his hat onto the back of his neck.

A woman answered the door, a baby in her arms. She had long, straight, folksinger hair, parted in the middle. She said nothing, just stood there looking at him. No fear, no objection to his presence, just a quietly sad smile on her round face.

"She's gone," the woman said at last. "Birch is gone. Scott took her to the bus two hours ago, before the storm broke."

"Gone? What do you mean, gone? Where could she go?"

"She said something about the East Village," the woman replied, shifting the weight of her baby onto her hip.

"How could you let a sixteen-year-old go to New York City by herself?" The words burst from Sam before he had time to hear them in his head and realize how strange they were, strange in their implication that the commune was responsible for her.

"I didn't want her to go," the woman said, "but Birch told us you wouldn't let her come home."

"I never said—I just said I didn't—I couldn't live with—oh, God, I didn't mean it like that! I never meant to send her away for good! I didn't mean—"

He raised a hand to his face, wiping tears away with quick, boyish swipes. The woman in the doorway put out a hand and gently rubbed his shoulder. He wrenched himself away and plowed through the mud back to his car. All the way back to Woodstock, the windshield wiper blades sang the woeful dirge, *Too late, too late, Sam Tate was too late.*

JEFFERY DEAVER is the *New York Times* bestselling author of numerous suspense novels, including *The Blue Nowhere* and *The Bone Collector*, which was made into a feature film starring Denzel Washington and Angelina Jolie. He has been nominated for five Edgar Awards from the Mystery Writers of America and is a two-time recipient of the Ellery Queen Reader's Award for Best Short Story of the Year. A lawyer who quit practicing to write full-time, he lives in California and Virginia.